A PL

STORIES OF SEL

A PLACE OF ONE'S OWN

STORIES OF SELF IN CHINA, TAIWAN, HONG KONG, AND SINGAPORE

EDITED BY
KWOK-KAN TAM
TERRY SIU-HAN YIP
WIMAL DISSANAYAKE

OXFORD
UNIVERSITY PRESS

OXFORD
UNIVERSITY PRESS

Oxford University Press is a department of the University of Oxford.
It furthers the University's objective of excellence in research, scholarship, and education by publishing worldwide in

Oxford New York

Athens Auckland Bangkok Bogotá Buenos Aires Calcutta
Cape Town Chennai Dar es Salaam Delhi Florence Hong Kong Istanbul
Karachi Kuala Lumpur Madrid Melbourne Mexico City Mumbai
Nairobi Paris São Paulo Singapore Taipei Tokyo Toronto Warsaw

with associated companies in Berlin Ibadan

Oxford is a registered trade mark of Oxford University Press

First published 1999
This impression (lowest digit)
1 3 5 7 9 10 8 6 4 2

British Library Cataloguing in Publication Data
available

Library of Congress Cataloguing-in-Publication Data
available

ISBN 0-19-591658-1

This project is supported by the Hong Kong Arts Development Council

Printed in Hong Kong
Published by Oxford University Press (China) Ltd
18th Floor, Warwick House East, Taikoo Place, 979 King's Road, Quarry Bay
Hong Kong

Acknowledgements

The idea for this anthology grew out of the joint work of the three editors in the project 'Self in Asian Cultures', coordinated by Wimal Dissanayake at the East-West Center, Honolulu. In the preparation of this anthology, we have been aided by a number of friends and colleagues. Our heartfelt thanks go first to William S. Tay (University of California, San Diego), whose work on contemporary Chinese fiction has all along provided inspiration for our research. We must also thank Howard Goldblatt (University of Colorado, Boulder), Donald A. Gibbs (University of California, Davis), Lucien Miller (University of Massachusetts), Jane Parish Yang (Lawrence University), Perry E. Link (Princeton University), Wong Yoon-wah and Edwin Thumboo (National University of Singapore), Poon Sing Wah (*Lianhe Wanbao*, Singapore), and Sarah Hsiang (*The Chinese Pen*, Taipei). All of them have supported us in many ways, including giving invaluable advice to us on the selection of texts for each section, and helping us to locate some of the authors or translators who have changed their addresses.

We would also like to express our appreciation and thanks to the Chinese Literature Press in Beijing for permission to reprint Fang Fang's 'Hints', Gao Xiaosheng's 'Li Shunda Builds a House', and Tie Ning's 'Ah, Fragrant Snow'; Singapore Association of Writers for re-publication of Cai Shuqing's 'The Poem of Spring'; and the Research Centre for Translation at the Chinese University of Hong Kong for inclusion of Han Shaogong's 'Homecoming?' and Xi Xi's 'The Drawer' in the anthology. We are also very grateful to the authors who have given us permission to include their works in this anthology. To all the translators who have taken time out of their tight schedules to help with the anthology, we owe a debt of thanks. Our thanks must also go to Joseph Owen Tam, Peter Yu, Jess Li, Ada Young, Jacky Leong, and Alisa Mak, research assistants at the Chinese University of Hong Kong, who helped type and proofread part of the manuscript.

Last but not least, we would like to thank the Hong Kong Arts Development Council for their generous support in the publication of this anthology.

Contents

STORIES OF (DIS/)LOCATION

Introduction

Self in Four Chinese Communities: China, Taiwan, Hong Kong, and Singapore

Over the past two decades, various efforts have been made to reconsider the emerging complex relations among Chinese writings and Chinese culture produced in different parts of the world. In the early 1980s some scholars in North America and Europe introduced the concept of 'Commonwealth of Chinese Literature'[1] as a way to rethink the commonalities and differences among Chinese writings in the contemporary period. In the early 1990s the concept of 'Cultural China'[2] was proposed to bring in broader historical and cultural perspectives in considering these relations. Despite such efforts at the philosophical and theoretical levels, readers have seen the appearance of a number of anthologies that have sought to put together the writings of the Chinese communities in China, Taiwan, and Hong Kong.[3]

In this anthology we have adopted a different approach, which is cultural and literary in orientation, by focusing on the Chinese short story as a kaleidoscope to examine contemporary Chinese cultural developments. Since the 1960s, the Chinese short story has made rapid headway, absorbing new influences, charting new territories, and experimenting with form, style, and technique. There is a new-found vibrancy and self-confidence in the modern Chinese short story that merits close and sustained attention. By the Chinese short story we mean the stories written in Chinese and produced in mainland China, Taiwan, Hong Kong, and Singapore. Despite the clear commonalities of language and shared cultural roots, the four communities present a number of socio-cultural factors that are unique to each, and which have endowed each community with a distinct identity.

In discussing the four communities represented in this volume, it is only natural to start with the Chinese mainland because it is historically the 'wellspring' of the Chinese peoples and Chinese culture. While the long and complicated evolutionary path of China as a nation is fascinating, the social transformation that has taken place in the country during the last five decades is even more interesting from the literary, social, and cultural points of view. After the Communist Revolution of 1949, a fundamental change took place in the social fabric of China, which reshaped all aspects of social life. Traditions were challenged; cultural legacies were frowned upon; Marxism-Leninism-Maoism was instituted as the official creed. A new selfhood based on socialist ethics and epistemology came into existence. This social transformation reached its calamitous peak during the Cultural Revolution (1966–76), when the entire country was swept by a wave of uncontrollable fury and social turbulence. It was not until the early 1980s, with the reinstatement of the 'Open Door' policy that the authoritarian rule of the Communist Party was considerably shaken. For a short period of time there was a sense of expectancy among the people, who anticipated the emergence of a more liberal society. Though this dream of a freer society was temporarily shattered by the events at Tiananmen Square in 1989, what occurred since then, and exerted a great influence on the people, was the further liberalization of the economy and the commercialization of their everyday life in the 1990s. Needless to say, these powerful and far-reaching social convulsions had a tremendous impact on the shaping and reshaping of personhood on the Chinese mainland. With the economic boom of the 1990s, China expressed a strong desire to be an active member in the world community. It is against this background of events that we have to read and assess the stories from the Mainland gathered in this volume.

As China gradually moves out of its self-imposed isolationism and seeks to become a partner in the new global society, questions of tradition and modernity, localization and globalization, nationalism and internationalism, socialism and capitalism, economic growth and political freedom begin to make a strong impact on the thought and imagination of the rulers and the ruled alike. The stories from the Chinese mainland included in this volume, in their different ways and with their divergent foci, register these vexatious issues which are closely related to the changing notion of personhood. China wishes to disavow orthodox Marxism, to adopt capitalism without giving up socialism, and to be inspired by the progress of smaller countries like Singapore, without, of course, abdicating its distinctiveness. It is against this backdrop of ambiguity, anxiety, and anticipation that the protagonists of the stories from China seek to live out their lives and invest them with meaning. Hence, it is hardly surprising that many of these stories seek to thematize the confusion of identities, the sense of bewilderment, the pulls of the past and the present, or the feeling of being self-exiled that almost always accompanies such ambivalence of feelings.

Many of the stories from China present as their sub-text the incalculable damage caused by the Cultural Revolution. The mindless violence, and the cultural and individual deracination that was set in motion by the Cultural Revolution, had a range of consequences on its people. Some turned inwards in an attempt to reconstruct a new personhood out of the fragments created by that cataclysmic event, while others engaged themselves in a quest for roots. The movement known as 'quest for roots' (*xungen*), represented by writers such as Han Shaogong, reflects this aspect of introspection and search for cultural meaning. Creative literature is a cultural practice that has a vital link to other institutions and representational practices of society. Along with the above-mentioned quest for roots goes the deeply felt need to recognize other voices that have been suppressed in the past by the monolithic party structure. The stories from China focus on the creation of distinct subjectivity and cultural meanings out of the traumatic past and the uncertain future. On the one hand, the Chinese government makes every effort to promote collective and unified national narratives, with the aim of erasing ethnic differences, and thus placing individuals squarely within the fold of the ideology of the imagined community. On the other, writers are by and large more interested in naming the fissures in the putatively unified national narrative and opening up discursive spaces of resistance. Here one may see the tension between national identity as a construction of power and the individual identity as perceived by the writers.

If we take a story like 'Li Shunda Builds a House' by Gao Xiaosheng, we see how the author points out, with unconcealed irony, how the much-wanted collective system is hollow and inimical to human flourishing. 'Li Shunda Builds a House' presents a picture of rural life in China—the life of the majority of Chinese untouched by modern Western civilization. The house Li Shunda wants to build represents a modest peasant's 'Chinese dream' inspired by the ideal of socialism. It is with this ideal that he becomes a selfless person, but in the end his own dream is never realized according to the socialist reasoning other people give him. He remains empty-handed until he finally understands, as other people do, that he has to think more for himself before he can think of others. The reader sees an overall picture of the relationship between the individual and the collective in socialist China through the image of an innocent peasant, Li Shunda. It is a comic story, but it is also a tragedy related not only to the socialist ideal, but also to the notion of confused self-identity. In a similar vein, the complexity embedded in the relations between power and identity, between self-assertion and social construction is presented vividly in the story 'Homecoming?' by Han Shaogong. The confusion of identity found in the protagonist, Huang Zhixian, is not so much the loss of self in rural China as the inability of self-assertion in the face of collective ideology in contemporary Chinese politics.

When one considers the literature produced in Taiwan, one finds a different situation. Within a short period of three decades, Taiwan has developed culturally from a totalitarian community to a modern democratic society. Taiwan presents us with a picture of a community that has progressed economically in a way that is truly astounding, brushing aside the anxieties and misgivings expressed by many. The annual per capita income on the Chinese mainland is approximately US$350; it is US$8,000 in Taiwan. This in itself indicates that, in comparison with the Mainland, Taiwan is both far more developed in its economy, and much more complex in its post-industrial socio-political developments. Many scholars have pointed out how Taiwan has succeeded in building up its fast-expanding economy on frail foundations since the 1970s. While the economic advances are wholly admirable, there are still unresolved political and social issues, such as the full democratic participation of the citizenry, tensions with the mainland, disenfranchisement of native Taiwanese, the refugees from the mainland, and so forth. With the new generation of leadership consolidated since the late 1980s, many welcomed the handing over of the reins of power from the older generation of the mainlanders, which has been accompanied by the rise of nativist identity in Taiwan. The political and intellectual landscape of Taiwan is indeed changing. A different set of questions related to the transition from nativism to cultural modernity, Chineseness, and cosmopolitanism are being raised. These find echoes in the eight stories from Taiwan contained in this volume.

Similarly, the effects of global capitalism on Taiwanese society, the importance of networks and roots in human relations, and the need for an identity based on more tangible, cultural boundaries are being articulated by literary intellectuals. It is against this backdrop of loss and achievements, tensions and successes that the stories from Taiwan are located. The new sensibilities, the new structures of feeling that have entered Taiwanese society, have been ably inscribed in Wang Wen-hsing's 'Flaw', which deals with a child's initiation and emotional growth in a transitional society. Furthermore, the representational space inhabited by Taiwanese writers and artists presents the contemporary reader with a site of intellectual vibrancy. Stories such as 'One Day in the Life of a White-Collar Worker' by Chen Ying-chen and 'Ximi in the Metropolis' by Chang Ta-chun capture admirably these unique experiences and modes of feeling. Taiwan's rapidly changing society and changing human relationships have often resulted in the loss of self in a person's quest of an anchor. Hence, the experience depicted in the story 'Earth' by Chang Shi-kuo is that of the importance of land to identity formation. The story, in this sense, is full of foresight that provides clues to the frustrations of the mainlanders who want to rebuild their homeland, and thus their identity, in Taiwan, as well as their tensions with the native Taiwanese. The problems of land, home, identity, and nativeness, prophetically portrayed in 'Earth', are among the irresolvable conflicts in the contemporary politics of Taiwan.

The economic boom has also made a great impact on Hong Kong since the 1970s, and in the 1990s it overtook its colonial master, the United Kingdom, in terms of per capita income. The Hong Kong government encourages free-market capitalism and the Chinese work ethic. Together with the great faith in family values, these seem to have worked to the advantage of Hong Kong. Hong Kong's role in international finance further serves to fortify its economic base. For Hong Kong, in the past, one of the pervasive and troubling questions had been its relationship with the Chinese mainland. Since July 1997, Hong Kong has become a part of China, but events leading to the handover gave rise to anxieties and tensions among writers, artists, and intellectuals. The selected stories from Hong Kong in this volume were written before the handover. In them are inscribed the uniqueness of Hong Kong, as well as the success that Hong Kong has achieved and the perils that it may have to face in the future. Its role in the new global and transnational society has had a profound impact on the shaping of personhood, and this finds articulation in the six stories included in this collection. A story like 'Earthworm, Sea Horse, and Fishmoth' by Ma Sha displays an intellectual's paranoid state of mind and his moral and cultural obsessions against the backdrop of a rapidly changing Hong Kong society. Distinctively different from the Chinese mainland or Taiwan, Hong Kong is a place less politically concerned with everyday life; writers present those aspects of life that have more to do with the universality of problems modern people have to face in their particular society. In the story 'The Drawer' by Xi Xi, questions of identity are posed as universal issues of displacement of subjectivity in a society that has become more and more dehumanized.

In the case of Singapore, one finds that it shares the economic success that characterizes Hong Kong and Taiwan, yet Singapore differs from these locations in that it belongs to Southeast Asia, is an independent country, and has a close but sensitive relationship with Malaysia. Nevertheless, the majority of Singapore's population is Chinese and traditional Chinese values play an important role in its social life. The cultural linkage with China has presented a dilemma in Singapore's search for cultural independence and a distinctive identity. On the other hand, the economic achievements of the last two decades and the creation of a welfare society, with education, housing, health care, and transportation readily available to its citizens, are remarkable in the magnitude of accomplishment. One has to recognize, however, that it is a highly regulated society with relatively little space for opposition or criticism. With the media securely in the hands of the government, the public sphere has very little to offer by way of honest critique. The government is efficient and free of corruption that mars most others in the region; but at the same time it is both autocratic and paternalistic.

The sense of being Chinese is important for many in Singapore, but it is less marked than in Taiwan and Hong Kong. Singapore is a multi-racial society with 15 per cent of the population Malay, 7 per cent Indian. Pointing out the differences between Hong Kong and Singapore, Ezra Vogel says that, 'If Hong Kong entrepreneurs thought of Singapore as a bit dull and rigid, Singapore leaders thought of Hong Kong as too speculative, decadent, and undisciplined.'[4] The English language, as well as the colonial legacy, also plays a significant role in Singapore society, and some of the most distinguished writers in the region write in English. The rapid changes in Singaporean society have produced contradictory pulls of the past and the present, and a newer subjectivity is formed as evidenced by the four selected stories from Singapore. In this sense, the story 'Wrongly Delivered Mail' by Yeng Pway Ngon can be read as a subtle record of the Singapore people's struggle not only to free themselves from the colonial past, but also to re-map the self in its search for a new identity.

The four Chinese communities represented in this volume, though sharing a common cultural heritage, have each taken a distinct path towards modernity and globalization, responding to the specific imperatives of their respective cultural geography. The way that citizens of these four communities seek to make sense of being Chinese in a rapidly changing world makes each place implicated in the destiny of others. These general observations should enable readers to focus more sharply on the stories themselves and locate them within the respective cultural discourses. Although we have chosen to describe the four places separately for the purpose of convenience, it must be emphasized that we are not positing a homology between state, nation, and culture. As a matter of fact, the most innovative short story writers in these places, as indeed those anywhere else, seek to break out of the single state-nation-culture boundary by focusing on the sub-nationalities and sub-cultures on the one hand and the supra-national and supra-cultural connections on the other. After all, a common pursuit among the Chinese living in different communities in the late twentieth century is the transition from tradition to modernity. In this process of cultural transformation and diversification, it is interesting to identify the global issues the Chinese self must face while striving to remain Chinese and local.

Earlier in our discussion we stated that the stories collected in this volume have to do with the question of personhood. Indeed, it is the organizing centre of the anthology and the topos that lends the collection its thematic unity. The concept of personhood is indeed both elusive and illusive; hence, we have decided to explore it under four sub-themes, namely, self, identity, gender, and location.

There are seven stories in the section on 'self', which is believed to be vital to one's understanding of society, culture, and literary representation. The self is at the heart of questions of value, beliefs, emotions, ideas of responsibility, and justice as well as social and cultural change. In his introduction to a special issue of the journal *Social Research* (Spring Issue, 1987), James Walkup maintains that a preoccupation with the self and its value is the only remaining tenet of Western tradition still capable of inspiring general assent. The concept of self, which has been at the base of philosophical thought in China, as epitomized in Confucianism and neo-Confucianism, is equally pivotal to an understanding of East Asian traditions of thought.

Most theorists of the self argue that understanding the self is understanding a location, a culture, a language, and a worldview. The concept of self, in this sense, has a certain normative element built into it. In the seven stories gathered under the theme of self, readers see the different and changing selves situated in specific temporal and spatial relationships in the four different communities. This situation, as well as displacement, of the self, whether in 'A Friend on the Road' by Su Tong, 'A Bone Stuck in the Throat' by Xin Qi Shi, or 'Ling and Long' by Soon Ai-ling, offers insights into the relation between self and other, between self and locality.

The concept of identity, on the other hand, is central to an understanding of personhood. It is becoming more evident that identities are by no means fixed, stable, unchanging, or unified. On the contrary, they are fragmented, fissured, volatile, and constantly make and re-make themselves in response to new challenges and contexts. Identities are constituted by diverse regimes of discourse and cultural practices. Identities are produced and re-produced in specific historical conjunctures, social formations, institutional sites, and cultural geography. The cultural critic Stuart Hall believes that identities are points of temporary attachment to subject positions that discursive practices create for us.[5] The six stories gathered under the rubric of 'identity', in their varying ways and from their diverse vantage points, underline the significance of these observations. 'Eyes of the Night' by Wang Meng captures the complexities of identity in modern society. Emphasizing the interplay of contrasts and counterpoint, the story textualizes the dramatic interaction between subjectivity and the locality of the world, the young and the old, the contemplative mind and the empty soul, material circumstances and inner life. The 'eyes' record in their retina the images connected to the hustle and bustle of the city, which produce in the protagonist a sense of bewilderment. It is a first-person narrative, in which the protagonist interprets not only what he sees in a big city, but also what he feels as an alienated, experiencing self. At the same time, the protagonist raises a series of questions about life and the place of his disoriented self in a changing society. Similarly, 'His Son's Big Doll' by Hwang Chun-ming, for example, depicts Kunshu the protagonist as an unsophisticated man. He is certainly different from most city-dwellers. He is the target of mockery of the townsfolk. For them, a man's identity is defined by his appearance. Kunshu, for his part, only needs recognition—recognition of him by his wife and son.

The eminent philosopher Charles Taylor has said that recognition is a vital part of identity, and that due recognition is not a courtesy that we owe people but that it is a vital human need. The heteronomous nature of identity is given form in each of these stories. Viewed in this light, the six stories centring on the notion of identity challenge the idea of identity being a referential sign of a unified and unchanging category.

The next topos related to personhood is gender. Until very recent times gender was not regarded as an essential component of personhood. However, with the increasing growth of feminism as a world-wide movement dedicated to the betterment of women's lives, more and more people are coming to appreciate the importance of gender as a significant aspect of personhood. Feminism and the need to highlight issues of gender have stirred the deepest creative impulses of Chinese female short story writers in interesting and complex ways. Some of the most innovative and memorable short stories emerging from mainland China, Taiwan, Hong Kong, and Singapore are by women writers. These writers perceive the need to change the existing gender relations in their respective societies and advocate for women a greater degree of freedom, and thereby re-define sexual difference. They clearly regard literature as a useful site for undertaking this much needed endeavour. All seven stories in this collection under the rubric 'gender' seek to deal with the complex ways in which social conventions and practices have served to further the interests of men and how the much-valourized ideals of femininity serve the interests of males. 'How Did I Miss You?' by Zhang Xinxin provides a picture of the gender confusion on the Chinese mainland today, where women seek to redefine themselves after their liberation from political patriarchy. 'A Place of One's Own' by Yuen Chiung-chiung depicts the sad world of divorcées and points out the importance of asserting oneself and re-possessing one's personhood to re-build one's life. In a less specific way, 'Curvaceous Dolls' by Li Ang presents woman's fantasy with Freudian overtones while discussing the woman's obsession with her own body. In Hong Kong as well as in Singapore, gender issues are represented more as women's unique experience and less as a social issue. Both of the stories, 'She's Woman; I'm Woman' by Wong Bik Wan and 'The Flower Spirit' by Wong Oi Kuan, explore female sexuality in relation to lesbianism, which is regarded by some as socially challenging and morally unsettling.

The stories dealing with gender capture for us in myriad ways the intersection of gender and culture. There has been a long-standing tendency—and fortunately this is being increasingly challenged—to talk of women's experiences in universal terms and generalize the experiences of Western middle-class women to include those of women in other parts of the world. However, the stories gathered in this volume point out the fallacy of such a mode of thinking and underline the need to explore carefully the interplay between gender and culture. In this way, the stories dealing with gender relationships in this volume serve to counteract the reductive images of Asian women. Instead, they unfold for the readers a world of complexity in which women's experience is both gender-universal and culture-specific.

The fourth topos of this collection, which is closely related to the concept of personhood, is 'location'. The concept of location works at a number of levels of intellectual apprehension. Firstly, it refers to the physical setting against which the stories take place. This is the most elementary level. Secondly, in such stories as 'Ah, Fragrant Snow', this physical space is traversed by issues of power, ideology, and tradition. Writers of these stories invest the physical space with manifold layers of meaning. As a matter of fact, location and dislocation play crucial roles in the six stories collected under the rubric (dis)/location in this anthology. Thirdly, in these narratives, location is not an impassive backdrop against which the stories take place; rather, it is constitutive of meaning. Finally, in psychological terms, dislocation also means dis-placement of subjectivity, and in this sense, both Tie Ning's story, 'Ah, Fragrant Snow', and Yu Hua's story, 'Distant Journey at Eighteen', can be read as examples of psychological dis-placement; the location is as active as any of the characters. In stories like 'Ximi in the Metropolis' by Chang Ta-chun and 'Transcendence and the Fax machine' by Ye Si, the reader comes to see how material developments in society have transformed the psycho-spatial dimension of the self into something hitherto unimagined. In 'The Poem of Spring' by Cai Shuqing, readers see the psychological effect of the interplay between temporal dislocation and memory in more basic and universal self-other relations.

At one level, the short stories collected in this volume can be read primarily for pleasure; at a deeper level, there are other intentionalities at work. In some of the places represented in this volume, the mass media are controlled by the state and the opportunity for frank and open discussions of socio-political issues is left to literature. Hence, the concept of public sphere assumes a great importance. Jürgen Habermas is chiefly responsible for popularizing this concept in academic circles in recent years. He says that the public sphere emerges as a consequence of the efforts of the bourgeoisie in the West to restrict the power of the absolutist state.[6] The public sphere thus provides a discursive space wherein public opinion, which challenges the authority of the state, can be generated through open and candid discussion. According to Habermas, the emergence of the public sphere in Europe was critically linked to the birth of genres, such as the novel and journalism.[7] It is indeed true that Habermas's concept of the public sphere bears the unmistakable imprint of European historicity; however, it is a concept that can be used productively if one is sensitive to the culture-specific itineraries of societies. As Mary Rankin remarks,

> Given the wide range of the term and the use of public outside of Western contexts, one may conceive of the public sphere as a broad category and treat Habermas' model as one specific manifestation. Even if the details of the bourgeoisie public sphere do not fit Chinese history, the idea of intermediate arenas in which open, public initiatives are undertaken by both officials and the populace seems useful in understanding the relationship between the two.[8]

That is why it is equally interesting to note how the stories collected in this anthology relate, in very important and complex ways, to the idea of the public sphere. In countries like the People's Republic of China and Singapore, where the mass media of communication are controlled by the state, creative literature becomes a vital part of the public sphere. Through the exploration of the idea of personhood, the writers of these stories interrogate such important notions as state, nation, modernity, bureaucracy, tradition, cultural heritage, womanhood, identity, location, cosmopolitanism, and the like. The way in which these interrogations are textualized in the stories has much to do with the purpose of the public sphere, and its role in societies that are reaching out towards participatory democracy. While one may certainly read these stories for the vitality and achieved art of these writers, the selected stories also register in a succinct way writers' attempts to address pressing issues pertaining to life in the contemporary world, especially those issues animating the four Chinese communities represented here.

Kwok-kan Tam
Terry Siu-han Yip
Wimal Dissanayake
1999

NOTES

1 A conference entitled 'The Commonwealth of Chinese Literature', organized by Helmut Martin (Ruhr-Universität, Bochum) and Joseph S. M. Lau (University of Wisconsin, Madison), was held in Günzburg, Germany, in 1986. A selection of the papers presented at the conference was published in the book *Worlds Apart: Recent Chinese Writing and Its Audiences* (Howard Goldblatt, ed., Armonk, NY: M. E. Sharpe, 1986). In the introduction, Howard Goldblatt quotes Marián Gálik in summarizing the difficulties of using the concept of 'commonwealth' to describe the commonalities of Chinese literature produced on the Chinese mainland, Taiwan, and Hong Kong, as opposed to the concept of 'community,' which 'expresses the identity of character, fellowship, sociability, common interests, and so forth' and also 'allows for differences and diversities, even polarities, of a literature written in a common language' (pp. 3–4).
2 The concept of 'cultural China' was initiated by Tu Weiming (Harvard University), first at the East-West Center in 1990, as a concept to investigate the cultural interrelations of the various Chinese communities in the contemporary period. Subsequently, conferences exploring the viability of the concept were organized. For example, a conference entitled 'Cultural China' was organized by the Department of Anthropology, the Chinese University of Hong Kong, in 1991.
3 In Chinese-speaking communities, particularly those of the Chinese mainland, Taiwan, and Hong Kong, there is a tendency to treat the literature of the three places separately. Thus most Chinese anthologies of contemporary Chinese literature would not put together the works from the three communities, but in the Western world, in journals as well as anthologies, there is always the attempt to put together the works of the three communities, not only for the sake of comparison, but also to show the common cultural problems facing contemporary Chinese.
4 Ezra Vogel, *The Four Little Dragons,* Cambridge, Mass: Harvard University Press, 1991, p. 81.
5 Stuart Hall, 'Who Needs Identity?', In Stuart Hall and Paul du Gay, (eds.), *Questions of Cultural Identity*, London: Sage, 1996, p. 12.
6 Jürgen Habermas, *The Structural Transformation of the Public Sphere,* Cambridge, Mass: MIT Press, 1989, p. 44.
7 Ibid., p. 45.
8 Mary Backus Rankin, 'Some Observations on a Chinese Public Sphere', *Modern China*, 19,2 (April 1993), p. 160.

Stories of the Self

1

Li Shunda Builds a House

By **GAO XIAOSHENG**
Translated by Madelyn Ross

Gao Xiaosheng 高曉聲 *(b. 1928) studied journalism and began his literary career in the early 1950s but was forced to give up writing in 1957 when he was labelled a Rightist.*[1] *He was then sent to the countryside to do hard labour for twenty years. He took up writing again in 1979 and has won a number of national awards for his stories. 'Li Shunda Builds a House' was awarded the* People's Literature Prize *for short stories in 1979. Among his best-remembered stories are 'The Broken Betrothal' (Jie yue* 解約*, 1954), 'A Lifelong Day' (Manchang de yi tian* 漫長的一天*, 1979), 'Chen Huansheng's Adventure in Town' (Chen Huanshang shang cheng* 陳煥生上城*, 1980), and 'Fishing' (Yu diao* 魚釣*, 1980), all of which have been translated into English. The general themes of his stories are about the sorrows and joys of the peasants in China. There is a taste of the seemingly bland in his writings, but as the reader tastes carefully, he will sense the bitter-sweet in them. Gao Xiaosheng is a member of the Chinese Writers' Association and is a professional writer with the Jiangsu*[2] *branch of the Association.*

1

There's a saying among peasants of the older generation: 'If you eat thin gruel for three years, you can save up enough to buy an ox.' It sounds easy enough, but it's really not. Think about it: if you have to go so far as to water down your rice for three years, won't you be skimping on everything else already? What's more, it's empty reasoning—if you can't afford to eat rice in the first place, then what can you have that's worth saving?

Li Shunda used to be in just such a predicament, and so before Liberation[3] he certainly never had any dreams about buying an ox. But after the land reform movement he began to have faith, and in the spirit of 'eating thin gruel for three years to buy an ox', he decided to build a three-room house.

How many 'three years of thin gruel' would it take to build a three-room house? He didn't know, but he believed that things were different since Liberation, and with a little scrimping and cutting corners it would be possible to accumulate some savings. This is why Li Shunda was full of confidence.

Li Shunda was twenty-eight then, with closely-cropped thick, black hair and a ruddy complexion. He was slightly above average height, and his broad shoulders and thick neck made him appear as sturdy as an iron pagoda. In his family of four (himself, his wife, son, and younger sister) there were three capable labourers, and they had received 6.8 *mu*[4] of good fields. Li Shunda felt so full of energy that he could dig a hole right through the centre of the earth, let alone build a mere three-room house! His steady, if not clever, eyes and a well-proportioned, broad nose rested heavily and stickleback-like above full lips; all these features clearly showed signs of his firm determination. Not even an ox could have pulled him off course.

Forget the ox: not even a train could have pulled him off course! Li Shunda's father, mother, and one-year-old brother had all died without owning a real home. They had come from generations of boat-dwellers who had fished the waters south of the Yangtze. After years of drifting far and wide, they had eventually lost all track of where their ancestral village was. By the time the family's wooden boat was handed down to Li Shunda's father, it was in terrible shape, with rusting nails and lots of holes. The reed covering was open to the sky. It was in no condition to weather a storm. It wasn't even good for fishing anymore, so the whole family was forced to find other work. Some managed by picking over leavings, some by exchanging sugar for rags, some by simply gathering snails; and all this work for just a few mouthfuls of gruel.

One cold day in the twelfth month of the winter of 1942, when Li Shunda was nineteen, the family's rundown boat pulled up along the banks of the river at Chen Family Village. The wind was blowing fiercely and the clouds looked ominous as Li Shunda and his fourteen-year-old sister went ashore, one to exchange sugar for rags and one to collect scraps. They walked over ten miles, and when they turned to head back at dusk they saw that the wind had died and the sky was slate-coloured. In no time, they were caught in a blinding snowstorm, hopelessly lost. Fortunately, they stumbled upon a rundown temple, and took shelter there for the night. At dawn they rushed back to Chen Family Village only to find that their boat had sunk under the weight of the snow, and their parents and baby brother had frozen on a peasant's doorstep. Evidently they had climbed ashore before the boat sank and gone from one door to another, pounding on them and calling for help. But in those times of chaos and war, with bandits everywhere, they had been mistaken for thieves and no one had dared open his door. Their cries had gone unheeded and they had frozen to death in the snow. Heaven has no eyes, the earth has no conscience, and the suffering of the poor is unthinkable . . . for lack of a house!

At the sight of the two children weeping and fainting over their parents' bodies, the poverty-stricken villagers were filled with remorse. They dredged up the sunken boat, using half of it for a coffin to bury the dead. The other half was turned over, belly up to the sky, and placed next to the graves. There it formed a shelter for Li Shunda and his sister, who lived on land from that day on.

When the war against the Japanese ended, the civil war began and with it came forced conscription into the Guomindang army. No one wanted to go, but the village headman had a quota to fill, and Li Shunda was preferred because he was an outsider and had no dependants. So he was forced to become a soldier and was paid three bags of grain in return for joining up. As he looked at their door-less shack, he feared his sister would be raped when he left her there alone, so he used the money from selling himself to put up a straw hut four paces long. Then, drying his tears, he set off for the war.

Although he'd sold his services to the army, he hadn't sold his life. So when he was moved to the front lines after three months, he immediately deserted and fled home. But the following year, the local officer made him sell himself into service again. Altogether, Li Shunda sold himself three times. With the money from his second sale he bought the land that his straw hut was built on, and the land where his parents were buried was bought with the money from his third sale. Ah, it was clear that even if he were to sell himself three more times, the money would somehow all keep disappearing.

The straw hut eventually brought some luck, for it helped Li Shunda get a wife. While he was away in the army, his sister had welcomed a homeless beggar girl into the hut to keep her company. When Li Shunda returned, he made her his wife and within a year they had a fat baby boy, and quite as good as anyone else's son at that!

When the land reform came, Li Shunda was given land, but no house. There had only been one landlord in Chen Family Village and his house was in the city, so it could hardly be divided up among those in the village. Li Shunda would have to think of something himself. He roughly calculated the needs of his family—one room for him and his wife, one for his sister (which could be given to his son after his sister was married off), one room for cooking and eating, and space to raise pigs, sheep, and store firewood. It looked as though his family would need a three-room house at the very least.

This was the goal that Li Shunda set his heart on after Liberation.

2

One might think that a 'liberated' pauper who sets his goal on building a three-room house is too short-sighted, or has insignificant aspirations. But as Li Shunda saw it, it was his faith in the Communist Party and the People's Government which allowed him to have what he thought was such a lofty goal, and the faith that it would really come true. He was ready and willing to follow the Party all the way. Everything he did was testimony to this fact. In his view, achieving socialism would mean 'an upstairs and downstairs, electric lights, and a telephone'. Most important was having the house. Personally, Li Shunda felt that having a two-room, one-storey house was better than having one upstairs room, so he would willingly forgo the 'upstairs and downstairs' part. Yet he wasn't quite sure if it was considered socialist to want to build only a one-storey building. He did approve of having electric lights, but felt that he could do just as well without a telephone—what use would it be since he had no relatives or friends to call him? Besides, his child would undoubtedly break it and then he'd have to spend money to fix it. In short, it would be a total waste. He spoke his mind freely on these matters in public and no one seemed to disagree with him.

None of the peasants in Chen Family Village looked down on his goal; on the contrary, some thought he was setting his sights too high. They warned him that as the locals say, 'ten *mu* of land and three rooms are tough enough to get anywhere in the world, let alone here.' Others said, 'You're going to have to sacrifice and suffer half your life to get this house built,' or 'Even though life is easier since Liberation, I'll bet it will still take you at least ten years of savings.'

True as this was, looking at the houses to the east and west of the area called Benniu on the Shanghai–Nanjing railway, their structure varied widely. To the west, 80 per cent of the homes were made of mud and straw; to the east almost all were of brick and tile. Chen Family Village was situated some 50 miles to the east of Benniu, and was the only cluster of structures in the area made of straw. So, although he was poor, Li Shunda had grown used to the sight of good housing after living amongst these surroundings. Ah, this honest man's reach really exceeded his grasp: building a three-room brick and tile house wasn't nearly as easy as it seemed!

When faced with others' skepticism, Li Shunda would always laugh and say, 'My task can't be any harder than that of the foolish old man who moved the mountain!'[5] When he spoke, the movement of his thick lips pulled his ponderous nose into motion too, making it look as if speaking required great effort. So even when he spoke of simple matters, his expression gave people the impression that he meant what he said.

From then on, Li Shunda and his family began a tortuous struggle, striving with their meager resources to farm every morsel of food and save every penny that they could. The fruits of their daily labour were extremely small, but they held firmly to the belief that every little bit counted, and remained surprisingly optimistic in the face of such hardship. Sometimes the income of Li Shunda's entire family was not enough to cover normal living expenses, and they would simply go a little hungry. Each person would reduce his daily intake of gruel by half a bowl each meal, considering the uneaten six bowls a 'surplus'. If it rained or snowed so heavily that no one could work, they would lie in bed all day to conserve energy, and therefore the need for food, eating only two meals instead of three. Then they would count the savings from the meals not eaten as their day's 'earnings'. When cooking, they added several soybeans to the pan instead of oil, for after all, they reasoned, oil is pressed from soybeans. To prepare snails, they would add a spoonful of rice broth, eliminating the need to add wine, since wine is made from rice in the first place. For years they raised chickens without ever saving any eggs to eat, selling them all instead. They even saved the meat that they placed on their parents' graves during the Qingming Festival to eat when transplanting began just before the Dragon Boat Festival in the fifth lunar month.

Whenever he had a free minute, Li Shunda would take up his old trade again: carrying sugar on a pole across his back and wandering through the village lanes trading it for rags, old newspapers, cotton wadding, worn-out shoes, and any other scraps he could get. Then he'd sort it all out and sell it to the purchasing station, often making a tidy profit. More often than not, he'd also be able to pick up cloth or shoes that his family could still use. When these had been worn out beyond repair, they would simply be put back in with the scraps to be sold. This practice saved the family a fair amount of money.

The sugar he traded came from malt that he bought and refined by himself very inexpensively. Although it cost him very little, his only son Xiaokang went for over seven years without even knowing what sugar tasted like, until finally one day some of the village boys goaded him into tasting a piece. He was caught in the act by his mother, who beat him like a thief until he cried for mercy, and made him swear never to do such a thing again. She kept repeating that he must never waste things, or he would destroy his parents' plans for building a house, and then he'd never be able to get himself a wife because there would be no place for her to live.

Li Shunda's younger sister, Li Shunzhen, was especially worthy of respect. At the time of the land reform in 1951, she was already twenty-three. The government had not yet begun to advocate late marriages, so according to custom she was of marriageable age. She was not only hardworking, docile, and honest, but also exceptionally pretty. She looked a lot like her brother, except that her nose was a little smaller and her lips a little thinner. These two slight differences, combined with her tall stature and oval face, gave her a delicate and attractive air. She had a number of suitors from neighbouring villages, but paid no attention to any of them, regardless of their eligibility or wealth. She insisted that she was too young to be married. She was determined to repay her brother for bringing her up, and she knew that it would be hard for him to achieve his goal without her help; if she married she would deprive him of a needed worker and her 1.7 *mu* share of land. Of course this would set back indefinitely his plans to build a house, so she dedicated these years of her life, which could have been some of her best, to helping her brother. She waited to marry right up until the end of 1957, when Li Shunda had already bought all the brick and tile he'd need for the house. Then, already twenty-nine years old, she married a thirty-year-old fellow who had remained single in order to support his destitute, elderly parents and crippled sister. Thus, all that awaited Li Shunzhen in her new family was more hardship and poverty. But she was quite used to it by this time, and seemed not to mind at all.

3

By the time his sister's marriage was all taken care of, time had already leapt forward into 1958. Li Shunda now lacked only the money to pay the carpenters and bricklayers' fees, but he figured that he'd have enough for everything within a year. Besides, the coming of the communes would be beneficial for him. When all land became publicly owned, he could pick out the very best plot to build on. What more could one want?

Li Shunda was not what one would call a real revolutionary, but rather a good follower. He followed Chairman Mao's teachings, did all he could to carry out Party directives, and considered anything that a Party member told him a direct order.

One morning, Li Shunda woke up to hear that the perfect society was about to be realized, and there would no longer be any distinctions between 'yours' and 'mine'. In the eight years since Liberation, the masses really had managed to accumulate some possessions—for instance, didn't Li Shunda already have the materials to build a three-room house? So why not try pooling everyone's resources to speed up the process of socialist construction? Our construction is for the benefit of all, so everyone should put all his energy into helping to achieve our goals. There is no more need for individual plans, for in the future everyone's life will be equally wonderful. Individual possessions amount to so pitifully little, wouldn't it be more glorious to contribute them all to this magnificent undertaking? No need to worry, every last item will become public property, we're all doing the same thing and no one will cheat you.

This theory was, no doubt, for the good of all. As Li Shunda thought about it, he felt suddenly enlightened, and lighthearted. Despite this, he couldn't help shedding a few painful tears when his bricks were taken to make an iron-smelting furnace, his wood used for making barrows, and even his remaining tiles taken to roof the collective's new pigsty. But he derived great comfort from thinking about the happiness the future would bring. Recent events had certainly changed his outlook on things. Now he felt that living in a multi-storey apartment building would be superior to living in a one-storey home. Grain could be stored above ground level so it wouldn't rot, and people living above the ground floor would be less prone to skin diseases from dampness. So it would be better to live in an assigned apartment, instead of asking for trouble by carrying the whole burden of a home on one's own shoulders, like a snail.

Thus did Li Shunda's thinking become totally liberated, and he happily gave the collective whatever they wanted. He wouldn't even grudge them his bed should they ask, since neither he nor his wife had had the luxury of a bed when growing up. The truth was his wife, the former beggar, had more misgivings about this new situation than he did. But the political atmosphere overwhelmed personal doubts, let alone a woman's misgivings. Her intuitions only brought her extra worry. She did, however, manage to hide away one thing—the family's iron cooking pot—so that it wasn't sent to the iron smelter for melting down. Therefore, when the communal dining hall system ultimately failed and was disbanded, their family alone was saved all the trouble of registering and standing in line to buy a new pot.

Finally, when there was no more money or capital left to throw around, people came back to their senses and made a new start at building socialism. Things had been done irresponsibly and sloppily, and there's no use in saying any more about it. But Li Shunda could not forget completely, and before the scenes of past mistakes were all swept away he would often go look at them, and sob at the sight of the smelting furnace that had collapsed, and the barrows lying abandoned in the untilled earth. He thought of all the blood and sweat of the past six years, the grain he'd managed to save despite his hunger, the sugar snatched from his son's hand, the waste of his sister's best years. . . .

4

Of course, all of the people welcomed the government's compensation policy. But the building materials taken away from Li Shunda had been used up by the collective rather than the state, and although the collective would also like to hand out compensation, they'd been left just as poor as anyone else. They had no materials left to return, nor even enough cash on hand to use as compensation. The cadres had no choice but to go out and do ideological work, raising the consciousness of people like Li Shunda, and urging them to accept only the tiniest compensation, in a spirit of self-sacrifice.

Although Li Shunda's losses had been substantial, his political consciousness was still able to be raised quite a bit. Until now, he'd never undergone such a serious and painstaking ideological education. The District Party Secretary, Comrade Liu Qing, a man of great integrity and prestige, came especially to see him and have a heart-to-heart talk. He explained that Li Shunda's possessions had not been embezzled, nor had anyone harmed him intentionally. The government and the Party had had the best of intentions: they had simply wanted to speed up the establishment of socialism and bring its benefits to the people sooner. The state and collectives had contributed far more towards this goal than Li Shunda had, and of course their losses were inestimably greater. But despite such huge losses, the state and Party were still determined to give compensation to individuals for their losses. Only the Communist Party would act in such a selfless way—it was certainly unprecedented in history. Only the Party would be so concerned about the welfare of the peasants. Please try to understand the Party's difficulties. They had to take care of the major losses for the moment, but they had learned from the experience of the past few years, so from now on development was sure to be even faster. As soon as economic conditions improved for the state and collectives, they would be able to make better provision for individuals. Although it was impossible to build a three-room house right then, it could be quite possible in the future, so one shouldn't lose hope. Finally, Comrade Liu Qing helped him make arrangements with the local supply and marketing cooperative, asking them to keep Li Shunda supplied with malt sugar to refine, so that he could continue to trade it for scraps and make a little extra money.

Li Shunda had always been an emotional fellow, and receiving guidance and concrete help from Comrade Liu Qing was enough to start the tears streaming down his face. Through his tears, he readily agreed to everything that had been said.

There was also the matter of Li Shunda's 20,000 tiles, which had been used for the roof of the production team's new seven-room pigsty. It would be ideal if they could be returned to him, but to do so at a time like this when new tiles were unavailable would leave the pigs out in the open. Besides, the tiles were fragile, and many would be broken in the process of taking them down. After much discussion, both sides agreed that—considering each other's difficulties—it would be better to leave the pigsty intact. But the production team would clean out two rooms of the pigsty for Li Shunda's temporary use as a home, until he could build his own place. The pigsty would certainly be sturdier than his current thatched hut, and being ten paces wide it would be spacious enough. The roof was almost four metres high, except towards the back where it was too low for a man to stand erect. But who needs to be able to go strutting around inside a house anyway? Besides, Li Shunda was used to crouching from having grown up hunched under the awning of the boat his family had owned.

So this was how the question of Li Shunda's compensation was settled. Although he seemed perfectly content after receiving all this guidance from the cadres, he had also learned a rather unusual lesson from the whole experience. Previously, the sight of rampant inflation in the old society had taught him that paper money was unreliable, so he had always spent his money on goods as soon as possible. But since this latest experience, he felt that in the new society, on the contrary, it was goods that were unreliable and assets were safer kept in the form of money hidden under a pillow. To tell the truth, it was thoughts like these that enabled alert 'leftists' to sniff out 'anti-Party sentiments', and would later get him in trouble.

From 1962 to 1965, thanks to the 'Sixty Articles on Agriculture' and the care Comrade Liu Qing had taken to see that he was kept supplied with malt sugar, Li Shunda had once again saved up almost enough to build a three-room house. But this time he didn't buy a thing, preferring to keep his assets in cash. He'd wait until he had everything needed to do the job from start to finish, then buy all the material and put up the house at once. This way he could avoid undue worry about making the same mistake as last time. Li Shunda was like many other peasants in this respect, very quick to learn from the lessons of the past. But spending too much time looking back makes one apt to stumble on unseen objects ahead. It's really hard to help someone make any forward progress if he's always looking back.

In those years goods were readily available and supplies practically limitless, but Li Shunda didn't dare buy a thing. Then suddenly the situation changed and things were again in short supply. Very few people were able to get hold of what they needed. Unfortunately, it was just around this time that Li Shunda finally had enough money to plunge ahead and buy everything, but it was too late. Once again he was left feeling like a fool. Yet it would be unfair to say that it was all his fault, for these days few people can be expected to have the wisdom of a wise man like Zhuge Liang.[6]

5

Under ordinary circumstances, Li Shunda felt that he was quite a devoted follower—always honest and sincere, and possessing genuine emotions. But when the 'cultural revolution' started, even he couldn't keep up anymore. How could you keep up with a situation in which you were surrounded by people everywhere loudly proclaiming 'Only I know the correct doctrine'? Who really knew who was right or wrong, good or bad, honest or insincere, red or black? Li Shunda got totally confused, and finally had to just squat down on his heels and give up trying to follow anyone.

The slogan 'all men have a sense of right and wrong' was prominent at this time, but in truth it was too simplistic for the experience of the 'cultural revolution'. One couldn't simply believe what a man said in his speeches; it was necessary to keep track of his actions as well. 'All men have a sense of good and bad' would have been far more appropriate.

Li Shunda's desire to build a house was causing him to feel uneasy. He realized that the spirit of the times was even more unusual than it had been in 1958. Then, some things had been destroyed, but that was the end of it. Now it had become a question of destroying some people, and one's involvement could really be a life-or-death matter. He certainly couldn't build the house in times like these, with no idea what tomorrow might bring. He was disgusted by it all, but at the same time felt lucky to have moved to a pigsty in the centre of town. If he'd still been living way out in his straw hut by the river bank, even the money under his pillow might have been stolen.

Li Shunda's thinking was not progressive, but if the times had only been more enlightened, maybe such a barbaric tactic would not have been used on him: a big tough-guy in the rebel faction came to his house for a visit one day, with a handgun tucked in at his waist and a copy of a little red book under his arm, accompanied by the leader of the production team. He was chairman of the commune's brick and tile factory, and he said, like a true friend, that he knew Li Shunda wanted to build a house but couldn't get the bricks, and he'd come especially to help him. He cursed the capitalist-roader Liu Qing who hadn't helped the poor and middle peasants. But luckily now the saviour had come along to set things right, and if Li Shunda would kindly just hand over 217 yuan[7] he'd take all the responsibility for seeing that 10,000 bricks were bought and delivered to him next month. He spoke so sweetly that it didn't even sound suspicious. Li Shunda reasoned that, after all, they were members of the same brigade and although they weren't on close terms they still saw each other often enough, and this fellow's reputation wasn't bad as far as he knew. Besides, in those days of revolutionary fervor, everyone was trying to do good, and people wouldn't be apt to cheat others. What's more, he had both a gun and a little red book, he'd come with the leader of the production team, and he seemed the image of friendliness, conviction, and authority. Even Li Shunda, who'd been cunning enough to escape from the army three times, couldn't stand up to such persuasive tactics, and before he knew it he'd handed over 217 yuan.

The following month, about the time when his bricks were supposed to arrive, Li Shunda's bad luck began. He was called to the commune's political headquarters to answer a few questions, and things went something like this: '1. Where are you from and what's your family background? 2. We know you were a soldier for the reactionaries three separate times. Hand over your gun immediately. 3. You're known to have made reactionary statements (for example: 'a one-storey house is better than a multi-storey structure', and 'it costs too much to fix a broken phone'). These are poisonous attacks on socialism.'

What followed needn't be elaborated, since it's known to all. Even when Li Shunda himself was let free he didn't have much to say about it. But two things were particularly characteristic. The first is that when he couldn't take it anymore and called out for help, it was the revolutionary chairman of the brick and tile factory who came to his rescue. In return for his help, Li Shunda privately agreed not to mention the missing 217 yuan to anyone again. The second is that the room in which he was held was extremely well built, and for the first time in his life he made a concerted effort to study construction, to form a clear idea of how his own future home should be built.

When he was released he limped home on the arm of his already nineteen-year-old son. When his weeping wife and sister asked him why he had been locked up and if he'd suffered much, he only rasped in laconic confusion, 'They are evil! My house!'

For a few years afterwards he wasn't able to work because of the pain in his lower back, and on overcast days his whole body ached miserably. One thought kept bothering him—although he'd never gone through such hard times before, his whole life had been pretty rough, stumbling along from one hardship to another . . . so why was he so delicate all of a sudden, not even well enough to work? Could it be that he really was a 'revisionist'? The thought shocked him. As far as he was concerned, it would be easier to turn into a cow or a horse than into a revisionist. Being a revisionist meant being a black pot, one that was no longer good for cooking, a worthless object to be lugged around endlessly on one's back. A revisionist was a label that never died, but was handed down through generations like an unwanted family heirloom. His son was nineteen already—how would he ever find a wife if he had to carry such a black pot around on his back too? And there was no family home either, nothing at all for him to attract a wife with.

When Li Shunda thought about all this, he became terror-stricken and superstitious. He remembered one of the many tales told to him as a child, about a man who could change into many different objects. The story-teller would whisper: 'And then one night, he suddenly turned into a. . . .' What's more, before each transformation he'd have a strange feeling, his whole body aching terribly all over, his flesh hot and dry . . . and so on. Therefore, whenever Li Shunda found himself in pain he would dread the approach of nightfall and sleep. He would lie awake with open staring eyes, trying to prevent himself from losing consciousness and being turned into a black pot. Because he was fully forewarned and cautious, he managed to ward off such a transformation.

During those sleepless nights, Li Shunda had to create his own entertainment in order to dispel his pain. He had no radio, and even if he'd wanted to read he only knew a few characters and couldn't afford to waste the lamp oil anyway. So his only recourse was to recall stories he'd heard in his youth, lyrics from plays, and folk songs passed on from the old to the young. During the day, as soon as he felt better, he'd shoulder a load of sugar and go out again to trade for scraps, constantly singing a little ditty to amuse the children. He claimed to have recalled this ditty during one of those nights of self-enforced sleeplessness. From the words, one can get an idea of what was really on his mind. He would sing,

Strange strange really strange,
There's an old man confined to the cradle;
Strange strange really strange,
There's a huge table stuffed in your pocket;
Strange strange really strange,
Look at the rat biting the cat;
Strange strange really strange,
Look at the lion bullied by fleas;
Strange strange really strange,
The dog sends the yellow weasel to guard the chickens;
Strange strange really strange,
That toad's got a piece of swan meat in his mouth;
Strange strange really strange,
A big ship's sunk in a tiny rainpipe;
Strange strange really strange,
A tall man can act as a short man's ladder.
Ai Ya Ya! Watermelon rind makes a hat for your scabby head,
No pearls, just piss inside the clam,
No air, just farts inside the ball,
Nothing but mud fills the fierce, robed idol.
So strange, so strange, so really strange,
A deadly snake coils inside the Buddha's statue,
Smelling the incense and putting on airs.

Everyone recognized this old familiar song about truly strange events. Each person who sang it usually added his own personal colour to it, throwing in whatever he felt to be most strange. But Li Shunda wouldn't admit to embellishing upon it at all. He was no writer—didn't even know how!—and anyway, what would have been the point of giving others something to use against him by revealing his own feelings? Although he wasn't brainy, his past experiences had made him aware that there was a certain type of person—whether a rebel in power or a powerful rebel—who would do anything to reach his objective . . . for example getting hold of his 217 yuan.

One day, while exchanging sugar for scraps and singing away in a neighbouring village, he happened to bump into a capitalist-roader doing labour reform there. It turned out to be none other than the former District Party Secretary Liu Qing! Liu Qing asked Li Shunda to sing the 'Strange Song' once more for him. Unsuspectingly, Li Shunda began to sing. The tragic, heavy, angry sound set even the air aquiver, and both men shed bitter tears.

6

A year passed and still he remained in poor health. Li Shunda began to feel disheartened and often wondered how much longer he had to live. Should he still trouble himself with his plans to build a house? Even the proverbial foolish old man had left part of the task of moving the mountain to his descendants, so why must Li Shunda complete the house all by himself? Besides, he would still be remembered for things like the money he'd managed to save and all his hard labour. On the other hand, the human spirit is stubborn and hard to fathom. Li Shunda thought of his son, past twenty now. Without a house he'd never find himself a wife, for who on earth would be willing to move into a pigsty! Unfortunately, Li Shunda's son would not have the chance to marry a beggar girl as his father had. But without a daughter-in-law, where would Li Shunda get a grandson? And without a grandson, where would he get a great grandson? When the good life of Communism arrived, would he leave no descendants there to enjoy it? So it seemed he had no choice but to continue planning to build the house, and as quickly as possible too. At least there was some time left, since his son had to wait until he was older to get married, in accordance with government policy.

After this period of wavering, Li Shunda recovered his determination and immediately got to work. He took his large wicker basket for scraps and trudged slowly and unsteadily from village to village, covering almost every road and alley in the county seat without finding any building material for sale. By asking at shops he finally found out that before he could buy a single brick, he would need certificates from all three local levels of authority. There seemed to be no way he could get around this requirement. He realized that before wasting any more time he'd better apply for a certificate at the production team, brigade, and commune. Luckily the day wasn't totally wasted even though he hadn't found any building materials, because he'd managed to collect enough scraps to sell for over 10 yuan.

His next step was obviously to get a certificate from the local cadres at the production team and brigade, but when they heard his request they just laughed at him and said: 'What good will a certificate do, when there's so little building material around for people's use? Even with a certificate you won't be able to buy a thing.' Li Shunda dared not believe them, thinking that they were just being obstructive. But he didn't dare argue either, for fear that he'd ruin his chances completely. So he waited patiently, camped out on their doorstep. No one took further notice of him, until dinnertime when he was discovered still hanging around and was asked to leave so that the door could be locked. He had to leave then, but was back again the next day. And so it went for three days, until finally a cadre told him impatiently: 'Since you won't listen to reason but insist on sitting here being a bother, I'll give you the certificate that you think will be such a big help.' And sure enough, Li Shunda was given his certificate and happily rushed off to the supply and marketing cooperative. The clerk took one look at his certificate and laughed just like the cadre at the brigade saying: 'Sorry, there's no material in stock.'

'When will you get some?'

'Dunno,' was the reply. 'Stop by and check whenever you have free time.'

From then on Li Shunda went there as faithfully as a pupil going to school, six days a week. But after six months of this, he still hadn't succeeded in buying even one brick. The clerk was actually good at heart, and although he pitied Li Shunda for his stupidity, he couldn't help admiring the man's stubborn spirit. Finally he whispered to him: 'Why not save your energy and quit coming here. People have been making revolution fiercely the past few years, and all the land is being "revolutionized", to the point where it's almost abandoned. When a few supplies do become available, there isn't even enough to go around for the cadres, let alone for you. If you were to get hold of something, it would be useless rubbish that no one else had any use for, and you'd have to pay full price for it too. You'd just be wasting your money. You'd be far better off to think of some other solution.'

This sincere advice was a terrible disappointment for Li Shunda, but he was extremely grateful nonetheless. He had no choice but to ask, 'What other solution?'

'Well, do you have any relatives or good friends who are cadres?' the clerk asked hesitatingly.

'None,' Li Shunda replied heavily, 'just my sister and brother-in-law, who are peasants.'

'Then you're out of luck,' the clerk said sympathetically. 'These days it's not what you know that counts, but who you know. No amount of official documents is worth as much as a few personal connections. If you don't have influential friends and relatives, your only other choice would be to buy on the black market.'

Li Shunda took this advice very seriously, and began planning how to get materials from the black market right away. He never suspected that perhaps the clerk knew very little about the black market himself, and didn't understand its complexities. The fixed price for 10,000 bricks was 217 yuan, but on the black market they would go for as high as 400 yuan, with payment required in advance. Then you had to wait at least six months for delivery, often to find that you'd simply been tricked. Li Shunda had made this mistake once and obviously wouldn't part with his money so easily again. So instead he spent three years running from one place to another trying to talk his way into a good deal, but with no success.

In the end it was the clerk who agreed to help him out by buying him a ton of limestone at the state's fixed price. This limestone had originally been scheduled for use in the silkworm house. But in recent years many mulberry fields had been enthusiastically replanted as rice paddies, and the few rotten mulberry trees left standing couldn't raise enough silkworms to make it worthwhile. So the limestone was worthless and the supply clerk took advantage of this situation to sell it cheaply to Li Shunda.

As a token of thanks, Li Shunda wanted to buy the clerk a pack of high quality cigarettes, but they were often difficult to get. By chance he happened to run into the former revolutionary chairman of the commune's brick and tile factory (who had risen to become a chairman of the factory revolutionary committee by this time). Li Shunda recalled that he always used to smoke good cigarettes, and reasoned that since the man had treated him so badly in the past he now owed Li Shunda a favour, so why not ask him for some cigarettes? Li Shunda unabashedly asked for the favour, and the chairman's reaction was equally straightforward: he took Li Shunda's 5 mao[8] and pulled an unopened pack of 'Da Qianmen' from his bag. Then, just before he handed them over, he deliberately plucked one out for himself, adding, 'This is my last pack; I wouldn't do a favour like this for anyone but you.'

So Li Shunda took the remaining nineteen cigarettes and offered them to the clerk, who adamantly refused them. Finally he smoked one so Li Shunda wouldn't lose face, but he insisted that he take the remaining eighteen cigarettes back with him.

On the way home, Li Shunda couldn't help thinking of how he'd done something wrong that day he'd never done before—he'd actually treated both a friend and an enemy to a cigarette. By dinner time he was really feeling angry, so he yelled at his son, a twenty-five-year-old helpless good-for-nothing, who made his father do improper things on his account.

7

A number of years passed quickly, and although Li Shunda's house wasn't any closer to being built, its fame had become quite widespread. Still, no problem is so large that it can't be overcome if one's mind is set on it, and the plight of the unbuilt house had moved not only the clerk but the Lord as well. The Lord in this case turned up in the form of Li Shunda's future daughter-in-law, Xinlai. Xinlai lived in a neighbouring village and had been involved with Li Shunda's good-for-nothing son Xiaokang for a long time. She was in love with him, and didn't mind if the family had a house or not—if it wasn't built until after their marriage, that was fine too. But her father was against the marriage; under no circumstances was he going to let his daughter be married off to live in a pigsty. He used his own life as a model example, pointing out that although he'd been poor, he'd still managed to build a two-room house before getting his son a wife. He cursed Li Shunda, calling him an incompetent fool. But Heaven likes to have her little joke, and teach those who talk too much a lesson. Within a year, most of the capitalist-roaders had been removed from power, and the new leaders were eager to literally 'change the face of the earth'. They decided to start with an unsightly river whose course was as crooked as an old man's back. They were set on using many thousands of labourers and tens of thousands of workdays to turn the river into a 'model river' that flowed straight as an arrow, so that even the higher creatures on Mars would look down at earth and marvel at man's greatness. But Xinlai's family home was right smack in the path of the proposed new river bed, nor was their two-room house the only one, so they were forced to move. The commune paid them a compensation of 150 yuan per room. After borrowing another 300 yuan, they were able—with some difficulty—to build another one-and-a-half-room house. But in the process, Xinlai's father lost a lot of weight and his hair turned almost all white from the worry. He also had to listen to his daughter admonishing him to 'learn from Uncle Li Shunda' who was both shrewd and patient, tucking away all his money safely under his pillow. He wouldn't build a house until he knew the time was just right. To such arguments her father had no reply, and finally he had to admit defeat, agreeing to let his daughter make her own decisions about marriage. Li Shunda was overjoyed, for he not only got a daughter-in-law, but also a strong theoretical affirmation of his actions. So on the night of his son's marriage he drank several glasses of wine and, feeling inspired, turned and spoke in riddles to Xinlai's father:

'Now I hold the cards in my hands, and the weak have become better off than the strong. Your house went up too fast. And with such chaos everywhere, people would rather live in cow sheds anyway. Even though I had to feed 10,000 bricks to that bastard of a brickmaker, I'm still less worried than you.'

He would have kept on talking but luckily his wife had a good warning instinct, and she piped up quickly: 'The silly fool just blabs on whenever he's had a few drinks. You'd think he'd remember the trouble he got into for talking too much before, and how it made his bones ache!' She managed to turn the conversation around with that remark, much to everyone's relief.

From then on, Li Shunda didn't waste any more energy trying to figure out how to buy construction materials. Instead he shouldered his sugar buckets and wandered here and there collecting scraps to earn a little money. But strangely enough he saw quite a number of houses being built during his travels. He couldn't help feeling jealous, and would always stop to ask what family was building the house and where they'd purchased their materials. The responses were extremely varied, and a separate book could have been written on the background of each house. But what everyone seemed to be covering up was the fact that they were all just cases of 'high officials having things sent to the door, lesser officials making use of their influence, and ordinary folk pleading with others'. Some of those poor folk actually envied Li Shunda, saying that he was the lucky one for avoiding all this trouble—a true hero of the times. A friend finally blurted out angrily:

'Every brick and tile I have had to be purchased on the black market. To build these two rooms cost me the price of building a four-room house! The day we were putting on the roof, that brigade party secretary—the one who relied on his involvement with the rebel faction to get power—invited himself over for a meal. Do y'know he had the nerve to say that if it hadn't been for the "cultural revolution" I'd never have been able to build a house? That bastard! Does he think I got my house the same way that he got to the top—through beating down others?'

By this time Li Shunda figured he knew just about everything there was to know about housing construction. But wonders never cease, and unusual events just keep occurring, rolling in like waves on the Yangtze. Who can help but be interested? It's understandable to skip over small matters, but it's a real pity to do so when marvelous incidents are involved. For instance, it became known that a certain brigade was preparing to tear down everyone's house in order to build a series of several-storey apartments called 'new village'. The material from the old houses was to be returned to the collective and the people would be paid for its value. Then whoever wanted to live in the new buildings could pay up and move in. Li Shunda felt greatly inspired when he heard of this, thinking that the ideal of 'an upstairs and a downstairs' was finally coming true. He impatiently shouldered his sugar buckets and rushed to the village to see for himself what was going on.

Although Li Shunda had often passed through this area before, everything was completely different now. In every alleyway, people were tearing down their houses and bringing all the materials to the edge of the public road where the first apartment was going up in a large field. Those families tearing down their houses were all talking animatedly, some even becoming fiercely emotional, and all were in agreement that this was the greatest event since the creation of the world. Some people were crying, probably because they were overexcited. Some of the tiles from the dismantled roofs were still covered with ash from the kiln and had obviously never even been rained on; yet here they were being 'emancipated' already. Seeing all this, Li Shunda felt that his twenty-nine years of vainly hoping for a house that had never been built had been a proper thing. Yet when he thought of these folks tearing down their houses, the fruit of so much labour, his own eyes began to brim over, and he sighed deeply, lowered his head, and began to walk away. Suddenly he heard someone call out: 'Hey, sugar pedlar!'

Looking up he saw an old man standing by the side of the road with a little girl in his arms, watching the construction. He looked very familiar but Li Shunda couldn't quite place him. The old man chuckled and said, 'What's this? Don't you recognize me?'

Suddenly Li Shunda recognized who it was and exclaimed quickly, 'Party Secretary, it's you! Are you still doing labour reform?' He felt sad as he realized that the old Party Secretary had aged beyond recognition in the few years since he'd last seen him. But surprisingly enough, the old Party Secretary seemed to be in high spirits.

Laughing, the Party Secretary answered, 'I'm still doing labour, but I haven't managed to reform yet. And you, have you come back collecting more material for your "Strange Song"?'

'Ai, you're making fun of me, Secretary Liu,' Li Shunda protested self-consciously. 'I came here to see the making of this "new village", "the upstairs and the downstairs". I didn't realize till today that the dividing line between old and new lies right here in these buildings, not in the question of whether or not to be collective.'

Party Secretary Liu took a quiet breath and urged, 'Say what you mean more clearly.'

'Of course it won't really matter if I explain it to you,' Li Shunda laughed. 'But then again, I don't want to break the law knowingly. I used to say that living in a high-rise isn't as good as having a one-storey house, and later this was judged to be reactionary. But now, when I see things like this, I still want to say what I feel. I mean, what's the point in tearing down perfectly good homes, some of them even brand-new, to build something else? Wouldn't it be better to put all this energy into planting more fields? These are questions people don't dare ask in broad daylight, but it sure keeps them awake at night!'

Hearing this 'reactionary' talk, the Party Secretary not only made no retort but even nodded his head in agreement, adding gravely: '"What's the point?" is a good question. You know, there are people who want to use all this as their ladder to self-advancement. As you well know, collectivization is the foundation of our new countryside.

But some people, in their attempt to "restore the old order", find the commune system easy to take advantage of. Open your eyes even wider. Just look at the situation—the poor and lower-middle peasants suffered for twenty years to build these small homes, and then the minute someone tells them to tear them down they have no choice but to do so. Nobody cares about what's important to the masses anymore. And yet the commune is still called a commune!'

Li Shunda felt enlightened by this speech, although he couldn't quite make sense of it all. He just stood there quietly, staring respectfully at this older man, with his mouth hanging open.

The old man gave an angry snort and stopped talking. He looked down at his little girl and pointed to Li Shunda saying: 'Say "Hello, grandpa!"'

The little girl did so, with warm affection. Li Shunda was greatly moved, and quickly broke off a piece of sugar and put it in her little hand, calling her a little darling. He was fifty-four years old now, an outsider who'd come to these parts in search of rags and scraps, and this was the first time that anyone had ever called him grandpa. It gave him great inspiration, and wiped out all other thoughts from his head.

From this time on, he and the old Party Secretary became fast friends.

8

During the Spring Festival in 1977, when Li Shunda took several sugar candies to visit the old Party Secretary, he first heard the news that Party Secretary Liu had been reinstated in his former post at the district office. Li Shunda was overjoyed at the unexpected good news, and after giving some candy to the little girl and eating some of the sweets her mother offered, he rushed off to the district office. He thought that maybe, with the current district Party Secretary as his good friend, he might finally be able to get hold of that building material he needed for his house.

His old friend greeted him warmly. But as soon as Li Shunda raised the question of building materials, the Party Secretary fell silent and coughed several times. Li Shunda trembled at the thought that this might be a bad sign. Then the old Party Secretary said slowly, 'My friend, I know all about your troubles. In the past when you sang your

"Strange Song", I agreed completely. So, now I don't think you and I can do this same type of "strange thing" ourselves, eh?'

Li Shunda blurted out, 'But Secretary Liu, I wouldn't do it if other people didn't. With everyone doing such things, why should I be the only one not to? That would be too hard on myself!'

Laughing, Secretary Liu explained: 'After ten years of chaos, it's not easy to change things. But now we must get to work and set things straight, or else the achievement of the state's plan will be merely empty talk. We can't do certain things just because other people do them. As the highest cadre in the district, I must be the first to set an example. As for the masses, let the singer of the "Strange Song" be first to set an example—how about it? Is that reasonable or not?'

On hearing this, Li Shunda was filled with mixed emotions. On the one hand he felt it would be greatly satisfying to take the lead in a rectification movement alongside the Party Secretary. But on the other hand, it would be such a disappointment to have a friend in a high position and not be able to take advantage of it. He had lived through the 'cultural revolution' and didn't want any more bitter lessons. After thinking a moment he spoke plausibly and at length:

'Secretary Liu, I'll do whatever you say. But let me say this first: OK, I won't do any "strange things", just as you've asked. But don't you waver either. Don't go opening "back doors" for closer friends than me or more important people than me. If you do, everyone will laugh at me for getting no profit out of our friendship, and I'll have to turn against you then.'

The Party Secretary laughed heartily and, taking out a pen and paper, he quickly wrote down Li Shunda's words. 'Listen while I read this,' he instructed, reading out an exact version of what Li Shunda had just said. Then he went on, 'Please take this and have someone write it up into a big character poster and paste it up in my office.'

Li Shunda protested, 'But I don't want to embarrass you!'

Secretary Liu insisted, 'Not at all. Actually, you'd be doing me a big favour. I've been dreading the time when high-ranking people will come and ask unsavory favours of me. If you put up this poster, you'll save me a lot of trouble in getting out of such situations.'

Li Shunda went off happily to follow instructions.

When winter arrived, Li Shunda's household suddenly began to bustle with activity. Party Secretary Liu Qing had done some 'work' on that ex-revolutionary chairman of the commune's brick and tile factory and told him to make adequate compensation to Li Shunda for the 10,000 bricks. The commune revolutionary committee also approved Li Shunda's request for eighteen concrete beams. And the good-hearted clerk at the supply and marketing cooperative informed Li Shunda that rafters were now readily available. This time it looked like Li Shunda's house would really be built! But to transport all these things, Li Shunda's family of four wasn't enough, so he asked his sister's family and daughter-in-law's family to help. Everyone was pushing and pulling and rowing and having a great time. Even Xinlai's father pitched in and worked up a merry sweat.

But there was one incident that spoiled part of this happiness. When it was time to transport the bricks from the factory, a surprising thing happened. Their boat was docked at the brick and tile factory, but no bricks were forthcoming. Instead, someone smiled insincerely and told Li Shunda, 'Your beams haven't been obtained yet so there's no use in taking the bricks back with you now. Better wait a little longer.' Li Shunda argued furiously, saying that the order for the beams had been given long ago. But this fellow seemed to know Li Shunda better than Li Shunda knew himself, and he kept asserting that there were no beams. Luckily, Xinlai's father rushed over and quietly informed him of what the fellow really meant when he said 'beams', as he'd learned from his own past experience with buying them. Li Shunda realized what was going on and went off immediately to the supply and marketing cooperative to buy two packs of the best cigarettes to give as gifts. Only then were things settled amicably and the bricks smoothly loaded. Later, when it came time to pick up the beams from the cement works, no one needed to give Li Shunda any more advice. He handed out a pack of quality cigarettes, in order to avoid being told that his rafters hadn't been obtained yet.

Li Shunda was truly indignant at having to resort to such corrupt tactics, and wouldn't have dared tell the Party Secretary about it. But he couldn't get it off his mind completely, and sometimes he'd curse himself, saying,

'Ai, I've really got to work on improving myself. . . .'

1979

NOTES

1 'Rightist' is a label used in the massive campaign that occurred in China in 1957, to purge dissidents.
2 One of the most culturally and economically developed coastal provinces in China, with Nanjing as its capital.
3 A term commonly used on the Chinese mainland to refer to the founding of the People's Republic of China.
4 A unit of measuring area. 1 *mu* = 0.667 hectares.
5 A Chinese fable that emphasizes the importance of determination and perseverance in human endeavours, which Mao Zedong used in the early days of the People's Republic of China to call for a general spirit of utopian optimism in building the socialist state.
6 The prime minister of the Kingdom of Su in the Three Kingdom Period (AD 220–280) of Chinese history. He has become a symbol of wisdom in Chinese culture.
7 A unit in Chinese currency. 1 yuan (RMB) = US$0.125.
8 A unit in Chinese currency. There are 10 mao in 1 yuan.

2

A Friend on the Road

By **SU TONG**

Translated by Lo Man-wa and Kwok-kan Tam, with Timothy Weiss

Su Tong 蘇童 *(b. 1963) was born in Suzhou and read Chinese literature at Beijing Normal University. His works of fiction cover a variety of themes dealing with gender, sex, initiation, and the urbanization of rural life in China. He is also the author of* Wives and Concubines *(*Qi qie cheng qun 妻妾成群*, 1989), which was made into the internationally acclaimed film,* Raise the Red Lantern *(*Da hong denglong gao gao gua 大紅燈籠高高掛*, 1990), directed by Zhang Yimou. Su Tong's short stories can be found in* Women's Paradise *(*Funu leyuan 婦女樂園*, 1991),* A Guide to Divorce *(*Li hun zhinan 離婚指南*, 1993), and the six-volume* Collected Works of Su Tong *(*Su Tong wenji 蘇童文集*, 1997). His novel,* Rice *(*Mi 米*, 1991), has been translated into English. As many critics have pointed out, Su Tong's fiction often deals with the inherent evils in the human mind. Su Tong is the editor of* Zhongshan 鍾山*, a magazine based in Nanjing.*

On the eve of the New Year I received a greeting card from Lijun, posted from a small, remote county in the north of Shaanxi. On it were drawn old-fashioned patterns of flowers and animals; its edges and corners, creased and torn during the postal route, were tinged with some curious, dusty yellow stains. Lijun posts a greeting card like this one every year, and with every year the place name on the postmark changes: Beijing, Kunming, Haikou, Yili, Harbin. This time it was Ansai County, an out-of-the-way place where few travellers had trodden. Obviously my good friend was still on the road. On the road—the style of life Lijun set for himself more than a few years ago.

I noticed that the style of the card's maxim was different from that of last year's. 'Bianxiang' ['Redirect']. Its abruptness and sharpness took me back a bit, and its message was difficult to grasp. The maxim that Lijun sent last year came to mind: 'Man thinks, God laughs.' Upon reading it I had felt a warmth, a kind of uncommon philosophical glow. Then I copied the maxim on cards to be sent to other university friends. Sometime later I discovered that Lijun's maxim was actually borrowed from Kundera, an exiled East European writer who had had a meteoric rise to fame in the West.

I looked up the phrase in the Chinese dictionary on my desk. Surprisingly, there was no entry for 'bianxiang'. I had no idea whether this was due to an unintentional omission or the ignorance of the dictionary editors. Nor could I figure out the moral behind the phrase, which was perhaps a physics term: What's 'bianxiang'? Well, why bother anyway? As some friends of mine advised: 'Don't take things too seriously with Lijun—just as you don't need to figure out why he went to Ansai County in the north of Shaanxi.' So I did not allow these things to trouble me because I knew that as Lijun's friend, I would continue to gain much from him.

In nearly every corner of China, Lijun has friends. I am just one of them, and yet looking back on our first acquaintance, I still feel a lingering regret. At that time both of us were studying at a university in the North. Usually he kept a low profile; only in philosophy and political-economics classes was he sometimes seen raising his hand and standing up, out of nowhere, to put incisive queries to the instructors. He spoke with a distinct Jiangjie[1] accent and a treble voice filled with conviction. On each occasion the girls sitting in the front row would turn their heads and look at him with admiration and affection. Lijun's dishevelled hair, his grave manner, and his acerbic eloquence made one think of luminaries such as Kant and Sartre in their youth.

Lijun had a passion for buying books and for this he often borrowed money. More often than not he failed to pay his creditors back. For this reason he had a mixed reputation at the university. Those who demanded their money back, but to no avail, called him a swindler. Those who had not had such a bad experience still admired him. Then it happened that Lijun borrowed 20 yuan from me, saying that only one copy of *Being and Nothingness* remained in stock and that it would be sold if he did not hurry to the bookstore. I could not turn him down, and the prediction of those poor creditors came true for me as well. I was hard up at the time, but I failed to get Lijun to pay the 20 yuan back. So you can imagine why I was exasperated when I found him drinking, all by himself, in a small restaurant off campus.

I sat down opposite him, resentfully watching him sip his alcohol, his eyes half closed. *Being and Nothingness* was placed between the bottle and a plate of deep-fried peanuts. Just when I snatched the book, I heard him sneer.

'Take it if you like,' he said, 'but you won't be able to understand it. Its truth is beyond the pale of the vulgar herd. You'll get nothing from it.'

'But you must pay me back,' I retorted. I put the book down, angry with myself for always seeming weak and mean-spirited in front of him.

'Don't talk about money with me. It's a word I detest.' His brows knitted, he pushed the bottle towards me. 'The drink's on me,' he said. 'Forget money. Forget college and its rules and its enclosing wall. Drink up whenever you feel like drinking. That's the only way to find peace of mind.'

Strangely, then, that was how I got broken in, and drank hard liquor for the first time. Becoming half-drunk, I heard Lijun say to me, 'Break through the enclosing wall. Go out to see the real world. Go out to find your true self.' And thus I was baptized like a devoted believer, and I became his most loyal friend.

On the road.
On the road.

Years earlier this slogan of Lijun was all the rage at the university, igniting our youthful ambitions. When it came time for graduates to receive their job assignments, it was exactly their idealistic passions that drove many classmates of mine to sign up for work in remote areas like Xinjiang, Qinghai, and Tibet. Lijun chose the latter, Tibet. His address at the graduation ceremony electrified the audience. 'Don't commend me. Don't praise me. I'm not answering the call of the fatherland,' he explained. 'This is just my personal desire. I need to be on the road. . . . '

'On the road', those words surged and resounded like pounding waves through the hall of the graduation ceremony. Even today the reverberations of that phrase still ring in my head.

A few years later when I happened to read a book, published in the 1960s, by an American author, Jack Kerouac, I suspected that Lijun must have taken his memorable slogan 'On the road' from this very novel. But it is pointless to dig too deeply. Lijun has certainly lived his words; he has been on the road a long time now, and so have his followers, my friends at the university.

Lijun sent me letters not long after he departed for Tibet. Enclosed were photos of him taken at the Potala Palace, with a yak train, or at the Tashilhunpo Monastery. He looked exhausted, yet his eyes still beamed with dreamy passion. In one photo there was a girl, short-haired and round-faced, who seemed unaware that she was in the picture. She was squatting in the lower left corner of the photo and gazing over her shoulder at Lijun, who was riding one of the yaks. Her expression, I thought, conveyed a trace of scorn.

In a letter sent sometime later, I learned that the girl was Lijun's first love. He hinted that there was nothing startling about this, and that they had already had that kind of intimate relationship. He said they might become a couple who shared the same ideals, just like Marx and Jenny. Before he came to the end of the letter he urged me, as he always did, to join him in Tibet.

'Take a close look at your city of lust and stinking money. Don't linger on there,' Lijun wrote. 'Come to Tibet. Come and breathe the pure fresh air.'

At one point Lijun managed to persuade me. I wanted to pack up and leave the drab and boring college. Yet before I could set off, numerous obstacles prevented me from going west. Today I know well enough what the real obstacle was: my profound irresolution and misgivings. And that is exactly where the essential difference between Lijun and me lies. So now I can only muddle along in this prosperous and noisy city in the south, while Lijun, like a free bird, flies high across the blue sky.

One night in an early winter while it was snowing lightly, someone knocked on the door of my unit at the singles' quarters. It was a stranger, a girl in a soldier's overcoat. The round face looked familiar, but I could not make out who she was. She took off her woolen hat, shook her jet-black hair, and announced: 'Greetings from Lijun. I'm Xiaomi.' The name rang a bell: the stranger in front of me was Lijun's girlfriend!

'I'm travelling in the south,' she said. 'Since I'm here it's only natural that I should stop by.' Xiaomi looked me up and down, then cracked a faint smile. 'As you're Lijun's friend, surely you're my friend too.'

The girl who came to my door in the middle of that winter night brought in a rush of chilly air. While I was worrying how to receive this uninvited guest, Xiaomi had already pushed off her mud-spattered leather boots and had sat down on my bed. I heard her say, in a mildly complaining tone, 'Why, it snows even in the south! I'm cold and hungry; could you give me something to eat?'

Just as I took out two packets of noodles, Xiaomi bawled: 'Instant noodles again!' Looking appalled, she stared at my hands. 'I feel like throwing up every time I see instant noodles. Don't you have anything else?' She curled her lips, adding grudgingly: 'You southerners are really stingy. You cannot hold a candle to us Tibetans. There, whoever our guest may be, we serve him only with our best.'

Xiaomi's words made me want to sink into the ground. I rushed to borrow some eggs from my neighbor, and a short while afterwards I stood watching a starving girl wolf down some half-cooked eggs. She told me, off and on, how Lijun was getting along. He was studying Tibetan religion, she said. But more often she talked about someone called Laogang. Gathering from her reverent looks whenever she mentioned his name, I could tell only that he was her idol, a sage rising above and rarely seen in our decadent times.

At about one o'clock in the morning, the volatile girl finally began to yawn. I took out a quilt, ready to put up for the night at the student dormitory. 'Where are you going?' Xiaomi asked, taken aback by my gesture. 'I'm going out to find lodging,' I said. 'You can sleep on the floor,' she replied, pointing at a place not far from her. 'That's our way in Tibet.' I shook my head, slightly embarrassed, and walked toward the door. At that moment the girl tittered and said, 'You're really feudal-minded. A man like you should take some lessons from Laogang.' I pretended not to understand. But deep down I was ashamed of my priggishness and sense of decorum.

One sunny morning, with a fresh cover of snow on the ground, Xiaomi jumped on a southbound train, leaving as suddenly as she had arrived. I never saw her again. Word of her visit must have gotten around, though. Lijun's Tibetan friends, on his recommendation, began to flood into my place like the spring tide. Sometimes a single visitor came, sometimes a small group. Before the end of the season I had received at least ten odd contingents. These friends of Lijun were either new acquaintances at Lhasa, or strangers who had met him on the road. Each of them brought a note written in Lijun's own hand—a courtesy to set against what turned into a disastrous outlay for me. I served them good food and good wine, and offered them my bed at night. I could barely make ends meet those days, so I had no recourse but to borrow money, here, there, everywhere. Sometimes the money I borrowed was in turn lent to the visitors. I knew it was doubtful whether they could pay it back. But I thought their cause was more important than mine, and they needed money more badly than I did.

It was an even colder winter night when Laogang knocked at my door. He was strongly built and robust, with a full, dusty black beard, although he spoke with a supple voice. Like a farmer from the north, he sat cross-legged on my bed. His tattered nylon socks smelled. 'Compared with Hegel, Sartre was shallow. Only a young and inexperienced fellow like Lijun would have blind faith in Sartre,' he blurted. Laogang kept rolling cigarettes with slips of paper, his mien easy and self-confident. I still remember that all of a sudden he jumped down while talking, went to the window and shook the security bars with his thick hands. 'Iron bars?' he said. 'Look at yourself, just like a prisoner!' I explained to him that all the windows of the quarters were like that. Suddenly he howled, 'No! Smash them! Only after you smash them can you be free!' The light sparkling in his eyes made me both awe-struck and perplexed.

Laogang came and went hastily. Just before he left he made it clear that I should donate money for his and Lijun's publication, *Thoughts on the Plateau*. I told him I did not have a cent. In fact, I had to beg food coupons from my students. Laogang grasped my left arm with a smile and pointed at the watch on my wrist: 'You still have a watch,' he observed. 'Quite a few of our friends have started to sell their own blood for *Thoughts on the Plateau*.' Fingering my watch, I could not make up my mind what to do. 'Don't become too attached to worldly possessions,' he advised, reassuringly. 'You should know that ideas are much more valuable than a watch.'

I could no longer resist. Later Laogang pawned the watch that my father had given to me, and just like that it disappeared from my possessions.

Gradually, I too gained a certain notoriety at the college and, like a disciple, followed the footsteps of Lijun's tragedy. I became swamped with debts. I avoided those people who had lent me money, while others avoided me as if I were the plague, fearing that I would hit them up as soon as I opened my mouth. I was in the doldrums. I knew that Lijun, although thousands of miles away, had cast a magic net over me. It was time to flee.

That's why I blame my change of post on him. It sounds ridiculous, but it is fact. In autumn I was teaching at a different college, and my life became quiet and satisfying. Certainly the main reason for this was that I had fallen in love. Xiaowei, my girlfriend, was outraged on hearing my occasional accounts of how Lijun had brought me such bad luck. 'How can you call him your good friend?' she objected. 'I wouldn't miss him if I were you. Just wait. See if I don't give him a piece of my mind if he ever rambles round this way.'

Anyway, Lijun did not visit, perhaps because I held back telling him of my transfer, or perhaps my replies had been all grudges and complaints, making him feel uneasy finally. Autumn passed, winter arrived and with it, to my surprise, a letter from Lijun. I had no idea how he got my new address. In this long letter he told me that his life had changed dramatically. Tired of each other, he and Xiaomi had parted. That news was no great surprise, but what shocked me was Lijun's remark that his affinity for Tibet had vanished, and that he would leave very soon on a walking tour of the Yellow River Valley. Lastly he told me with gusto that a poet-friend would come to visit me on New Year's Eve. He believed that I could learn something from talking with this poet-friend of his. He added that he expected him, although living in destitution for the time being, to be a future candidate for the Nobel Prize; such were Lijun's visions!

Still another friend of Lijun's was descending my way. Panic gripped me. As if confronted by a mortal enemy, on New Year's Eve I went hastily with Xiaowei to her grandmother's house and stayed there for several days. When I came back, I found the cement entry at the door of my unit littered with cigarette butts of varying lengths. I imagined the poet waiting and waiting at my door, lighting cigarette after cigarette to help him bide the time, but I could not make out how I felt. Then I picked up some scraps of paper, already torn to shreds, from among the cigarette butts. They looked like improvisations. Unfortunately I couldn't piece them together; only the scribbled words on one strip looked familiar. I read them aloud: 'On the road, on the road.'

There are conflicting stories about why Lijun left Tibet. A few of my classmates, having come back from that region, told me that Lijun, depressed after he lost Xiaomi, took to drink. One day when he awoke from a stupor he heard a Shaanbei[2] folk song, dismal and primitive, on the radio. He was deeply moved. It was the song that took his mind off the pain of his lost love. It was also the song that made him finally set out on a long journey of roaming about China.

They told me that Xiaomi was a girl of easy virtue. She left Lijun and went to Laogang. Half a year later, Laogang, a learned and contemplative man, tired of her and left her in turn. Xiaomi went south to Guangdong. She cast off once and for all the life she used to live, and ended up in a coastal city, reportedly engaging in a taboo trade.

Nowadays, more and more often, friends who are faraway come to mind. They are like floating islands, drifting in all directions. They move farther and farther away from me. Whenever Lijun, who is roaming about China, sends me a postcard showing the natural beauty of the north, south, east, or west; whenever I see a different place name on the postmark, be the mark blurred or clear; whenever I read Lijun's maxims or words of advice, charged with the same passionate conviction as ever, a feeling of loss wells up inside of me.

For me, youth is a cluster of wild roses, some in bloom, others already withered and fading.

Five years after my university graduation, I married Xiaowei. Our wedding night happened to be a wintry night, with blowing and drifting snow. I sat near the stove with my newlywed, listening to some piano music of Chopin. Somebody knocked on the door of our small house, and Xiaowei ran to open it.

There, in front of her, stood a stranger, a young man in an old soldier's overcoat. He looked even younger than us; on his hair, his eyebrows, and the backpack on his shoulder was a layer of snowflakes.

'Who are you looking for?' Xiaowei inquired, keeping the door half ajar. On her guard, she looked closely at the uninvited guest.

'I'm Lijun's friend.'

The young man outside took a letter from his overcoat pocket. 'I came from Daxing'anling,' he explained. 'Lijun told me to pay you a visit.'

Xiaowei did not move; her hand held the door firmly. Then I heard her say to him, indifferently: 'We don't know anyone named Lijun. I'm afraid you've come to the wrong house.' When she had finished speaking, she began to shut the door. I could see the young man's face, illuminated in the background; stunned and disappointed, he stepped back. Xiaowei barred the door.

It never occurred to me that Xiaowei might act that way. She leaned on the door and after a moment's silence, explained: 'That's the only way. Such a small house, and it's so late. Such a cold and snowy night. I didn't want to take in such an odd visitor.' She raised her head, looked at me and remarked: 'His feet were soaked with mud. He would have soiled the carpet.'

She should not have treated my friend, not even a friend of a friend, in that way. But I said nothing. I knew that in these matters, one's wife surely has a mind of her own.

1992

NOTES

1 A short form for Jiangsu and Jiejiang Provinces.
2 A province in the wild northwest part of China.

3

Flaw

By **WANG WEN-HSING**
Translated by Chen Chu-yun

Wang Wen-hsing 王文興 *(Wang Wenxing, b. 1939) was born in Fujian, China, but moved to Taiwan with his family in 1947. He received a BA in foreign languages and literature from National Taiwan University, and MFA from the University of Iowa. He is currently a professor in the Department of Foreign Languages and Literature at National Taiwan University. His genius in writing was already evident in his undergraduate years. In 1960 he and his friends founded the journal* Modern Literature *(*Xiandai wenxue 現代文學*) and he was, for a time, its chief editor. As can be seen in his writings, Wang Wen-hsing is an advocate for the use of Western techniques, such as stream-of-consciousness. He has published two collections of short stories,* Dragon Tower *(*Long tian lou 龍天樓*, 1968) and* Fifteen Short Stories *(*Shiwu pian gushi 十五篇故事*, 1979), as well as two novels,* Family Catastrophe *(*Jia bian 家變*, 1972) and* The Man With His Back to the Sea *(*Bei hai de ren 背海的人*, 1981). Wang Wen-hsing is noted for his innovative language and insight into the psychological workings of his characters. His third novel, a sequel to* The Man With His Back to the Sea*, will soon appear in book form.*

I must have been eleven that year, because I had just enrolled in junior high. At that time we were still living on Tong'an Street, our earliest home in Taipei, and had not yet moved to Tonghua Street, after which we moved again, to Lianyun Street. But it has always been my impression that the earlier the home, the better it seemed; every time we moved, it was to a less attractive place. Perhaps it was the nostalgia for early childhood, strongest for the earliest years, that gave rise to such an illusion.

Tong'an Street was a quiet little alley, with less than a hundred families along its entire length. Slightly curved around its middle, the street stretched all the way to the great grey river at the end. Actually, viewed from the vantage point of the river bank, there were very few pedestrians on the street, which, with its pale body and meandering path, was virtually a small river itself. Such was the tranquil picture when I was eleven. Later, as small cars were allowed to pass through the street, the atmosphere of quiet seclusion was lost altogether. My present reminiscences hark back to the era before the arrival of the cars.

In any event, on Tong'an Street at that time cats could be seen strolling lazily along the tops of the low walls, from one house to the next. The whole landscape was filled with glistening green foliage and delicately fragrant odours from the profusion of flowers and plants growing in the front yards. Flowers especially took to Tong'an Street; they bloomed in the spring and in the fall. Most unforgettable, however, were the evenings, when silent street lamps illuminated the darkness of the road. Night seemed even quieter than day. The little grocery stores, unlike their counterparts in the crowded city, closed at half past nine. Midnight began at half past nine. Night enjoyed its deepest and longest sleep on this street. Light breezes rustled among the leaves, while remote stars twinkled in the skies, and after a few hours, night passed and day broke. In the early morning mist, the owners of the small grocery stores, still unlike their counterparts in the city, began taking down the wooden panels of the shops.

In spring that year, a young seamstress opened a shop at the end of the street near the river. It was at a time when Taipei, still untouched by affluence, was just beginning to prosper, and a number of three-storey buildings could be seen cropping up here and there. Ever since the previous winter, we children had been watching with interest the construction of such a building on the vacant lot in front of our houses. Our feelings were excitement mingled with sadness. We were excited because, as children, we felt an immense satisfaction with all novel experiences—new sights, new sounds, new objects, new undertakings—and sad because we were losing our favourite playground for after-school ball games. The building was completed in spring, and the young woman moved in. The house consisted of three compartments, and was three storeys tall. The young woman and her family occupied the entire compartment on the right, while the second and third floors served as family rooms. It was said that she owned the entire building and we children had naturally assumed that she would occupy all the space herself, but it turned out she reserved only one compartment for her own use and offered the others for rent. A week after they had been taken she changed her mind and sold them off. We felt a slight twinge of regret for her, that she had been able to occupy only a part of the building.

I was a precocious child then, although I looked at least two years younger than my eleven years. Like all underdeveloped children, however, my mental growth compensated for my physical weakness by being two years beyond my age. One day, I discovered that I was in love with the young woman. The realization dawned upon me during spring vacation, right after the soft spring showers, in the blossom-filled month of April.

Being a sensitive and inward child, I had an instructive fear of glamorous and sophisticated women, and took only to those with kind faces (I still do even now). The woman at the dressmaking shop was exactly the type I like.

She was about thirty-five or so, and did not wear much make-up (this was very important). She wore neither rouge nor powder on her face and only a tiny trace of lipstick on her lips, which were often parted in a warm, white smile. Her eyes were not only beautiful, but, even more important, glowed with gentle kindness. My love for her stemmed not only from approval of her looks, but was rooted in sincere admiration for the goodness of her character as well.

Love in a precocious child, like a heavy blossom atop a frail stem, was a burden too heavy to bear. Only then did I realize the consuming nature of love; if the blazing flames were the joys of love it was the burning of the fuel itself which made these flames possible. I found it impossible that true happiness could consist in achieving joy from the masochistic burning of one's own self. Although I had been in the world for a mere eleven years then, I had undergone enough minor suffering to be able to devise a means of avoiding pain: if you happened to form an emotional attachment to a certain thing or a certain person, the best thing to do was to immediately look for a fault therein, upon which you would then be able to withhold your affection and thus lighten the burden. During the next few days, I often concealed myself directly opposite her shop and scrutinized her with cold detachment, in an effort to discover some ugliness in her. But the longer I watched, the more beautiful she seemed. I realized then that love had so deeply embedded itself that there was no way of uprooting it. I would have to live with it.

It was already the last day of the spring vacation. I made up my mind to enjoy it to the full by playing outdoors for the whole day. Early in the morning, I went over to our new playground (which had been relocated at the vacant lot in front of the garbage heap beside the grocery store) to wait for the other children to gather. We started our ball game much earlier than usual that morning—it must have been before eight o'clock, for our shrill cries woke an office worker living in one of the wooden buildings. Still clad in his pajamas, he opened the window and leaned out to scold loudly. Our ball often hit the ragged old woman who kept a cigarette stand next to the garbage heap. She tried to chase us away with a broom, but she lacked the strength and energy and could only stand brandishing her broom like a sentinel in front of her stand, hitting out at whoever ran near her, but we were all careful to stay away. On top of it all, Ah-Jiu's pet mongrel kept dashing among us madly. For some reason or other he seemed to have picked me for his target, jumping on me repeatedly and causing me to fall several times. It was only when Ah-Jiu's mother appeared and summoned him and his four brothers back to breakfast that we finally broke up the game and dispersed. The sun had splashed the entire street golden by then. Thick greenery clustered over the tops of the plaster walls. Market-bound housewives were already holding summer parasols to ward off the sunlight, whose beams had become so strong lately that some buds were bursting into flower before their time. I felt thirsty and wormed my way into Liu Xiaodong's yard in order to drink from their faucet. Water flowed over my face and neck, where I left it for the sun to dry. As I passed the dressmaking shop, I saw the young woman standing in the doorway talking with another lady, teasing now and then the baby the latter held in her arms. I climbed up the incline at the end of Tong'an Street, walked down the steps on the other side, and headed for the river.

The river under the sunlight was alive with undulating glitter, like a million thumbtacks rising and falling in rhythm. On the opposite bank, two ox-carts were crawling along the sandy beach. Standing under a newly budding tree, I could smell the fragrance of the baked earth along the river bank and feel the coolness of the river breeze on my skin. As I walked away from the tree, I raised my voice and started singing 'Crossing the Sea in Summer'. Keeping time with my hands, I went singing all the way up the river. I walked into a bamboo grove, found a relatively flat patch of land, and lay down.

In front of me stretched the river, glimmering through the bamboo leaves; at my back was a piece of farmland as colourful as a Persian rug. The huge patches of green were rice paddies; big blocks of rich dark brown were earth freshly plowed but yet unsown; slender strips of light green, like the thin glass squares used under microscopes, were bean tendrils, while the golden patches were vegetable blossoms, swaying in the spring breeze. The short dark figures of the farmers could be glimpsed working in the distance, and occasionally the faint odour of manure drifted in from the fields.

I lay quietly, thinking of all kinds of whimsical things, but they were all happy thoughts. I allowed my fancies to roam like the breeze-driven clouds in the sky. I turned over, and, resting my chin upon my arms, gazed at the river through the bamboo leaves. I thought of the young seamstress. I had no one in whom I could confide my love, only the river. Later this river also became the witness to my pains in learning to swim. I would often steal away from home, make my way alone to the river under the summer sun, and, bracing myself against fears of drowning, would try to teach myself the art of floating above water. But I never did succeed. I gave up my efforts finally, because I no longer had the courage to struggle.

The river could not respond to my confidences. I returned to my former position on my back and covered my face with a handkerchief.

I lay until the sun had travelled directly overhead, then removed the handkerchief and sat up. Thinking that my mother would be waiting for me to go home for lunch, I stood up and headed for home. The farmers had all disappeared from the fields. Probably they too had gone home to eat.

At home I saw our Taiwanese amah. She had not gone home yet and was still doing the ironing. As soon as she saw me, she asked:

'Young Master, have you seen my Chunxiong?'

I replied that I had not.

'Weren't you playing with him outdoors?'

I said I was not.

'I can't think where he could've gone. I told him to come and help me mop the floors, but there hasn't been a trace of him all morning. My Chunxiong just can't compare with Young Master, Ma'am. Young Master is smart, and works hard; so young and already in junior high;

he'll be in senior high next, and after that, a top official,' she said, shaking out one of my father's shirts.

Our amah often praised me thus, remarking that I would proceed to senior high school after finishing junior high. She could not imagine a college education beyond that of senior high, so after that, I was to become a high official.

Mother answered her in broken Taiwanese, 'It'll be the same with you. Chunxiong will also go to school, also earn money and support you.'

'Thank you, Ma'am, thank you. But I was born to suffer, Ma'am. Chunxiong's father died early, leaving me alone to raise him. I have no other hopes, only that Chunxiong will be like Young Master, work hard in school, study in junior high, and afterwards in senior high. No matter how hard I have to work, even if I have to wash clothes all my life, I want him to be educated.'

'He won't disappoint you,' my mother replied.

Amah only sighed.

That kind old woman. I still remember her broad tan face, like a piece of dark bread, warm and glowing, the perfect blending of simple goodness and unpretentious love. Where she had gone, no one knew. As I grew older, gentle people like her were harder and harder to come by. They are not the kind to adapt easily within an increasingly complex society, I suppose. I also recall another minor detail about her, the result of the peculiar powers of childhood observation: I often noticed her bare feet, with ten stout toes fanning out, pattering along on the shining floors of our house. The reason I found this extraordinary perhaps was that we all wore slippers in the house and there were many pairs of spare slippers in the hallway reserved for guests. Amah probably had never become used to this alien custom and thus never wore any. I often mused to myself then that even if she consented to wear slippers like the rest of us, where would we find such a large pair to fit her?

That was the last day of the spring vacation. Another detail I remember was that I went out and bought a diary that afternoon. A certain fascination for the surrounding phenomena, interest for the musings within my mind (for my newly-sprung love), and for spring itself urged me to imitate Liu Xiaodong's elder brother and keep a diary. All my thoughts for the day were faithfully recorded that evening in the first entry of my diary.

After the spring vacation, love continued to plague me, as if urging me to some action, to do something which would bring me closer to her, albeit only in my feelings. I thought of taking something to her shop and asking her to mend it for me (a sorry means of courtship, I admit). But that shop of hers took only women's clothing. I could not think of anything else, so one day I finally brought along a Boy Scout jacket with a missing button to her shop.

Her shop was tastefully furnished. Pictures cut from Japanese fashion magazines adorned the walls, and a vase of bright red roses stood on a small table in one corner. Four girls were sitting in the room, talking and laughing among themselves as they treadled on machines spread with pieces of brightly coloured material.

'What do you want, little one?' A round-faced girl wearing a string of imitation pearls lifted her head and asked.

'I want a button sewn,' I said, turning to the seamstress, who stood at the table measuring a dress, 'Can you do it?'

The woman took my jacket and said: 'Ah-Xiu, sew the button on for him.' She handed the jacket over to the round-faced girl, then turned and went on with her measuring.

I felt the sorrow of rejection.

'Which button is it?' the girl asked me.

I told her, with my eyes on the woman.

'How much?' I asked the woman.

'A dollar,' replied the girl.

The woman seemed not to have heard my question, for she did not even lift her head. My grief sank its roots into the depths of my heart. But after a while I saw the woman put on a pair of glasses, and curiosity took the place of sorrow. I found it strange that she should wear glasses, as if it were the least probable thing in the world. I did not like the way she looked with glasses; she no longer looked like herself. Moreover, she was wearing them too low. They made her look old and gave her an owl-like expression.

Suddenly aware that I had stood gazing in the shop much longer than necessary, I asked the round-faced girl:

'Can I come back and get it later?'

'No, stay. It'll be ready in a minute.'

I waited nervously in the shop for her to finish. I glanced again at the pictures of the Japanese women on the walls. They were all very pretty, with dazzling smiles, but strangely, their eyelids all had only single pleats. I looked again at the roses in the corner. They were still flaming red. Feeling that they seemed to be redder than roses usually were, I took a more careful look and discovered that they were plastic flowers.

After a while, a boy came down the stairs, munching a piece of fruit. He was taller than I, also in a Boy Scout uniform, and was wearing a pair of glasses. With sudden intuition, I realized this was her son. I had seen two smaller children with her, but had never seen this one; like all newcomers to the neighbourhood, he never came out to join our games. Amidst surprised confusion I, who was secretly in love with his mother, watched him as he went upstairs again with a water bottle.

After the button had been replaced, I hurried out the door with the jacket. In the doorway I met our amah coming in. Afraid that she would report me to my mother, for I had come to the shop without her knowledge, I slipped away as unobtrusively as I could.

Despite the fact that I had been received with cold indifference at her shop, and that I had seen a son of hers who was much older than I, my love did not change; the love of a child does not change easily. I still gave her all the passion of my eleven years.

Thus I loyally allowed my love to continue, without hope, without fulfilment, and without anyone's awareness. This hopelessness, however, coloured my love with a nuance of melancholy beauty. Actually, I could not tell whether this sense of futility gave me sorrow or happiness. But I was sure of one thing, that with such love I was happier than adults in one respect. I was spared any unnecessary anxiety; I did not have to worry over the fact that one day my love would suddenly come to an end. As long as my admiration existed, my love existed. Looking back now, I should say I was quite happy then.

The trip I made to her shop, I recall, was the only time I undertook such a venture. I never found another opportunity; besides, for some reason I suddenly lost all courage, and found myself deeply ashamed over the incident. Whenever I thought of myself going into her shop on the mere pretext of replacing a button, my shame would grow until the experience became a positive terror, causing me to sweat in anguish. For three days afterward I did not have the heart to pass in front of her shop. Courage is a strange thing: the first plunge should never be merited as true courage until tested by subsequent attempts.

Although I was never in her shop again, I was often in front of it. Opposite her shop was a dry-goods store, which sold all kinds of tidbits for children and at which I frequently stood vigil. Munching on a cracker, I watched as she moved around in her shop. Sometimes I would see her husband, a man of thirty-something, riding a motorcycle and said to be working in a commercial bank. Strangely enough, I never felt a trace of jealousy for this man. This showed, I suppose, that I was still a long way from maturity. I did not seem to realize the full significance of the word 'husband'. I thought of him as merely another member of her household, like her brother, her uncle, or her brother-in-law. But should she be talking with another man, for instance if she chatted momentarily with the barber next door, my jealous rage would lead me to visualize the barber lying on the ground with a dagger in his heart.

Thus the days slipped by, one after another, like the turning pages of my diary. Soon it was summer and the end of the school term approached. I began to worry about my grades; I was very weak in algebra, and was afraid I would not be able to pass the finals. My algebra teacher had already warned half-jokingly that he expected to see me again next semester. I shook with fear; I had never in my life had to repeat a grade, and now the threat loomed large. Yet mingled with the anxiety was a sense of unbound expectation, expectation for the freedom, the happiness, and the unlimited possibilities of the summer vacation. Under the dark shadow of the finals, I sat for hours on end with the algebra text in front of me, but, instead of studying, I often simply gazed at it anxiously. I grew thin and pale.

Finally, the heavy, burdensome finals were over. All the students hurled themselves into the free skies of the summer vacation like birds escaping from captivity. I was merely one ecstatic soul among thousands. Countless youngsters, burdened by the exams, had eagerly awaited the arrival of the summer vacation and, in waiting, had imagined that it would never become a reality, otherwise their joys of expectation would have been cancelled by the pains of suffering.

That first morning of the vacation, I opened my eleven-year-old eyes to the riotous singing of birds and a world brilliant with sunshine. Exams were a thing of the past. No matter how badly I did on them, they were no longer on my mind. All children, perhaps, are unable to worry over the past. Sitting up in bed, a shiver of excitement told me beyond a shadow of doubt that the summer vacation had finally arrived. That certainty did not come from any indication on the calendar, but from a certain sound, a certain odour, a patch of sunlight, all distinctively characteristic. I heard the shrill buzz of cicadas, saw the reflection of a basin of water shimmering on the ceiling, smelled the cool fragrance of mothballs as my mother took out our winter clothing from the trunks and laid them out in the sun—and I knew that this was it. Happiness was that child as he jumped out of bed.

Each year with the awareness of summer came the reminder to sort out our fishing gear. We would rummage among the coal bins in the kitchen and come out with a slender bamboo pole which our mothers had put aside (and which we had painstakingly whittled ourselves), take it to the bathroom and, with great effort, try to clean it, thinking of the great catches in store this year, although for the most part we were only able to catch frogs.

I found my fishing pole that day as usual, and cleaned it up as before. But holding it in my hands I all of a sudden felt that it was much too homely. It was my own handiwork, of which I had once been so proud, but now I saw its crudeness. I felt that I needed a brand new fishing pole, a bona fide one, not a plain home-made one like this. I wanted one with a reel, a bell, and one that was gracefully pliant like a whip. I made up my mind to ask my father to buy me one. I had high hopes of getting it, because I had an indisputable reason: I was *eleven*.

I threw my fishing pole back into the coal bin.

I headed for the garbage heap to look for my friends. It had been two whole weeks since we played our last ball game, all because of the final exams. Our mothers would not let us play.

I passed by the dressmaking shop, hoping to catch a glimpse of the young woman, but today her shop was closed. She must be out with her family. I felt a little disheartened. I saw her every day, but one day in which I did not was enough to give me that feeling of emptiness.

My friends were already in the middle of a game. I hurriedly joined in and immediately became involved in the ferocious battle. We played happily until noon. The side I was on lost and they blamed me, while I blamed myself for joining the wrong side. But we all determined valiantly to fight again tomorrow and win. As I walked home, the dressmaking shop was still closed. Again I experienced disappointment.

At home my mother was complaining over the fact that Amah had failed to show up that morning to do the laundry, and that if she was too busy to come she should have sent Chunxiong over with a message. Then she turned upon me and said that I had disappeared all morning like a pigeon let out of the cage; she wanted me to go and look for Amah, but she could not even find me. I was surely headed for trouble if I played like that every day, and I should not spend all my time in ball games even though it was the summer vacation. Naturally, these words were ones I liked least to hear.

After lunch I felt drowsy. The white-hot sunshine outside made it hard to keep my eyes open; in the room a few flies were buzzing intermittently upon the dining-room table. Unconsciously I dozed off for about ten minutes. Awaking, I gazed at the bright sunlight outside the window and the flies on the table in the room and a familiar sensation dawned upon me. How could I have forgotten? Summer vacations were always boring after all.

Just then Mrs Liu, who lived next door, came over for her daily chat with my mother. With hair curlers bobbing she stepped in the doorway and asked:

'Is your mother at home, little one?'

'I'm in the kitchen, Mrs Liu,' my mother called. 'Find a seat and I'll be out in a minute.' But Mrs Liu had already traced the voice into the kitchen.

Then they both emerged. My mother's hands were covered with soap suds. She found a piece of cloth and started wiping them.

'How come you're doing the wash yourself?' Mrs Liu asked as she sat down.

'Amah didn't show up today. I thought I might as well.'

'That's what I came to tell you,' Mrs Liu said, setting her curlers bobbing again. 'You know what's happened to Amah? She's lost all her money. Twenty thousand dollars of savings, and she lost it all last night. No wonder she's sick.'

'Oh? Is that so? I didn't know she had so much saved up,' my mother remarked in surprise.

'All the money she earned by working day and night as a washerwoman, saved up bit by bit. She says she was saving for her son's education. Bad luck that she should lose it all. But this time lots of other people on our street were hard hit too. Mrs Ye lost ten thousand—seems like she just put the money in a couple of days ago—and it being the money for the fuel coupons of her husband's office at that. Mrs Wu lost three thousand. It's all that witch's fault, and now the whole family's skipped.'

'Who're you talking about?'

'That woman in the dressmaking shop. You can't imagine how unscrupulous she is. One hundred fifty thousand, gone just like that. Who'd believe she was capable of doing such a thing? Everyone saw that her business was good and trusted her, saw that she offered higher interest, of course, and never dreamed she would suddenly skip out like that. Sheer betrayal, that's what it is.'

'Unbelievable,' my mother mused. 'She seemed to be such an honest person. Oh, poor Amah, what is she going to do . . . ?'

I did not stay to hear my mother finish. I ran out of the house and headed straight for the dressmaking shop.

The shop was still closed. A few women were standing near the doorway chatting. I stood gazing at the shop as pieces of the conversation nearby drifted into my ears.

'They left in the middle of the night. No one knows where they are now.'

'They could report her to the police, have her arrested.'

'No use. All she'll have to do is declare herself bankrupt, and she wouldn't have a care in the world. Besides, now that she's got the money, the law can't touch her.'

'It was all planned,' another said. 'You notice she was in a hurry to sell most of this building as soon as she moved in.'

'They say she sold this shop of hers last week too.'

A few maids were peering in from the windows on the right. I went over and looked in through a small pane of glass: the room was empty, all the sewing machines and the furniture were gone.

'Just imagine, she didn't even pay the girls their wages. How mean can one get?'

Hearing this I suddenly felt my ears burn with anger.

Mrs Liu had already left when I got home. Seeing me, my mother murmured:

'Unbelievable, just unbelievable. People are getting worse and worse. More people get rich and more cheating goes on. People are getting prosperous, but if morals go bad, what's the use of all this prosperity? Luckily we aren't rich; otherwise, who knows? We might also have been duped.'

Our family was not rich. My father was teaching in a high school then, and, in Taiwan, a teacher was by no means well off. But was Amah well off? Why cheat her out of all her money? And those girls who had worked for nothing, why deprive them of their wages?

I went with a book up to the rooftop that evening; I had decided to heed my mother and do a little studying. The sky above was a soft quiet blue. I sat on the reddish tiles and leaned my head against the railing.

I could see the dressmaking shop down across the street. The door was still closed; the chatting women had gone.

Thinking of the young woman, of her comely yet gentle face, I found it hard to believe that she was a fraud. But she *was a fraud*. Every time I told myself the truth, my heart contracted in pain.

I still cherished my love for her. I wanted to keep that love. I closed my eyes and thought of her lily-like face—yet I was always reminded of her flaw. I saw the ugliness of that face; and the flower hung down and withered.

Dusk slowly enveloped Tong'an Street; wisps of pale smoke began to curl from the chimneys nearby. The scene in front of me got misty, and I discovered that my eyes were filled with tears.

Oh, youth, perhaps my sadness then was due not only to a woman having disappointed me, but to the discovery that some element in life had been deluding me, and had been deluding me for a long time. The sorrow and anguish of the discovery disturbed me deeply.

From that day on, I understood a bit more; I learned that disillusions were an integral part of life, and that more disillusions were to come. From that day on, I forgot the beauty of that woman, although I never could forget the details of this incident. No wonder; that was my first love.

1964

4

One Day in the Life of a White-Collar Worker

By **CHEN YING-CHEN**
Translated by Lucien Miller

Chen Ying-chen 陳映真 *(Chen Yingzhen, pen-name of Chen Yongshan* 陳永善*, b. 1936) comes from a missionary family in Taiwan. He obtained a diploma in English from Tamkang College (now Tamkang University) in 1960. He is unique among his generation of Taiwanese writers in that he has addressed himself to the most sensitive social and political problems in Taiwan. He was detained for alleged anti-government political activities in 1968 and released in 1975 after an amnesty was granted. His early short stories can be found in the Chinese journals* Modern Literature *(*Xiandai wenxue 現代文學*), and* Literature Quarterly *(*Wenxue jikan 文學季刊*). In 1984, he founded the magazine* Ren-Chian Magazine *(*Renjian 人間*). So far he has published five volumes of short stories, which form part of a fifteen-volume series of his critical and literary writings. While his early fiction focuses on the life of intellectuals and their sense of rootlessness in the disintegrated world of the Chinese, his post-imprisonment fiction is marked by its social awareness, in which the individual is often placed against the disorganization of native civilization with the invasion of multinational corporations in Taiwan that changed the pattern of life of many white-collar workers.*

The piercing jangling of the telephone on the headboard woke the man with a start. He removed the eye shades that shielded him from the light, and grabbed for the phone. Despite the drapes between his bed and the sliding glass door, the light from the mid-summer morning sun was so bright it blinded him.

'Hello . . .'

'Hello,' he said. Being so abruptly roused from a deep sleep made his heart beat anxiously.

'Olive. That you?'

'Umm,' he mumbled. Suddenly he was awake. 'It's me.'

'Still sleeping, eh?'

'Ah,' he said, sitting up in bed.

'If you can sleep this late, you're no longer upset.' The man on the other end of the line chuckled. Olive picked up the pack of cigarettes from beside the phone, thrust the receiver between his left ear and shoulder, and struck a match.

'Actually, I was awake for a while.' He smiled sociably and affected a relaxed tone. 'Then I went back to sleep.'

'Good. After a good night's sleep you should be more clear-headed. We'll just forget all about what happened yesterday. From now on no one is allowed to mention it again.'

Olive didn't answer. A phone call from Bertland Yang was something he had not expected. Being stroked by the boss caused a modicum of meek-spirited joy to well up within Olive, despite his reserve.

'I told Mr Talmann this morning that you had three days off. Maybe you ought to go some place for fun.'

Olive smoked silently and imagined Bertland Yang's sly face, with its gold-rimmed glasses. B.Y., as he was called, had just turned forty, but already he was bald on top.

'The only thing is, we're really busy right now, as you know. Nobody is able to handle your end. So if you could come in tomorrow and take care of things for a stretch, I'll give you a two-week deferred leave.'

Olive continued to smoke slowly, saying nothing. He thought of himself the day before in Bertland Yang's office swearing angrily, his voice lowered:

'If I say I'm quitting, that's it. If I don't mean it, my name isn't Huang Jingxiong![1]'

'You're talking nonsense!' B.Y. had exclaimed, his face showing both anger and solicitous concern. He had hastily gotten up from his chair to shut the office door.

Olive recollected yesterday's scene while half-listening to B.Y.'s voice pleading with him over the telephone: 'Come on, Olive, come on. . . .'

He began to feel tied up in knots. 'No,' he said finally. 'I don't want to.'

'I'm not saying come now. Tomorrow. If you really can't. . . .'

'No.' Olive repeated calmly, though his voice sounded hesitant. 'No. I can't come.'

'O-live!'

He did not reply.

'You're not making any sense! Listen to me. I've already arranged for your leave. If you don't want to come in tomorrow, it doesn't matter.'

Olive considered hanging up, but he continued listening silently to his caller saying things like 'For heaven's sake don't do anything rash,' or 'I'll take care of everything for you,' until finally B.Y. hung up himself.

Olive looked at the clock: it wasn't quite ten past nine. He threw his cigarette butt in the ashtray beside the bed. As usual, Grace had neatly set out breakfast and the morning paper on the tea table in the bedroom before she left for work. He got up, washed, and ate breakfast, and after skimming the paper aimlessly, strode into the living room.

He had not anticipated that, with his wife gone and his child at school, the apartment would be so quiet. He sat down on the white plastic-covered sofa, his back to the living room window; he wanted to read the newspaper he had carried with him from the bedroom. Unexpectedly, the silence of solitude nettled him and became a thunderous roar. He put down the paper. The wallpaper looked as fresh as on the day they had moved in, eighteen months ago. Each month he had to pay two hundred dollars interest on the condominium. When the site for the building was being excavated, he had figured out that if he were promoted to assistant manager that year, he could shorten the payment period from ten to six years.

Now the thought of the possible promotion to assistant manager depressed him. He pictured the empty office next door to Bertland Yang's, which was kitty-corner from his own. This vacated office had been within his reach, and then suddenly had vanished over the horizon like some fleeting scene from a movie. Yesterday afternoon around three o'clock, Julie, B.Y.'s skinny, dimwitted secretary, had tossed a copy of some official document on his desk. Just then he was very annoyed trying to locate a sum hidden somewhere in his account books; but he picked up the copy, figuring he might as well stop what he was doing. The original letter had been typed on a fancy electric typewriter, and he read every word:

> This is to announce that as of 15 July, Edward K. Zhao will assume the duties as assistant to the company's accounting division's manager, Bertland Yang.
>
> Mr Edward K. Zhao graduated from Campbell College in the United States in 1974 where he received his master's degree in business administration. That same year he joined the New York branch of Morrison Mutual, Ltd., and was made head accountant. In 1976 he was assigned to Morrison's Asia-Pacific headquarters in Manila. Presently, Taiwan Morrison is fortunate to welcome Mr Zhao to his new post, where he will render assistance on questions of finance.
>
> On this occasion it is appropriate to note the following: this appointment is one of the important signs of Asia-Pacific's concrete help in implementing Taiwan Morrison's plans for the future expansion of production. I sincerely believe that all the division managers, as well as all the personnel working for this company, will join me in offering congratulations to Mr Edward K. Zhao.
>
> Signed
> Samuel N. Talmann

Olive placed his copy of the announcement on the corner of his desk, then buried his head between the manila covers of a monthly income statement. A second later he looked up again and began cracking his knuckles loudly. Then, a page at a time, he gathered up the report he was going through. He stood up and carefully folded his copy of the announcement and placed it in his left breast pocket. His entire face had turned white, even his thin lips, ordinarily as red as cherries.

He walked directly into Bertland Yang's office.

'How about it? Is the report almost finished?' B.Y. asked.

As they faced one another, Olive was certain B.Y. could see how distraught he was—his features were contorted with irrepressible shame, anger, and frustration. B.Y.'s casual question instantly caused Olive to lose control of the little self-restraint he had left. He pulled the copy from his pocket, tore it into four pieces, and threw them on B.Y.'s desk.

'There's no sense in everybody cheating each other like this,' Olive said, suffering unbearably.

Immediately B.Y. put his cigarette out in an ashtray heaped with cigarette butts. 'Sit down, sit down,' he said.

Olive remained standing quietly. He looked past B.Y.'s face to the window behind him. On the opposite side of the street was an office building that was nearly completed. Four or five workmen stood on the scaffold in the sweltering summer sun.

'I should have talked to you first, okay,' said B.Y. 'Olive, they wanted to put someone in, so they did it. What could I do?' B.Y. opened his drawer and took out a pack of Rothmans, offering one to Olive. Olive raised both hands and shook his head. B.Y. took the cigarette himself and lit it. Olive noticed that several brands of foreign cigarettes were laid out in the drawer. Bertland Yang's taste was varied—Kent, Dunhill, More, Salem—he smoked them all.

'For the past several days I've been busy and upset,' said B.Y. 'I didn't have the chance to let you know ahead of time. Honestly, I consider you a member of the family. You understand, don't you?'

Olive sneered but said nothing. He kept standing as before, then gazed down at his brightly polished black shoes.

'You've been with me a long time, Olive,' said B.Y., 'and I've filled you in on a lot of things. Haven't I explained it before? Foreigners are here at the most for three or four years. I've been on very good terms with our company director, Rong. That old boy and I are going to be here forever. . . . Do you understand?'

'I quit,' Olive said.

B.Y. looked at him askance. 'I've always trusted you the most, and I've watched out for you.'

'I quit,' Olive repeated.

'You quit?' exclaimed B.Y., infuriated. 'Just let me see you try it!'

'If I say I'm quitting, that's it.' Olive's eyes were red-rimmed with anger and the hurt over being wronged. 'If I don't mean it . . . my name isn't Huang Jingxiong!'

He turned and was about to go, but B.Y. called out and stopped him.

'What kind of nonsense are you talking?' B.Y. asked, offended. He closed the door to his office.

Olive looked out the window, saying nothing. In the brilliant sunlight, the workers were painting the building across the way a milky white, stroke by stroke. Occasionally they would chat or wipe sweat from their foreheads with the handkerchiefs tied around their necks. Having the office door closed made the cool air inside more concentrated. Olive began to feel the coolness of the sweat that had collected on his forehead.

Only then had B.Y. let Olive know that Edward K. Zhao, the man coming to take over as assistant manager, was Rong's nephew.

'Just recently the old boy was inquiring after you,' B.Y. said. 'In fact, he really appreciates you. He often says that your poise and talents aren't typical of native Taiwanese.'

Olive recalled the time B.Y. had introduced him to the always mysterious Rong:

'How are you General Rong?' Olive had said. B.Y. had told him beforehand that old Rong liked people to address him as 'General'.

'Fine, fine,' Rong replied. The general quickly looked Olive up and down as he spoke, and nodded his head slightly.

Rong was a retired general. He had a swarthy complexion, a head of coarse silver-white hair, and thick, bushy eyebrows that hung over his sunglasses. He and Mr Bottmore, now the president, were together in the Sino-American army stationed at the Chinese front during the Second World War. After the Korean War, Bottmore retired from the Pentagon. Capitalizing on his war experience in the Far East, he took a position with Morrison's Asia-Pacific division, owned by a leading armaments firm, and was rapidly promoted. He was solely responsible for the planning and establishment of Taiwan Morrison. Accordingly, Bottmore's wartime friend, General Rong, was selected as the major Chinese stockholder and director; his was the ideal name under which purely American funds could be legally changed into joint Sino-American capital.

'As long as Bottmore is president of the main company, then the old boy will remain head of Taiwan Morrison. You get it, don't you?' B.Y. asked. 'Foreign general managers last three, maybe five years. That's nothing. General Rong needs me, and I need you. Understand?'

That General Rong needed Bertland Yang was patently obvious to Olive. Many a time B.Y. had handed Olive a thick stack of receipts from the general. B.Y. didn't need to say a thing: right away Olive would meticulously record these bills as proper company expenditures. And that B.Y. needed Olive was equally obvious. 'Take these accounts and get rid of them,' B.Y. would say, as though nothing were going on. Olive would then expunge the accounts from the record, so that even the auditing agency sent from New York couldn't find anything. He had also established a secret account: B.Y. was deceiving the parent company and investing in several manufacturing and business firms that did business with Taiwan Morrison.

By this time, standing in B.Y.'s office, Olive felt dispirited.

'You follow me?' B.Y. went on. 'Young people ought to learn to keep a low profile. Understand? Are you going to quit? If you do, you're the only one who will take a beating, and all for nothing. You get me? All you need to do is keep plugging along, and before long everything will be ours. Do you follow me?' B.Y.'s questions were solicitous and earnest, his words flowing smoothly. Olive just stood there silently staring out the window, watching the workmen on the scaffolding risk their necks turning the coarse surface of the skyscraper milky white inch by inch. In the afternoon sunlight the building looked radiant.

After seeing B.Y., Olive had walked out of the office without so much as glancing at his own desk, then gotten on the escalator and gone home.

For over ten years, he thought, the same monotonous routine of going back and forth to the office. Before coming to work for Taiwan Morrison, Olive had marked time with several companies. Five years ago he had secured a spot in Morrison's spacious, elegant, and fully air-conditioned offices. Never in all that time had he experienced being idle and alone at home on a Wednesday morning, as he was now, a time when one was supposed to be going to the office. To a white-collar worker, he thought, home was like a hotel—someplace you went back to in order to sleep. For the past ten years, all his creative energies and the very essence of his existence had been centred on his work at an office. The first year at Morrison he was promoted from accountant to main accountant. He was made head of the credit division his third year; that same autumn he was placed in charge of the income accounts section.

As time passed, he became the confidant of the aggressively ambitious Bertland Yang, and during this same period Olive started to set his hopes on becoming assistant manager. A high salary, a car—such amenities were really secondary. Olive yearned to have the assistant manager's chair because it meant a lighter work load, because at last he would have the abundance of freedom and drive necessary to work on the documentary film he had never been able to complete while in college.

Musing in this way, Olive stood up. He glanced at a shelf of well-worn books on film in the bookcase against the living room wall to his right. A special three-volume collection of pioneer works by André Bazin and others on Fellini and Antonioni was there, along with the basic text, *Young Film-maker*. All these were books he had been addicted to reading in college, and they were the source of his dreams. He was in the film club at college and was insane about shooting movies, but had no camera of his own. He wrote scripts for club members who had cameras and would stand behind them, making modest but earnest suggestions about shooting the films. After helping edit in the preview room, he would return home all alone at night, riding his dilapidated bicycle. It was during these lonely rides, when he was poor and hopelessly longed for a camera of his own, that he got the idea of using the bicycle as a theme for a documentary. The first shot would be of the revolving wheels and the endlessly rolling road below. . . .

At the time Olive was discussing marriage with Grace, he was working in a tiny advertising agency. Grace's family of course expected to receive the customary betrothal present from the groom's family. So, for recompense, he finally drummed up his courage and suggested to Grace—a recent graduate of a junior teacher's college whose love for him was quite conventional—that she ask her family to give an eighteen-millimetre movie camera as a dowry. After the wedding, and right up until the time he joined Taiwan Morrison—two years of bliss and financial hardship—Olive was intermittently involved in shooting a film, some fifty feet long.

Last night he had thought again of that movie, pigeonholed for almost four years, and that out-of-date camera. He had tossed and turned, his mind whirling:

—The camera's been set aside for so long. Take advantage of this free time, and shoot a few more feet. . . .

—Start with the revolving wheel, then move to the lunch-box mounted behind the seat. Next, the most menial white-collar worker is seen riding the bicycle and disappearing down a street filled with private cars, taxis, and buses. At the end, the camera shifts to a shot of skyscrapers that look like a huge forest of building blocks. . . .

—That bastard Bertland! The way he cheated me for so long, for so many years. . . .

—What about the future? The money Grace has saved over the last three or four years will give me a year and a half of security. So probably there's nothing to worry about. . . .

—White-collar work, hardly anybody realizes what a huge hoax it is. How many talented, ambitious men have been destroyed by a ridiculous feeling of security?

—Bertland, don't imagine I'm easily set aside. I know every invoice, the story behind every phony account. I'm familiar with your shady dealings with customs officials and manufacturers and business firms. Damn it! Don't think I'm an easy mark!

At some point, several hours past midnight, he had, at last, fallen into a deep sleep. Originally he had planned that in the morning he would take out his camera, which was locked away, and clean it. But the call from B.Y. had distracted him. I'll polish it up this afternoon, he thought to himself.

Olive sank back into the sofa; he looked over the living room which his efficient wife had made sparklingly clean. He recalled the place they had rented when they were first married. There was only room enough for a new bed, a dresser, and two plastic clothes closets. The kitchen, bath, and living room were shared with other tenants. Two years later he had rented a little place on a rather noisy, narrow lane. It was over 700 square feet and had a living room and kitchen they could call their own. At this time, he became the father of a baby girl they named Lily. Three years later, when he joined Taiwan Morrison, he was solvent enough to carry the burden of paying the interest, and so was able to obtain the 1,300-square-foot apartment they had now. And so, ten years had gone by, a life made up of countless treks to and from the office. He sat on the couch quietly staring at a flower arrangement Grace had made. Although it was a bit withered, there was a pleasing artistic flair about it. A feeling of something he could not express pervaded his being, a sense of crushing emptiness.

Near noon he began listlessly reading André Bazin's *Essays on Film*. Here and there he would come upon such statements as: 'the theme of De Sica's *The Bicycle Thief* is thus marvellously and infuriatingly brief and to the point—in the world in which workers exist, the poor must steal from one another in order to survive'; or, 'In the West the Italian cinema can command a large audience of morally sensitive persons because of the significance it attaches to realistic portrayals. Once again this world is bedeviled by forces of rancor and fear; in a world where truth itself is not loved, but is considered some kind of political symbol, the Italian cinema has produced a radiant humanism which has transformed the world. . . .' Olive felt shocked and on unfamiliar terms with what he was reading, even to the point of anger. He tossed the book on top of the tea table. He wandered through the living room, Lily's tiny bedroom, and the kitchen, looking all around him. Before long he thought of friends he did not see very often, and he decided to make some phone calls.

'Busy?' he asked the first person he rang.

'Yes,' said the voice on the other end of the line, without a trace of regret. 'Real busy.'

Another, who was an older alumnus of Olive's college, responded: 'Just this minute I'm working on a $250,000 advertising job. No time, hey. We're trying to change completely the value concepts of Chinese and their consumption habits. When that happens we can get rid of one American import in particular. Get rid of it! Busy, eh?' He was the manager of a firm's research and development.

'What! You're enjoying your peace and quiet at home?' asked a former classmate. He specialized in buying up Taiwan-made athletic equipment to export. Naturally, Olive did not dare mention he had resigned. He said he was on vacation.

'Ah, the *annual leave*!' his friend exclaimed, using the English term. 'You high-level, white-collar workers sure live better than we do.'

Olive chuckled and said: 'An American company—vacations are part of the system.' Unexpectedly, he found himself relishing mentioning this difference.

'You go ahead with what you're doing,' Olive went on in a lonely voice. To his surprise, his old buddy hung up gladly, adding a parting shot:

'It's really tough to make a living this year. Hey, I work myself to death just for a bowl of rice. . . .'

Suddenly Olive felt friendless and isolated, as though everybody had abandoned him. He had come to the realization long ago that the whole world was a huge and powerful, well-meshed machine which he could not comprehend. The world followed the machine's revolutions, never stopping for a second, and always making harsh, grating noises. With each dawn, countless people rode motorcycles, squeezed into buses, or walked in a mad rush to find their tiny places within the great machine. Then, exhausted again after eight or ten hours, they went back to what was called 'home', the absurd, lonely, quiet place where Olive was now. The only difference was that they each followed their own way of supporting themselves and of sustaining those who one day, like themselves, would grow up and join the anxiety-ridden world of the white-collar worker.

The sudden ringing of the phone caught Olive in an alienated mood, unable to order his thoughts.

'Hello,' he said.

'Olive. Ah, you haven't gone out.' It was B.Y. Olive immediately felt elated.

'No,' he said. 'It's too hot.'

'I want to ask you to lunch. You choose the place.'

'Thanks, but that's not necessary. How come you're acting so formal?'

As soon as Olive opened his mouth, he realized he had made a mistake. B.Y. was a bright, perceptive person; of course he knew that Olive had the goods on him. Olive hoped B.Y. wouldn't take his refusal to dine with him as a threat.

'I've already invited someone else,' Olive said. 'But,' he hastened to add, 'whether I go back to work or not, we're still friends.' Then he sighed heavily and kept his mouth shut. He used not to be skilled at lying, but from numerous occasions in the past he had learned at critical moments to lie, and insincere hypocritical words would flow glibly from his lips.

'Okay, that's all right,' B.Y. responded. He sounded somewhat agitated. After a pause he said: 'Okay. As a matter of fact, there is something I want to talk to you about. But it isn't urgent. We can talk it over tonight.' And he hung up.

Suddenly Olive was hungry. He wanted to find a quiet spot and eat by himself. He was beginning to feel a little as if he were on vacation. He changed his clothes and locked the door as he left. Outside the air-conditioned apartment, the depressing heat and dust of Taipei suddenly hit him full in the face. He undid the top buttons of his shirt and, squinting his eyes, walked along the red brick road in the scalding sunlight. He hadn't gone more than a couple of steps when he stopped beneath the shade of a maple tree, next to a taxi stand, and tried to get a taxi. He waved to one in the distance that looked freshly painted, a bright blue. As he got in, he gave the cab driver directions:

'Go past the second section. I'll get off by the Bank of Florida.'

The air-conditioned cab gradually made him comfortable again. Just a few years back he had been one of those white-collar workers who had to jam into a bus to get to work, or walk, even on a hot day. The year he was made head of the credit division, he was given the privilege of taking a taxi to work and turning in travel expenses, since his work took him outside the office for credit checks. From then on, taking cabs became a habit. As time went by, he would fill out reimbursement forms for taxi fares that were not necessarily incurred on official business. Soon he had turned into a person who refused either to pile onto buses or to walk. Even if his destination was only a ten-minute walk away, he could not help hailing a passing cab.

Olive got off at the entrance to the Bank of Florida. Harvey's Western Restaurant was located on the top floor of the bank building. He picked out a table with an excellent view of the imposing Washington Building nearby, and sat down. Taiwan Morrison was on the ninth floor of the Washington Building. To Olive, the view from the top floor of the bank of the street scene below was full of charm, like a scene in a movie. The skyscrapers surrounding the intersection were of every height and shape. In the sunlight they thrust straight up against the sky, and looked secure and serene as they cast shadows like variegated designs. By contrast, the people and vehicles on the streets below were a river flowing rhythmically in obedience to the traffic signals. In the sunlight the Washington Building stood apart from all the rest, with its ochre marble and singular design. The inevitable street noise was cut off by Harvey's double-paned windows. The forest of silent, majestic skyscrapers and mighty buildings bathed by the summer sun, the sweeping tide of people, cars sandwiched together like teeth in a comb, and motorcycles threading their way among them—they all were reflected in the restaurant window, a silver screen on which they played their silent parts in an exquisitely vivid manner. I really ought to make a movie, Olive conjectured idly.

'Sir, something to eat or drink?'

'I'll eat,' Olive replied, still gazing outside. He drew out a cigarette, then realized he had no light.

'Could you give me a book of matches?' he asked, raising his head.

He was a bit startled to see the young girl with an oval face. He took the menu from her.

'I think I'll have dinner "A",' he said, handing the menu back without opening it. 'Is it steak or pork chops today?' he asked, looking at her intently.

'Pork chops.'

'Would you change the pork chops to braised prawns, please?'

'All right,' she said. She was hugging the menu against her chest, just about to leave.

'And a small bottle of beer,' he said, smiling. 'Are you new here?'

'Yes,' she replied.

As she walked away, Olive stared after her. She wore a uniform with a floor-length skirt. All of a sudden this waitress reminded him of Rose, even though this girl's figure and age were different.

Rose also had a round face, full lips that pouted slightly, and a rather broad, fleshy nose. But she lacked the gleaming, white, evenly-spaced teeth of this new waitress, which made her immediately attractive as soon as she opened her mouth. Rose's experience and profession naturally gave her a casually seductive charm that this other woman lacked.

Not long after Olive was promoted to head of the credit division, opportunities for social get-togethers with factory and business people suddenly multiplied. When he visited a brothel for the first time in his life, he met Rose.

'What's your Chinese name?' he asked her.

'Call me Rose, that will do,' she replied. 'You're not a census taker.'

Gentlemen callers were forbidden from inquiring after a prostitute's real name—something Olive did not understand until much later. Nevertheless, Rose did not mind his unintentional breaking of the taboo. They had fun drinking together under the dim lights. Drinking was something he was really good at, and it gave him a lot of self-confidence. Olive's sense of composure during his initial outing to the floating world was one that first-time guests seldom enjoy.

'Hey, you couldn't be from my home town, Puli, could you?' asked Rose, staring steadily at Olive.

'And if I was?' he asked.

She silently smoked a cigarette. As he lit it for her, he noticed how her full lips pouted slightly.

After that Rose would sometimes give him a call. Often it was just after she had dried out.

'My phone's right at the head of the bed,' she would explain. 'You must be awfully busy. I really shouldn't bother you.'

Once when she called her voice was muddled and despondent. He could hear her coughing hard, trying to clear her throat.

'How about cutting down on your smoking?' he suggested.

She burst into tears, then tried to control her sobbing.

'What's the matter?' he asked. 'What happened?' But she just kept on crying.

'It's nothing,' she said finally.

'Do you want me to come see you?' he asked.

'No! From now on you shouldn't come to this sort of place so often.'

He sighed deeply.

'Just don't mind me calling, that's all,' she said.

'Phone whenever you like,' he told her.

'I'll call as seldom as possible. That's what I'll do,' she said. 'Thanks.' She hung up.

Olive began to eat the first dish. He had always been fond of Harvey's cold plate of tender beef tongue. He slowly savoured his first glass of cold beer, then craned his neck to look around the dining room for the waitress with the oval face, but he couldn't spot her. By now it was almost two o'clock, so the number of patrons in the dining room had diminished. Sitting at a table towards the rear of the room were four Japanese having an uproarious conversation.

And that was how, after some initial awkwardness, Rose had quickly slipped into his life. From that time on, he was no longer the prudent, self-deprecating employee who wormed his way onto public buses. Instead, he became a relatively clever and worldly, minor boss, one who used a taxi instead of walking and had a mistress to boot. When he joined a financial co-op[2], Rose readily put up $2,500.

'This isn't right,' he said.

She stuffed a check into the pocket of his trousers, which were hanging on the wall.

'I've gotten together all the money I need,' he said.

'This $2,500 is to go toward two walls of your study,' she said, undressing as she walked into the bathroom. She closed the door.

'But you can't use it to build your and your wife's bedroom,' she shouted. Olive could hear her enjoying a good laugh behind the bathroom door.

Six months later she suddenly left. No quarrel, no grief. Later he heard she was living with an American soldier and ended up leaving Taiwan with him. At first he intended to take the whole business as a joke, but he couldn't help thinking of her. After a while, he went crazy. Passion and jealous rage completely possessed him. Often, in the morning before the others got to the office, he would dial the number she had left for him, and again after they had gone home in the afternoon. Once he telephoned Rose's former apartment, a place where women like her lived crowded together.

'Hello. . . .' The woman's voice was unfamiliar, naturally.

'Did you think you could end the affair simply by going away?' He spoke in English.

'What you talking now?' The woman on the other end said in pidgin English.

'You know what I'm talking about, sweetheart,' he said. 'Fuck, I want you. . . .'

'Baby, you come see Dolly, hey? Come and try me. . . .' She burst out laughing in delight.

Olive hung up, the tears streaming down his face.

To be sure, Olive's heartache and despondency did not persist all that long. Suddenly and unexpectedly one day he was promoted to head of the income accounts section—the stepping-stone to becoming assistant manager of accounting. He had his own little office and a car. Many times when there was a fairly high-level company meeting, he would sit alongside the divisional managers—sometimes even with the top administrator of manufacturing in the Taoyuan area. It was as if he had been elevated overnight to a higher status. The work of assistant manager—just one step away—was basically doing reports on joint planning, training, and analysis, and was of such a nature that he would find he had somewhat more free time. Unexpectedly, the bit of training he had gotten from reading movie criticism in college would really come in handy every time he had to write an analytical report in English. As far as he was concerned, the really vital thing was this: as soon as he was able to move into the assistant director's office, he would really have the time to resume his creative work on the documentary film he had put away ten years before. With all this to think about, Rose faded from his memory.

As he set aside the plate of braised prawns only half-eaten, a pair of white hands suddenly reached past him, nimbly clearing away his cup and dishes. He looked up at once. Again there was that oval face. But this time, no matter how intently he stared at her, it was clear she was quite a different person from Rose, whose image he conjured up from a spotty memory. Feeling low, he directed his gaze out the window. The sun seemed fiercely bright and hot. In the white heat the Washington Building stood straight up, oblivious to all else— 'like a contemporary marble sculpture,' Mr McNell had said.

That autumn, something happened that no one could have predicted. Unexpectedly, Mr McNell, who was then general manager, brought Kenneth Zhao from the Rotary Club and appointed him assistant manager of accounting, unilaterally acting to fill the position to which Bertland Yang had devoted all his cleverness and eloquence to get approved and established. Before long, the affair between Mr McNell and Kenneth, his homosexual lover, was bandied about all the associations of top-level business executives in Taiwan, and also within Taiwan Morrison itself. Rumours and gossip began to circulate, repressed yet insistent, like a spring that has begun to bubble.

Yet, no matter what the particular circumstances were, what had happened meant that Olive had lost his chance, which had been only one step away. For him it felt just like missing a catch and having the ball whistle by and sail away.

This appointment was a setback to Bertland Yang as well, and he reacted like a poisonous snake, which quickly coils up when aroused and prepares for a lethal attack. He became preoccupied with stratagems and, again like a snake, worked without making a sound. First, under the guise of safeguarding sound morals, he got General Rong to join him in overthrowing the faction supporting Mr McNell. After that, he posed as someone sympathetic to homosexual love, and ended up encouraging Mr McNell and Kenneth to rent a room so they could live together. Once Mrs. McNell, the betrayed wife, fell into B.Y.'s carefully devised trap, both she and General Rong signed a hefty dossier of incriminating evidence, and the president of Morrison in New York, Mr Bottmore, was informed of the charges.

'Excuse me, Sir. Do you prefer coffee or tea?' asked a young waiter obsequiously. His face was covered with acne.

'Make it tea,' said Olive.

He noticed that the oval-faced waitress was now slumped in a dark corner of the dining room. A newspaper covered her head and shaded out the light. She had sprawled face downwards over a table and was taking a midday nap. Mr McNell's appearance came to Olive's mind, as it often did: a full head of silver-white hair, large, slightly protruding eyes, and well over six feet in stature. He liked to wear tight-fitting dark pants. By comparison, Kenneth was pallid and slightly overweight. A dignified-looking person, but not handsome. It was said that he had been a translator during the Korean War. After the war he left the American PX and joined Huntington Electric. He had met Mr McNell at the Rotary Club.

Mr McNell ended up leaving Taiwan, and the way he left was one people could not easily forget. When he and his wife were divorced, he provided very generous alimony. In keeping with the refinement of one with a Harvard doctorate, he tactfully refused a transfer by the main office to take over the territory around Pakistan. Over the preceding ten years in this multinational company, he had been sent all over the world. Based on his first-hand experience of managing these subsidiaries, he had published three volumes of poetry, essays, travels, and fiction, and each year the royalties from his moderately productive writing were considerable. Yet he threw away his career, wife, and children, and drifted to Africa with his doleful Kenneth, so young and pale.

The assistant manager's office across from Olive's and next to B.Y.'s was vacant once again. The hope which had swung like a pendulum far out of reach was suddenly within Olive's grasp. Just at this time he received an aerogramme written in an unfamiliar hand from the States. He opened it suspiciously, then realized it was from Rose.

She told him that he reminded her of a physics and chemistry teacher she had had in junior high school. 'He taught me not to feel ashamed of being poor,' she wrote. 'After graduation he visited my simple village and said I ought to take the high school entrance examination. And he offered to pay the tuition.' But, she went on, 'In fact you are not my teacher, the man I will never forget, the only one I have really loved.' She wrote that when she was forced into prostitution, she knew that 'he could not blame me.' At that time he contracted a liver ailment and died very young.

Nearly a third of the letter was a discussion of whether Chinese or foreign men were superior.

'Chinese men are relatively more intelligent, but they are third-rate lovers. They don't dare love. They make lots of conditions. And you aren't any different. . . . Some foreign men are nothing but savages, but they're not afraid to love. My American husband, Paul, knew all about my profession and that I'd been pregnant with another man's child. But he said he wanted me and would marry me. . . .

'Lastly, I want to tell you my Chinese name, Zhou Ah-Mian. My teacher, my one love, is the only person in the whole world who ever told me that Zhou Ah-Mian was a pleasant-sounding name.' Then she added: 'When I was working on North Sun Yat-sen Street in Taipei, of course I couldn't use my name. It wasn't because I was ashamed, but because I cherished it.'

Rose had filled the two sides of the aerogramme with densely packed writing, no two characters the same size. On the envelope she had written in very crooked letters her address in Iowa. He wanted to write her back a very friendly letter right away, but he put it off for a day or two, and then, what with this anxious period of time working with B.Y., he totally forgot about her.

Olive lit a cigarette, and with his left hand slowly turned his glass filled with iced tea. He noticed that the ice cubes, suspended in the middle and seemingly unaffected by his movements, did not turn with the glass.

'Chinese men . . . don't dare love. And you aren't any different.' That comment especially stuck in his mind. He sighed and then smiled helplessly to himself.

After Mr McNell had gone, the New York office sent a man named Talmann from the Asia-Pacific headquarters in Indonesia to be president of Taiwan Morrison. He was three years older than B.Y., prematurely bald, and sported a goatee. At a glance one could tell that he was an energetic, sophisticated sort. Olive still remembered how B.Y. endeavoured to feel him out, the wily octopus reaching in every direction with long, boneless, clinging tentacles. Finally, one day B.Y. got hold of a huge pile of Mr Talmann's bills and gave them to Olive to record in an account book.

'This guy is easy to feed.' B.Y. said, as though nothing was up, but the wrinkles around his eyes and the corners of his mouth indicated that he was brimming over with delight. 'He's not choosy. Eats anything, large or small.' B.Y. broke into peals of laughter.

Following B.Y.'s movements step by step, Olive could see ever more clearly the extent and depth of corruption in business. When he had first started work, Olive was one who had always relied on textbooks for his knowledge of concepts such as 'American business enterprise is a manifestation of modern rational management'. A person like himself, who had stuffed his mind with such ideas, was astonished by reality.

Last spring B.Y.—his face suffused with a constant happy smile—delightedly told Olive that the company had sent his dossier, along with plans to assign him a car, to the Manila office with the request that these be forwarded to New York for approval.

'This time we'll be neighbours for sure,' B.Y. had said.

For a brief time Olive was ecstatic when he went to the office each day, and his efficiency on the job was extraordinary. But in less than a week, B.Y. called him on the intercom and asked him to come to his office.

'There's a couple of items of news to tell you,' said B.Y. 'Neither one is too good.'

Olive smiled, relaxed, and sat leaning on B.Y.'s desk.

'Mr McNell is dead.'

'Eh!' Olive exclaimed.

'Suicide.' B.Y. placed the edge of his hand like a knife against his throat and drew it suddenly to the right.

'Ssssst,' he said, 'like that.'

'Oh!' said Olive, shaking his head.

B.Y. offered Olive a cigarette; Olive gave him a light.

'The other news is that the head office wants the subsidiaries in each country to follow a "capital reduction plan".'

'Oh,' said Olive.

'They want us to reduce personnel expenses. Whew! What can I do but close the office next to mine, temporarily?' He winked at Olive and smiled. All Olive could do for the time being was to smile with him.

'Don't worry,' B.Y. assured him.

'Hmm,' Olive mumbled.

'It would be best not to worry. The whole thing is nothing but externals,' B.Y. went on. 'Who says Americans don't bother with externals?' He asked in a low voice, and smiled again.

Olive sipped his iced tea in little mouthfuls. Until today the CRP (the English abbreviation for 'cost reduction plan') had been in fact just a matter of 'externals'. There was no way to stop Bertland Yang and General Rong, two bottomless funnels of cash who spent money endlessly. On the other hand, the two of them would go to any length weeding out insignificant items, such as paper and ball-point pens in order to trim expenditures. And the position of assistant manager of accounting, which Olive had considered a well-cooked duck simmering in the pot, took wing and flew away.

As a matter of fact, Olive thought to himself, his loss of complete loyalty to B.Y. and trust in him could be dated from the moment B.Y. sacrificed the assistant manager position in order to push the cost reduction plan.

He turned his head and looked at the Washington Building, standing tall as always in the glaring summer sun. Opening his eyes wide, he tried to figure out which was B.Y.'s office window. He counted up and down, left and right, as if he were afraid of making a mistake while proofreading a large report.

'B.Y., you are a cheat,' he whispered to the office window he guessed belonged to Bertland Yang. Actually, Olive had long since lost his anger. What flooded his heart now was the thought of the wandering Mr McNell, who had cast away all that the world considered precious. He thought of Rose: even given her profession, she cherished real love, and for her it wasn't taboo to condemn the 'love' of men who were cowardly and unjust. Suddenly he felt melancholy. He looked at his watch. It was just a little after three o'clock. He waved his hand for the waitress. He did not know when the oval-faced woman had woken up, but just then she was playing cards with another waitress. She walked over.

'My cheque,' he said.

'Oh.' She brushed her shoulder-length hair to the side and spoke as though there were something on her mind. 'They say you work at the Washington Building. . . .'

'That's right,' he replied.

'At the Washington Building.' She talked as she was clearing the table. 'Do you want to charge it, or. . . .'

'No,' he said, standing up. 'This time I'll pay for myself.'

After Olive got home from Harvey's he slept soundly. When he awoke it was already past five o'clock. He fetched his camera, which he had left in the closet, and cleaned it in the living room. Although he had not shot any film in seven or eight years, he gave it a maintenance check at least once a year. After Lily and then Grace had gotten home, he finished the job. The quiet apartment, which made him feel strangely uneasy and lonely that day, was once again filled with all sorts of sounds: his wife cooking in the kitchen, a TV cartoon coming from Lily's room, and their voices intermingling with the noise.

Grace was concentrating on making a sumptuous dinner. The previous night he had told her he wanted to resign from Morrison and cut back on his activities so as to get some rest. He also mentioned his decision to take advantage of the opportunity to make a film.

Her response, unexpectedly, was a straightforward and genuine 'That's good.'

'Why?' he asked.

'Because from now on I won't have to worry about going to the company's formal banquets,' she laughed. 'I'm never comfortable wearing evening clothes, and besides, I can't speak English fluently like the other managers' wives.'

Olive forced a bitter smile.

Tonight he reminded her of something else. 'There's still the interest to pay on this place,' he said.

'When are you going to show movies?' asked Lily. Whenever she saw her father adjusting his camera or projector, she always made a fuss about wanting to see the two small reels of her parent's wedding and herself as a newborn baby.

'Time for dinner now,' said Grace. 'After we eat you can see them.'

'And besides, there's what we need to live on. . . .' he went on.

'No problem for the time being,' Grace assured him. 'I figured that out when I was at school today. We can buy a piano and I can take students in the evening. A good way to get some income, no?'

He did not respond. Yesterday, right after he had sworn in his rage that he would quit, he realized that in fact he had long since fallen into the great formless net of daily drudgery in which every white-collar worker was caught.

They prepared to watch movies as usual. Lily, barely able to contain herself, was poised waiting to turn off the lights. Olive put the film on the reel adeptly, then switched on the projector light. 'Ready!' he shouted.

Lily snapped the lights off, scrambled to her favourite place on the sofa, and looked ahead, eyes wide open. The projector made a faint whirring sound that filled the living room.

On the screen appeared a narrow, rundown little lane. The camera moved forward gradually, then there was an appealing shot as it followed the alleyway twisting upwards and to the right. A tiny balcony suddenly zoomed into view and Grace, the newlywed, came strolling out and leaned against the railing. Her hair fluttered in the breeze. She gazed east, then west, all the time wearing a wooden expression.

Olive started to laugh.

'You absolutely insisted that I not stare at the camera so the movie would seem more natural,' she said. 'But instead I look funny.'

The scene abruptly switched to an interior. Grace and her girl friends were sitting on a sofa in the living room the couple had shared with other tenants. They were going through a photograph album. The turning of the pages and the explanations of the pictures were all highly exaggerated. Olive watched himself walk into view, a veteran movie star. He was young and slender and had long hair. Without a trace of self-consciousness, he directly faced the camera and spoke, a serious expression on his face. Behind him, Grace and her friends tittered and covered their mouths, then began clapping enthusiastically.

'What are you saying, Daddy?' asked Lily.

'Ask Mama,' he said.

'Mother doesn't know,' Grace said. 'Ask Daddy.'

Olive lit a cigarette and inhaled deeply. The black smoke coiled in the flickering light of the projector. Olive remembered the situation clearly. He had placed his camera carefully on a table and then walked into the picture he was shooting. He had faced the camera and said: 'Huang Jingxiong, China's great documentary film-maker-to-be, marrying at age twenty-five. While he was living at this humble little apartment, he made his first movie. . . .'

'Why is it that life then was full of a different kind of vitality?' he said in a subdued voice.

'What?' Grace asked.

Olive shook his head and kept smoking silently. The film moved from scene to scene without any breaks: there was Grace, pregnant, walking in a cultivated field; looking through a book on infant care in bed; sorting through baby clothes her family had sewn. And finally, Lily wailing vociferously, suspended in her mother's arms. . . .

Suddenly Rose was on the screen with her oval face, broad nose, and thick, pouting lips. Olive was astonished. He wanted to shut off the projector, but quickly realized that if he did it would look suspicious.

'Hey, who's that?' Lily asked, fascinated.

'Yes,' asked Grace. 'Who is that?'

Olive smoked his cigarette calmly and explained that this was an experimental film made by one of the students in the film and drama department at the university. Because this student had no projector of his own, he borrowed Olive's; he had left his film on the projector reel.

'Although it was just practice,' Olive remarked nonchalantly, 'in terms of skill it appears remarkably well done.'

Every so often in the film Rose would tug nervously at her then-fashionable miniskirt. One moment she fondled flowers in a vase, the next she would furtively glance at the camera. She was not photogenic. Now she was sprawled in a rattan chair, and the natural lighting revealed the voluptuous figure beneath her winter clothes. She was stubbornly refusing to look at the camera. Her right leg was crossed over her left, and she kept jiggling it slightly. All of a sudden she flew into a rage, grabbed a thick magazine, and flung it at the camera with a powerful swing. At that moment the film stopped, leaving only the bare white screen and the faint clicking of the movie projector.

Lily turned on the light.

'Who is that, huh?' she asked.

'Some woman Daddy doesn't know,' Olive replied.

'Why did she throw that book?'

'I guess because she doesn't like to read,' he said.

Grace and Lily both started laughing. Grace considered his 'film art' something sacred. Obviously, she suspected nothing about the part with Rose in it. Olive began reversing the film, and the projector made a rapid, swishing sound.

On the day he received the letter Rose sent from America, Olive had taken home this same film, which had been kept locked up in his office. He watched it secretly all by himself once while his wife and daughter were out. But now to have that scene shown in front of his family—Rose throwing a magazine at him—for the first time the incident hit him where he hurt and reminded him of his shame.

He vividly recalled that while he was shooting the film he asked Rose to slowly undress.

'No,' she said. She obeyed his orders not to look at the camera, but she also stiffened her neck in refusal.

'If you don't want to take everything off, strip down to your underwear. That will do,' he cooed, all the while continuing to film. 'You have a beautiful body. Really.'

'No,' she said.

'How could you of all people be bashful?' he laughed.

Suddenly he saw her face the camera directly and throw a thick magazine at him with all her might. He stopped filming immediately. She sat as before, twisting her dress between her fingers, weeping.

During those years he had been a dreamer. A star of ambitious hope had kept beckoning to him as it glittered above the horizon. He had experienced boundless passion as well. But before long he became a lowly slave to that fickle door of the assistant manager's office, that narrow, lacquered teakwood door which had closed, then opened, and now had shut him out at last. He had been a minor actor in an ugly, rotten drama directed by Bertland Yang, a man consumed by lust.

While Olive was soaking in the bathtub and getting into his pajamas to go to bed, a sense of regret and a spiritual ache—long since unfamiliar to him—spread throughout his being. His compunction and pain led him to decide to seek some kind of new existence.

'For the time being there'll be no problem,' Grace was saying as she brushed her hair in front of the dresser mirror.

He looked at her in the mirror as he lay in bed, and fell silent.

'I think something's bothering you,' she said.

'Oh, it's nothing.'

No more B.Y. or General Rong. No more rotten schemes, and no more coveting the assistant manager's black artificial leather chair. Life will be really different, no doubt about it, he thought to himself.

Just then the telephone rang.

'Olive. . . .' It was B.Y.

'Yes,' Olive said.

'I just returned from General Rong's house. He said that his precious nephew had called this morning from overseas and told him he didn't want to return to Taiwan. He's resigning from Morrison.'

'Oh,' said Olive.

'This Edward Zhao said that if he went back to Taiwan at this point in time, he would have no way of getting a green card. Ha-ha.'

'Oh.'

'Let's not talk about that now. With you gone only one day I realized that Joe and Nancy can't handle anything. The income accounts are in a big mess. . . .'

'Oh,' said Olive.

'What do you say?'

'I'll come have a look tomorrow!' Olive yelled, his loud voice angry.

B.Y. hung up with a chuckle.

Grace stared at Olive quietly. 'Who was it?' she asked.

'Bertland.'

She turned around again to look in the mirror. 'Does he want you to come back?' she asked.

'Mhmm,' he responded.

'How can they afford to lose you?' Grace smiled very contentedly to her face in the mirror, her make-up off now. She saw Olive jump out of bed and leave the bedroom.

'What is it?' she asked. 'I already locked the front door.' The living room light went on. A moment later she called again: 'What are you doing, huh?'

'I'm putting away the camera and projector,' he said in a low voice.

'Mhmm,' she said.

1978

NOTES

1 Olive Huang's Chinese name.
2 A private 'chain-letter' method of raising funds in Taiwan. Members pay a certain amount into a common fund every month. Each person takes a turn using capital from the common fund while continuing to contribute the required amount.

5

Earthworm, Sea Horse, and Fishmoth

By **MA SHA**
Translated by Kwok-kan Tam, with Timothy Weiss

Ma Sha 馬沙 is the pen-name of Li Ten 李登 (Li Deng, b. 1946). He graduated with a diploma in English at Hong Kong Baptist College in the early 1970s and worked as a TV programmer in Hong Kong. His short stories can be found in the literary column of Express Daily *(*Kuai Pao 快報*), a Hong Kong newspaper. He is also a film critic and has written regularly for the Hong Kong film journals,* Montage *and* Cinema. *He is currently a free-lance columnist, writing under the pen-name 'Kamala' 卡馬拉 (camera), for many magazines and newspapers in Hong Kong, including* Next Magazine *(*Yi zhoukan 壹周刊*) and* Ming Pao Weekly *(*Mingbao zhoukan 明報周刊*). His knowledge of the cinema gives his fiction the flavour of highly effective visual images, and makes him distinctly unique among Hong Kong writers.*

I

His hair was his dream, crawling out from his skull into the daylight; I let mine grow, longer and longer. The beard was his fixed asset, whereas my only current assets were the few lice residing in my private parts. Every evening when he went to work at the press, he was like a beast just emerged from his burrow; during the day I buried myself in deep sleep.

He lived in a dank, dark basement, the only source of light descending from two windows above the sidewalk outside. Through these openings to the world came the hustle and bustle of the city, together with its polluted air. During the day, they served as a small screen showing myriad shapes of legs passing to and fro. Occasionally, upon awaking, I would lie in bed and stare up at this odd assortment of animal forms—long ones, short ones, skinny ones, chubby ones. Based on their manner of grooming, I would try to figure out the appearance of their masters and make up comic stories about them.

But apart from this, he lived a sunless, soundless, colourless, odourless existence. I, too, resigned myself to my allotted niche, leading a self-sufficient unisexual life. He relied on semi-blind eyes, behind thick myopic glasses, to grope around in the dark world of his self, cultivating an opaque solitude.

II

The earthworm, also known as the 'crooked eel' or the 'wriggling worm', is a species of invertebrate in the phylum Annelida, also classified as Vermes. Having neither ears, eyes, nose, teeth nor feet, it is a nocturnal creature that bores its way into the earth for its shelter, feeding on soil and producing an excrement beneficial to farming. Its body is made up of 150 segments; hermaphrodite, it has a pair of ovaries in the thirteenth segment and two pairs of testes in the tenth and eleventh segments respectively. The chapter 'On Nature' in *The Book of Rites of Elder Dai* states: 'The earthworm has neither sharp claws nor teeth; nor does it have a strong, sinewy body. It feeds on loam from the heavens above and drinks yellow-spring water from hell below; this signifies its righteousness and single-mindedness.' Yang Quan's *An Essay on the Nature of Things* adds: 'Scrupulous and free of desires, the earthworm is the only true ascetic hermit. Even a virtuous and determined person cannot be compared with it.'

III

Sitting next to me was a teenager, feeding a baby in his arms. The son was attentively sucking his milk; the father was attentively feeding his baby. Sitting opposite was a young girl who looked at the father and son with a smile; beside her was an old woman, who looked at the father and son with a smile for one moment and at the young girl, also with a smile, for the next. She stared at them. I ate my ox-tongue spaghetti absent-mindedly. Leaving behind his wife and young son, the father had gone to the United States to incubate his ambition. At the end of a year the egg had hatched finally, yielding a Master of Arts degree. He returned to Hong Kong to look for a job, and half a year had now passed without any sign of hope. He killed time at home by playing hide-and-seek with his son and singing nursery rhymes. His wife went to work during the day and did not return till the evening. His son, who resembled a fair, chubby-looking doll made of dough, was originally entrusted to the care of a mother-in-law. But now the father had nothing much to do during the day and wanted something with which to occupy himself, so he took care of the baby as a means of killing time and relieving boredom. The day passed without notice amidst the baby's wow-la wow-la cries. Time seemed to be going backwards; he seemed to be reliving his days in the United States, baby-sitting for extra income, doing a job that was natural for a woman, but less so for a man.

The father and son sitting beside me had not altered their facial expressions, as if they had somehow turned to stone.

IV

The sea horse, also known as 'dragon seed' or 'horse-head' fish, is so named because from the side its head looks like a horse's. A species in the family of vertebrate jawfish, its length ranges from one inch to one foot, and its colour varies from brown to silvery white. A hard, ring-shaped coat protects its body, whose tapered abdomen is wider than its tail, itself resembling an elephant's trunk in miniature. The sea horse is wont to swim upright and rest with its tail curled round seaweed. A homogamous animal, the male has a pouch in its belly where, after mating, it keeps its fertilized eggs for forty-five days until they hatch, thus performing the reproductive functions of the female.

V

He dreamed a dream of his room. No, it was not really a room, for there was not a single piece of furniture in it, but rather, books only, like a large, tightly packed case devoid of surrounding space. He was completely buried in books. The books around him suddenly opened and closed, each one like a mouth, all of them trying to bite him unceasingly. Then, after a while, they all suddenly disappeared, leaving only the four walls around him, naked and empty. A horse stood on the floor. It was not really a horse, but a species of ox. No, it did not seem to be an ox. It was the skeleton of an ox. Two flowers had sprung from its eye sockets. Two morning glories. The ox skeleton was dancing. No, not really dancing, but its forelimbs were shuffling to a certain rhythm: look forward and kick, one, two, three; kick hard, one more, two more, three more. . . . It was the cancan. He was so frightened that he suddenly woke up. The books in the room: Chinese, English, French, German, Japanese, Spanish books, photography books, major archaeology books, novels, classics in medicine, etc. All were in good order without any sign of disruption. His room was more like a library than a room. The shelves were filled with books. The wardrobes were—in addition to the clothes within—also stuffed with books. The writing desk had books piled on top of it and beneath it. So had his chair, on the seat and below the seat. There were books stacked beneath his bunk bed. He slept on the lower bed, part of which was occupied by books. He had gotten used to sleeping with his body facing outward and would not turn inward for fear of overturning the books which had piled up high along his back. His wife occupied the upper bed, and he would climb to the upper level two or three times a week. That is to say, he would leave the enjoyment of Faulkner, Abe Kōbō, Proust, Kroetz, and the like for two or three nights per week. Your wife does not seem like your wife. She is like a rare book that you love too much to touch. He did not like this analogy made by his friends. Every morning when he washed his face in the bathroom, he would carefully examine himself after a night's rest. He would discover several more grey hairs, which, like burglars, had stealthily poked out half of their bodies and peeped through his forest of dark hair. He was particularly careful inspecting his face, which looked unusually pale as a result of his long bouts of reading. There was a face in the mirror. It was his face, but did not seem to be his face. It was merely a face, and not his face. It looked like someone else's face. Gradually he felt that he both had a face and had no face at all. No, it was definitely not a face; it was only an old edition of another book.

VI

Moth, a worm in the wood. The *Etymological Dictionary of Ancient Chinese Scripts* devotes an entry to it, while the *Duan Annotation* contains this brief gloss: 'Living in the wood and feeding on the wood. The modern term was moth-eaten.' The moth larvae in books are called 'fishmoths'. The classic *Erya Annotation* elaborates: 'Cicada: yellowish at first, it has a silvery powder on its body when it is fully grown. Thus it is called silverfish, though nowadays it is called fishmoth.' Its tail has three hairs, all of equal length.

1976

6

A Bone Stuck in the Throat

By **XIN QI SHI**
Translated by Benzi Zhang and Terry Siu-han Yip

Xin Qi Shi 辛其氏 *is the pen-name of Kan Mo Han, Maureen* 簡慕嫻 *(Jian Muxian, b. 1950). Born and educated in Hong Kong, she currently works at an institution of higher education in Hong Kong. Xin Qi Shi started her writing career in 1969 when her essays were published in* Chinese Students' Weekly *(*Zhongguo xuesheng zhoubao 中國學生周報*). Her first short story, 'The Wedding' (Hunli* 婚禮*), was published in 1979. Her essays have been published in two collections entitled* At Holiday Time *(*Meifeng jiajie 每逢佳節, *1985) and* Writings on the Theatre *(*Xianbi xise 閒筆戲寫, *1998). Her published works of fiction include* The Blue Crescent Moon *(*Qingse de yueya 青色的月芽, *1986) and* The Red Checkers Pub *(*Hong gezi jiupu 紅格子酒舖, *1994). In her works there is a strong flavour of Hong Kong's local life that spans the 1960s through the 1990s.*

It had been a week of thunderous rain. Like a punctual visitor, heavy showers of rain had been with us every morning and afternoon for the whole week, as if our days were somehow incomplete without its presence. That morning, however, was different—the sky was unusually clear and bright. Since I believe that fine weather always helps to brighten up one's day, making one feel happy and light-hearted, I decided to put aside the unhappy feelings I had had the day before. It seemed pointless to remain angry and upset over a problem for which one could find no immediate solution. On such a fine day, I thought I should perhaps reconsider my attitude toward Peter Chen and also the way I handled our relationship. As I was deeply immersed in my thoughts, the bad news found its way to my office.

I had gone to bed late the night before and so I was still half asleep when I arrived at my office in the morning. The clacking sound of the typewriters, like an effective stimulant, brought my attention back to my work. I sorted and filed the letters and papers that had piled up the day before, and locked up those documents stamped CONFIDENTIAL in blood-red ink. I made appointments by phone with a number of people whom my boss wanted to see, and checked with the airline about the time and date of the arrival of the 'inspector general' from the bank's headquarters in the United States. The Head of the Research and Analysis Department called to see my boss and I managed to send him away by saying, 'My boss has an important meeting this morning,' although I was perfectly clear that there was no such meeting scheduled for the day.

It was past ten and yet there was still no sight of my boss. Peter Chen's office was adjacent to mine; his office door opened into my room. So Peter Chen had to pass by my office every day to make his way to his office. That day he was already two hours late. Perhaps I was over-sensitive, but every time I looked at my colleagues in the outer room through the glass panel, I felt somehow that work morale was getting lower and lower. A number of them were whispering to one another with their glances cast in my direction from time to time. Like other offices of many similar corporations, the Credit and Investment Department of this American bank was rife with secrets and rumours which could spread through the entire office building in a couple of hours, in a much exaggerated or elaborated form. The boredom of routine office work was often enlivened by gossip of all kinds. Power struggles in the senior administration, promotions and transfers in middle management, or news of office romances could add some flavour to the otherwise dull and mechanical existence in the office. In a place where human relationships were so complex, people seemed to have no right to privacy. The huge glass wall on one side of my office allowed me a clear view of my colleagues working in the general office, and yet very often it was this same piece of cold glass that gave me the most unpleasant feeling. At times when I was pressed by my workload or office politics, I might look up from my desk, mistaking myself for a fish swimming back and forth in an aquarium—my every movement was always under public scrutiny. I was so used to my colleagues' spying eyes and surveillance that after three years of practice, I had developed a superhuman ability to return any spiteful glances that came my way. It was my developed self-defence mechanism that had enabled me to keep my head above water while I served in Peter Chen's Credit and Investment Department.

I must admit, in recollection, that the idea of quitting the job did occur to me in my early days in the department. I was not a young girl fresh from high school with little experience of society. I have had setbacks in my so-called 'emotional' life. A heavy workload, complex human relationships, or gossip that spread like infectious disease never overwhelmed me. As a matter of fact, when I found myself in a new environment, I would double my efforts to meet new challenges with enthusiasm and to adjust to changing circumstances. After all, I had changed jobs several times before taking on the present one. As a woman who had no intention of getting married, I put all my attention and energy into my career and longed for a stable job with good prospects. That's why I considered myself fortunate when I got the present job in the bank. I felt very excited and hoped that I would eventually climb up the ladder to the position of Senior Personal Assistant. It is a long road to go from secretary, to senior secretary, to personal assistant, to senior personal assistant. Some people may have no respect for such petty ambition, but for a high school graduate like me with one year of secretarial training, what else could I expect? I am fully aware of my own limitations and so I never demand much from life. Now that I am about to turn thirty, all I want is a secure life, a well-paid job, a nice little flat, and a man who loves me. It's just natural, I suppose.

So before I accepted this job in the bank, I told myself that there was not much time left for me should I wish to accomplish something in life. Since it was not easy to secure a job in such a respectable company, I decided that in no circumstance would I quit the job rashly. However, things seldom turn out the way one wishes. I soon found myself pondering the idea of resignation, not because of the endless tedious office work, but because of my boss Peter Chen. He was a slender man with a bald head—a man in his early forties who headed the Credit and Investment Department.

I remember the first day I reported to work. Mr Chen summoned me into his office, which was furnished with a two-seater sofa and a coffee table. (I learnt later that only heads of departments were provided with such furniture. It was an indication of their status in the company.) He briefed me on his working style and some work procedures, and then stated that he expected me, his personal secretary, to accompany him to social functions whenever necessary, and that I should dress up elegantly for such occasions and behave in a sociable and graceful way. As he spoke, he sized me up, looking me up and down. I was filled with anger at that moment. What was that supposed to mean? I would not mind attending social functions if it was part of my job duty, but it was a different matter to be stared at in such an insulting way. And yet I had to control my emotions, especially since it was not easy to find such a fine job these days. At this time of worldwide economic depression, I must have seemed quite capable to have beaten ten highly qualified competitors to get the present job. Certainly the bank would never hire a person who was good for nothing. Besides my professional competence, I suppose my good looks also added some weight to my success in getting the job. Although I was annoyed by Peter Chen's remarks, I managed to leave his office with a feigned smile on my face. He even patted me gently on the shoulder to show that he was looking forward to a happy work relationship with me.

Put crudely, the work of a secretary is not much different from that of a maid. A secretary has to serve her boss, trying to read his mind and attend to his needs and wishes. She has to mind every detail, and her work may range from scheduling important meetings to getting a piece of soda biscuit or half a tablet of aspirin for him. A secretary should not state her positions but should only cater to the needs of her boss, taking her boss's interest as her own. She has to adjust herself according to circumstances. In this respect, a secretary may be a complete failure as a person, but she can still be the most accommodating, top-notch secretary in her boss's eyes. The tension between these two roles troubled me for quite some time when I first worked as a secretary. A secretary may know that her boss is playing such nasty tricks behind the back of a colleague or competitor that the person eventually loses everything, and yet she is forced to put her conscience aside. She continues to draw her salary by protecting her boss, trying by all means to conceal the truth, and in doing so she finds herself becoming more like an accomplice in crime.

I had thought of changing my occupation, but what else could I do? My qualifications and experiences were all related to secretarial work. I could anticipate a grim future for myself should I quit my job. And then I would never be able to realise even my very petty dream. All these years, I had been changing bosses one after another and struggling through my career. I was tired of all these changes and eventually I learnt my lesson. Now I could see my situation from both sides. I came to understand that neither my insistence nor assertion would make me happy. I saw that all my friends, classmates, and colleagues could, despite the irresolvable tensions involved, manage their lives and careers in harmony, and gain fame and wealth in the course of time. My insistence on principles would get me nowhere; it could only mean self-defeat or wasted energy. For years, I made little progress in my career. My unnecessary insistence on principles left me stuck in my previous position as a petty Personal Secretary II. When I found that everyone had safely landed on shore, and I was still drifting along in the currents of the sea, clinging naively to some flimsy seaweed for life, I came to see my own stupidity. And what a fool I must have been in the eyes of the people ashore. Having played the fool for all these years, I decided to make a change. So, when I applied and was offered the present position as Personal Secretary I in this bank, I knew my opportunity had come and I must grab it. But that was also the beginning of my troubles.

They all started one night about three months after I joined the bank. Peter Chen and I were coming out from a client's reception when he suddenly made a suggestion that went beyond the realm of propriety. Having refused him in very firm terms, I thought of quitting my job right away. This was a very painful decision for me. I thought about my decision over and over again, only to be left with a splitting headache, which prevented me from going to work the next day. And yet Peter Chen phoned me up at home to apologize, saying that he had been overjoyed by the deal he so successfully made, that he had drunk too much the night before, and that he had said inappropriate things which he did not mean at all. I knew that I had lost nothing in that case, and that it was indeed difficult to find another fine job. I also knew that even if I was to resign then, I still had to work with Peter Chen for a month, so I decided to stay and take things as they came. That decision of mine, however, had put me in his trap—a trap with no escape.

From that day on, Peter Chen was very respectful, courteous, and attentive to me. Although he was my boss, this 'gentleman' filled my days with his generous gifts. Sometimes I had to stay late to finish some urgent work, or to work overtime, drafting letters in shorthand form in his office—correspondence work that could not be done during normal office hours because he was in meetings. On such occasions, we would concentrate on the work at hand and yet, from time to time, he would suggest that I take a break. He would hand me a glass of water, talk about some insignificant matters, or just chat with me. My professional training had made me an excellent listener. He would talk about his family history or his own life, and yet he never mentioned his wife. I came to learn that he had no children. I could not know for sure how a career-minded husband managed his relationship with his wife. As a matter of fact, Peter Chen spent more time with me than with his wife. I had no intention of playing the role of an interloper, because it was not in my nature to do things that hurt others. I often reminded myself that my relationship with Peter Chen could only be that of a co-worker. It was true that I came to know a lot about him and learnt many things about his life, owing to my work as his secretary. We shared the same goal, which was our dedication to work. Such enthusiasm allowed us to perform our best on the job, thus increasing our chances for promotion and securing our power in the organization.

It was true that Peter Chen had great affection for me because I could shoulder with him problems in our Department. I became his extended right-hand, managing everything in his office so that he could concentrate his energy on planning strategies and lobbying work—things that helped pave the way for his future promotion. Everyone in the bank knew that he had his eye on the vice-presidency of the bank at its Hong Kong headquarters. I believed it was his life-long goal. If it were in his capacity to get the president's position in the bank, he would have tried all means to transform himself into a red-bearded, green-eyed Caucasian for it. However, fate had it that he was born at the wrong time and conceived in the wrong womb, so that the highest position a Chinese employee like him could ever reach in the bank was as vice-president. As a matter of fact, what drove me to work so hard was exactly the same kind of aspiration. Things in the world, however, seldom take a single course. What seemed to be an extremely simple matter might suddenly turn into a complicated mess.

I can't recall precisely when my colleagues began to look at me in a strange manner. Whenever Peter Chen stood before me giving job instructions or just chatting, colleagues in the outer office would start exchanging knowing glances and pretend to look in my direction in a casual way. And when I passed by them on my way to the washroom, they would suddenly stop their heated discussion as if I was an untouchable porcupine. Eventually I learnt from colleagues in other departments that there was gossip about Peter Chen and me. And such gossip became more interesting and exciting when I suddenly fainted in my office one day and was rushed to the hospital, where I was advised to stay for two days. Rumour had it that I was not only Peter Chen's mistress, but I also had an abortion in the hospital. The best way to deal with these annoying rumours, of course, was not to take any notice of them. But I was left to wonder whether Peter Chen was aware of such rumours or not because he remained calm all the while and did not seem to be disturbed by anything at all. Certainly it would be awkward to discuss the matter with him. I had confidence that I was armed with an arrow-proof 'shield', protecting me from the spiteful and inquisitive glances. Since Peter Chen had hinted that he would promote me to become his personal assistant by the end of the year, I thought I should not think of quitting my job at such a crucial point in my career. But I found that my 'shield' could only guard me against those busy-bodies in my office. It was hardly effective when it came to approaches from Peter Chen's neurotic and hypersensitive wife.

Mrs Chen called up Mr Chen five or six times a day and she treated me in a very rude way. If Peter Chen happened to be out when she called, she was always suspicious about my account concerning Peter Chen's whereabouts. Once Peter Chen did not go home for the night and I found Mrs Chen marching into my office the next morning, bombarding me with her curses and words of gall. Although my office door was closed, the scene immediately set my colleagues into another round of heated discussion. Had I been Peter Chen's mistress, I would not have minded bearing such retribution. But in this case I was only a victim suffering under a false accusation and there was no way for me to defend myself. I was most upset because Peter Chen's response to his wife's accusation was one of ambivalence. He neither denied nor accepted the charges, thus putting the three of us in an awkward situation. I did not know what Peter Chen was up to, but I was so mad that I nearly burst with anger. No matter how I explained things to her, Mrs Chen would have only one retort: 'The two of you know exactly what you have done.'

For that I openly protested to Peter Chen, demanding him to clear up this unnecessary misunderstanding immediately. He just responded to my complaint with a smile, asking me what was so bad about being his mistress. He continued to say that he liked me very much and that he would like all the rumours to be true. With great confidence, he told me that he would be promoted to the post of vice-president either by the end of the year or by early next year the latest. He continued to say that if I stayed with him, I would rise with him to the second most important position in the Hong Kong head office. I certainly understood the implications of his remarks. I knew that he had never given up hope on his amorous intent since my firm rejection of him in the past. He had been trying by all means, making various promises, to make me surrender. He was too self-confident and could never imagine that any woman would ever refuse his advances. All the while he put on a modest and gentle look in order to have me fall into his trap. It seemed that I had two choices before me: one was to give up my chance of promotion and quit my job; the other was to give in to Peter Chen and become his mistress.

I had sound knowledge of his personality based on his working style and his unscrupulous practices when it came to fame and gain. Peter Chen was one who could not accept failure with grace, and for this reason he always moved with great care and caution so as to avoid any loss or defeat. A move he made today might not show its effect until much later when the time was right. He would never engage himself in any losing battle. His calculating mind and self-confidence made him the most arrogant person I had ever known. His interpersonal communication skills were so ingenious that he could keep his smile while stabbing a person in the back. And the poor person would die without even knowing who delivered the fatal blow. He would pull every string to befriend anyone whom he could exploit. Being such a smart person, he would go about his plan in a neat and tidy way so that there was no trace left for suspicion. That was why he was generally regarded as a 'loyal and trustworthy' friend. In these instances, I was often the executive helping him to carry out his plans. I was aware that I knew too much, and that that might put me in a dangerous position. Peter Chen was not a person who believed in the so-called professional ethic of confidentiality. For him, there was no easier way to control a woman than to control her heart by developing an amorous relationship with her. If I became his mistress, got promoted, accepted his money, and allowed him to buy me a flat,

I would never be able to untangle myself from his net. I would inevitably become one of the pitiful pawns in his master plan. I was fully aware of my own needs as well as my predicament. I could not easily give up the chance of promotion that was promised me nor could I act against my own will. That left our discussion inconclusive and our relationship remained undefined and ambivalent.

Meanwhile, Mrs Chen became increasingly sensitive and neurotic. She phoned me up one night looking for her husband. The fact was, Peter Chen and I had parted right after the business appointment that evening, and I had no idea about his plans for the rest of the night. Ever since I sensed a change in the way my colleagues looked at me, seeing me not merely as Peter Chen's personal secretary but also as his mistress, I found myself dumbstruck. I felt deeply wronged and I wanted to voice my frustrations, but there was no one to hear me. Most people chose to accept the groundless gossip as fact, and my attempts to clarify the issue only made me a laughingstock. I found myself under great pressure, and my heart was filled with conflicting feelings. It seemed that an invisible force was pulling me into a whirlpool. I was terribly afraid—afraid that I would give in to that force one day. I did not like Peter Chen's calculating personality, but he had been very nice to me. When you spend a lot of time with a man, day in and day out, you come to see both his strengths and weaknesses. Although I kept reminding myself that ours was merely a work relationship, no one could guarantee that it would stay that way forever. At any rate, my relationship with Peter Chen continued to develop under such a gloomy atmosphere, like the overcast sky.

Sitting in my 'fish-bowl' office made of cement walls, I noticed that my colleagues in the outer room were again whispering to one another and their eyes met mine with questions and curiosity. My years of experience told me that they must have been wondering about Peter Chen's lateness to work. In Mr Chen's eighteen years of service in the bank, he had never been late to work. Instead, he was always the first to show up at the office in the morning and the last to leave in the evening.

When we parted that night, he had not mentioned having any appointments on the following day. Did the decision made by the Board of Directors come as such a hard blow to him that he broke his years of habit of showing up early at work? Or did he feel so ashamed of himself after my open criticism on his moral depravity in the presence of another manager that he kept away from the office? That particular Board meeting meant a lot to Peter Chen. Before the meeting, he had secretly assessed his potential competitors and concluded that he was the most qualified candidate for the position of vice-president at the Hong Kong head office. The decision of the Board, however, proved him wrong. Someone else got the position, and Peter Chen's dream of promotion vanished like bubbles. And by sheer coincidence, something else happened on the same day.

When I entered the washroom at noon that day, I overheard the conversation between two female colleagues. They were chatting about my affair with Peter Chen and I came to know a secret that had been known to all but me. To my great surprise I came to learn that the tattler who spread rumours about my affair with Peter Chen was none other than Chen himself. It was the inquisitive busy-bodies who, in the process of verifying the sources of the rumours, found out that everything originated from Peter Chen. Since it was his own narration, people thought that it must be a reliable account of the affair. Although I had often been puzzled by the possible sources of such rumours in the past, it had never occurred to me that they could have come from Peter Chen himself, that it was he who set up the whole thing and put my reputation at stake.

I was determined to bring this into the open with Peter Chen, demanding him to admit that all these rumours had been a terrible mistake. When Peter Chen returned to his office from a business appointment that evening, before having been informed of his failure in the promotion exercise, I purposely detained the branch manager from the Marketing Department who had come to see Peter Chen to talk about some sales promotion. When their business talk was over, I invited that manager to be my witness as I pressed Peter Chen to straighten out our relationship and redress the damage and injustice done to me. I challenged him for his ill intent in spreading rumours about the two of us and I told him to his face that he was morally base and shameless. Peter Chen's face looked red and pale in turn, and the witness looked embarrassed and awkward and started fidgeting. Finally the branch manager found an excuse to flee like the wind from the scene. Peter Chen admitted that he had invented all the stories about himself and me, but he had only told them to one colleague. But the fact remained that these stories were made known to every one in the bank. I decided, there and then, that I would give up my wild hope of promotion to personal assistant because circumstances would no longer allow it. Although I was not and had never been Peter Chen's mistress, public opinion already had it that I was an immoral woman with no integrity. I could not, however, act like one of my classmates, who willingly and openly led the life of a kept woman. So I considered quitting my job there and then.

With my mind preoccupied by my possible resignation, I started clearing the papers on my desk. At that moment, Mr Guo, a member of the Board of Directors and also an intimate friend of Peter Chen's, came to break the disheartening news about the Board's decision to Peter Chen. Then Mr Guo left, leaving behind him a silent office with no sound to be heard. I had no idea what Peter Chen was doing in his office. Since we had just had a row and I was still extremely upset about the whole matter, I was in no mood to find out what he was doing. It was already 6.30 in the evening when I finished my work. As I was gathering my things to leave, Peter Chen came out from his office, looking quite depressed. He apologized for his deeds and invited me out for a drink. I looked at him and felt that it would be cruel to refuse him at a time like that. And yet I warned myself that I should check my behaviour, that I should not engage myself with him in anything other than work. This was particularly crucial at a time when the office was rife with the scandalous rumours about us. He then walked listlessly out of the office and out of my sight. At that moment he gave me the impression of an old and worn-out fellow, although in reality he had just turned forty.

I spent a sleepless night at home, wondering whether it was appropriate for me to quit at a time when Peter Chen felt most dejected. If I were to wait for a while and continue to work with him, how should I handle the complex relationship between us in the absurd situation already set? Should I abandon my dream of moving higher up in my quest for fame and gain? Would I regret my own decision later in life? Would there be better opportunities awaiting me if I chose to work in another company? I spent the whole night going through questions like these, only to find myself feeling strained and dizzy in the morning. My mind was not clear and my whole being seemed to be moving in a trance.

Fortunately, the weather was exceptionally fine that morning. The sunlight on the glass walls of the building opposite gave the building a glittering outlook, and images of objects were reflected on it in distorted forms. The midday sun baked Victoria Harbour with its intense heat. I concentrated on my work, trying my best to forget the unpleasant experience of the day before. I could not figure out why Peter Chen did not show up for work. Doubtless to say, colleagues found it exciting to speculate on the cause of Peter Chen's absence. Rumours spread quickly that he deliberately chose not to show up at work that day as a sign to show his disappointment over his failure in the promotion exercise. At noon, when everyone was discussing excitedly the plausible reasons for Peter Chen's absence, the bad news reached us from the Personnel Office: Peter Chen had died the night before.

I could never believe that Peter Chen would commit suicide because of his defeat in the promotion exercise. He was simply not that type of man. My common sense told me that given time to gather his strength, he would have returned for another battle and would not have given up until he had attained his goal. Nonetheless, death easily got him when he least wanted it. All of his ingenious schemes, after all, could not protect him from his cruel fate. What is more, his death turned out to be absurd and incredible.

The night before his death, Peter Chen was nearly drunk when he returned home and emptied a bowl of fish soup. A piece of fish bone got stuck in his throat. In great pain and confusion, he tried to drink some white vinegar to dissolve the bone, only to find he had gulped down sulphuric acid by mistake. The acid burnt his throat and oesophagus, and caused fatal damage to his internal organs. He was pronounced dead less than an hour after the accident.

For years Peter Chen had worked hard and waited for his chance to land the vice-president's position in the bank. It was not usual to have that position open and available. And yet to everyone's surprise he was not only defeated in the competition but also killed in an absurd way, thus giving away his own post to others. The following few days after his death, everyone in the office—whether friend or enemy—showed signs of grief. Behind their masks of grief and sorrow, however, were their own plots and schemes. I was sure that Peter Chen would have put on the same hypocritical attitude if the deceased had been someone else in the office. Ironically, misfortune had also taken Peter Chen unprepared. After a brief moment of general disbelief, what happened in the office was a series of discussions and speculation, some of which were inevitably directed at me. My colleagues all watched me in a curious and aloof manner as if they were observing someone who had suddenly lost support in life and had to struggle for survival in the open sea. In their eyes, I was not only a person stripped of power and influence but also a poor mistress stripped of a rightful name. I found this most unbearable because the whole situation was so absurd and yet I had no way to rectify it. As far as I was concerned, I could not say whether Peter Chen's death was good or bad for me. It could be good because I would never become his mistress, and that saved me from a bad investment that would not guarantee a profit. On the other hand, it could be bad for me because I could never redeem my reputation now that Peter Chen was dead. Furthermore, my hope for a promotion was dashed to pieces and all my labour lost. But what remained most annoying were not my colleagues' inquisitive looks nor their sarcastic remarks, but the hysterical behaviour of the bereaved Mrs Chen.

I tried to get colleagues to go with me to Peter Chen's funeral service, but in vain. They gave me all sorts of excuses. It really made me mad to see them conveying their condolence in a casual manner and expressing their sympathy in an indifferent way. They all left my office in silence with their heads lowered as if they were filled with deep grief. I was so annoyed that I yelled at them, saying 'I was not Peter Chen's mistress, so stop treating me in this way'. But it was no use. They treated me in a more attentive and tender way and asked me to calm down, saying that time would cure me of my loss. I found myself alienated and finally decided to brave the world by going to the funeral parlour on my own. In a simple outfit, I showed up at the funeral parlour. Upon the prompting of the master of the funeral service, I made three bows before the picture of the deceased. I was conscious of the strange eyes staring at me in an accusing way from all directions. Since everyone thought that I was the mistress of the deceased, I also started to wonder whether I really was or not. Out of spite, I decided to play my part as Peter Chen's mistress and moved to sit in the front row. To my surprise, I even shed a few tears although I could not tell whether the tears were for Peter Chen or for my own self.

With an expressionless face, Mrs Chen knelt on one side of the funeral hall, looking pale and thin. She had her eyes on me all the while and sometimes when our eyes met, I felt very sorry for her. I wanted so much to convince her that I had never had any sexual relationship with her husband. Even if Peter Chen had been unfaithful to her, it had nothing to do with me. Without my knowing, I had been made a scapegoat. It seemed, however, hard to get a jealous and hate-ridden woman to listen to her rival's explanation. Apparently it was too late for that. All of a sudden, Mrs Chen sprang at me like a hungry beast and slapped me hard on both cheeks. I had no time to do anything except to say 'You have been mistaken,' and then I was ushered out of the funeral hall by some kind-hearted but nosy people attending the funeral service. In this way I was denied my right to confess the truth in public by the good will of these people. But vaguely I knew that everything I tried to do would prove futile.

With her financial support gone, the bank arranged for Mrs Chen to take up a post in the Import and Export Department in one of its branches. There would be no chance of meeting Mrs Chen because our offices were located in different parts of the city. And yet like a ghost she would appear from time to time in my neighbourhood, repeatedly saying the same thing: 'Give me back my husband.' At first, I tried to be patient and bear with her, until it proved too much and I had to call the police to free myself from her endless harassment.

One night when I returned home from a friend's dinner party, I was surprised to find Mrs Chen lying drunk at my doorstep. I took her inside the house, helped her clean up the dirty stains on her clothes, and let her have a cup of ginger tea. After vomiting several times, she finally came around. With bloodshot eyes, she stared at me and muttered a whole chain of unintelligible nonsense. Then she suddenly became very excited and told me that it was she who had caused Peter Chen's death. She had loved her husband deeply. They had been classmates in high school and had been in love for ten years. Later things changed, and Peter Chen became a different man as he began to enjoy fame and wealth in his increasingly successful career. She could not bear the pain of being neglected, nor could she stand the endless lonely days. Furthermore, she could not give away her husband to some other woman. She told me that she hated me because everyone said I was her husband's mistress.

The day Peter Chen died, she had decided, as usual, to prepare a nutritious fish soup for him although she had no idea whether or not he would come home that night. She kept the live fish in the bathtub only to find it had disappeared shortly afterwards. She later discovered that the fish had jumped into the toilet and got stuck there. Only the tip of its black tail could be seen sticking out. Since the fish was very slippery, she had no way to get it out. So she got a plumber to help her. The plumber suggested that either they save the fish intact by knocking down the toilet, or they dissolve the fish and flush it down the toilet by using a corrosive liquid like sulphuric acid, which would leave no trace of the fish. She took his second suggestion. With half a bottle of sulphuric acid poured into the toilet, she saw the fish instantly dissolve before her eyes and that scene excited her and gave her an idea. Straight away she went back to the market to buy another fish, together with another bottle of sulphuric acid. . . .

Mrs Chen took a deep breath before she continued her story. She said that the bottle of sulphuric acid was meant for me. If Peter Chen didn't come home that night, she would use the sulphuric acid to get rid of me. Things, however, did not work out that way. Everything was set up in the wrong way. It so happened that Peter Chen returned home that night and in a half-drunk state finished the fish soup prepared by his wife. When he got a fish bone stuck in his throat, he became extremely irritated and violent, yelling at his wife. In a state of panic and confusion, Mrs Chen handed him the bottle of sulphuric acid, mistaking it for a bottle of vinegar. And that ended Peter Chen's life in such an extremely absurd manner. In tears and sobs, Mrs Chen concluded that if it were not for me, the whole tragedy would never have happened. I reassured her in a serious and sincere way that I had firmly declined her husband's amorous proposal although he had expressed his selfish desire for me. It was perhaps true that her husband and I did become very close owing to our work relationship, yet we had never had the kind of lewd relationship that she had imagined. Mrs Chen listened to me calmly and I thought for a moment that she was finally willing to accept my explanation. To my surprise, she suddenly scolded me in a righteous tone for being ungrateful. Her husband was just dead and right away I seemed to have forgotten all the favours he had done for me. In a way, one could say that her husband had sacrificed his life for me and now I seemed to be denying everything. How could I be so heartless and cruel?

Mrs Chen's accusations left me dumbfound on the spot. I could no longer make a distinction between truth and falsehood. I felt dazed because things seemed to have all turned upside down. I had tried hard to clear my name as somebody's mistress; it had been tiring and exhausting. Why bother to explain and clarify? I believed that the title 'Peter Chen's mistress' would accompany me for life. After such a night of turmoil, Mrs Chen eventually calmed down and fell asleep. However, when I woke up the next morning, there was no sign of her in the house. She had left, and it wasn't until six months later on Christmas Eve that I came across her again. It was in the departure lounge at the airport that I noticed her from a distance.

After Peter Chen's death, the bank had undertaken a major management restructuring. I had no wish to stay because the newly appointed manager of my department was even more base and indecent than Peter Chen. He always tried to take advantage of me by using various work-related excuses. When I refused him, he would make a lot of insulting remarks, which almost always alluded to my 'relationship' with Peter Chen. I found this unbearable and so six months later I submitted my resignation and freed myself from my nightmarish days in the bank. I chose to take a trip to Europe to visit a couple of friends there, with the hope of starting a new life by leaving the shadows of the past behind me. The pursuit of fame and wealth is a dangerous trap. Since I wished to keep a clear conscience, I had to get away from that environment without a second thought.

The departure lounge of the airport was packed with vacation-goers on Christmas Eve. When the time for my boarding was announced for the third time, I suddenly discovered a familiar face. It was Mrs Chen, dressed up in a gorgeous way. Arm in arm with the new vice-president of the Hong Kong head office, she made her way towards the boarding gate. I couldn't believe my eyes because the new vice-president was a married man. I found the whole case ridiculous and sad. It seemed as if I had been caught in an extremely absurd dream.

1983

From: A Place of One's Own: Stories of Self in China, Taiwan, Hong Kong & Singapore Ed. Kwok-Kan Tam, Terry S. H. Yip, Wimal Dissanayake Oxford Univ. Press 1999

7

Ling and Long

By **SOON AI-LING**

Translated by Amy Tak-yee Lai and Kwok-kan Tam, with Peter G. Crisp

Soon Ai-ling 孫愛玲 *(Sun Ailing, b. 1949) was born and educated in Singapore. She graduated from the Chinese Department of Nanyang University. Her works of fiction have been widely anthologized, and can be found in the collections,* Green Green the Willow Wind *(*Lu lu yangliu feng 綠綠楊柳風*, 1988),* Ten Miles of Biluo Fragrance *(*Biluo shili xiang 碧螺十里香*, 1989), and* The Jade Pin *(*Yuhun kou 玉魂扣*, 1990). She received the Gold Lion Award for fiction in 1985. She also won the Singapore International Book Prize for 1989–90. She has taught secondary school and at the Institute of Education in Singapore for many years. After obtaining a PhD from the University of Hong Kong, she moved to Hong Kong and is currently teaching Chinese at the Hong Kong Institute of Education. The story 'Ling and Long' was first published in 1986 in the Shanghai magazine,* Mengya zazhi *(*Buds 萌芽*) in 1993, and won an award for Best Overseas Chinese Fiction in 1994.*

Value judgements are normally based on feelings and past experience. They can be good, if they help a person to build up a firm sense of their 'self'. Yet they may also destroy a person, though even this is not necessarily bad. After all, a value judgement will have been formed through someone's own logical processes of thought and decision. A human being possessing the capacity for thought and decision should have no regret at being a human being.

14.00 sharp!

A traffic accident!

On the highway.

In the car sat two women with their hair cut short, both in black evening gowns exposing their bare shoulders.

One rested her hands on the steering wheel. Blood dripped from the corner of her mouth. Her face was turned aside. She was dead.

The other had her seat belt on. Her head hung low. She sat firmly in her seat.

Similar faces. Same dresses. Same style of ear-rings hanging over their shoulders: a moon on the left, and a star on the right. Around them, dead silence. Street lamps shone upon the two moons and the two stars, giving them radiance and lustre. A quiet glow.

Ling and Long: lovely and exquisite.

The Chu family had a pair of twins. Both were female. They were named Ling and Long, meaning, in English, Lovely and Exquisite: the elder was Ling, the younger Long. They were born in the year 1960.

Ling and Long's mother was called Lianhua, their father Hengchang. One day, when Ling and Long were three years old, Lianhua was driven to tears in front of her two daughters. The twin dolls, both dressed in pink gauze, were sitting on the bed and rolling their jet-black eyes. They had just finished their bath and their wet hair was combed to one side. Both were crying at the same time: 'Mum! Mum! Mum-cry-cry.'

Hengchang, hearing the cry of Lianhua, hurried to the scene. Lianhua pointed at the two dolls:

'I feel nervous and a bit scared in front of my two daughters, really. Which is which?'

'Let me see. This is Chu Ling. Her eyes are more lively and lustrous. This is Chu Long. Her eyes are less radiant and her body lacks spirit.' In this way, Hengchang decided the fates of his two daughters.

'I think they are becoming more and more alike! How can I distinguish between them?'

Hengchang consoled her:

'Don't worry. Fetch me a pair of scissors, and I'll cut the hair short on one of them.'

After looking at the two babies for a while, he chose Chu Long and said:

'Good girl, I'll cut your hair short, so your Mum can recognize you.'

There was no obvious reason why Hengchang should choose Chu Long. Even he himself could not have said why he did not choose Chu Ling instead.

Chu Long remembered clearly how her Dad's face became suddenly strange and enormous, and how, with a series of annoying sounds, the pair of scissors was transformed into something like one of those large, noisy machines for trimming wild grass. Her father murmured:

'What a good child you are.' Chu Long, too, felt that she was good. She didn't struggle or try to jump down from her chair. What about Mum? In the mirror she found her Mum holding Chu Ling and sitting on one side of the bed, while she looked at Dad, who was cutting her hair. The scissors produced a loud, sharp noise, and the floor was soon covered with her scattered, black hair. A whole floor covered with long and short scraps of hair, so irregular, seemed to reflect the injustice of the situation. After Hengchang had cut short Chu Long's hair, he kissed her. Angrily, Chu Long brushed away the traces of his kiss with her little hand, with a force so hard that her face was even more crimson than ever.

After that the twin sisters were easily distinguished.

Ling and Long were now five years old and it was time to go to kindergarten. Lianhua, in an attempt to please Chu Long, bought her some hair clips so that she could hold back the fringe of short hair that hung irritatingly over her forehead. She also spent a lot of time and effort in taking care of Chu Ling's long, bright hair, knitting it into plaits or tying it up into a pony tail. When Chu Long saw this evidence of her Mum's love for Chu Ling, she hated those hair clips even more. Once she'd left home and got on the school bus, she would take off all those clips and throw them out of the window. Or she would just twist them out of shape and throw them onto the floor. She begged her mother:

'Mum, let my hair grow long, please!'

'Your sister already has long hair. If you do, too, how can your Mum distinguish between the two of you?'

'I will tell you who is who!'

'Don't cry. Mum will buy you a doggy!'

'I don't want a doggy. I want to have long hair.'

Then Chu Long tried to persuade her father. By sitting in his lap.

Every day when Hengchang returned home from work, Chu Ling and Chu Long would run to him. Every time he picked up Chu Ling first and lavished kisses on her, while Chu Long stood there with her head raised, watching them and feeling the time pass so slowly. When her Dad did finally pick her up, her longing to be picked up and hugged was already gone. Whenever Hengchang sat down, Chu Ling was always the first to reach him, rushing into his arms, while Chu Long would at most finally perch upon his knee, or let him hug her shoulders while she stood at his side. Only when, as at the present moment, Chu Ling was asleep, did Chu Long have the chance to sit for a while in her Dad's embrace. She caressed his face with her little hands and asked him intently:

'Daddy, I want to have long hair. Is that okay?'

'No. Don't you look pretty good now? Daddy loves you to look this way.'

'But I don't. I want to be like Chu Ling. I want my hair to grow long till it hangs down to my waist.' Chu Long touched her waist and indicated her hair's ideal length.

'Come on, don't quarrel. We'll wake up Chu Ling.'

Though Chu Long didn't really want to, she still followed her father about. She watched him crouch on the bed smelling Chu Ling, kissing her and, when she woke up, picking her up. Chu Ling rubbed against him in his arms until his clothes got all creased. Chu Long watched them quietly.

Chu Long woke up from her dreams. As she opened her eyes tiredly, she vaguely saw Chu Ling's ear-rings shining under the moon. She cried in fear: 'Chu Ling. Chu Ling.' Chu Long loosened her seat belt, and begged to the point of hopelessness: 'Wake up! Wake Up! Chu Ling, please wake up!' She wanted to call Chu Ling back. When they were children, they used to play the game of doctor and patient, and Chu Ling loved to pretend to be dead and refused to open her eyes. Chu Long started to get frightened: she caressed Chu Ling, but the latter had already stopped breathing. Chu Long watched Chu Ling wildly, while her spirit detached itself from her body.

It was their tenth birthday. Girls of ten are already at the age of maturity. According to Brown the psychologist, a human being who has reached the age of eight has already developed 80 per cent of her intelligence. When Ling and Long reached the age of ten, their bodies had already started to mature and blossom; they were almost pubescent. Chu Ling always represented the school in story-telling and speech competitions; Chu Long always represented the school in writing and general knowledge competitions. Both of them played the panpipes. On Children's Day, they both stood on the stage, one on the right, the other on the left. Chu Ling played the pipes horizontally, and Chu Long vertically, and one after the other they played 'The Crescent Moon Shining over the Nine Islands,' smoothly and suavely. They also both played the flute. At their school anniversary, they played 'Su Wu Herding His Sheep,' one being responsible for the higher pitch and the other for the lower, and they fully expressed the spirit of the wilderness.

On the night of their tenth birthday, Lianhua sewed two gauze dresses, each in a different style, for Ling and Long. The one for Chu Ling was a six-piece dress, with pink lace, lantern-sleeves, and round collar; the one for Chu Long had light blue lace and cup-sleeves. Looking at the dresses, Chu Long locked the door of their room suddenly. She put on the pink dress and looked into the mirror. Her short hair rested neatly on the nape of her neck. Her eyes, usually dim and shadowy, became extraordinarily lustrous because of the dress she was wearing.

There was a loud knock at the door. Chu Long opened the door. When Lianhua found her wearing the dress that was made for Chu Ling, she cried: 'Why are you wearing Chu Ling's dress? The blue one is yours. Take that one off. It's not yours!'

'I don't want to!'

Hengchang, hearing the quarrel, hurried to the scene. Lianhua pointed at Chu Long:

'This child is becoming more and more rebellious. You see, she is wearing Chu Ling's clothes. That blue one is hers. But she won't wear it.' Hengchang crouched down and spoke to Chu Long:

'Chu Long, you can't take something that is not yours. Take off the pink dress and return it to Chu Ling. The blue one is yours.'

'No.'

Seeing that her parents were angry, Chu Ling picked up the blue dress and said: 'Mummy and Daddy, please don't be angry. Let Chu Long wear the pink dress. I can have this blue one.'

'Ai-ya! See what a good girl Chu Ling is! Chu Ling really is Mummy and Daddy's darling.'

'Chu Long is no good. Chu Long does not listen to her parents. Daddy doesn't love her. Neither does Mummy.'

Hearing this, Chu Long took off the pink dress and tore at it as hard as she could. Lianhua was both scared and furious. She scolded her:

'Are you crazy? Why are you tearing the dress?'

'Chu Long, do you want me to beat you? You won't stop? All right! Now you've destroyed it, you can put this torn dress on for your birthday.' Hengchang grabbed at the dress and made her put it on. Then he picked up the camera on the table and took a photo of Chu Long. In the photo, one of Chu Long's budding breasts was laid bare.

This was her tenth birthday photograph.

After that, Chu Long refused to be manipulated any longer. She let her hair grow long. She spent most of her time studying, and seldom talked to her parents. Looking back to what had happened on Ling and Long's tenth birthday, both Hengchang and Lianhua felt they had gone too far. So they tried to please Chu Long from time to time. But Chu Long's obstinacy had already dismissed the whole issue. She knew well that her parents were good to her these days. After she graduated from high school at the age of sixteen, she went to England to continue her studies. During her four years in England she no longer cared about the length of her hair. Yet scenes from the old days would at times appear before her eyes, and these scenes haunted her and she could not escape from them.

It was looking at Chu Long's photo that made Hengchang realize that he had hurt her, for the photo seemed to carry the evidence of his own sin. He had not in fact intended to harm his daughter. In fact, he did not know why he had been so angry at the time. He seemed to have been possessed by a devil when he had taken that photo showing one small, budding breast of his daughter.

Lianhua, too, felt sorry for what she had done. From that day on, she seemed to live by the whims of Chu Long. She even seemed to be a little frightened of her. She had not expected a cold barrier to be raised between herself and the child whom she had borne.

Chu Ling got married when she was twenty. Her husband, Zhao Yifu, was ten years older than she. Zhao Yifu was a barrister who had an interest in old cases and knew how to apply the tricks of defence of the old days to the present. They gave birth to a daughter the following year, who was named Zhao Jun. Hengchang and Lianhua doted on her and helped Chu Ling to take care of her. Since

Zhao Yifu disliked being disturbed by his baby's cries after a long day's work, Zhao Jun naturally stayed at her grand-parents' house. After her return from England, Chu Long led a quiet life at her parents' house, and so had more contact with Zhao Jun than Chu Ling herself. It felt strange that she could get to like this baby girl. Not only did she often feed her at night, to pass the time she also played with her during the day. On weekdays Zhao Yifu loved to drink and chat with his friends at clubs after work, and on Sundays he used to play golf with them. As Chu Ling had to accompany him, she had hardly any time to spare for her own child.

When Chu Ling and Chu Long were twenty-two years old, they both went to the Christmas dinner organized for the alumni of Saint Stephen's College. Chu Ling loved organizing things. She ordered an evening dress of the same kind for both Chu Long and herself, with long, off-the-shoulder sleeves, and embroidered with Belgian black lace. The lace spread down to the black, crinkled skirt, which looked like a black lantern reaching down to the knees. Lianhua saw the dress and said it did not suit Chu Long: 'Chu Long should wear a more conventional type of dress.' But Chu Long took no notice of her.

Chu Long lay on the bed and looked at the evening dresses hanging side by side on the outside of the wardrobe. She sighed and felt deeply that Chu Ling loved her. Ever since their tenth birthday, Chu Ling had known how to love her. Long thought: 'This is the first time we have owned the same dress. It's been given to me by Chu Ling. Whatever she has she wants me to own as well. When we were young she got the same rubber for us both, and together we put the rubbers to our noses to sniff their perfume. She also got the same photos of pop stars for us both . . . Thomas riding on his motorbike and showing us his cheerful smile. On the back she wrote: Thomas loves you. Chu Ling knows how to love me. We have come from the same egg.'

Chu Ling came into the room. Her newly cut hair was the same as Chu Long's. She said: 'I went to your hairdresser. He said we look alike. Now I've had my hair cut the same way it's even harder to tell the difference between us. Tonight let's play a trick on all those old classmates who haven't seen us for years. Let's see if they can recognize us now. Come on! Get up, let's put on our dresses and see first if we can trick Mum. Quick!' Chu Long was aroused by her urgency.

The two of them took off their clothes in front of the mirror. Chu Long put on a strapless bra. Chu Ling appreciated her own body in wonder. When she saw Chu Long, she smiled and said:

'One does not wear a bra with this type of dress.' As she said this she helped Chu Long take off this burden from her body. Standing side by side, they looked into the mirror. Chu Ling's new hair style was exactly the same as Chu Long's. Chu Ling said: 'We look so alike. Our faces, ears, shoulders. See, Chu Long! We have beautiful shoulders. And our breasts, though not big, are so firm.' As she said this she held onto Chu Long's shoulders from behind. Thus only Chu Long appeared in the mirror. After that she jumped out and stood in front of Chu Long, and so in the mirror there was then only Chu Ling. Then she said: 'We two merge into one.'

Chu Long said: 'Don't play anymore. Mum is waiting outside.'

Lianhua was frightened when she saw them, asking: 'Who is who?'

Chu Ling remained silent. Lianhua pointed at Chu Long and said: 'You are Chu Ling!'

'I'm Chu Long!' Seeing that Chu Ling was the first one to be wanted by her Mum, Chu Long was not pleased.

'Haha! How come Mummy can't even recognize her own children?' Chu Ling clapped her hands.

'Don't laugh. From the time you two were born Mum has been afraid of mixing you up.' That was true. Mixing up her two children had been the nightmare of Lianhua's whole life.

Chu Long got into her car and sat in front of the steering wheel. She put her exquisite black leather handbag on the back seat. Chu Ling also got into the car. They cried almost at the same time: 'You are using the perfume Poison!' At that moment, Lianhua shouted from the doorway: 'Be careful on the road!'

Just as the car had past the junction, Chu Ling shouted: 'Let me drive!'

'Can you?'

'Of course! Stop!' Chu Long had to stop. Chu Ling opened the door, got out, and walked to the other side of the car, while Chu Ling moved to the other seat. Chu Ling could not wait to get into the car. Her excitement was at its peak.

'I feel so good now. I don't know why. Just because I'm going to play a trick on some people, I'm happy!'

'You don't act like someone who's married with children!'

'Don't be such a killjoy. Laugh! Laugh right from the very bottom of your heart! Be happy, not for other people or things, but for yourself!'

'Now I discover there is indeed a lesson in laughing.' This time Chu Ling was really pleased by Chu Long and smiled.

'Yes! Be happy, Chu Long. Don't you know you look really beautiful tonight. I love you, Chu Long, I love you!' Chu Ling shouted.

'You've gone crazy!'

Chu Ling laughed. Chu Long turned her face toward her and their eyes touched. It was at this moment that the car was making a quick turn. It veered off the road and overturned.

Chu Long woke up again. Vaguely, she heard her mother moaning: 'Chu Ling, Chu Ling, my darling. Please wake up! Wake up!' Chu Long struggled and dimly she heard her mother say again: 'Chu Ling, have pity on me. I have lost Chu Long. Please don't abandon me. My God! I don't demand much, but please return one of them to me. I did not intend to have many children. It was you who granted them to me. That one is gone. Please save this one for me.'

Chu Long wanted to open her eyes and answer: 'I am Chu Long, not Chu Ling.' But that didn't work. Chu Ling was really gone. She wanted to find Chu Ling. It was just like when, as children, they played hide-and-seek. Chu Ling used to hide in a secluded place. Since Chu Long could not find Chu Ling, she cried as she walked along. Then she felt afraid. She feared that Chu Ling might have been caught by the witch. So she cried and cried, and then Chu Ling appeared. And Chu Long cried loudly: 'Chu Ling! Chu Ling!'

Chu Long heard Lianhua cry: 'Are you Chu Long or Chu Ling? You can't be Chu Long. I saw her drive the car when you left. The one dead in front of the steering wheel must be Chu Long, not Chu Ling.'

Though Chu Long's eyes were closed, her mind remained clear. Ever since she was very, very young she had wanted to be Chu Ling. Now she had the chance—a chance given her by Mum, a chance bestowed by Heaven. Once endowed with this name 'Chu Ling,' everything of Chu Ling's would be hers and she would receive compensation for everything of which she had been deprived. She wanted to be Chu Ling. Now she was determined. She hardened her heart, opened her eyes, and cried out: 'Mummy! I am Chu Ling!'

Lianhua stared at Chu Long: 'Chu Ling! You've woken up. That's wonderful. But now poor Chu Long is gone.' Chu Long thought: 'Is it only now that she has any pity? It was needed long ago.'

'Where's Daddy?'

'He's gone to the funeral parlour to deal with Chu Long's funeral. He thought the dead one was Chu Ling. But I said it was Chu Long. I found both of you when I was out in the car.'

Chu Long thought: 'Clever Daddy. He knew the difference.'

Hengchang took care of the coffin and was very sad. He felt that his dead daughter was now closer than ever to him in his heart. He was tormented with the agony of one who has lost the person he loves most of all. He had never realized that he had, unconsciously, loved Chu Long so much. It even felt strange that his love for her should be so profound. He was suffering a nameless, indescribable agony. He looked at the 'Chu Ling' who stood next to the coffin staring at the one who was dead. She seemed gloomy and dull, typical of one who had been shocked beyond all limits. He went forward to give her support; he told her to sit down, kissing her deeply on the forehead. 'Chu Ling' stared at him strangely and as her eyes met his he had the feeling that they were not Chu Ling's tender eyes; they seemed instead like those of Chu Long. He was mesmerized. But he soon dismissed this passing fancy, telling himself that it was because of the tremendous shock that Chu Ling had suffered that she had become like Chu Long. He could not then help shedding tears.

When Zhao Yifu brought Chu Long back home, he treated her as Chu Ling. He did notice how clumsy and unsure she had become. She'd forgotten that he had fried bread with his bacon and eggs for breakfast. She'd forgotten that he drank his black coffee without sugar. She'd forgotten that he brushed his teeth after breakfast. She'd even forgotten his office phone number. She seldom spoke; her eyes were lustreless. One of the strangest things were those boring magazines that she read. Yet he was not suspicious, thinking of her weird behaviour as due to the shock of the terrible tragedy she had suffered. Sometimes her speech, though simple, contained a great deal of wisdom. She had said:

'We two seem to be separated by a thick wall of glass.'

'If we go on not talking our relationship will die.'

'Speaking a lot does not necessarily make people more intimate.'

That night he found he wanted her. So he went to her, and did the whole thing slowly. She had never been that shy before. She let him act like her master, responding strangely as he touched every inch of her body. He felt that she was mild and tender and that, like a plant, she needed water. She co-operated with him so well that he was not as quick and impatient as in the past. He did feel she was a bit cold, but that did not affect the main thing. So he started to thrust urgently, rolling with her body on the bed. That was the first time he had done it thoroughly. It made her cry hysterically, and this in turn woke him up. He remembered that in the past Chu Ling did not cry, but only gasped. When he let her body go she hid her face in the pillow. He went to bathe as usual. As the water ran down his body, he seemed to see blood dissolving into the water. He was not quite sure since the water flowed off quickly. He returned to the room, switched on the lamp, and found small blotches of blood. A thought darted through his brain like lightning: 'It's not Chu Ling.'

He turned her body over. Her eyes, full of hatred, met his. She wriggled to the corner of the bed and, her body curled up like a shrimp's, fainted. He watched her fearfully. The earlier convulsions and the surprises that had come afterwards made his brain ache. For the first time in his life he failed to think rationally with his brain, falling instead into a sleep of exhaustion.

When he woke the next day, Chu Long was no longer in her room. He turned the whole thing over in his mind carefully, and became determined to keep Chu Long. She suited him even better than Chu Ling. He was willing to defend her and to protect her. In fact, Chu Ling no longer occupied so favoured a position in his heart. She was so simple and shallow. It was true that she had many good qualities, her sociability and the way she flattered him for instance. But she had become increasingly inadequate with her tendency to expose all her weak points in front of others, licking their boots, and being friendly with whomever's wife.

Zhao Yifu was almost shocked by the way he analyzed Chu Ling. He should now, at this moment, be feeling sad. Yet what he was doing was calculating his dead wife's deficiencies.

Chu Long rushed back to her parents' house. Hengchang and Lianhua saw her drawn face. She twisted up that face, on which the word 'agony' was engraved, while both her hands and her legs trembled. She gripped Hengchang tightly, trying hard to speak to him, but she could not produce a word. Hengchang wrapped her in his arms and shook her:

'What has happened to you?'

Chu Long nodded, and then shook her head and forced her mouth open in an attempt to speak. Hengchang shouted:

'Go and fetch a glass of water for her!'

She finished the glass of water her mother gave her, and then opened her mouth and said:

'I . . . I . . . I am Chu Long.'

She was dumb when she had finished.

Lianhua, hearing what she said, wailed immediately: 'The dead one is Chu Long. You are lying! You are lying! The dead one is Chu Long, not Chu Ling! Oh no! Not Chu Ling!'

Hengchang, too, was in agony: 'The dead one really is Chu Ling!' He mourned together with Lianhua for Chu Ling, for themselves, and for their fates.

Zhao Yifu, Chu Hengchang, and Lianhua discussed the serious problem facing them. Hengchang told Yifu:

'Chu Long wants to be herself.'

'So you want me to expose her identity?'

'What would that lead to?'

'A charge under common law as well as the law of the Republic.'

'That's serious!'

'She could be said to have deliberately assumed another person's identity. She could also be accused of fraud.'

'Could we use the traffic accident as an excuse, and say she was not in her right mind?'

'But when she left the hospital the doctor had confirmed that she had suffered no brain trauma. She had been wearing her seat belt.'

'But she fainted!'

'That was due to fear. I saw the record of her brain scan. Everything was normal.' Zhao Yifu then continued:

'For me, it is not wise to report this to the police. It would certainly lead to a charge. She would have to produce a good reason for assuming Chu Ling's identity. Chu Long studied abroad and was better qualified than Chu Ling. So what could the reason be? This type of case often takes one or even two years to settle, and she would certainly be put in jail. It would certainly involve you two. One of you claimed that the dead one was Chu Long, while the other took Chu Long's identity card to the Births and Deaths Registration Division. Finally, she is only twenty-three years old. How could she face her colleagues and friends?'

'So what can we do?'

'Go on as it is. Don't bother about it.'

'But your wife is Chu Ling, and she is Chu Long!'

'I know. But all we have to do is keep that to ourselves.'

'We must have incurred a double debt to your family in our previous lives. Now we must repay you with both our daughters.'

'Why shouldn't you say that I owe you a debt twice over, and must therefore endure both your daughters?' Yifu's sophistry silenced Hengchang.

When Chu Long had desired to be Chu Ling, she had not anticipated that it would involve so heavy and painful a cost. She had thought that heaven wanted to pay her back for the psychological burden of those twenty years; she did not realize that she would have to pay by using her body as a sacrifice for the rest of her life. She did not realize the pain that would be involved in this silent sacrifice. When Zhao Yifu wanted her, she at first trembled and then, suffering shock, almost lost consciousness. The most dreadful thing was that he knew she was not Chu Ling. She found herself falling endlessly into a bottomless pit from which she could never extricate herself.

She gripped Hengchang and embraced Lianhua:

'I want to be Chu Long again, not Chu Ling!'

'Child, you can't be Chu Long anymore.'

'Chu Long, please. Don't go on like this. I can't bear it.' Lianhua, weeping, implored her.

She had chosen the path of no return.

Now, the only thing that could offer Chu Long comfort was Zhao Jun. When the two year-old Zhao Jun cried, 'Mama mama,' she would clasp her in her arms, enjoying the feeling of a kind of steadiness. She spent two whole years at home, educating Zhao Jun and bringing her up. She did not return to Zhao Yifu. When Zhao Jun went to the kindergarten she went out to work.

Every day as usual Hengchang went to work as an assistant at the jeweller's. Every night he went to the drama workshop and played the *zheng*. His musical instrument now had twenty-five strings instead of twenty-one and so could play twelve different tunes. His skill with the instrument, whether in pressing, plucking, rubbing or pushing, had reached a near-professional standard. Time passed in the rubbing and pressing of the strings. He always thought of the days when Chu Ling was still alive and he had taught the twin sisters to play the flute and panpipes. But now only Chu Long was left. She especially loved the flute. She played 'A Plum Blossom' with elegance and solemnity, expressing its mood with refinement. She wanted to express the joy contained in the piece. Yet the one who understood her could hear only her sobbing.

1993

Stories of Identity

8

Eyes of the Night

By **WANG MENG**
Translated by Donald A. Gibbs

Wang Meng 王蒙 *(b. 1934) made his name in 1956 as a sensitive writer with his personal style and keen observation in his first work, 'The Young Newcomer to the Organization Bureau' (Zuzhibu lai le ge nianqingren* 組織部來了個年輕人*, 1956), which probed the issue of bureaucracy under the socialist system. For this work, he was labelled a Rightist in 1957 and sent to Xinjiang to do hard labour. He returned to the literary scene in the 1970s, after twenty years of silence, with a number of stories dealing with explosive subjects, which include 'Bolshevik Salute' (Buli* 布禮*, 1979), 'A Spate of Visitors' (Shuoke yingmen* 説客盈門*, 1980), 'The Butterfly' (Hudie* 蝴蝶*, 1980), 'Voices of Spring' (Chun zhi sheng* 春之聲*, 1980), and 'Kite Streamers' (Fengzheng piaodai* 風箏飄帶*, 1980). For his positive attitude toward modernism and the stream-of-consciousness techniques, Wang Meng became a focus of controversy in the early 1980s. Wang Meng has been on the editorial committee of* People's Literature 人民文學*, and was Minister of Culture before the events at Tiananmen Square in 1989. He is the author of the controversial story 'Hard Porridge' (*Jianying de xizhou 堅硬的稀粥*, 1992). His works can be found in the ten-volume* Collected Works by Wang Meng (Wang Meng wenji 王蒙文集*, 1993).*

Street lights, of course, are all turned on at the same time. Chen Gao knew that, but he still had the sensation that they were two rows of lights shooting out from his own head, two long, long streams of light so long that you couldn't see the ends of them. The locust trees overhead cast stark shadows everywhere. People on the sidewalk waiting for the bus also cast their own shadows, multiple shadows at that, some dark, some light.

Trucks, automobiles, trolleys, bicycles, horns honking, chatter, laughter. It takes night-time for a big city to show off its energy and its uniqueness. At first the lights are faint and scattered, but then those attention-getting neon signs and devices like the revolving poles in front of barber shops come on. And you see permanents, long hair, high heel shoes, low heel shoes, short, form-fitting dresses, and there is the scent of cologne and face cream. Cities these days, like women, are just beginning to pretty themselves up, and already there are people who won't sit still for it. That's interesting.

For more than twenty years Chen Gao had not been back to this big city. For over twenty years he had remained in a small, remote provincial town where one-third of the street lights never came on at all, and of the two-thirds that did have good bulbs in them, a third of them never got electricity. Was this because of negligence or because the electricity allocation was haywire? A small matter in any case, for nearly everyone there lived by the old pattern of rural life anyway, working from dawn to dusk. By six in the evening all the offices, factories, shops, and restaurants were closed for the day. Evenings, people stayed home cuddling their babies, smoking, doing laundry, or saying the kinds of things that are no sooner said than forgotten.

The bus arrived, a blue one, the long, articulated type. The conductress was talking through the loudspeakers. People squeezed their way off, and then Chen Gao and others squeezed their way on. There were no empty seats, but still it felt good just to get on board. The conductress was a young woman with a healthy glow on her face and a bright, clear, resonant voice. In Chen Gao's small, remote provincial town she would surely be picked as the announcer for the culture troupe programmes. In a series of smooth, practised movements, she deftly pressed the switch to close the electric doors, snapped on her shaded, gooseneck lamp for checking tickets, punched several tickets. Then 'snap' again—and off went the lamp. Street lights, tree shadows, buildings and pedestrians all flashed by the windows until another stop was reached. Her clear, resonant voice announced the station. 'Snap,' on went the lamp, and again the crowds surged off the bus and a new crowd promptly surged on.

Two youths in worker's garb were among those who got on, keyed up in animated discussion: '. . . the crux of it all is democracy, democracy, democracy. . . .' Wherever he had gone throughout the entire week of his stay in the city this time, Chen Gao had heard people talking about democracy. It was about as common as people in his small, remote provincial town talking about a leg of mutton. This was probably because food supplies in the cities were relatively plentiful so no one had to worry much over a leg of mutton. 'How enviable,' Chen Gao thought, smiling to himself.

But of course there really is no conflict between democracy and mutton. After all, if there is no democracy, mutton reaching the lips can always be snatched away. While on the other hand, any democracy that cannot help people in small, remote provincial towns get more and meatier legs of mutton is just so much hot air. Chen Gao had come to the city to attend a conference on writing short stories and plays. After the downfall of the Gang of Four,[1] Chen Gao had written five or six short stories that some had praised as showing greater maturity and versatility, while others said—and there were even more of these—that he still hadn't achieved the level of his work of twenty some years ago. Having to pay disproportionate attention to the leg of mutton no doubt was regressive for writers, although one has to admit that gaining an awareness of the crucial importance and urgency of mutton is, in itself, a great advancement and a matter of personal benefit. The train bringing him to the conference had halted at a tiny country station for an hour and twelve minutes because a man who had no proper identity cards, but who did have a high-priced leg of mutton to peddle, was crushed under the wheels while trying to get the best price for it. In order to get a head start on selling his mutton, the fellow ended up risking his life by ducking under the car in order to make a shortcut across the tracks. Just then the brakes had slipped a bit, causing the train to roll slightly, killing the poor fellow. The event weighed heavily on Chen Gao.

In the past Chen Gao had always been the youngest to attend this sort of conference; now he was somewhat older than most, and also somewhat more countrified, more weathered in complexion and less refined. When the comrades of the younger generation whose shoulders were so much broader than his—tall fellows with large, prominent eyes—delivered their speeches, they always expressed fresh, bold, sharply defined, lively new ideas. They could really make one see the light, make one feel good all over, really fire a person up, stir people to action. This resulted in literary issues somehow never quite getting discussed, and no matter how strenuously the conference organizers tried to lead the discussion to the central issues, everybody ended up talking mainly about how the Gang of Four had got their foothold, how to oppose feudalism, or else they talked endlessly about democracy, law, morality, and the social climate, about how more and more young people were gathering in the public parks to dance together to the accompaniment of electric guitars, and how the park administrators were trying every trick they could think of to ward off such calamities, everything from announcing over the p.a. system every three minutes that dancing was prohibited to collecting fines from the dancers. They even tried clearing out the park two hours before closing time.

Chen Gao also spoke his piece at the conference. Compared with the others, his statements were low-key, things like, 'Bit by bit, from our own individual efforts, we can get things done.' How marvelous, he mused, if but half the things presented in the conference could be realized. No, one-fifth. No, even a tenth! The thought roused Chen Gao to life, but then, it also gave him pause.

The bus reached the terminus, still jam-packed with passengers. Everyone freely ignored the conductress's plea to show tickets as they filed off the bus, despite the note of irritation and impatience that had crept into her voice. Along with others who must have been newcomers to the city, too, Chen Gao conscientiously held his ticket up high for the conductress to see, even though she never so much as glanced at it. As he dismounted, he tried to press the ticket into her hand, but even then she didn't bother to take it from him.

Under the bright lights of the bus terminus, he took out a small address book, folded back its blue-grey plastic cover, checked an address, and then began asking directions. He directed his inquiry toward one person, but to his surprise quite a few people at once began volunteering directions. In this respect, at least, he felt that city people had managed to preserve some of the traditional old respect for courtesy. Thanking them, he took leave of the well-lit terminus, and after several twists and turns came to a neighbourhood that was a maze of new apartment buildings.

To say that it was a maze is not to imply any great complexity; indeed, the confusion was precisely because of its simplicity—each building looked exactly like its neighbour. The balconies were all piled up with things. Pale blue light from fluorescent tubes and yellow light from ordinary light bulbs shone out from all the closely clustered windows of all the buildings in exactly the same degree of brightness. Even the sounds coming from the windows were identical. Apparently an international soccer game was on television—the Chinese team must have just scored, for a roar rose simultaneously from the spectators at the stadium and from those watching at home; people screamed wildly as applause and shouting rose to a crescendo, like a giant wave. The veteran sports announcer Zhang Zhi, so well known to audiences, was also shouting for all he was worth, although, as everyone knows, any description is entirely superfluous at such times. From still other windows came the sounds of hammers pounding on doors, vegetables being chopped, and children scrapping, with the threatening voices of their parents in the background.

All these sounds, lights, and material things were crammed together in these apartment buildings, which stood like so many match-boxes put on their ends. This sort of congested living seemed strange to Chen Gao; it was really hard to imagine what it would be like, living here, and it even struck him as a little comical. The tree shadows, reaching as high as the buildings themselves, spread a thin layer of mystery over the strange lifestyle he now beheld. In his small, remote provincial town, the most you would ever hear at night was the sound of a dog barking, and so familiar was he with all of them that he could tell from the bark alone what colour the dog was and who it belonged to. Beyond that, in his town there was only the sound of heavily laden trucks passing through the night, their headlights piercing the eyes with such brilliance you were blinded for a time after they passed by. All the houses and buildings near the road vibrated each time a truck rumbled by.

Chen Gao began to feel some regret as he walked here amidst this maze of identical apartment buildings.

'I never should have left that long, brightly lit boulevard, never should have left that noisy, packed but still cheerful bus, or that street where everybody was striding so purposefully along the sidewalks. How fine all that was.' And yet, here he was in a place like this. Better never to have left the government hostel in the first place. Could have argued the whole evening with those young fellows. All of them struggling to make heard his own particular remedies for dealing with the problems left behind by Lin Biao and the Gang of Four. Always talking of Belgrade, Tokyo, Hong Kong, and Singapore. After dinner they invariably were good for a plate of shrimp-flavoured chips, a plate of peanuts, and they'd order up litres of beer, too, to relieve the heat and give a boost to the conversation. But instead, he had ridden a bus for heaven knew how long, getting who knew where, fumbling around trying to find who only knew what kind of a place, looking up God only knew what sort of person, and all in order to take care of something that was none of his business in the first place.

Actually, there was no mystery at all as to what he was doing; it was a perfectly legitimate thing, an obligation, in fact, but the trouble was, he was simply the wrong person for the job. For him to take on something like this, well, you might as well have him go on stage to do ballet, to be the prince in *Swan Lake*.

As he walked along, there was just the trace of a limp in his step, something you wouldn't notice unless you were looking for it—a memento left him from the 'Sweep Away Everything' period.

These upsetting thoughts brought to mind the time twenty or so years before when he had first left this city. On that occasion, too, there had been the sad ache of being set apart from others. It was because he had written several short stories that at the time had been regarded as too outspoken, and that were now regarded as having been too soft spoken, something that put him on a swing oscillating for a long time between being, as Chairman Mao had put it, one of 'the 95 per cent of the people who are good,' and one of 'the 5 per cent who are bad'—a dangerous game, certainly.

According to what they had told him at the bus terminus, the very apartment house he was now approaching was the one he was seeking. Quite clearly, however, construction was still underway; it looked as though they were preparing to lay some sort of piping. No, not only pipes, because there were some bricks, tiles, lumber, and stone there as well. Maybe they were going to put up one or two single-storey buildings, or maybe dining halls. And of course they quite possibly could be public toilets. In any event, there was a wide trench that he probably could not jump across, not that he would have had any trouble with it before being 'swept away'. Better search around for a plank to bridge it with. He grew impatient as he walked the length of the trench without finding any. Clearly, he had come here the wrong way. Go around or jump? Well, he wasn't that old. He backed off a few paces, and then, one, two, three. . . . Bad luck. Soft sand ruined his footing just as he jumped, landing him in the bottom of the trench. Fortunately, there were no hard or sharp objects there. Even so, it was ten minutes or more before he had fully recovered from the pain and shock of his fall. Smiling, he brushed off the dirt from his clothes and slowly inched his way up out of the trench. Once out, his very first step put him in a deep puddle. He extricated his foot with a squish, but not before his foot and sock both were soaked through, feeling gritty, like eating rice with sand in it. As he looked up, his eyes were drawn to a light bulb fastened to a crooked, leaning post beside the building, and forlornly glowing orange-red in the surrounding darkness. This electric light, at this place, at this time, struck him as a tiny question mark, or maybe an exclamation point, written on an enormous blackboard.

As he walked closer to the light, again a great wave of cheering swelled out from the windows, and this time whistles were intermixed with the cheers. Probably the foreign team had just kicked in a goal. He drew closer to the entrance to check the number over the doorway more closely, wanting to be absolutely sure he was at the right building. Still not satisfied, he hesitated at the entrance, hoping to confirm the address from a passerby, even though just standing there idly made him feel awkward.

Before he had left for the city, one of the comrades in his remote provincial town, one of the local leaders he felt particularly close to, and whom he respected very much, had taken him aside and given him a letter and instructions to look up a certain leader in the city. 'We're old army buddies,' he confided in Chen Gao. 'In the letter, I've explained to him that our Shanghai sedan is the only car we have, and that it needs repairs. Our staff and driver have been all over trying to get parts, but from the looks of it, there's no way we can get it fixed anywhere in the whole province. What we need are a few key parts to get it going. This old army buddy of mine is in charge of a vehicle maintenance unit. He's always said, "leave anything to do with vehicle repairs up to me," so go look him up, and after you get in touch with him send me a telegram. . . .'

It was just a very ordinary thing. You look up someone you know personally—an old friend, someone in a position of authority—to repair a car for someone else who is also in a position of authority and is regarded in his own unit as someone of good character and prestige. The car belonging to his unit, of course, is in any event state property.

There was no reason why Chen Gao should not have acceded to this veteran comrade's request. As someone who well understood the importance of a leg of mutton, Chen Gao never really developed any doubts about the necessity of having to convey this letter to the comrade in the city. Since he was coming to the city anyway, he naturally felt an obligation to do his best for his local unit. But after having accepted the assignment, he began to feel awkward about it, as if he were wearing shoes that didn't fit or trousers of different coloured legs.

It seemed almost as if the comrades in that small, remote provincial town could read Chen Gao's mind, for shortly after arriving in the city, he began receiving one telegram after another from them, urging him to hurry up with the job.

'Anyway, it's not for myself. Besides, I've never ridden in that sedan, nor will I ever ride in it after this,' he had encouraged himself, while making his way along that great boulevard with its two long streams of light, after leaving those friendly fellow passengers on the bus, after leaving the bus terminus that was lit as brilliantly as a stage, and while he was winding this way and that through the dark side streets, falling into the trench, crawling out, wiping the dirt off his clothes, filling his shoe full of mud. And now, at last, here he was.

After verifying the street address and the building number from two youngsters passing by, he mounted the steps to the fourth floor, located the correct door, and stood before it gathering himself together, catching his breath. Then he gave the door as soft a knock as he could, a delicate, civilized rap, one calculated to be just loud enough.

No response. Yet there did seem to be some sound inside. He put his ear to the door. Music, it seemed like. Stifling the split-second's urge to blurt out in relief, 'Well, no one's home,' he forced himself to give the door another good knock.

His third knock brought a response. Footsteps approached, 'thump, thump, thump', from inside. The built-in lock squeaked as it rotated. Finally, the door was opened by a young man with unkempt hair and a bare chest. He wore only a pair of cotton undershorts, which revealed the thighs. On his feet he wore a pair of foam-rubber thongs. His body glistened with the sheen of the well-fed.

In a tone of voice that barely concealed his impatience, the young man asked curtly, 'Yeah?'

'I'd like to speak with Comrade —,' Chen Gao replied, giving him the name written on the envelope entrusted to him.

'He's not home,' the young man grunted, and would have closed the door had not Chen Gao so earnestly stepped forward. Making an effort to speak the city dialect as perfectly and as politely as he could, Chen Gao made a brief self-introduction, concluding, 'And are you, may I ask, a relative of Comrade —?' (He figured the boy must be —'s son, and in point of fact, it was quite unnecessary in addressing a member of a generation so much younger than himself to use the honorific form 'may I ask?')

'Might I venture to have a few words with you to explain why I have come, and might I prevail upon you to convey a message to Comrade —?'

In the dark corridor, one couldn't actually see the expression on the young man's face, but one could sense that he frowned and hesitated before answering curtly, 'Well, come in.' Turning on his heel, he receded into the apartment without so much as nodding or beckoning to the visitor, the way nurses do when they tell a patient it's his turn to go in and have his tooth pulled.

Chen Gao followed the flop, flop, flop of the boy's thongs, his own steps sounding squeak, squeak as they filed down the pitch black hallway into the apartment. A door on the left, a door on the right. Quite a few doors, actually. Think of that, one door opening into so many other doors. One door was opened revealing a soft light within. Soothing music was playing, and there was the warm smell of liquor.

A coil-spring bed, an apricot-coloured silk comforter, neither made up nor folded back, but all bunched up in a heap in the middle like a wheat dumpling. A floor lamp had a metal stand issuing a cold, repellent glitter. Through a half-opened door on the bedside stand, he could see ball-bearing door stops. Any number of friends in his small, remote provincial town had asked Chen Gao to try and get some door hardware like this, but he could never find them for sale anywhere. Back home, big wardrobe chests with doors that needed those things were just coming into fashion in a big way. Then his gaze shifted slightly to take in the wicker chairs, a lounge, a round table, and on it a fancy tablecloth exactly like the one in Hatoyama's dining room in the fourth act of the revolutionary opera *Red Lantern*.

A four-speaker portable tape recorder. Imported. Hong Kong music. Soft voices, clear pronunciation—exaggerated even—and sensuous. Whenever you hear that kind of mushy stuff, you can hardly keep from laughing. If you took that tape back to his small, remote provincial town and were to play it for them there, why, it would probably frighten them more than a cavalry charge. Of all the things in the room, it was only a common drinking glass half filled with water that struck Chen Gao as something familiar, something close to his own life. Seeing it was almost like running into an old hometown friend in a foreign country. Even if you never were so very close at home, or even if there had been some friction between you, under such circumstances you'd become thicker than ever.

When Chen Gao spotted a worn stool near the door, he pulled it toward him and sat down. His clothes were still soiled from his fall. He began explaining the purpose of his visit, but halted after two sentences, thinking the young man would lower the volume on the tape recorder. He stopped and started several times until he realized the young man had no intention of turning it down. The strange thing about it was this: Chen Gao, who had always been a pretty good talker, now seemed to have lost his tongue. He spoke haltingly, in disconnected phrases, and sometimes his speech went completely awry, as when he meant to say, 'We want to ask Comrade—to take care of this for us,' but instead heard himself saying obsequiously, 'We would be honoured if you could do us the favour of looking into it,' almost as if he were applying to the young man for a pay supplement. At one point he intended to say, 'At the moment, I just want to get in touch with him,' but instead blurted out, 'I want to line things up with you.' And even his speech had changed so that it sounded more like a dull blade sawing elmwood than his own voice.

Having spoken his piece, Chen Gao pulled a letter from his pocket. The young man remained slouched in his chair, motionless, while Chen Gao, who was about twice his age, had no choice but to take that letter, written by a comrade in a position of authority, in his own hand, in a far-off place, and carry it across the room to the young man. As he handed it to him, Chen Gao got a better look at the annoyed, arrogant, ignorant expression on his pimpled face.

The young man opened the letter, scanned it, and smiled contemptuously, all the while tapping his left foot in rhythm with the beat of the Hong Kong music. Tape recorders and Hong Kong music were new to Chen Gao, but he by no means found them disgusting, nor was he necessarily against that style of singing. On the other hand, he wasn't convinced, either, that music of that sort amounted to anything, so his own face also bore a contemptuous expression on it, even though he did not realize it.

'This fellow Y — (the comrade in a position of authority in Chen Gao's distant and remote district who had written the letter), is he really my father's old army buddy?' (The young man had not troubled to introduce himself, so one could not be completely sure whom the reference to 'my father' actually indicated.) 'How is it I've never heard my father mention him?'

Feeling the insult, Chen Gao replied, 'You're pretty young, you know. It's possible your father never told you about. . . .'

'My father says anytime someone wants a car repaired he becomes an old "army buddy",' the young man interrupted.

'You mean to say your father doesn't know Y —? Why, he went to Yanan in 1936. Last year he published an article in *Red Flag*. . . . His older brother is the area commander in Z — district. . . .'

Chen Gao, despite himself, blurted out these credentials too hastily, and particularly, the minute he brought the prominent general into it, he suddenly felt his eyes blur and became conscious of beads of sweat running down his spine.

This time the contempt on the young man's face was twenty times what it had been before. Nor could he keep from laughing out loud. Chen Gao, feeling disgraced, looked down at his own feet.

'Let me put it to you this way,' the young man said, rising to his feet, adopting a posture of authority. 'If you want to make a deal these days, it takes two things. First, you've got to come up with something. What do you propose to offer?'

'Propose to offer . . . ? Why, I suppose . . .' Chen Gao replied, speaking more to himself than to the young man, 'I suppose we have legs of mutton. . . .'

'Mutton won't do,' he scoffed, once again laughing.

By now, however, his contempt had run its course and had become pity.

'The second thing—and let me put it to you straight—you need to know the ropes on something like this. You don't really need to go through my father at all. If you can come up with something to offer, and if you have someone who knows how to handle it, it doesn't make any difference whose name you use to pull strings.' Then he added, 'My father's been sent to Beidaihe[2] on the coast for a while.' He was careful not to say 'taking it easy'.

Chen Gao found himself at the door unable to recall just how he had left the room. Just before stepping out into the hall, he hesitated and instinctively cocked his ear to one side. The tape recorder was now playing real music, a Hungarian waltz. In his mind he envisioned a single leaf dancing in circles over a dark blue alpine lake surrounded on three sides by tall, snow-covered peaks; beside the lake was his small, remote provincial town. A white swan had settled in peaceful repose on the surface of the lake.

Chen Gao raced through the dark hall of the apartment building and plunged down the stairway. Was the pounding in his ears his footsteps or his heart? Once clear of the building, he again saw above him that dim light bulb shining out like a question mark, or was it an exclamation point? But now it suddenly appeared bright red, like a devil's eye, a hideous eye able to metamorphose its beholder, reducing birds to rats, horses to gnats.

Chen Gao easily leaped the ditch. The television announcer was now speaking in a relaxed, intimate voice of the next day's weather forecast. In no time he reached the bus terminus. As usual, a large crowd had gathered to wait for the bus. A group of women night-shift workers were noisily chattering about the bonuses at their factory. One couple waited for the bus side by side, arms around each other. If the old fogey moralist 'Mr. Siming' in Lu Xun's story 'Soap' were to see this today, he would suffer yet another shock at the decline of Confucianism.

Chen Gao climbed into the bus and took a position near the door. This time the conductress was a woman already past youth. She was so bony and spare you could almost see her skinny shoulder blades protruding inside her thin blouse.

Through twenty years of frustration, twenty years of remoulding, Chen Gao had learnt many valuable lessons and had also lost certain things that he should never have lost. Through it all, however, he had never lost his love for bright lights, his affection for night-shift workers, his love of democracy, bonuses, legs of mutton. . . . Suddenly the bell sounded, and shsss . . . the three doors closed, one after the other; the tree shadows and street lights swiftly receded as the bus picked up speed. . . .

'Tickets? Tickets anyone?' But no sooner said, than 'Snap!' Out went her goosenecked lamp, long before Chen Gao could reach for his change.

'She must think all her passengers are night-shift workers with monthly passes,' mused Chen Gao.

1979

NOTES

1 The 'Gang of Four' refers to the clique formed by Wang Wenhong, Zhang Chunqiao, Jiang Qing, and Yao Wenyuan who seized the highest political power in China during the Cultural Revolution. Their downfall took place in 1976.
2 An exclusive resort.

9

Homecoming?

By **HAN SHAOGONG**

Translated by Martha P. Y. Cheung

Han Shaogong 韓少功 (b. 1953) was born in Hunan. He worked in a rural commune during the Cultural Revolution. In 1974, he was re-assigned to a cultural centre, where he began writing short stories. In 1978 he entered Hunan Normal University and graduated four years later with a degree in Chinese. Han Shaogong is one of the most noted writers in China, not only for his innovative literary style and subjects, but also for his association with the movement for the quest of cultural roots that occurred in China in the late 1980s. In his pre-1985 works, Han is mainly concerned with the history and tradition of Chinese culture and he sees writing as a process of reflecting reality, but in his post-1985 works, he is more concerned with the questions of identity and the shaping of the self in relation to power and ideology. He is now a professional writer, and he has published five collections of short stories. His works have also appeared in English translation. He has won literary prizes in China and Taiwan.

People have often observed that, sometimes, when they visit a place for the first time, they find it familiar, yet they don't know why. This was what I felt now.

I was walking. Much of the dirt track had been washed out by water running down the slope, leaving jagged ridges of earth and mounds of pebbles, like a body stripped of skin and flesh, with sticks of dry bone and lumps of shrivelled innards fully exposed. There were a few rotting bamboos and a frayed length of the curb-rope of some buffalo or cow—a sign that a village would soon come into view. There were also some dark motionless shadows in the small pond beside the track. They looked like rocks at first glance, but a closer look showed them to be calves' heads, with eyes that were staring furtively at me. Wrinkled and bearded, these calves were born old, they had inherited old age at birth. Beyond the banana grove ahead loomed a square blockhouse, with blank staring gun embrasures, and dark walls that looked as if they had been charred by smoke and fire, as if they were the coagulation of many dark nights. I had heard that bandits had been rife in these parts in the past. If they weren't put down, there would be nobody on the land in ten years' time—so it was said. No wonder every village had its own blockhouse, and the houses of the mountain folk were never spread out but huddled together, sturdy, with mean little windows set high up to make it difficult for thieves to climb in.

All this looked so familiar and yet so strange. It was like looking at a written character: the harder you look at it, the more it looks like a character you know, and yet it doesn't look like the character you know. Damn! Had I been here before? Let me guess: follow the flagstone path, go round the banana grove, and turn left at the oil-press, and perhaps I'd see an old tree behind the blockhouse, a ginkgo or a camphor, struck dead by lightning.

A little later, my guess was proved correct. Down to the hollow in the tree trunk, and, in front of it, two boys at play burning grass.

I ventured another guess: behind the tree, a low cow-shed perhaps, several heaps of cow-dung at the entrance, and a rusty plough or a harrow under the eaves. I walked over, and there they were, clear as day. Even the granite mortar and the pestle lying aslant, even the sand and the few fallen leaves in the mortar seemed vaguely familiar!

Of course, there was no muddy water in the mortar in my imagination. But come to think of it, it had been raining; the water must have dripped from the eaves. At this, a chill rose from my heels and crept all the way up to my neck.

No, I couldn't have been here before. Definitely not. I'd never had meningitis, never gone mad, and my mind was still in good shape. Had I seen this place in a film, then? Heard it mentioned by friends, perhaps? Or dreamt about it . . . ? I searched my memory frantically.

The even more puzzling thing was, the mountain folk all seemed to know me. Just now, when I was cautiously picking my way among the boulders in the stream, my trouser legs rolled up, a man carrying on his shoulder two young trees tied into the shape of an 'A' came towards me from upstream. Seeing how precariously I was balancing myself on the rocks, he threw me a dry branch pulled from a melon shed by the roadside and, much to my surprise, gave me a big grin, showing his yellow teeth.

'You're back?'

'Yes, I'm back. . . .'

'Must have been over ten years?'

'Ten years . . . .'

'Go and take a rest in my place. Sangui is ploughing the seedling beds in front of the house.'

Where was his house? Who was Sangui? I was bewildered.

I went up a gentle slope. An expanse of eaves and tiled roofs and a doorway rose up before me.

I saw in the distance a few figures threshing something on the ground. As I went up to them, I could hear the rhythmic clacking of their flails—a few loud clacks, then a softer one. They were all barefoot and had close-cropped hair, their faces were glazed with jagged trickles of brown sweat. As they moved about, patches of sweat on their cheeks gleamed in the sun. Their short jackets hung loose on their bodies, exposing the smooth skin on their bellies, and their navels. Their trousers also hung low on their hips. It was not until I saw one of them move towards a cradle and start breast-feeding a baby, and then noticed the earrings they all had on, that I realized they were women. One of them stared at me in amazement.

'Isn't this Ma. . . .'

'Glasses Ma.' Another reminded her. They all giggled, amused by the name.

'My name is not Ma. I'm Huang. . . .'

'Changed your name?'

'No.'

'Still such a tease? Where did you come from?'

'From the town, of course.'

'A rare visitor! Where's sister Liang?'

'Which sister Liang?'

'Your wife. Isn't she called Liang?'

'No. My wife is called Yang."

'Did I remember it wrong? No, I can't be wrong. In those days she even told me her surname was the same as my family's. My family is from Sanjiangkou, Liangjiashe,[1] you know that.'

What did I know? Besides, what had that Liang, whatever her name, got to do with me? It seemed as if I'd wanted to go and find her, and ended up here somehow. I'd no idea how I got here.

The woman threw down the flail and showed me to her house. The threshold was high and solid. Innumerable people, young and old, must have trodden on it and sat on it to wear down that depression in the middle. The grain of the wood spread out on the threshold like yellow moonbeams, a fossil of yellow moonbeams. Kids had to crawl over it, grown-ups had to turn their bodies at an angle and lift their legs high before they could bring themselves in through the doorway. It was dark inside, you couldn't see a thing. Only a thin ray of light managed to creep in through the tiny high window, slicing open the damp darkness. The place smelled of chicken droppings and swill. It took a while for my eyes to adjust, to make out the walls and beams that were covered with ashes and soot, and the outline of an equally sooty hanging basket of some sort. I sat on a wood block, mildly surprised that there were no chairs, only benches and wood blocks. The women, young and old, packed the doorway, gibbering and jabbering. The one who was breast-feeding her baby was not at all inhibited by my presence. She pulled out her other long heavy breast and gave suck to her baby, the nipple of the one she had just removed from the baby's mouth still dripping milk, and she smiled at me.

They were saying some strange things . . . 'Young Qin . . .' 'No, not Young Qin.' 'No?' 'It's Young Ling.' 'Oh yes. Is Young Ling still teaching?' 'Why doesn't she come and visit us?' 'Have you all gone back to Changsha?' 'Do you live in the city or the country?' 'Have you got any kids?' 'One or two?' 'Has Young Luo got any kids?' 'One or two?' 'Has Chen Zhihua got any kids?' 'One or two?' 'What about Bearhead? Has he found himself a wife?' 'Does he have kids? One or two?' . . .

It was obvious that they had mistaken me for a certain 'Glasses Ma' who knew people by the name of Young Ling and Bearhead and the like. Perhaps that chap looked very much like me. Perhaps he, too, hid behind his glasses looking at people.

But who was he? And did I need to worry about that? The women's smiling faces told me there was no need to worry about food and shelter for today. Thank heavens! Let them take me for this Ma what's-his-name. I could easily handle their 'One or two?' questions, surprise them a little, or make them nod their heads in sympathy now and then. No sweat really.

The woman from Liangjiashe brought in a tray with four large bowls of sweet tea. I learnt later that this meant 'peace all the year round', the four bowls standing for the four seasons. The rim of the bowl was dark and grimy, and I drank without touching it with my lips. But the tea was good and tasted of fried sesame and glutinous rice. She picked up from the floor two dirty garments belonging to her children, put them in a wooden tub, and carried it into the inner room. And so her sentence was cut into two: 'We haven't had news of you for a long time, Old Shuigen said . . . (it was quite a while before she emerged from the room) . . . you were thrown into jail soon after you left us?'

I was so shocked I nearly scalded my hand with the tea. 'No, I wasn't. What jail?'

'Old Shuigen doesn't know a thing then. What rubbish he talked! My poor father-in-law was in a terrible flap. He burnt lots of incense sticks for you.' She covered her mouth in a fit of giggles, 'Oh! I'm going to die laughing.'

The women all burst out laughing. The one with a spread of yellow teeth added, 'He even went to Yang's Hill to pray for you to the Buddha.'

Rotten luck! Incense sticks and the Buddha! Well, maybe that chap Ma really had fallen into the hands of some evil spirit and was doomed to end up in jail. And here I was, sipping tea in his place, laughing like an idiot.

The woman served me another bowl of sweet tea, her free hand holding the wrist of the one carrying the bowl, as she had done before. Part of the local etiquette, I suppose. But I hadn't yet finished the first bowl. There wasn't much tea left, but the sesame and the rice were still sitting at the bottom of the bowl, and I had no idea how to eat them politely. 'He missed you, he said you were kind and just, and you had a good heart. He wore your padded jacket for many winters. When he died, I turned it into a pair of trousers for our little Man. . . .'

I wanted to talk about the weather.

The room suddenly grew dark. I turned round and saw a dark shadow almost completely blocking the doorway. It was a man, naked to the waist, his bulging muscles hard and angular like rock, not smooth and curved. He was carrying something which looked in silhouette like a buffalo's head. The shadow loomed over me. Before I could see the face clearly, he dropped what he was carrying with a loud thud, and I felt the file-like surface of two enormous palms rubbing my hands.

'It's comrade Ma! Well, well, well. . . .'

I wasn't a caterpillar, why was I scared stiff?

He turned towards the brazier and the flames lit up the side of his face. I saw a big grin, a black gaping mouth, and arms sporting green tattoos.

'Comrade Ma, when did you arrive?'

I wanted to say that my name wasn't Ma but Huang, Huang Zhixian. And I hadn't come to revisit this place or to explore it out of a sense of adventure.

'Do you know me? (Does he mean 'recognize'? Or 'remember'?) I was in Spiral Hill building roads the year you left. I'm Ai Ba.'

'Ai Ba. Yes, yes. I know you.' What a contemptible answer. 'You were the team leader then.'

'No, not the team leader, I recorded work points. And do you still know my wife?'

'Yes, yes. I do. She was good at making sweet tea.'

'I went to chase meat with you once, do you still know? ('to chase meat', does it mean 'hunting'?) I wanted to make some offerings to the mountain gods, but you called ('said'?) I was superstitious. And what happened? You stumbled into some poisonous grass and got nasty boils all over your body. You also came upon a muntjac deer. It ran between your legs, but you missed it. . . .'

'Yes. Yes, I missed it, by an inch. My eyes aren't very good.'

The black gaping mouth exploded into laughter. The women stood up lazily and, swaying their heavy hips, left the room. The man who called himself Ai Ba took out a bottle gourd, poured the drink into two large bowls, and invited me to drink. The wine looked murky. It was sweet, but it also had a bitter, burning taste. I was told it contained medicinal herbs and tiger bones. He turned down my offer of a cigarette, and rolled his own with a bit of newspaper. He drew a deep puff and the paper burst into a bright flame. He wasn't at all worried, he didn't even look at it. I watched him anxiously, and it was a while before he blew out the flame in one leisurely breath, the cigarette still intact.

'We have good times now, plenty of meat and plenty to drink. At the Spring Festival, every household slaughtered a cow to celebrate.' He wiped his mouth. 'That year when every village had to be run on the Dazhai[2] model, nobody got paid anything. You know all about that, of course.'

'Yes, yes I do.' But I wanted to talk about the good times.

'Have you watched Delong? He's now our chief. He went to Zhuomei Bridge to plant trees yesterday. Mayhap he'll come back, mayhap he won't, and then mayhap he would.' Then he started to talk about things and people that puzzled and bewildered me: so-and-so had built a new house, sixteen feet high; so-and-so, too, it was eighteen feet high; so-and-so was about to build one, also eighteen feet high; and so-and-so was laying the foundations, mayhap it'd be sixteen feet high, mayhap eighteen. I listened nervously, trying to work out the implications his words might have. I found the vocabulary used by the people here somewhat peculiar: 'see' became 'watch', 'quiet' became 'clean.' Then there was the word 'gather'—did it mean 'rise'? Or did it mean 'stand'?

I felt a bit tipsy and made a show of enthusiasm at every mention of the figures—sixteen feet, eighteen feet.

'You haven't forgotten us in the mountain then. You've come back to watch how we're doing.' He took another pull at his cigarette, and for a moment or two the bright flame again drove me to distraction. 'You know, I've kept the books you gave out when you were a teacher here.' He went rat-a-tat up the stairs and a long time elapsed before he came down again, cobwebs in his hair, beating the dust off a few yellow tattered sheets of paper. It was a mimeographed booklet with the front and back cover missing, a sort of primer probably, and smelt of damp and tung oil. It contained what looked like night-school songs, a miscellany of agricultural terms, the characters '1911 Revolution', Marx's essays on the peasants' movement, and a map. The printing was crude, the characters were huge and the pages stained with ink blots. I didn't think there was anything great about these characters, I knew how to write them myself.

'You were really down on your luck then. You looked quite starved, just a pair of eyes in your gaunt face. But you still came here to teach.'

'Oh! It was nothing. Nothing!'

'It was the last month of the lunar year. Heavy snow, freezing cold.'

'That's right. So cold my nose nearly froze off.'

'And we still had to go and work in the fields, using pine torches to light our way.'

'Ah, pine torches.'

All of a sudden, his manner grew mysterious. The two bright patches on his cheeks and the cluster of drinker's spots drew close to my face. 'Tell me, did you kill Shortie Yang?'

What Shortie Yang? My skull suddenly contracted, my mouth and jaws went stiff, and I shook my head vehemently. My name simply wasn't Ma, and I'd never met anyone called Shortie Yang. Why did I have to get sucked into a criminal case?

'They all said you killed him. Served him right. That slimy two-headed snake!' He snarled. But, seeing me shake my head, he stared at me, incredulous, disappointed.

'Can I have another drink?' I tried to change the topic.

'Sure, sure. Help yourself.'

'There are mosquitoes here.'

'Yes. They pick on strangers. Shall I burn some straw?'

He lit some straw. More people had arrived in groups to see me and were greeting me with the usual polite questions about my health and my family. The men lit the cigarettes I offered them and went to sit by the door or by the wall, puffing away noisily, smiling but saying little. Now and then they exchanged a few remarks about me among themselves. Some said I had grown fat, others said I had lost weight; some said I had aged, others said I still looked 'young-faced' and it had to do with the rich food I ate in the city. When they finished smoking, they took their leave with a smile, saying that they had to fell some trees or to apply manure on their fields. A few kids had gathered round me, they stared hard at my glasses for a while and then dashed off into hiding, screaming in an ecstasy of fear and excitement, 'There are little devils inside! Little devils!' A young woman was standing by the door chewing a blade of grass and watching me with an absorbed expression, her eyes glistening as if with tears, I had no idea why. Feeling awkward and uneasy, I turned and fixed my eyes politely on Ai Ba.

I had been through scenes like this already. Just now when I went to take a look at their opium fields, I met a middle-aged woman. She looked terrified as soon as she saw me, the colour draining from her face like a lamp suddenly going dim, and she quickly pulled up the back straps of her shoes, lowered her head and changed direction to avoid me, I didn't know why.

Ai Ba said I ought to pay a visit to Third Grandpa. Actually, Third Grandpa had passed away. They said he had died from a snakebite not long ago. But his name still cropped up in conversation, and his desolate little house still stood beside the brick-kiln. Flanked by two tung trees, the house was leaning precariously to one side and looked as though it would collapse at any moment. Around the house there were weeds waist-high. They were creeping up the front steps with sinister determination, their tongue-like blades quivering, waiting to swallow up the little house as if they were about to devour the remaining bones of a clan. The padlocked wooden door was full of black holes bored by worms. I wondered whether the house would have become so dilapidated if its master had been alive. Could it be that the man was the soul of the house and when the soul was gone, the body would rot in no time? A rusty lantern lay overturned in the grass, its surface dotted with white bird-droppings. Close to it stood a broken earthenware jar. When you touched it, mosquitoes swarmed out buzzing. Ai Ba told me that this jar was used for pickling vegetables and that in those days I often came here for Third Grandpa's pickled cucumber. (Did I?) The plaster on the walls had flaked off, leaving only the barest outline of a few large characters, 'Eyes on the world'. Ai Ba said I had painted them on. (Had I?) He picked a bunch of herbs and studied the birds' nests in the tree. I peered at the inside of the house through the window and saw a basket half full of lime standing in one corner, and what looked like a large round tray. A closer look told me it was an iron barbell disc, badly rusted. I was amazed—how could an unusual piece of sports equipment like that have found its way into the heart of the mountain? How did it get here?

But there was probably no need to ask Ai Ba—I'd given it to Third Grandpa as a present. (Had I?) And I'd given it to him so he could make it into a hoe or a harrow, and he never did. (Was that right?)

Someone up the slope was calling his cow, 'Wuma—Wuma—'. And the faint tinkle of cow bells came from the woods on the other side. They had an unusual way of calling cows here. It sounded like a sad desolate call for mama. Perhaps the walls of the blockhouse had turned black because of this dismal wailing.

An old woman was coming down the hill, a small bundle of firewood on her back. She was bent almost double and with every step, her hoe-like protruding chin dipped as if it was digging at the ground. She looked up at me, her cloudy pupils pressed hard against her upper eyelids, and gave me a long stare that seemed to go right through me to the tung trees behind. There was no expression on her face, just lines and wrinkles so deep I was stunned. She glanced at

Third Grandpa's little house and then turned round to look at the old tree at the entrance to the village. 'The tree has died too,' she mumbled to herself all of a sudden. Then, step by step, she trundled off, dipping her chin, and the thin silvery strands on her head were pressed down by the wind, pressed down by the wind.

I was now sure I'd never been here before. And I couldn't figure out the meaning of the old woman's remark—it was unfathomable, like a deep dark pool.

The evening meal was a grand feast. Chunks of beef and pork the size of a palm were brought out in a large bowl extended at the rim with straw hoops. The meat, underdone and greasy, was stacked up high in the bowl, one piece on top of another, like a pile of bricks in a kiln. People must have eaten like this for thousands of years. Only the men could sit round the table. One of the guests did not turn up, but the host put a piece of rough straw paper at the empty place and served food to the absent guest all the same. During the meal I asked about their fragrant rice but they refused to talk about the price, insisting I should take some as a present. As for the opium, they had had a good yield this year but the national pharmaceutical agency had a monopoly on it. At this, I decided not to pursue the matter further.

'Shortie Yang had it coming to him.' Ai Ba slurped a spoonful of soup, put the spoon back at its sticky place on the table and turned his eyes to the meat bowl again, tapping the table with his chopsticks. 'Fat-arsed, plump-pawed, he couldn't do a thing. And he wanted to build a house. The bloody schemer!'

'Damn right you are! And who hasn't been tied up by that bloody rope of his? See, I've still got two scars on my wrists. That fucking son-of-a-bitch.'

'How did he die? Did he really bump into a blood-sucking demon and fall over a cliff?'

'You can be mean and ruthless, but you can't beat Fate. And yet some people are never content. They want more than heaven gives them. Hongsheng over at Xia's Bay is like that too.'

'Shortie even ate rats. It's diabolical!'

'Absolutely! Never heard anything like it in my life!'

'Rotten luck for Bearhead too! Shortie slapped him hard on the face twice. Bags of dye they were, I saw them with my own eyes. Wasn't even good enough for dying cloth, only good for painting clay Buddhas. But Shortie insisted it was gunpowder.'

'Well, it had something to do with Bearhead's class background too.'

I plucked up my courage and interposed, 'Did the higher-ups send someone to investigate?'

Ai Ba said, chewing a piece of fat noisily, 'They did. They fucking did! They even tried to question me, but I slipped away in time, saying that I'd to go and look for a hen that had gone missing. . . . Hey, Comrade Ma, you haven't touched your drink! Come, come, help yourself to more meat.'

My throat tightened as he thrust another chunk of meat on me. I had to make like I was going to get some more rice and, as soon as I was in the shadow, I threw the meat to a dog squeezing past my legs.

After dinner, they insisted on letting me take a bath. I wondered whether it was a local custom, and warned myself not to behave like a new-comer. There was no bath-tub, just a tall barrel big enough to hold several cauldrons of hot water standing in the corner of the kitchen. After I got in, the women still moved about in front of the barrel, while the woman from Liangjiashe kept adding water into the barrel with a gourd ladle. I was so embarrassed I ducked down each time she came close to me. Only after she left the room with a bucket to feed to pigs did I quietly let out a sigh of relief. I soaked for so long I was dripping with sweat. The water must have been boiled with wormwood for the mosquito bites on my body had stopped itching. A lard lamp hung above me, emitting a pale blue glow in the steam, giving a blue tint to my body. Before I put on my shoes, I looked at this blue body of mine and was suddenly overcome with a peculiar feeling: the body seemed a stranger, seemed alien. I had no clothes on, and there was no one here but me, so no one to cover myself up for or pose for, not that I could have done so anyway. There was only my naked self, the reality of my own self. I had hands and legs, so I could do something; I had intestines and a stomach, so I had to eat something; and I had genitals, so I could produce children. For a while the world was shut outside the door; when I was out there I was always busy wherever I went, and never had time to look at myself and think. The chance union of a sperm and an ovum had, in the distant past, brought one of my ancestors into existence; the chance meeting of this ancestor and another ancestor had brought about yet another fertilized ovum, making it possible for me to come into existence generations later. I, too, was a bluish fertilized ovum connected to a string of coincidences. What was I in this world for? What could I do? . . . I was thinking too much, and too foolishly.

I started to wipe dry an inch-long scar on my calf. I had received the injury in a football pitch, where I was hit by a studded boot. But, no, I was wrong, it seemed. It seemed that I'd got the scar from a nasty bite by a short, dwarfish man. Was it on that rainy misty morning? On that narrow mountain track? He was coming towards me holding an opened umbrella and I was scowling at him. He was so frightened he started to shake. Then he went down on his knees and swore that he would never do it again, never, and that Second Sister-in-law's death had nothing to do with him, nor was he the one who had stolen Third Grandpa's buffalo. In the end he fought back, his eyes starting out of their sockets, and bit my leg. He jerked and pulled at the curb-rope round his neck. Then, abruptly, he stretched out his hands, and they began scratching and digging into the earth like two scuttling crabs. I didn't know how long it was before the scuttling crabs gave up their struggle and became quite still. . . .

I did not dare to think anymore. I didn't even have the guts to look at my hands. . . . Did they smell of blood and carry the marks of a cow rope cut deeply into the flesh?

No, I told myself with desperate finality, I'd never been here before, I'd never known any short, dwarfish man in my life. And I'd never seen any pale blue glow, not even in my dreams. Never.

The central room was now filling up with people. An old man came in, trampled out the pine torch, and said he had come to repay the two yuan he owed me for the cloth dye he had asked me to buy. He also invited me to dine and to 'bed the night' in his place tomorrow. This led to a heated argument with Ai Ba who said that since he was going to fetch the tailor tomorrow and had already prepared the meat, I should go to his place tomorrow, there could be no question about it.

While they were still arguing, I slipped out of the house. Stumbling on the uneven road, I made my way towards the house 'I' used to live in. I wanted to see it. Ai Ba said it was the cow-shed behind the old tree. It had been converted into a cow-shed only the year before last.

I walked past the tung trees again and once again I saw the weeds that were about to swallow up Old Grandpa—that silhouette of the tumbledown thatched hut. It was watching me quietly, coughing through the caw of the crows, whispering softly to me through the rustling leaves. I even felt a hint of alcoholic breath in the air.

You're back, my child? Grab yourself a chair and sit down. Didn't I tell you to go away, far, far away, and never come back again?

But I miss your pickled cucumber. I've tried to make some myself, but it isn't the same.

Why miss those humble things? I only made them because I knew you were starving and down on your luck. You worked in the fields all day, and you were so hungry you pulled the broad beans from the stalks and ate them raw.

You cared for us, I know.

Who doesn't have to be away from home sometime in his life? I know what it's like, I only did what I could.

I remember that day when we were sent to gather firewood. We only brought back nine loads, but you put it down as ten to give us more work points.

Is that so? I don't remember.

And you kept insisting we should shave off our hair. You said that hair and beards drank blood and that letting them grow was bad for our health.

Did I? I don't remember.

I should have come to see you earlier. It never occurred to me that things would have changed so much and that you'd be gone so soon.

It was time to go. If I'd lived on I'd have turned into a grand old monster. True, I loved a drink or two, but I've had enough and now I can sleep peacefully.

Won't you have a cigarette, Grandpa?

Go and put on the kettle if you want a cup of tea, Young Ma.

I left the smell of alcohol behind and moved on. Holding the guttering pine torch and thinking about what I had to do in the fields the next day, I made my way home, accompanied by the sound of frogs splashing into the pond. But now there was no pine torch in my hand and my home had turned into a cow-shed. It looked so desolate, so unfamiliar. I could not see it clearly in the dark, I could only hear the cows chewing the cud and smell the strong odour of warm cow dung on the straw in the shed. The cows took me for their master and the whole herd pressed forward, jostling one another, making the gate of the pen creak. As I walked, I heard echoes of my footsteps from the earthen wall of the shed, as if someone was walking on the other side of the wall, or perhaps even inside the clay of the wall. And that person knew my secret.

The dark mountain cliff opposite looked even more imposing and a lot closer at night, so close it was suffocating. It had curtained off the starry sky, leaving only a tiny uneven slit. Looking up at the tiny opening that was so high and so far away, I felt strongly the pull of the earth, as if I was being sucked in by a strange unknown force and was about to sink, sink into a deep crevice in the earth, down, down.

A huge moon appeared. The dogs in the village seemed frightened and started to whine. Treading on the moonlight seeping through the leaves, treading on tiny moonlit circles that were like algae, like duckweed, I went towards the stream. I thought to myself: there could be someone by the stream, a young woman perhaps, with a leaf held between her lips.

There was no one by the stream. But on my way back, I saw the silhouette of someone under the old tree.

The night was so beautiful, it needed just such a silhouette to complete the picture.

'Is that you, brother Ma?'

'Yes.' Surprisingly, I didn't feel at all flustered.

'Have you come from the stream?'

'You . . . Who are you?'

'I'm Fourth Sister.'

'Fourth Sister! How tall you've grown. I wouldn't have recognized you if I ran into you outside the village.'

'You moved about in the big world, that's why you think everything has changed.'

'How's your family?'

She suddenly went quiet and turned to look at the oil-press. When she spoke again, her voice was strained, 'My sister, she hated you. . . .'

'Hated me. . . .' All tensed up, I darted a glance at the path leading to the light and the open space, ready to run. 'It's . . . it's hard to explain. . . . I've told her. . . .'

'Then why did you put corn into her basket that day? Didn't you know what that meant? How can you put things in a young woman's basket just like that? When she gave you a strand of her hair, didn't you know what that meant?'

'I . . . I didn't understand. I didn't know your customs. I . . . I wanted her to help me, so I let her carry a few cobs of corn.'

Not a bad answer, I thought. I'd probably muddle through.

'Everyone was talking about the two of you. Were you deaf? I, too, saw you teaching her acupuncture. I saw it with my own eyes.'

'She was keen. She wanted to be a doctor. Actually, I didn't know much about acupuncture then, I just messed about with the needles.'

'You city people can't be trusted.'

'Please don't say that!'

'It's true! It's true!'

'I know . . . your sister is a nice girl, I know. She sings beautifully and sews well. Once she took us to catch eels and she caught one every time she put her hand into the water. She cried when I was ill. . . . I know all that. But there are lots of things you don't understand, and it's hard to explain. I'll be busy rushing about all my life. I . . . I've got my career.'

So 'career' was the word I finally chose, although it sounded a bit awkward.

She covered her face and started to cry. 'That man Hu, he was so vicious.'

I thought I knew what she meant, so I ventured an answer, 'So I've heard. I'll make him pay for it.'

'But what's the use? What's the use?' She stamped her foot and cried even more disconsolately, 'If you'd said a word or two in those days, things wouldn't have come to such an end. My sister has become a bird, she comes here day after day to call you, to call you. Can't you hear?'

I looked at her in the moonlight. Her thin gaunt back was heaving gently, the nape of her neck was smooth and the white scalp at the parting of her hair was shimmering in the dark. I really wanted to wipe away her tears, grab her by the shoulder, kiss the white scalp like I would my sister's, and let her salty tears drop onto my lips and swallow them.

But I checked myself; this was a strange story and I didn't dare to lick it lest it should burst.

There really was a lone bird calling in the tree. 'Don't go, brother! Don't go, brother!' The sound, solitary, desolate, shot high into the sky like an arrow and then dropped swiftly into the mountains, into the forests, into the dark clouds in the distance and the noiseless thunder and lightning. I lit a cigarette, watching the storm.

'Don't go, brother! Don't go, brother!'

I left the village. Before I left, I wrote Fourth Sister a letter and asked the woman from Liangjiashe to pass it on to her. I said in the letter that her sister had wanted to be a doctor, and although she didn't become one in the end, I hoped Fourth Sister would fulfil her sister's wish. After all, one's life is in one's own hands. Would she like to sit the exam for the medical school? I'd send her lots of material to help her prepare for the exam, I promised. And I said I'd never forget her sister. I told her that Ai Ba had caught the parrot from the tree and I'd take it with me and let it sing every day at my window and be my friend forever.

I felt as if I had run away from the village, for I left without saying goodbye to anyone, without taking the fragrant rice either. But what did I want the rice or the opium for? It seemed that I didn't come for those things. I felt suffocated—by the village, by my own inexplicable self. I had to run away. Turning back to take a last look at the village, I saw again the old tree that had been struck dead by lightning standing behind the blockhouse, its withered branches stretching out like convulsing fingers. The owner of those fingers had died in a battle and turned into a mountain, but he was still struggling to hold up his hands, to grasp at something.

I stopped at an inn in the county town and soon fell asleep amidst the babble of the parrot by my bedside. I had a dream. In it, I was on a dirt track in the mountain, walking. The track had been so badly washed out by water running down the slopes that it looked like a body stripped of skin and flesh, leaving exposed sticks of dry bones and lumps of shrivelled innards to bear the trampling of the straw sandals of the mountain folk. The road seemed to go on forever. I looked at my calendar watch—I had been walking for an hour, a day, a week . . . but I was still on the same track. And no matter where I went afterwards, I always had this dream.

I woke with a start, got up three times to drink some water, and went to the toilet twice. Finally, I phoned a friend. I had wanted to ask him whether he had managed to 'wipe out' Mad Cao at cards, but I found myself talking to him about exams for self-study courses instead.

My friend called me 'Huang Zhixian'.

'What?'

'What do you mean what?'

'What did you call me?'

'Aren't you Huang Zhixian?'

'Did you call me Huang Zhixian?'

'Didn't I call you Huang Zhixian?'

I was stunned, my mind a complete blank. Oh yes, I was in an inn. In the passageway, mosquitoes and moths were fluttering about the dim light bulb, and there was a row of makeshift beds. Just beneath the mouthpiece of the phone there was a fat head snoring. But was there someone called Huang Zhixian in this world? And was this Huang Zhixian me?

I'm tired, I'll never be able to get away from that gigantic 'I'! Mama!

1985

NOTES

1 Liangjiashe is the name of a village in Sanjiangkou. Both are imaginary place names supposed to be in Hunan Province, China.
2 A production brigade in Xiyang County, Shanxi Province; the pace-setter for agriculture in China, during the Cultural Revolution.

10

His Son's Big Doll

By **HWANG CHUN-MING**
Translated by Howard Goldblatt

Hwang Chun-ming 黃春明 *(Huang Chunming, b. 1939) has had a rebellious character since childhood. He had to transfer several times from one school to another for his 'misbehaviour.' He only finished his tertiary education after attending three schools, finally obtaining his teacher's certificate from Pingdong Normal College. Since then he has had a number of jobs ranging from that of a day-labourer to a high-salaried executive, yet he seldom stays in one job for longer than a year. Many of his stories made their first appearance in the literary supplement of the* United Daily News *(*Lianhe bao 聯合報*) and the magazines* Youshi Literature and Arts *(*Youshi wenyi 幼獅文藝*) and* Literature Quarterly *(*Wenxue jikan 文學季刊*). He has published five collections of short stories,* His Son's Big Doll *(*Erzi de da wan'ou 兒子的大玩偶*, 1969),* The Young Widow *(*Xiao guafu 小寡婦*, 1975),* Sayonara-Zaijian *(*Shayounala zaijian 莎喲娜啦，再見*, 1974),* The Gong *(*Lo 鑼*, 1985), and* I Love Mary *(*Wo ai Mali 我愛瑪莉*, 1979). He writes generally from his own experience with themes about humble people in their humble lives. For this reason, he is labelled a 'nativist' writer, as opposed to the Western-inspired modernist experiments that were popular in Taiwan in the 1960s and early 1970s. His keen observation of rural life in Taiwan offers the reader an opportunity to see how individuals react to a rapidly changing society.*

In foreign countries there is an occupation called the 'sandwich-man'.[1] This line of work one day suddenly made its appearance in the little town, but no one could come up with a fitting term, nor knew what it was supposed to be called. Eventually, someone—just who is not known—coined the term 'adman' for a person engaged in this work, and once the term became known in town, everyone, young and old, quickly grew accustomed to saying 'the adman'. Even babies cradled in their mothers' arms would stop crying and fussing and raise their heads to look around whenever their mothers called out: 'Look, here comes the adman!'

The sun, like a fireball rolling along overhead, followed the people below, causing the perspiration to flow freely. For Kunshu this sort of hot day was particularly unbearable, for he was attired from head to toe in a strange costume that made him look like a nineteenth-century European military officer. He was the centre of attention not only because of the way he was made up, but even more so because of this heavy costume. But then that was what this job of his was all about—attracting attention. The sweat coursing down through the make-up on his face gave him the appearance of a melting wax statue; the false moustache stuffed up into his nostrils was soaked with sweat, making it necessary for him to breathe through his mouth. Only the waving feathers atop his high conical hat gave an appearance of coolness. He longed to escape the heat by walking under the arcade, but the movie advertisements he was carrying over his shoulders made this impossible. Two more ad-boards had recently been added below the original advertisements: the one in front proclaimed the virtues of Hundred-Herb Tea, the one behind plugged a tapeworm medicine. As a result, when he walked down the street, he looked like a puppet on a string. The added load was more tiring, of course, but he consoled himself with the thought that the additional money was worth the increased fatigue.

He had regretted going into this line of work from the very first day, and he was eager to find another. The more he thought about what he was doing, the more ridiculous it seemed. He laughed, even if no one else did, and this self-imposed mental torment was forever on his mind, increasing in intensity as his fatigue grew. He'd better find a new line of work. But then he had had the same thought for more than a year.

In the heat, the glare of the asphalt road ahead made it impossible for him to see anything. Off in the distance everything was shrouded in a bile-coloured haze, which he dared not even try to look through. For if he were actually to collapse there, as he feared he might, that would be the end of it for him. He summoned up all his willpower to struggle against the pall of colour before his eyes that seemed bent on hounding him to death. Damn it! This is no job for a man. But whom was he to blame?

'Say, boss, since this movie-house of yours just opened, it won't hurt to give it a try. Try it for a month, and if I don't produce results, you don't have to pay me. I can take your movie ads to the people far better than any billboard. What do you say?'

'What sort of costume do you have in mind?'

It wasn't so much what I said as it was my pitiful look that aroused his sympathy and made up his mind.

'If you'll give me the go-ahead, you can leave everything to me.'

Getting this damned job was the most exciting thing that had ever happened in my life.

'Well, you finally got yourself a job.'

Damn it! Ah-Zhu was so happy about this job she was in tears.

'Ah-Zhu, now you don't need to get an abortion.'

It's only right that Ah-Zhu was in tears about this. She's a strong woman—that was the first time I had ever seen her cry with such helpless abandon. I knew she was very happy.

At this point in his thoughts Kunshu couldn't keep from shedding tears himself; they flowed unchecked, partly because he didn't have a hand free to wipe them away and partly because he was thinking, *What the hell, no one can tell if it's sweat or tears anyway!* This thought seemed to encourage his tears to flow faster. Under the scorching sun he felt the two lines of hot tears flowing down his cheeks, and for the first time in his life he experienced the satisfying relief of an unrestrained cry.

'Kunshu, just look at yourself! What in the world have you turned into? You don't look like a proper man or a proper ghost! How could you let yourself come to this?'

On the evening of his second day on the job, Ah-Zhu told him that his uncle had come several times that day. He was changing his clothes when his uncle came shouting his way in.

'Uncle. . . .'

I should have stopped calling him Uncle long ago. Uncle! Uncle be damned!

'Don't you call me Uncle, the way you're made up!'

'Uncle, hear me out. . . .'

'What's there to say! Is this the only job around? I believe anyone willing to be an ox can find a plow. I'll tell you to your face—I want you to get the hell out of here and not bring disgrace down on your community. If you don't heed my warning, don't be surprised if you're disowned by your own uncle!'

'I've been looking everywhere for a job. . . .'

'What? You looked everywhere and you came up with this ridiculous dead-end job!'

'There wasn't anything I could do. I tried to borrow rice from you, but you wouldn't. . . .'

'What? Is that my responsibility? Is it? I don't have rice to spare. I bought that rice little by little. Besides, what does all this have to do with that ridiculous job of yours? Stop talking nonsense! You. . . .!'

Nonsense? Who's talking nonsense? That makes my blood boil! Uncle! So what? Screw him!

'Then just leave me alone! Leave me alone leave me alone leave me alone!'

He's driving me crazy!

'You dumb beast! Okay, you dumb beast, if you want to defy me, go ahead and defy me. From now on I am no longer Kunshu's uncle! We're through!'

'If we're through, we're through. With an uncle like you, I'd starve to death anyway.'

A good reply. How did I ever think of a reply like that? As he left he was cursing a blue streak. I really didn't feel like going to work the next day, not because I was afraid of offending my uncle, but because for some reason I was in the dumps. If I hadn't noticed the tears in Ah-Zhu's eyes, reminding me of my promise to her—'Ah-Zhu, now you won't have to have an abortion'—and how I had already thrown away the two packets of medicine, I'm sure I wouldn't have had the courage to walk through the door.

Thoughts. They were the only things that helped Kunshu get through the day; without them, the passage of time would have been agonizingly slow as he made his dozen or so rounds every day, from early morning till late at night, up and down every street and lane in town. His mind was active as a natural result of his loneliness and solitude. He seldom thought about the future, and even when he did, it was only about the practical problems of the next few days.

Mostly he thought of the past, a past that he judged by present-day standards.

The blazing fireball overhead followed him as he left the asphalt street. The bile-coloured pall was still there a short distance ahead of him, and he was troubled by the sinking feeling that engulfed him. The mood of anxiety thus forced upon him was a little like the feeling he had every morning at dawn: as he lay on his bed, watching the first rays of the sun seep in through the cracks in the wall amidst the surrounding darkness, the stillness, and that dampness peculiar to this house, his mood would change suddenly from one of tranquillity to one of fear. Though this was something he had grown accustomed to, it was almost like a brand new experience each day. His monthly income didn't amount to much, but it was certainly no worse by comparison than the income from other jobs. It was the tedium and the ridiculous nature of the job that nearly drove him mad. But without the money it brought in, his family's rudimentary livelihood would have presented an immediate problem. So what was he to do? Finally he would force himself to climb out of bed uneasily and, with a certain sense of shame, sit down at Ah-Zhu's little dressing table, take some face powder from the drawer, and rub it onto his face before the mirror. Looking in the mirror with only half of his face painted, he would smile sorrowfully as waves of vague emptiness surged through his mind.

He felt that all the water in his body was gone—he had never been so thirsty! The prostitutes in the red-light district next to the elementary school were standing around food stands snacking in their pajamas and wooden clogs. Others were sitting in doorways making up their faces or just leaning in the doorways or buying their heads in comic books to pass the time. The few families that lived in this red-light district either barricaded themselves behind tightly closed doors or had put up fences in front of their homes; as an added measure, each house sported a sign alongside the door with the words 'Regular Household' painted in large red letters.

'Hey, the adman's coming!' one of the prostitutes called out from a food stand. The others turned their heads to look at the signboard hanging in front of Kunshu. He mechanically approached the food stand.

'Hey! What's playing at the Palace Theatre?' one of the prostitutes asked as the adman passed by.

He mechanically walked past them.

'Have you lost your marbles? That guy never talks,' one of them said laughingly to the prostitute who had asked the question.

'Is he a mute?' The prostitutes began chatting among themselves.

'Who knows what he is?'

'I've never seen him smile either. His face is always lifeless.'

He was only a few steps away from them, and their words pierced his heart.

'Hey! Adman, come here! I'm waiting for you,' one of the prostitutes yelled, running after him. Amidst the ensuing laughter, someone said:

'If he really does come to you, it'll be a wonder if you don't die of fright.'

He continued walking away from them, but he could still hear the prostitute's provocative comments. At the end of the lane he smiled.

I'm willing. If I had the cash I'd be willing. I'd choose the daydreamer leaning up against Xianle's door.

Passing through this red-light district helped him forget his fatigue for the moment. He saw by a clock on the street that it was nearly three-fifteen. He had to hurry to the train station to meet the passengers coming in from the north. This was all part of his arrangement with the boss: he had to mingle, for instance, with the factory workers as they left work and the high-school students when school was out.

He had managed his time so that he didn't have to rush or take any shortcuts. As he emerged from the Eastern Lights area and turned toward the train station, the passengers he had come to meet were just then filing out of the exits, so he approached them from the shady side of the street. This was one of his methods of operation: the heat was still so intense it could bake a potato, and the departing passengers scooted across the open area and quickly moved under the sheltered arcade where the transport company was located. The only people who were at all interested in him were a few out-of-towners. He wouldn't have known what to do if it hadn't been for the encouragement he received from those few unfamiliar, curious faces. He was confident that he could look at any of their faces and tell you who was from out of town, who was local, and exactly when and where they were most likely to appear.

But no matter how things looked, he could not hold onto this job by relying solely on these few unfamiliar faces. Sooner or later the boss was bound to find out. The reaction of the people in front of him made his heart sink.

I've got to think of something else.

A conflict was raging in his heart.

'Look! Look over there!'

During my first days on the job, everyone looked at me with the astonishment of someone seeing a ghost.

'Who's he?'

'Where'd he come from?'

'Is he from our town?'

'Can't be!'

'Yo! It's an ad for the Palace Theatre.'

'Where in the world is he from?'

I'll be damned! What's so interesting about me? Why don't they pay more attention to the ad? In those days I was an object of real interest to them—I was a riddle. Damn! Now that they all know I'm Kunshu, and the riddle has been solved, no one pays me any more attention. What's it all got to do with me anyway? Isn't the ad changing all the time? But the gleam in those cold, curious eyes!

It was all the same to Kunshu—being the centre of attention and being ignored were equally painful to him.

He made a sweep around the train station, then meandered back to the street in front. Unable to reconcile the conflict of an inner cold and an outer heat, he reacted only with a few inward curses. The bile-coloured pall reappeared some five or six metres ahead of him, and his throat was so parched it seemed about to crack. At that moment his home exerted a powerful pull on him.

She won't fail to make tea for me today because of what happened last night, will she? Ai! I was wrong not to go home for lunch, and I should have returned home for tea in the morning. That'll only add to her misunderstanding. Damn it anyway!

'What are you so mad about? And why take it out on me? Can't you lower your voice a little? Ah-Long's sleeping.'

I shouldn't have taken my anger out on her. It's all the fault of that cheapskate—he wouldn't go along with my suggestion to change the costume. 'That's your affair!' he had said. My affair? That damned dog-turd. This costume, which I made out of a fireman's uniform, has lost its appeal. Besides, it's not the sort of thing to be wearing in scorching weather like this!

'I'll talk as loud as I please!'

Whew! That was going too far. But what was I to do with all that anger inside me? I was bushed, and Ah-Zhu wasn't using her head. Why couldn't she put herself in my place instead of arguing with me?

'Are you trying to pick on me?'

'What if I am?'

Damn it, Ah-Zhu, I didn't mean it!

'Really?'

'Stop it!' Then he had added gruffly: 'Shut up or I'll . . . I'll slug you!' He had clenched his fist tightly and slammed it down hard on the table.

It must have worked, because she shut up. I was worried that she would try to stand up to me, and I wouldn't be able to stop myself from hitting her. But I really didn't mean it. Honestly, I shouldn't have frightened Ah-Long awake. The way Ah-Zhu held the crying child tightly in her arms was enough to tug on anyone's heart-strings. My throat's so dry I can't stand it, and it doesn't look like I'll get any tea today. Serves me right! No, I'm too thirsty.

Occupied with thoughts of what had happened last night, before he knew it he was standing in front of the door to his house. He was shocked back to the here and now. The door was slightly ajar, and as he nudged it with his foot it swung open lightly on its hinges. He laid down his ad-board, tucked his hat under his arm, and entered. The big teapot was on the table beside a bamboo food cover, a big green plastic cup covering the spout. She had made tea! A warm feeling flooded Kunshu's heart—he was greatly relieved. He poured himself a full cup of tea and gulped it down. It was the ginger tea with brown sugar that Ah-Zhu had been preparing for him every day since the beginning of summer, and which was waiting for him each time he passed by the house. Someone had once told Ah-Zhu that ginger tea is a good tonic for a tired man. He was so thirsty he filled the cup again, but he felt his heart filling with anxiety. Normally it didn't bother him if Ah-Zhu wasn't there when he came home for tea, but thoughts of his unreasonable loss of temper with her the night before unsettled and distressed him. He put down the cup and looked under the food cover and into the rice pot, discovering that nothing had been touched. Ah-Long was not asleep in his bed, and the clothes Ah-Zhu had washed for others were neatly folded—Where was everybody?

When Kunshu left that morning without eating breakfast, Ah-Zhu was unable to check the deep concern in her heart. At first she wanted to call him back to eat breakfast, but she hesitated a moment, and before she knew it, he was already across the street. They hadn't spoken a word. As always, she strapped Ah-Long onto her back and went out to wash other people's clothes. She was so disturbed she didn't know what to do with herself, so she scrubbed the clothes extra hard—so hard that the movements of her body made it impossible for Ah-Long to cram into his mouth the soap dish he was holding to satisfy his sucking instinct. He threw the soap dish away and cried angrily. Ah-Zhu continued to scrub the clothes hard, evidently unaware that the child was crying more and more loudly; in the past she had never let Ah-Long cry so pitifully without paying him any attention.

'Ah-Zhu,' the mistress called to her through the bathroom window overlooking the washroom.

Her head lowered, Ah-Zhu continued to scrub the clothes.

'Ah-Zhu!' The amiable woman was forced to raise her voice.

Startled, Ah-Zhu stopped her work and straightened up to hear what the mistress had to say. Then she suddenly became aware of Ah-Long's cries and reached back to gently pat his bottom with a wet hand. She cocked her head to listen to the mistress.

'Didn't you know your baby was screaming?' Her voice, while mildly reproachful, was as amiable as ever.

'This child of mine. . . .' There was really nothing she could say. 'Even with a soap dish to play with he still cries!' She lowered her left shoulder and looked back at the child. 'Where's your soap dish?' Quickly discovering the cast-off soap dish on the floor, she bent over, picked it up, rinsed it off, and handed it back to Ah-Long. Then she stooped down again and picked up the clothes, but before she could begin scrubbing, the mistress spoke to her:

'That's a brand new dress you have in your hands, so don't scrub so hard.'

Ah-Zhu could not remember how she had been washing the dress, but there didn't seem to be any call for this reminder by the mistress.

After finally managing to hang up all the clothes, Ah-Zhu rushed out onto the street with Ah-Long on her back. She threaded her way through the marketplace and the main section of town, looking up and down the streets anxiously, searching for Kunshu in vain. She racked her brain thinking of places where she might find him. Finally she caught a glimpse of him off in the distance, carrying his ad-board high as he walked down People's Rights Road toward the Town Hall. She ran after him in high spirits, and before long his back was fully visible to her. She lowered her left shoulder and put her face up close to Ah-Long's.

'Look, Ah-Long, there's Daddy.' The way she pointed at Kunshu's back and her tone of voice had the qualities of cringing inferiority. There was too great a distance separating them for Ah-Long to know what was going on. Ah-Zhu stood by the side of the road and followed Kunshu's back with her eyes until it disappeared at the crossroads. At that moment the outermost layer of anxiety was stripped from her heart. She wondered what Kunshu was thinking, for there had been a message in his not eating. Still she received some consolation from the sight of him carrying his signs as usual. But the mixture of this relieving thought with those other disturbing elements produced a confusion in her mind even more unbearable than her original fears. Seeing Kunshu like this only changed her mood—it did nothing to lessen her anxiety. She decided to go over to the next home and wash their clothes.

The moment she came home after finishing her work, she went over and removed the lid of the teapot: the pot was still full and the rice porridge had not been touched, proof that Kunshu had not been home today. Something was definitely wrong. Or so she thought. She had intended to put the sleeping Ah-Long to bed, but now she could not. She rushed back outside, closing the door behind her.

The heat of the fireball overhead was intense, and most of the pedestrians had sought refuge under the arcade, making it much easier for Ah-Zhu to look for Kunshu. At each cross-street she stood in the intersection and looked in both directions until she determined that he was not there. Finally she spotted him near the lumber yard on Chiang Kai-shek Avenue North heading toward the Temple of the Goddess of the Sea. She followed him discreetly at a distance of seven or eight houses, being careful lest he turn around and see her. Noticing nothing out of the ordinary about his behaviour from the rear, she hid herself behind arcade posts several times, closing the distance to two or three houses, and continued to watch him. Still nothing out of the ordinary. Nonetheless, she felt very uneasy over his refusal to eat or drink. And she was not reassured by what she was seeing. Convinced that something was wrong, she feared that something had come between them.

She suddenly felt a need to see him from the front, figuring that a look at his face might tell her what she wanted to know. So she followed him to an intersection, and when she saw that he continued walking straight ahead, she ran on ahead several blocks and hid herself behind a pedlar's stand near the Temple of the Goddess of the Sea. There she waited for Kunshu to appear. The pounding of her heart increased as she impatiently awaited his approach. When he drew near, she quickly squatted down behind the pedlar's stand, ignoring the inquisitive looks on the faces of bystanders, and looked around the stand to see Kunshu as he passed in front of her. In that brief instant all she could see was the profile of his sweltering face, the tracks of perspiration reminding her that she, too, was sweating profusely. Even Ah-Long was bathed in sweat.

This pursuit had stripped away some of the layers of worry inside her, but the innermost layers were so sensitive that the slightest touch was painful. Ah-Zhu now placed all of her vague hopes on the noon meal. After finishing her washing at the last house, she went home and prepared lunch. Then she sat down to wait for Kunshu, the baby Ah-Long at her breast. But she began to grow restless when he still had not appeared after some time.

With Ah-Long on her back, she went out and found Kunshu on the road leading through the park. More than once she nearly found the courage to go up to him and beg him to come home to eat, but each time, as she started to draw near to him, this courage left her suddenly and without a trace. So she just kept her distance and tagged along behind him, quietly and forlornly. Street after street, lane upon lane, she followed him, blaming herself for having talked back to him the night before, which had so far cost him two meals and his tea as he walked the streets on this sweltering day. Every few steps she had to wipe away her tears with the end of the carrying cloth strapped around her back.

When she finally saw Kunshu turn toward home, she was so happy she grew somewhat tense. Taking a different road, she arrived ahead of him and stationed herself at the mouth of the lane opposite their place, where she could observe how he approached the house and see whether or not he ate lunch. Here came Kunshu. He stopped for a moment in front of the door. When Ah-Zhu saw him finally enter the house her tears were flowing so heavily that she covered her face with her hands and leaned her head against the wall for support, feeling a great surge of relief. She could see his every movement inside the house and could guess what he was feeling at the moment—he was probably looking for her anxiously. This thought gave her a sense of well-being.

Just as Kunshu was about to leave the house, Ah-Zhu, feeling depressed and unable to wait any longer, with Ah-Long on her back, entered quickly, her head downcast. (At the very moment she was bounding across the street, filled with the happiness of having seen him drink some tea from her vantage point across the street, his feeling of depression had been almost overwhelming.) The two of them seemed to shed a heavy emotional burden simultaneously—he having seen his wife walk through the door, she having seen her husband drink some tea. Ah-Zhu kept her head lowered as she busied herself with removing the food cover and filling Kunshu's rice bowl. He slipped the signboards over his head and placed them off to the side, then sat down at the table after unbuttoning his shirt. He ate his food in silence. Ah-Zhu filled her own rice bowl, sat down opposite him, and began to eat. Since they did not say a word to one another, all that could be heard in the room was a munching sound like that made by hogs at the trough. When Kunshu got up and refilled his rice bowl, Ah-Zhu quickly raised her head to catch a glimpse of his back, then just as quickly lowered it again and resumed eating. When she in turn got to her feet, he caught a hurried glance of her back before looking away as she turned back around.

Finally he could stand this oppressive silence no longer:

'Is Ah-Long asleep?' He knew quite well that Ah-Long was sleeping on his mother's back.

'Yes.' Her head remained bowed.

More silence.

He looked at Ah-Zhu, but when he thought that she was about to raise her head, he immediately looked away. He broke the silence again:

'The blacksmith shop at Red-Tile Corners caught fire early this morning. Did you know that?'

'I know.'

Her answer cut short what he was going to say. He paused for a moment.

'Two children were killed on the street this morning right in front of the noodle shop.'

'Huh!' Her head shot up, but she quickly lowered it again when she saw that he was just about to raise his head from his rice bowl. 'How did that happen?' She was eager to know, but her tone of voice lacked the excitement of her initial exclamation.

'Some sacks of rice fell off an oxcart and crushed the kids hanging onto the back.'

Ever since beginning this line of work, Kunshu had more or less become Ah-Zhu's exclusive reporter of local news. He reported to her daily and in great detail everything that occurred in the town. Sometimes he came to her with an extra news flash like, for instance, the time on Park Road when he saw a long line of people stretching from the side entrance of the Catholic church all the way to the street. He rushed back home to tell her that the Catholic church was distributing free flour, then returned that evening to find two large sacks of flour and a can of powdered milk lying on the table.

Though a note of awkwardness was discernible in their conversation, they had now reestablished a line of amicable communication. Kunshu buttoned his shirt, checked his equipment, and, to keep the conversation going, asked: 'Is Ah-Long asleep?'

What a dumb question. I already asked that!

'Yes,' she answered.

But Kunshu, utterly embarrassed by his own question, didn't even hear her response. Wanting to get out of there in a hurry, he left hastily without even turning his head back. As Ah-Zhu walked over and stood in the doorway to watch her husband walk off, she rocked the baby on her back and gently patted his behind with her hand. The whole reconciliation process had taken about half an hour, during which time their eyes had never once met.

The wall of the Farmers' Association granary was not only high, but it also seemed to people to be uncannily long. Because of this huge wall the winds swirled round and round the area. The wall also cast a great shadow over the low houses across the way, and this was where Kunshu was headed. He was feeling much better now, and there was no longer a bile-coloured pall anywhere in front of him as far as he could see. With the numbness gone from his shoulders, he could once again feel the weight of the ads draped over his head. Calculating the time of day, he cursed the length of time remaining before nightfall, for he wanted very badly to take Ah-Zhu to bed. Experience showed him that that was all they needed to remove any bad blood between them. Actually, the removal of these marital ill feelings was an incidental benefit; he didn't know why, but whenever the animosity between them grew to a certain level, his sexual desires were aroused. The sun-drenched day became the object of his curses.

As sparrows chirped incessantly around the granary, he thought back to his childhood, when the land beneath this row of low houses had been completely vacant. He remembered how he and several of his playmates had often come here to shoot sparrows—he had been an excellent hand with a slingshot.

He was being scrutinized by several sparrows perched on the telephone wires, and though he turned his head to look at them, he didn't slacken his pace, so that the angle of his head and eyes changed with each step. He was suddenly brought up short by the sound of running footsteps approaching him from behind. He turned his head, just as he had done in years past when he was watching out for the old man at the granary. This reflex amused him. The old man had died long ago, when Kunshu was still shooting sparrows, and they had found his body near the well beside the granary. With these thoughts in mind, he gradually left the sparrows on the telephone wires behind him.

A group of children playing in the mud by the side of the road left their games and ran toward him giggling and laughing. They kept a safe distance from him as he walked along, those in front walking backwards and facing him. Prior to the birth of Ah-Long, he had been angered by the constant pestering of children on the street. But now things were different: now he would make faces at them, which not only delighted the children, but somehow also gave him great pleasure. It was the sort of feeling he had every time he played with the laughing Ah-Long.

'Ah-Long! Ah-Long!'

'Go on, get out of here. You don't have to be cute with him.'

'Ah-Long, bye-bye, bye-bye. . . .'

This is how Kunshu took his leave of them nearly every day. Whenever Ah-Long saw his daddy walk out the door, he would cry and make a scene, sometimes trying to keep him from leaving by bending over backwards in his mother's arms. Then it would be up to Ah-Zhu to say things like, 'He's your child, and he'll still be here when you get back,' before Kunshu would reluctantly drag himself away.

The boy really likes me.

Kunshu was very happy. This job had enabled them to have Ah-Long, who in turn enabled him to endure the hardships the job forced upon him.

'Don't be silly! Do you think it's really you that Ah-Long likes? What he thinks he has is somebody who looks like you do now!'

At the time I nearly misunderstood what Ah-Zhu was saying.

'When you go out in the morning, he's either asleep or else I've put him on my back to go out and wash clothes. During most of his waking hours you're made up like you are now, and when you come home at night he's asleep.'

It's not as bad as that, is it? But the boy is shying away from strangers these days.

'He likes the way you dress up and make faces at him. It's no secret that you're his big doll.'

Oh! I'm Ah-Long's big doll, his big doll!

The child walking backwards in front of him pointed and yelled: 'Ha-ha, look here, quick. The adman, he's smiling. The adman's saying something and his eyes and mouth are all twisted!'

I'm a big doll, a big doll.

He was smiling. The long shadow he cast ahead of him did not seem at all like a man's shadow, because of the ad-boards over his shoulders. The children were making a game of stepping on his shadow. One of the children's mothers was calling to him from somewhere far behind Kunshu; the child reluctantly stopped what he was doing and looked up, then enviously looked at his playmates, whose mothers were not calling an end to their play.

Kunshu inwardly admired Ah-Zhu's cleverness, musing over her metaphor: 'A big doll, a big doll.'

'Born in the year of the dragon, what better name for him than Ah-Long—Little Dragon?'

If Ah-Zhu had had any schooling, she would have been a good student. But then if she had had schooling, she wouldn't have married me.

'Xu Ah-Long.'

'Is this the way you write *long*—dragon?'

That fellow who handled birth certificates was really something—he knew perfectly well that I only asked him to fill in the form because I don't know how to write, so why did he have to ask that in such a loud voice?

'It's dragon, like in the solar cycle.'

'He was born in June. Why didn't you come and report it earlier?'

'We only named him today.'

'Since you didn't report the birth within three months, there's a fine of fifteen dollars.'

'We didn't even know we were supposed to register.'

'You didn't know? I'm surprised you knew how to make a baby.'

He really shouldn't have made fun of us like that. He said it so loud that everyone in the Town Hall was looking at us and laughing.

High school students on their way home from school, more serious than adults, carefully read the movie bills on his board. Some even discussed the movies, though one of them remarked: 'What's the use? The military instructors won't let us go see them!' Kunshu didn't comprehend what the boy meant, but he was happy just looking at their bulging book bags, and he was filled with heartfelt admiration.

No one in our family has been to school for three generations. But Ah-Long will be different. The only thing that worries me is that he might not do well there. I've heard it costs a fortune to put a child through school! What a lucky bunch of kids they are!

Two rows of trees lined the sidewalks, one of them throwing spotted shadows onto the street. The workers emerging from the industrial district at the far end of the street lacked the enthusiasm of the high school students; fatigue written plainly on their faces, they walked in silence, the few conversations among them carried on in hushed tones, the rare laughter subdued. Before taking on this job, Kunshu had applied for work in a paper factory, a lumber factory, and a fertilizer factory, and he envied these people their work and the regularity with which they walked down this cool tree-lined road at the same time every day on their way home to rest. Not only that, they had Sundays off. He didn't know why he had been turned down for a job. He had thought long and hard about it, but the answer escaped him.

'How many in your family?'

'Only my wife and me. My parents are both dead. My . . .'

'Okay, okay, I know.'

That's odd. How could he know? I haven't finished. Damn him! After waiting in line all that time for an interview, is that all I'm going to get—two or three questions? Some of the men weren't even asked anything. He just nodded his head and smiled, and they walked off looking very satisfied.

Dusk.

Kunshu looked up at the sun, which was sinking into the sea. The sight quickly filled him with happiness. When he returned to the Palace Theatre, the manager was outside looking at the movie notices. He turned around and said:

'Ah, you're back. Good, I've been looking for you.'

This came as a shock to Kunshu; finding himself momentarily speechless, he finally managed to say: 'What's up?'

'I want to discuss something with you.'

Kunshu quickly tried to grasp the intent of the manager's words and the significance of his cold manner. He carefully leaned the ad signs against the bare wall below the theatre announcement, then removed the boards that sandwiched him. The hand in which he was holding the tall hat was trembling. He wanted desperately to postpone what was coming, but he had exhausted his supply of delaying tactics, and it was time for him to say something. He turned around with great apprehension; his hair, which had been wet but was now dry, stuck to his scalp, and the white powder that had covered his forehead and cheeks had run with the perspiration and was now caked in his eyebrows and the hollows of his cheeks. The skin that showed through was so rough it looked diseased. Finally, he unmindfully removed his false beard and stood there staring blankly ahead, like a strange muted mannequin.

'Do you think this sort of advertising is producing any results?' the manager asked.

'I . . . I . . .' He was so nervous he couldn't speak.

I should have known. This is it!

'Maybe we should try something else.'

'I think so,' Kunshu responded without knowing what he was saying.

If the damn thing's finished, that's just as well. What future is there in this line of work anyway?

'Can you handle a pedicab?'

'A pedicab?' He was crushed.

Shit!

'I . . . I don't think so,' Kunshu continued.

'There's nothing to it. You'll get the hang of it in no time.'

'Uh-huh.'

'I'm thinking of switching to a pedicab for advertising. In addition to riding around on the pedicab, you'll continue to help out until we close at night. The same wages.'

'Right.'

Whew! That was close! I thought I was finished.

'Tomorrow morning you go with me to the shop to fetch the pedicab.'

'What about these?' He pointed to the signs leaning against the wall, but what he really wanted to know was, could he stop using make-up.

The manager pretended he didn't hear him and walked inside.

Stupid! Why did I have to ask that?

He felt like laughing, but didn't know just what was so funny. He hadn't a clue. He opened his mouth wide as though to laugh, but no sound emerged. On the road home he casually carried all of his equipment over his shoulder, which unexpectedly drew astonished looks from passersby; the townspeople had never seen him like this before, with his tall hat tucked under his arm.

'Take a good look, it'll be your last chance.' He was so exhilarated he felt he could actually fly.

What a ridiculous job! He remembered when he was a child, and a traveling moving-picture show had come to town from somewhere—oh, right, it was a show at the steps of the church—and he, Ah-Xing, and some other friends had climbed up an acacia tree to watch. One of the moving pictures had shown an adman dressed up just like him being pestered by a crowd of children. It had left a deep impression on their young minds, and afterwards they had often dressed up like that to play games. *Who would have thought that as an adult those games would turn into reality for me? That's really funny.*

'Damn that short movie scene and its damned consequences. It's damned funny.' As he walked down the road with his thoughts, he mumbled incessantly to himself.

Scenes of past events came to his mind one after the other.

'Ah-Zhu, if I don't find a job soon, you'll have to get rid of the baby you're carrying. This medicine is supposed to work during the first month of pregnancy. Don't be afraid—it'll all just come out in the form of blood and water.'

That was close!

'Ah-Zhu, now you won't have to have an abortion.'

If that's the case, then if I hadn't seen the outdoor movie, Ah-Long might not be here today! It's a good thing I climbed that acacia tree.

The strange thing was, this job that he had tried so unsuccessfully to give up and which had been the object of his curses, he now viewed with a certain degree of affection. But affection is all it was. The inner happiness he was feeling now easily won out over all other emotions.

'Kunshu you're back!' Ah-Zhu called out loudly with an uncharacteristic exuberance as she saw her husband off in the distance making his way home.

This took Kunshu completely by surprise. How in the world could Ah-Zhu have found out? If he weren't so preoccupied, Kunshu would have viewed this display of affection by Ah-Zhu as too sudden and too bold; usually, this sort of thing caused him prolonged embarrassment.

As he drew nearer, but not yet near enough to say anything, Ah-Zhu blurted out: 'I knew your luck would change.' She seemed unwilling to hold anything back. This time Kunshu was really stunned. 'Can you handle a pedicab?' she continued. 'It doesn't make any difference anyway. You'll get the hang of it in no time at all. Jinchi wants to sub-lease his pedicab to you. As for the details. . . .'

Now he understood the coincidence, and he decided to play a joke on her. 'I know everything,' he said.

'I figured as much when I saw the way you were walking home. What do you think? It doesn't sound bad, does it!'

'No, it doesn't sound bad, but. . . .' He was barely able to keep himself from telling her the happy news. He stopped just as the words were about to tumble out.

Ah-Zhu pressed him anxiously: 'What's the matter?'

'If the manager doesn't want us to do things this way, I don't think we ought to accept Jinchi's offer.'

'Why?'

'Just think: if it hadn't been for this job, I'd hate to think what our lives would be like. Ah-Long might not be here today. Now if I give up this job the moment a better one comes along, that's going a little too far, isn't it?'

He had thought this up on the spur of the moment, but once it was out, the seriousness and importance of what he was saying came to him in a rush, and he grew dead serious. Ah-Zhu, in turn, was gripped by fear, not because she understood what he was saying, but because of his change in demeanour. Obviously disappointed, she nonetheless gained support from her sense of right and wrong. She followed her husband into the house in silence, feeling, in the midst of her bewilderment, a newborn respect for him. Perhaps she was able to accept his explanation so readily because of what he had said about Ah-Long.

They ate diner that night together as usual, the only difference being the silent, mysterious looks Kunshu gave Ah-Zhu from time to time. Though somewhat puzzled by these looks, she was completely reassured by the twinkle in his eye. She was very conscious of the fact that she had already planned their whole future once he began riding a pedicab, without any thoughts for the well-being of the man who was making it all possible, and she felt terribly guilty about this. Kunshu decided to wait until he came home at night, following the last show, to give Ah-Zhu the good news. He put down his rice bowl and walked over to look at Ah-Long, who was fast asleep.

'That child sleeps all day long.'

'It's a good thing he does. Otherwise, I wouldn't be able to get a thing done. The Goddess of Childbirth has been a big help by giving us such a good child.'

He left to go to work at the theatre.

He regretted not having told her the truth right away, because now he didn't know how he would be able to stand the long three-hour wait until closing time. Maybe for other people this was just a commonplace matter, but to Kunshu, who could no longer contain himself, anxiety was bubbling up inside him.

I nearly told her while I was taking my bath. Wouldn't it have been better if I had?

'Why have you flattened out your hat?' Ah-Zhu had asked him.

Ah-Zhu has always been clever, and she knew there was something in the air.

'Oh! Have I?'

'Do you want me to straighten it out for you?'

'No need.'

She was trying to look right through the hat to see if she could discover some secret.

'Oh, all right, straighten it out.'

'How could you be so careless as to ruin the hat like this?'

Go ahead and tell her and be done with it!

Musing over past events like this had already become a habit with Kunshu. He couldn't have changed if he had wanted to. He sat listlessly in the office, thinking about isolated incidents in his life. Even thoughts of events that had caused him pain and discomfort at the time today somehow brought a smile to his face.

'Kunshu.'

Lost in his thoughts, he didn't move.

'Kunshu.' This time it was louder.

He turned around in surprise and smiled awkwardly at the manager.

'The show's about over. Go open the exits, then give a hand at the bicycle rack.'

The day was finally coming to an end. He no longer felt tired. When he arrived home, Ah-Zhu was outside walking around with Ah-Long in her arms.

'Why aren't you in bed?'

'It's too hot in there. Ah-Long couldn't sleep.'

'Here, Ah-Long, let Daddy hold you.'

Ah-Zhu handed him the child and followed him inside. But to their surprise, Ah-Long began to cry, and no matter how Kunshu rocked him or played with him, he wouldn't stop. Indeed, the crying grew progressively louder.

'Silly child, what's wrong with Daddy holding you? Don't you like Daddy? Be a good boy and don't cry, don't cry.'

But not only was Ah-Long crying hard, he was bending backwards, struggling to get out of his father's arms just as he tried to twist out of Ah-Zhu's arms each morning when Kunshu was leaving for work in his costume.

'Naughty boy, why are you crying? Daddy's holding you. Don't you like Daddy anymore? Silly child, it's Daddy! It's your Daddy!' Kunshu kept reminding Ah-Long. 'It's your Daddy. Daddy's holding Ah-Long—look!' He made faces and funny sounds, but all in vain. Ah-Long was crying piteously.

'Here, I'll hold him.'

As Kunshu handed the baby back to Ah-Zhu, he felt his heart suddenly sink. He walked over to Ah-Zhu's dressing table, sat down, and hesitantly opened the drawer. He removed the powder and looked deeply into the mirror, then slowly began making up his face.

'Are you crazy? What are you making up your face for now?' Ah-Zhu was completely mystified by Kunshu's actions.

A momentary silence.

'I . . .' Kunshu's voice was trembling. 'I want Ah-Long to recognize me. . . .'

1968

NOTES

1 English in the original.

11

The Leaper

By **CHANG CHI-JIANG**
Translated by Nancy Du

Chang Chi-jiang 張啟疆 *(Zhang Qijiang, b. 1961) was born in Taiwan and brought up in a military residence compound. Although he graduated from National Taiwan University with a degree in business, his interest lies in writing. He has written short stories, poems, essays, scripts, and cultural critiques. He has published two collections of short stories,* The Visage Like a Blooming Flower *(*Ru hua chuzhan de rongyan 如花初綻的容顏*, 1991) and* The Novel, Novelist and His Wife *(*Xiaoshuo, xiaoshuojia he ta de taitai 小說，小說家和他的太太*, 1993) and a volume of essays,* A Guide to the Blind *(*Dao mang zhe 導盲者*, 1996). Chang Chi-jiang has won many literary awards, including prizes for the best short story from the* Central Daily News *(*Zhongyang ribao 中央日報*) and the* United Daily News *(*Lianhe bao 聯合報*). He is currently vice-chairman of the China Youth Creative Writing Association.*

Suddenly, he was on the rooftop. He extended his arms out like a bird spreading its wings, while his body swung left and right like a white cloud. From our vantage point, looking at his blurry visage against the light, we seemed to see a halo materialize above his head. He stood proud and tall on the summit of the fibreglass building. . . . How was he planning to jump?

I kept wiping the sweat off my forehead and chin, and cleaned the dust that had gathered on my spectacles. An involuntary shiver went up my spine. I had heard so much about the legend of the 'leaper' but it was the first time I was actually going to witness his outlandish behaviour. Come to think of it though, when I wrote my news article I was not sure I would be using a word as concrete as 'witness'. My reason was simple. From the instant I laid eyes on this person, things began going amok, though I can't put my finger on what exactly. All of a sudden I could see, flashing fantastically past, the thoughts and images that always raced through my mind during this period when the 'Leaper Fiasco' was the talk of the town.

A month ago, when news of his first leap broke in Kaohsiung, my instinctive feeling was: scam. It was definitely a scam or gimmick of unclear intention, a trick to camouflage the con. There was nothing new under the sun for people on the editorial desk. As a seasoned reporter with over ten years of experience, I did not take for granted as truth what appeared to have happened, or one man's version of a story. In other words, the so-called 'noise principle' or 'newsworthiness' of events is often determined by us (the 'word manufacturers', a term we used to poke fun at ourselves), and by how readers make sense of what they read. What did I mean by the 'noise principle'? Based on my own experience, I often fail to understand the causal relationship between noise and fact. Does fact exist before noise? Or did the overwhelming wave of voices come together to form fact? It was like the dialectical relationship between the chicken and the egg. Or the Big Bang theory explaining the birth of the universe: did the bang first occur in existing space or did the explosion create space? From this angle, news should be called 'views'—articles that spring from the mind's free interpretations.

Based on misconstrued evidence or overheard rumours, for many years we reporters produced headlines, exclusives, or inside stories that were born in the morning and died in the evening. Three years ago, when I was still covering parliamentary news, I became extremely gifted at interpreting what high-level officials said (we termed it 'A Phrase a Day') and dissecting the actions and thoughts these political animals were attempting to hide. (Perhaps, we had resorted to becoming the megaphones for these politicians?) With my professional knack of smelling something fishy and assessing an even more than politically correct outcome, I could sometimes even forecast the comings and goings of prominent officials, the occurrence of internal strife, splits among political parties, and affiliations and link-ups between factions. During that time, we would end up drunk every night at the karaoke bars or pubs. There was an implicit consensus that we were in the vanguard, shouldering the problems of society:

the violent episodes in parliament, the bloodshed and struggle in the streets . . . none of which was as real as our glasses of wine and loud voices; or should I say the toils of this world existed only in our glasses.

Once, when I was on the brink of inebriation, I offhandedly composed a nonsensical, awkward 'Presidential' address, only to see an exact replica of it the next day on the front page of the morning paper.

For these reasons, I gradually found myself turning into a cynical member of the riffraff, unable to believe lightly in word of mouth or written narrative. (When I read the papers I only read the real estate and pornographic-related advertisements. I tried to savour spontaneous and illicit consumption impulses sparked by the exaggerated and flowery language.) From another angle, I was also like an exorcist in reverse, one with the cold contempt of an agnostic who spread the word of the devil wherever I went. The dichotomy between truth and lies, the murky territory between vagueness and clarity made me sick to my stomach with the notion of 'accurate news' standards—did it imply an accurate rendition of news or was it just an accurate transfer of rumour to readers who could not tell black from white? This explains why a month ago, when slightly intoxicated I heard the stoned Chen go on about the miracle of the leaper (his words flashed like twisted gamma rays on the swirling clouds of my consciousness), I shook my hand crudely at him and downed two shots of tequila consecutively (at the same time, I had come up with the draft of a sensational, reflective, and subversive piece on civilization with headlines that would read: 'The Toppling of Newton's Apple Basket'). I stared at the pair of Woody Allenesque spectacles that rested on the bridge of Chen's nose and said, 'Wake up, man, don't tell me what's news, okay? Have you forgotten that we're the damn thing itself?'

I was wrong. The leaper event was not only one that rocked the three major metropolises, but also 'new news' that left the old-timers questioning all they thought to be true. For news people like us who doubted everything, it really seemed like a breath of fresh air. It shook the foundation of our old ways and our professional sense of judgement.

Speaking for myself, at least during the period when the leaper went 'on circuit', I temporarily stopped numbing myself on alcohol, cigarettes, and the buying and selling of the same stocks all in one day. Every night I used to stay holed up in my room, either in a daze, snickering, or walking around in circles. I reread the books I failed to finish ten years ago. The laughable thing was that as I descended deeper into depression, I started forgetting I was no longer married. The grievances, old unsettled scores between my ex-wife and I, were suddenly like star bursts light years away. I felt like a captain on a Star Trek mission, staring at the dying rays of light in the pitch dark night when I was actually reminiscing about the times of remote antiquity before earth was formed.

The person swayed, he looked like he was about to drop straight down, gasps sounded from the crowd. Miss Li from the newspaper that covered public TV (for the life of me, I couldn't remember her name, just like I couldn't remember my wife's birthday) grabbed onto my arm and moved her head towards the back of my shoulder. After a while she decided to shut her eyes. I didn't dare avert my eyes, not even to blink, I did not want to miss this opportunity to witness for myself what would happen. But perhaps I was concentrating too hard; blurred images appeared before me and I saw double. The entire building began receding as far back as Kuan Yin Mountain. I massaged the bridge of my nose and that familiar sense of despair flooded over me. Behind the man, a circle of light slowly spread, pushing downwards, then ascended like waves of light at high tide. Was the man moving? Or was it the sky? Perhaps it was the earth picking up speed rotating? Or was it merely the trembling of my paralyzed body?

'You're the one that should wake up,' Chen told me a month ago. 'Look at you, the divorce has taken the earth from right under you. Nothing interests you. Let's leave out the sense of morality and conscience for the time being. Whatever happened to your journalistic passion, that determination to get to the bottom of all things? Have you seen the magic of David Copperfield before?'

Apparently, that evening at the pub on Fuchou Street, which was open around the clock, the daily scenario replayed again. Two stinking drunks slugged the hell out of each other, then fell together in an embrace and howled like cows. But later Chen forgot all this took place, while I could only forget the pain of having two of my front teeth knocked out by him. All the rest, every shaking, quaking word he uttered, was as vivid in my hazy, crazy memory as the pulling of wisdom teeth.

'Five years ago, I witnessed how David Copperfield made a real live 747 disappear into thin air. Of course I knew it was a trick of the eye, but the question remained, why did our naked eye, or more explicitly, why did our minds fail to spot the flaw? I kept thinking to myself, was David Copperfield a kind of "magician" or was this a kind of truth called "David Copperfield"? Zhang, open your eyes, stop dozing, how can you call yourself a physics major? Get a good look at the guy leaping off these buildings, he's even weirder than David. I mean it, when you next get the chance, go and savour his magic. . . .'

My eyes were opened wide enough, but not to spot the truth; rather I was hoping to detect the uncertain, incredible, or inexplicable blind spot in the visual chaos. I believed the value of scientific research was not only in proving positive theories but also in showing negative outcomes—at least then you managed to determine the level of ignorance in man. Undeniably, the rumoured leaper had aroused my intellectual interest; he also stimulated a hidden fire within. I spent a whole month searching through caseloads of data with my magnifying glass. I tried to find the crack in physics. What did I want to prove or deny? Did I want to prove with suspicious eyes the affirmation that lay hidden in my consciousness? Or was I trying to use affirmation to enhance my embedded sense of emptiness? Perhaps I should affirm Chen's forgetfulness, and begin to doubt the true origin of that voice that was ingrained in my consciousness (the truth was that a sober Chen could not have come up with those pearls of wisdom). So who was actually speaking? Who borrowed Chen's drunken mouth to utter those enlightening words to me?

Propelled by what was mostly a force greater than me and a fraction of my own initiative, I began studying the tricks of the leaper. The headlines of those few days were really a sight for sore eyes, flamboyant phrases like 'Defying the Limits of Gravity', 'Anti-world, Anti-gravity', 'Water Flows Upwards?', 'The Sky Above the Dead Sea', 'The Devil's Camouflage', 'Newton Must be Crazy', filled the pages. Suddenly, this island seemed to revert back to the far-off Middle Ages when sky-heaving and earth-shaking theories brimmed over. From the old mouldy textbooks I dug out, all the new or classic theories, schools of thought, rules, used rationalizations to seek a balance to find terra firma amidst the tilting of the earth. Yes, the magic of Galileo—different matter falling and hitting the floor at the same instant—was just the result of throwing a few balls down the leaning tower of Pisa in front of a large crowd. Newton's apples, why could they not rise and fall like the moon and become stable and fixed satellites orbiting the globe?

Old Wang from the political section reminded me that this crisis was not a scientific issue but a political incident. 'Although I don't know how he manages it, the whole thing's a metaphor, an ironic form of protest. Haven't you noticed? The background to his first jump in Kaohsiung, the high-rise "Landmark of Southern Taiwan", was the shallow political billboard of the cash-cow legislator. The next few times in Taichung, he chose estates belonging to a well-established businessman-politician: the consortium building of the mayoral faction and the designated stretch of land for new banks under construction to facilitate the "Asia-Pacific Regional Financial Centre". Isn't it clear where all this is pointing to? That kid magician is highlighting the absurdity of our times through his own absurd antics. He is using his symbolic behaviour, and our dumbfounded reactions, to testify to the injustices and unfairness of this society.'

Was this the case? To be honest, I failed to spot his protest and the ironic intention behind it, but I had become increasingly paranoid nonetheless. The kid magician suddenly smiled. Two rows of white sparkling teeth broke through his tanned face. It was a youthful, primitive smile which made it even more difficult to decipher. It resembled the embarrassed, goofy, yet slightly arrogant smile of the 'Baseball Prince' Liao Mingxiong when he hit a home run. (It was really strange. Whenever I saw the little white ball career through the evening sky like a shooting star, I would question the reality of the home run. The movement of the ball was contrary to the rotation of the globe, and the globe rotated around the sun while the sun and other fixed stars were rotating in the Milky Way, as the Milky Way spun round and round.) On the 29-inch TV screen, I suddenly witnessed the phenomenon of 'beads, big and small, bouncing off a tray of jade'.[1] By god, what was happening to my eyes? How was it possible to see changes in his expression from a slanted distance ten storeys below? Perhaps I needed to install a high-resolution computer lens, or better, the compound eyes of an insect.

According to descriptions given by reporters from the different newspapers, the identity of the kid magician was as unclear as his motive for jumping. The reporters could not get an exclusive or special interview with him (most of the pictures in the newspapers were blurred side shots or a view of his back), neither could the police catch this violator of public safety. They could only assess from his dark brawny physique and overly agile movements that he was probably not a kid that grew up in the cities, nor did he resemble a coolie, miner, fruit farmer, or fisherman. Old Li from the literary supplement insisted the kid was an aborigine and, what's more, a native Taiwanese spokesman who harboured historical resentment. Half a month ago on the mahjong table, even Old Li, who was on a winning streak, almost blundered when he was busy defending the kid. 'I swear, the kid's here to seek revenge for his forefathers. For hundreds of years, these aborigines have suffered at the hands of the Fukienese, Hakka, and Mainlanders. In their eyes, we're all the same load of shit. We're building high-rises that are almost as tall as their goddam Alishan Mountain. Think about it, we can dig up their ancestral graves, wreck their hometown, strip their women of underwear—why can't they topple our foundation of civilization? Royal flush by my own hand, another round for me boys, get ready to take off your underwear. Heck, how come it's a fucking "white-block"?'

From the devil-may-care attitude of the kid, Miss Li deduced the 'native' elements contained in the spirit of this native Taiwanese man. She used the example of a gutter: 'When I was little, there was this huge gutter, like a cliff in the back alley of our old house. On the two sides of the gutter, there was only a small space of less than half a metre wide for people to pass through. I was really scared of that long alley and that gutter back then. Every time I passed through I'd experience the fear of falling from a cliff. But the weird thing was, grown-ups always passed through nonchalantly like kings walking on flat ground. Later I realized, the reason grown-ups did not feel "fear" was probably because they had no sense of the "gutter". Haven't you found, as you grow older, more and more things confuse and worry you, while fewer and fewer seem to really frighten and scare you?' I only noticed how her elbows, as if by chance, brushed me three times. She said, 'By the same token, that man's acting like there's no one around him. Is it because his eyes are blind to the high-rises, blind to the buildings, so he can't see civilization, nor you and me?'

I quietly examined the flat features of Miss Li's face and the thin lines around her eyes. Well, she must be thirty-something (did a thirty-something man like myself appear like a fifty-something person in her eyes?). Nonetheless, her irises suggested the inward spreading of a concentric spectrum; they resembled annual tree rings with clearly defined colours. The closer you got to the centre, the more clearly you saw the earth-shattering pitch black; the closer you got to the soul, the younger you seemed to be.

At that instant, I suddenly felt her black eyes dissolve into an inky gutter impossible to cross. While afraid of falling off the cliff, I stayed cowering on the half-metre-wide embankment, unable to proceed or retreat; my wife stood on the opposite shore far away, casting cold eyes on me.

Maybe Miss Li was right. The leaper had mistaken city for jungle and saw the leaps off buildings as swinging from one tree to another. Or maybe he was actually a magician trying to interpret a higher level of science through an unorthodox form of magic. Who's to know?

What about myself? What was I a member of the new, homeless class of poor who continued to bob along with the weighted stock index, to do? For ten years, I went from the political section, to the social section, to the securities section of the newspaper. I'd seen more than my share of hat tricks in politics and witnessed the formulae of love and hate among the masses as well as the rise and fall of the money market; my only unchanging focus was the volatile stock market. Was I a gambler? A speculator? Or an obsessive adventurer with suicidal tendencies? Each day, from nine till noon, I'd throw myself almost exhaustingly into the bear and bull struggle of the stock set. I'd ride every wave and every cycle whenever there was a stock crisis. Time and again I'd experience the thrill of what was likely found in Sisyphus' legends. When the leaper made his first appearance, I was oblivious to it as I was busy playing bear at the securities company on Kuanchien Road (that was the day of the big Kansai earthquake) and thinking of ways to stall my wife who was determined to leave me. It was a big day on the lunar calendar, suitable for the opening of markets, transactions, and divorce but ill-suited for marriage. The index had fallen more than 200 points and I'd earned a 20 per cent difference for three individual stocks. But my marriage index had hit rock-bottom that morning. I was completely oblivious at noontime when I received the 'goodbye' message from my wife. A puzzling, abstract image had materialized on the screen on my beeper. It was identical to the huge upward leap and splintering of that day's line graph. When I discovered the world was crashing about me, I turned around abruptly and was shocked to see the deadly still monitor staring at me like a big gaping black hole, the remnants of my emotions and feelings hurled into that abyss.

The night before, after a suffocating round of the silent treatment, my wife asked me in a voice devoid of emotion, 'What will you do without me? I mean it—what will happen to you?'

It is only now, as I continue to stare at the bottomless sky (an impulse to hug the floor wells up) that I finally make out the answer that I couldn't get out then:

'I'll fall.'

A palmful of warmth covers my tightly held fist. I was startled, afraid to move, not daring to press back, neither feeling it was right to let go. The hand holding onto mine seemed calmer, or maybe more nervous. The owner of the hand arched her neck stiffly and stared at the strange space that we faced together. Half a month ago, when the Miss Li in question heard I was claiming to 'unravel the leaping trick of the kid magician' (really it was when she learnt of my divorce), she suddenly came to me babbling about Einstein, the theory of relativity and what have you, and expressed her willingness to be my voluntary research assistant. Since then she has embarked on a tightrope game of the heart. Perhaps out of cowardice, or perhaps feigning ignorance, I didn't ask her her birth date, her eight cyclical characters, blood type, horoscope, interests, or habits; I'm also too lazy to find out the sad story behind this sentimental little woman. Frankly speaking, I don't even have the energy to get her into my bed. The more we came into contact, the more I missed my wife who had virtually the same look in her eye; I only felt the absurdity and loneliness of worldly affairs and human foibles. I knew at a very early stage that Miss Li was not interested in the leaper, she was here to admire 'the leap down' by a middle-aged divorcé like myself. The problem was, even though I could feel the heat from her body and the centre of our palms that melted as a result of irresolute sweat, I was still suspicious. Was she holding me up? Or, weak as I was, was I extending the tentacles of consciousness and grabbing onto a piece of driftwood?

Chen suddenly emerged from the crowd, coming towards me and winking at me. Around us, it was getting more and more crowded. Nanking East Road was already choked, not even the police cars could get through. Hundreds of camcorders and cameras were set up and properly adjusted. On the upper left side of the corner on I-Tung Street stood our frowning chief editor and Old Wang and Li with their hands on their hips. Our chief editor was saying something forcefully; was he saying a prayer or cursing? All the reporters had rushed over; the colleagues at our news bureau were 'forced out' as well. Or rather, this time round we were not tracking him, for he had come to us. The fibreglass building beneath the leaper's feet was none other than our very own news agency.

Perspiration clouded my spectacles again. Right then, the cries that came to us from all four sides made me raise my head hastily. The young kid was suspended in midair, his two legs kicking like he was bounding in air. My god! Was he attempting to bungee jump? Why couldn't I see the rope behind his ankles or the steel wire behind his back? Did he not know about gravity? The next moment, he had safely 'landed' on the ground. In the midst of thousands of people in Nanking East Road, he made a perfectly executed landing.

How was it possible?

It was about this 'performance' that I'd heard thousands of rumours and read thousands of articles, but if I hadn't seen it with my own eyes I'd have found it incredible. I always thought the secret of the leaper was not in the leaping action itself, but rather that he might be 'flying' or he might have anti-gravity devices, like an invisible parachute, so he could swirl down like a falling leaf. But I was wrong. He really did jump, just like in the scenes showing incredible moves in martial art movies. One step and he had covered hundreds of metres, one blink and he was in front of you (I swear I did not blink). From start to finish, I didn't even get a good look. I cannot tell you how he 'edited' the series of continuous movements that eliminated most of the normal processes of physics.

Lord, who was willing to teach that barbarian the way to get from roof to ground level, via the stairs or the elevator, step by step, floor by floor? It cannot or should not be with an agile leap of the body, just as the tower of civilization was built and gathered height floor by floor, layer by layer, from the bottom up. This is the way of logic.

But who was willing to tell me what had happened to the life of a guy like me? Why was my family broken? Why did the woman who loved me for ten years but to whom I could still not say 'I love you' leave me without a backward glance, and just at the time when I discovered I could not live apart from her? Looking back, why was my life filled with scars, deep pits much like the 'abysmal openings' that occur when the stock market skyrockets or crashes? Where will a free-falling body that has lost its centre of gravity finally land?

Perhaps I was holding on so tightly that I failed to notice, my right fist gradually experienced spasms and turned cold. But I warned myself not to let go, not to relinquish the last hand to hold mine in this lifetime. Yes, I should face the woman next to me bravely. . . . But no! Miss Li was no longer next to me, she was ten metres ahead of me with an automatic camera in her hand snaking towards her news object. The photographers and policemen around me were also crowding in on the kid magician. I looked down and saw my right hand actually holding onto my left, so tightly my joints had turned white and the veins on the back of my hands were bulging. My ten fingers were locked together in a rope knot that could not be undone (I started remembering, twelve years back, the feelings I had the first time I held my wife's hand).

Cries and applause rang out in the crowd. During the time I was lost in my own thoughts, the kid had 'rewound' himself and was now gracefully back on the roof, his arms were widespread and he had that same arrogant, wings-wide-open look of before. It was like he'd never descended. But what really pained me was the fact that at this moment, while he was far off on the top of the building, he seemed also to be right before my eyes. Where had the theory of perspective disappeared to? What happened to our training in visual aesthetics? Was he a giant that could not be contained? What about myself? Was I a midget of custom and prejudice?

It finally dawned on me: even if the leaper performed this act a hundred times in slow motion I would still not get it. Just as, even if I were married a hundred times, I would still not be able to truly grasp my wife's desire and my own selfishness. I suppose in this lifetime I would probably never fathom the degree of my own ignorance, nor understand the self I've been saddled with all my life.

Another gasp goes up from the crowd, a series of heart-wrenching cries rings out. It was my turn to scream, and very probably I was the only person screaming in the entire area.

In front of me, the hundred-metre-tall obstruction, the building that had housed and fed me for over ten years, the newspaper agency known as the 'New Age Antenna' was busy collapsing from top to bottom, and shattering floor by floor. . . .

1996

NOTES

1 This is a line out of a famous Tang-dynasty poem. It alludes to the sound of the Chinese lute.

12

The Drawer

By **Xi Xi**

Translated by Douglas Hui and John Minford

Xi Xi 西西 is the pen-name of Cheung Yin 張彥 (Zhang Yan, b. 1939). She was born in Shanghai, but grew up and received her education in Hong Kong. She has a teacher's certificate from the Grantham College of Education and has worked as a primary school teacher. Her pen-name is a pictorial metaphor for a girl playing a Chinese game of 'aeroplane hopping', similar to hopscotch. It is also a Chinese metaphor for writing when the writer's pen jumps from one square to the next on the writing paper. From this the reader learns something about Xi Xi's attitude toward life and writing. Xi Xi won the fiction award given by the Hong Kong Arts Development Council in 1997.

Xi Xi began writing in 1965 and published her first story, 'Maria' (Maliya 瑪利亞) in the Hong Kong magazine Chinese Students' Weekly *(*Zhongguo xuesheng zhoubao 中國學生周報*), for which she won a prize. Now she has published six collections of short stories,* My City *(*Wo cheng 我城*, 1979),* Cross Currents *(*Jiao he 交河*, 1981),* Deer Hunt *(*Shao lu 哨鹿*, 1983),* Spring Prospect *(*Chun wang 春望*, 1983),* A Girl Like Me *(*Xiang wo zheyang de yige nuzi 像我這樣的一個女子*, 1984), and* Beard With A Face *(*Huzi you lian 鬍子有臉*, 1986), a volume of poetry,* Stone Chimes *(*Shi qing 石磬*, 1983), and two novels,* Lamenting Breasts *(*Aidao yufang 哀悼乳房*, 1992), and* Flying Carpet *(*Fei zhan 飛氈*, 1996). Some of her stories have been translated into English and have appeared in the collections* A Girl Like Me and Other Stories *and* Floating Clouds. *Xi Xi's fiction is rich in style and deals with a variety of subjects that are typical of life in Hong Kong.*

I have a drawer. I keep in it the little things I may need to use in the course of the day: coins, a bunch of keys, a watch, stamps, a half-empty packet of cigarettes. It's only a small drawer. Sometimes I pull it all the way out, tip it upside down and sort everything through. When I do this there's always a sound of something rolling away: a button, or a pencil stub. Rolling. From the desk down on to the floor, from the floor to some unknown place. If I can see it, I pick it up. If I can't, I just let it be.

When everything is tipped out of the drawer, some things do not roll; they just make a sort of clattering sound. It may be my lighter; or that tiny round mirror of mine. I can no longer remember how that little mirror got into my house, how it has managed to monopolize that corner of the drawer for so long. I only know that it has become part of my life. Every day without fail, when I open the drawer I see it. And once I see it, a voice seems to rise from some strange place: Hallelujah, we are alive.

I go to work every day. Even on Sundays, I have somewhere to go. That's why I have to open my drawer every day. I have to open it for my purse, my cigarettes, my keys, and my ID card. Each time I open the drawer, I see my mirror lying face-up in the corner, like an unruffled little pool of water. And in the mirror, I see myself.

No one else has ever opened my drawer. Other people have their own drawers. My drawer is entirely mine. In that little drawer of mine lives my mirror; and in my mirror, me. It's become a habit with me now, after all this time, not to rush straight to my keys or purse first thing when I open the drawer. And I'm in no hurry to put my lighter and cigarettes into my pocket. Instead, I glance quickly at the mirror lying in the corner of the drawer, to see if I am there or not. The mirror has never failed me; I always know I'm not lost, I have been living in my drawer all along, safe and sound.

In point of fact, after all this time, now, whenever I open the drawer, what I see is no longer a mirror, but me. Oh, that must be my nose . . . and those are my ears on either side of it. . . . I feel comforted: I know that both my nose and my ears have been living peaceful, comfortable lives in my drawer all along. And I push the drawer lightly in, so as not to disturb their peace and quiet.

For many years I have not known where I am, and have been much afflicted by melancholy as a consequence. I have not known where I am in this infinite universe. But gradually I have come to know. Very gradually. I have finally arrived at the truth of the matter through all my daily openings of the drawer. The fact is, I have been living all along in my drawer. The knowledge that I actually have a place of domicile in this universe has brought me an incomparable sense of happiness. No more need for me to lament the futility of life, to see myself as a drifting soul, a passing phantasm.

By the side of my mirror in the drawer lies my ID card. Every day, before I leave home, I open the drawer, take out the ID card and put it in my pocket. Then I take out one or two other bits and pieces—my purse, my ball-point pen, and so on and so forth. When I return from the outside world, I open the drawer again, put back the ID card by the mirror, and then place the odds and ends of the things that I use in the day back in the drawer, one by one.

The other day I went shopping for a pair of shoes. I chose the type of shoe I wanted, and the salesman asked me if I'd brought my pattern with me. That suddenly made me think of an ancient fable. I said to him, do you take me for an idiot? What do you think today is, April Fool's day? Why should I need to bring my pattern with me to buy shoes? I've brought my feet. Look! But the salesman insisted on my producing my pattern. They only accepted patterns, not feet. What good were feet? That was what they said. You could only prove something about your feet by producing your pattern. Your pattern had a photo of your feet on it, it had your toe prints, the date of birth of your feet, their race and nationality, their colour, their names and aliases in Chinese and English, their shape and measurements. And their Civil Registration Number. What good were your actual feet? Only your pattern could prove that your feet were yours.

This encounter taught me that my pattern was my feet. In a similar manner, I have learnt that my ID is me. So I put my ID away in my drawer every day with extraordinary care. My drawer is my only domicile in this infinite universe, and I must protect it as best as I possibly can. I worry about my house catching fire, about hurricanes and storms, about earthquakes. These calamities would mean ruin for the drawer. If my drawer were gone, where would I be able to be? If the drawer were gone, my ID would be gone too; if my ID were gone, I would be gone too. Likewise, if the drawer were gone, so would my mirror; if my mirror were gone, so would I. No wonder I have taken out such an expensive insurance policy for my drawer.

That's it. For so many years, I haven't known who I am, where I am, where I come from, or where I'm going to. I have thought hard about all these questions, but to no avail. Now I've got the answers.

The questions that have perplexed me for so many years have vanished like wisps of smoke. I don't have to ask any more who I am, where I am, where I come from, where I am going to, how I should go on living. I am not troubled by these questions any more.

Who am I? I have only to open my drawer and my ID tells me who I am, in great detail. Where am I? Again, I only have to open my drawer and look into my mirror. Haven't I been living comfortably in my mirror all along? Haven't I been keeping my mirror carefully in the drawer all along? Where am I? In my drawer, of course. It hardly needs saying. As for where I come from, from the Immigration Department, of course. And where am I going to? To the Registry of Births and Deaths, of course.

Yesterday, I ran into some friends of mine on the street. They'd arranged to have coffee together at a café, and asked me whether I would like to join them. Like to? I said. How could I know? I'd have to go home and consult my drawer. And then they asked me whether I would go swimming with them on Sunday. I said I didn't know that either. I'd have to go and consult my drawer.

That's it. If you ask me whether I like lying in the sun on the grass, I have to go and consult my drawer. If you ask me whether the apple I'm eating is sweet, I have to go and ask my drawer. If you ask me whether I am happy or not, I have to go and ask my drawer.

1981

13

Wrongly Delivered Mail

By **YENG PWAY NGON**

Translated by Eric K. W. Yu and Kwok-kan Tam, with A. T. L. Parkin

Yeng Pway Ngon 英培安 *(Ying Pei'an, b. 1947) began his writing career as a poet and essayist in Singapore, and recently has also turned to fiction. After graduating from the Chinese Department of Ngee Ann Institute, he founded the journals* Chazuo *(*Teahouse 茶座*),* Qianwei *(*Avant-Garde 前衛*), and* Woniu *(*Snail 蝸牛*), and has since been owner of the Caogen Bookstore. In 1968 he published his first collection of poetry* On the Operation Table *(*Shoushutai shang 手術枱上*) when he was a third year student at Ngee Ann Institute.*

As Yeng Pway Ngon says, his essays on Singapore society are often more widely read than his poetry, though he likes to write poetry. By writing on Singapore society, he is forced to leave his ivory tower to face the stark reality in which the masses live.

I've disappeared for almost a year, and no one knows where I've been. In fact, this goes quite beyond my own expectations.

It all happened like this. You know, I'd been hoping to leave this damn place. Many people thought that life here didn't suit me, mainly because it's not the air I wanted to breathe. Already stuck here for more than ten years, I feared that I'd go mad if I stayed on. I ought to get out before I go mad, I thought. Otherwise I wouldn't be able to make it! What could I do? My income was so low and distant travel meant expenses. In my bank account there was never more than a hundred dollars. All I wanted was to go to America. Though American dollars had been depreciating, my savings would not allow me to go there in any case. But I saw a ray of hope. I'd seen a beautiful ad in the cinema saying that the bank would help people in need, that bankers would serve you all their lives. So I followed the instruction in the ad and went to a bank manager, identifying myself, and told him that I'd like to borrow five hundred dollars.

I don't know how to describe the manager's facial expression. The subsequent plot didn't go exactly like what's in the ad. Although I tried my best to act out my part, the manager didn't hand me a cigarette or a cup of coffee. Well, I didn't care about coffee, but then I didn't get the money, either.

I was enraged. If he didn't kick me out first, I'd have mercilessly beaten him up. From then on, I no longer trusted advertisements. This world is full of liars.

In desperation I thought of the only viable way at last. I went into the post office, bought some stamps from the woman at the counter, stuck the stamps on my forehead, and asked if she could send me to America.

Hearing this the woman panicked. She explained to me that they only delivered mail, never people. I asked how much additional money was required to pack me up and said that I was willing to pay.

This woman must have been a lazy Singaporean. She argued with me for a long time, refusing my request. Eventually, she called a few tall, big men to deal with me, including policemen. I complained of the poor service there. Although the poster with smiles was still pasted on the wall, they were not for me. On the contrary, they abused me. Obviously, the courtesy campaign was over.

The scene, as I remember, got more and more confused, ending with a blow to my head. I passed out.

When I came to I found that I was tied up. I thought perhaps they'd finally tied me up in order to mail me to America. Afterwards, I found that I was wearing a police uniform of the colonial era. This really drove me crazy. If it's not the case of time flowing backwards, it's got to be the whole world going crazy, I thought. For I'd never thought of becoming a policeman, especially a policeman of the colonial era.[1] Besides, I was still a boy, not old enough to be a policeman.

How despicable! Without my consent, they forced on me a job I didn't know. I was a decent chap and wouldn't do anything bad. Although I had no political beliefs, I never thought of serving colonialism and oppressing the people.

At last they let me walk freely. I gradually found out that, as a policeman of the colonial era, I had no authority of office. Everywhere were policemen like me. There were only a few civilians, who were said to be nurses and doctors. I learnt after exhaustive inquiries that I was in a madhouse, and people called me an inmate.

On what grounds did they send me here? Was it misdirection of the mail? Or hadn't I paid enough postage? No matter what, no one had any reason to mail me to a madhouse.

Now that I was here, I didn't want to make a fuss. Life here, however, was bad enough. The doctors were eccentric, evasive, and sneaky. Obviously people were driven mad by them. For it's they who called people lunatics.

The most exciting thing about the place was to discover Mr Chen, a former classmate of mine. Chen sang the same song every day: 'I am a thrush.'

He sang very seriously, so that some girl students who visited us thought that he was innocent and pitiable. This proved that he was not mad. He sang repeatedly: 'I am a thrush.' It showed that he was aware that he was locked up here and not free. So he was clear-headed.

I did ponder this question. I asked Chen why we were imprisoned here and on what grounds they called us madmen. Chen said that it's because we didn't behave normally. I thought this was laughable. What on earth was normal? What counted as insanity? Was Hitler normal? What normal things had he done and why hadn't anybody suggested putting him into a madhouse? Hey, what's the use of psychologists? Perhaps only mass killing and large-scale torturing of people were recognized as behaviour of genius! I'd better stay here for good.

To Chen, I was innocent, for everyone had the freedom to go somewhere else, especially to America, a place of freedom. I told him possibly my method was wrong. I hadn't pasted enough stamps, and didn't write the addressee. Therefore I couldn't blame them.

Chen said that it's ridiculous to send someone to the madhouse because he didn't pay enough postage. And he started worrying. The letters he wrote his girlfriend probably all came back here. It's no surprise that his girlfriend didn't write him back. He's sorry that he wronged his girlfriend.

It's lucky that they didn't send me to Iran, I said. I don't like Khomeini. I don't object to other people with such a surname; I just don't like Khomeini. I can't understand what he says, and his beard is too long. He's also too old, and there'd be a generation gap between us.

Chen told me why he was sent here. A psychologist thought Chen believed himself to be a thrush, that Chen had a thrush's ideology. I asked if Chen had ever wanted to become a thrush. Chen said he loved freedom and liked singing. The doctor thought that he spoke the bird's language and was unfit for the world outside, so he recommended him to come here.

Chen believes that it's not wrong to be a thrush. He's a very sober bird and shouldn't be locked up here. He ought to be happy as a bird. Unfortunately, it's rather sad to be merely a thrush in a cage. Having articulated this, he couldn't help feeling down. So he started singing loudly: 'I am a thrush!'

What's more sad is that Chen was only a thrush fit for a cage. Once, the window of our cell was opened. Chen thought the moment of flying towards freedom had come. Elated, he flapped his wings and flew out of the window. But as his wings never grew any feathers, he fell immediately to the ground and broke his back. He regretted that because he'd been locked in the cage for too long, he had lost the strength to fly.

When I paid him a visit in the ward, he looked very depressed. In a low voice, he sang: 'A thrush with no wings, how can it fly away?' He sang haltingly, obviously without much strength. As he finished, he said to me, his face wet with tears: 'I'd rather be a vegetable. If there's some soil on the bed, I'll certainly take root and sprout.'

I comforted him: 'Don't give up. You may ask the doctor for physiotherapy. Maybe you can regain your strength and fly.'

He kept shaking his head and tears rolled over his cheeks. What else could I say? We sat silently for a while.

I said to him before I left: 'It's not that bad. From now on you no longer have to eat grasshoppers. Grasshoppers are difficult to swallow, and they're not nutritious.'

He didn't answer. When I went to see him later, he didn't speak any more, only stared at me, eyes in tears. The nurse told me not only did he keep silent, he also refused to eat or drink. Vegetables, I know, do not talk. Looking at his face with deep depressions, protruding cheek bones, and listless eyes, I was deeply saddened. There should be someone to water him, I thought.

Chen soon died in that ward, a tragic character. It was not easy to be a vegetable, for the room got no sunlight, and he withered away.

Chen's death made an enormous impact on me. If a man wants to become a bird, he will be seen as a madman. And yet those people who were originally birds swagger around and keep on living unmolested. I've got lots of proof that some of our supervisors are in fact parrots transformed into humans. Although they know human speech, they talk nonsense. They just blindly imitate the boss's words and have no ideas of their own. Of course they sometimes use bird language, not to mention the fact that birds' thoughts fully occupy their brains.

How ridiculous! A few parrots control this world, and control even people's livelihood. What future is there for human civilization? Is this world actually a birds' world? Probably the world is coming to an end. And it's not surprising that Chen wished to become a bird.

At last, I left that place. Honestly, if it were not for Chen's death, I'd have preferred to remain here for good. Knowing how so many normal people outside die and suffer, I'd rather have retired prematurely and enjoyed the rest of my life inside.

Before my departure, I went through close examinations by psychologists. They interviewed me, and found that I had very good reasoning power. One day it was like this: I was brought into a small room. The one who talked with me was introduced as a doctor. He seemed to be a bit nervous. Apart from that, however, there wasn't anything remarkable.

'We're sorry that you were sent here,' he laughed neurotically. 'But I hope you understand that we did this because we love you. You were then unfit for the world outside.'

'Love means never having to say sorry.' I said, and I smiled too, with more or less the same expression as his.

'Very well! No. . . .' The doctor hesitated for a while: 'What I'm saying is, I want to ask you a question, to see if you're . . .'

'Normal,' I supplied the missing word.

'No—well yes, if you're fit for the outside world.' The doctor pulled out a white handkerchief, then kept dabbing at sweat on his forehead. The air-conditioner was making a humming sound.

'I'll try my best to tell you what I know,' I said.

'Very well.' The doctor paused. From the drawer he took out an electric torch and turned it on suddenly. A strong light stabbed into my eyes, and I was so scared that I almost fell from the chair.

'Sorry!' The doctor stood up, not knowing what to do.

'It's okay!' I calmed down, turning my chair to the right position. 'My eyes are sensitive. I'm always afraid of light, especially when it suddenly gets in my eyes.'

'Hm!' The doctor sat down, cleared his throat, and then said slowly: 'If I throw this light onto that small window, do you think you can climb up along the light beam?'

I looked at the small window, which was at least ten feet high.

'No,' I answered solemnly.

'Why not?' The doctor smiled, full of confidence.

'If you suddenly turned off the electric torch when I was half way through,' I said, 'wouldn't I fall down?'

So I passed the exam and left the madhouse in peace.

1979

NOTES

1 There was a time when inmates in madhouses in Singapore wore uniforms of the policemen of the colonial era.

Stories of Gender

14

How Did I Miss You?

By **ZHANG XINXIN**
Translated by Nienling Liu

Zhang Xinxin 張辛欣 *(b. 1953) was born in Beijing. She is one of the most talented women writers who rose to fame in China in the 1980s. Like many Chinese who grew up during the Cultural Revolution, Zhang Xinxin's education was interrupted and she had to join the exodus to the Great Northern Wilderness*[1] *in China's Siberia in 1969. She became an army nurse while there, and later worked as an administrator for the Communist Youth League. In 1979 she entered the Central Academy of Drama, Beijing and graduated in theatre-directing after four years. At the Academy she had the opportunity to direct Arthur Miller's 'Death of a Salesman'. She later joined the Youth Art Theatre, Beijing, and also worked for television. Many of her works deal with the status of women in contemporary China, the confusion in gender after the Cultural Revolution, and the loss of identity as a result of the crisis of belief upon the collapse of the socialist system.*

It was another late Saturday afternoon as the streetcar moved from one stop to another along the familiar, noisy avenue. She was busy selling tickets as usual, clipping them and pushing them through the throng of passengers. She was wearing a straight, loose greatcoat with a collar of camel hair and, if it had not been for the neutral professional tone of her voice trying to cover up its femininity, one would have had no way of telling she was a woman for she was buried under a sea of blue-uniformed passengers. Now, she was hopping up and down in the doorway, stamping her suede boots laden with heavy mud, heckling the passengers to move on quickly, or even trying to push them along. At one point she encountered some roughnecks who immediately yelled, 'Ah, the lady is tough' or 'Aiyo, mistress you're pushing against my back!' Like puppies that had had their tails trodden on, these boys would seize any chance to get themselves worked up. As soon as they had yelled the words, they discovered that it was a woman. Yet they would not excuse her, not at all, but even went so far as to let out a barrage of curses and profanity more prolific and harder to take than the foul language of street girls. Nevertheless, she walked away as if she had not heard. . . .

When taking a breathing spell she was hardly noticeable as she stared through the window at the melting snow drifting away; but in her eyes something uncommon glistened.

'Put them here!' yelled a woman to her husband as they got on the bus. She was indicating to him to put several large frozen fish on the ticket counter. The woman was worker Huang Yun.

'Yo, are you still here?' Huang Yun asked. 'Is it you who's written a play? I saw the poster in the Xidan market. Many kids from our factory went to see it. They even asked me about you. They wanted to know your name and all about you. How are things going? Too many choices make one dizzy. You think Li Ke is too nice? It's all right then! Going to Beijing University? Beijing Normal? Four years? It's too long. Tomorrow I'll be busy again, having company. Our house has an extension which the renovation brigade built. . . . I'm not very good at dealing with those sort of things; he's the one. . . .' Huang Yun suddenly stopped in mid-sentence, as if frightened by her own words.

Brought back to the present, the ticket-seller looked at Huang Yun with surprise. 'What's the matter with you?' Huang Yun asked. 'You're so absent-minded, a completely different person now.'

'I'm paying attention.' She smiled faintly. She was hoping that Huang Yun would shut up.

Though she was watching closely the passengers inside the bus and the goings-on outside, she was simultaneously fidgeting with her hands as she listened to Huang Yun's crisp rapid talk. Her mind was following an unknown path, persistently searching for something. . . .

Where are you? Even if I had told you the truth, it would have been too late!

In my imagination I arranged meetings in another world; yet in reality I have few chance meetings. I know I am saying things that will offend many young men, make them feel sad, or make them disdainful of me, but it is my deeply felt anguish that there are so few men worthy of one's love.

It is said that there is a disparity between the number of women and the number of men, but I often feel another kind of despair.

I have no expectations from those young men who are so bold in their way of pushing onto the bus and so indifferently self-absorbed when one calls out to them to give seats to other passengers in need. I do not pay attention to those flaunting street youths who display the latest hair style and fashion when there is not a trace of cultivation in their expression. They and I are of the same generation, yet we are altogether unlike one another in thoughts and feelings. Of course they will not think much of me either.

I could never have any feeling for a man like Huang Yun's husband, no matter how competent and capable he was.

But Li Ke is such a perfect, nice person; it puzzles me why I chose him. We were schoolmates at elementary school. For many years our fathers were both teachers at the same school. Our personal files were like those of twins who even shared the same dress codes. Yet our personalities are entirely different. When we were together I used to burst out laughing, excited by our talk. He would sigh, 'You, you haven't changed at all. For that reason your problems with the organization remain unresolved.' He looked as if he were awfully unlucky. Yet his innocent face seldom showed any marks of pain, because he had had it easy. He had transferred to a biology major in the 'Darwin' department. He got five points[2] for each of his courses, as he had in his elementary and middle schools. He was then awarded the 'Three Excellences'[3] certificate. Pity, he had never shown any interest in insects, birds, flowers, and fish. He had never shown enthusiasm for any major subject, nor any ambition. He always lived well, very proper, and made a good impression on people. He was like a well-behaved rabbit; because the social system required a diploma, he ran accordingly within the bounds marked out by white lines. Yet I, a stubborn tortoise, still crawling slowly on another line not far from the starting point, was following my own feelings and beliefs.

Sharing common customs and background, we became dearest friends. My elders and friends all considered that he was the most suitable person for me. Yes, he was a good person. We got along very well. I couldn't find fault with him. I had thought it over; living with him I would have a peaceful life. There would never be the possibility of his changing heart or of getting into trouble. But love can only be fulfilled after a trial. I know, because I have loved before. The experience of love I had was different from this. With Li Ke, I was often distracted. He had told me sincerely that I had a kind of self-sufficiency which encouraged him. Ah, I was not being watchful over him. I was only whipping myself relentlessly to get ahead. I was racing with myself. I did feel that I was growing too fast, but undeniably, in front of him I felt self-confident. We were not like lovers, but siblings. When he gave me that look of admiration and unconditional trust, I felt a quiet loneliness, helplessness, and a kind of sadness because we couldn't have a natural rapport or sharing of life.

Later, when looking out of the bus window, this idea would unexpectedly flash across my mind. Maybe among those who had crossed my path there was one who could be really close; but we had missed each other forever.

I found you. Yet I also lost you. Why? Was it because of the play I'd written? Because I pushed you? Maybe . . . Ah! Maybe, from the beginning, unwittingly there had been this omen that I would have to lose you.

It was a crowded Saturday evening. The middle door was jammed open so I jumped down to repair it. When I returned to the front door, there were a great many people surging around it and I couldn't squeeze myself on.

Inside the boys all roared at once, 'Wait for the next bus: There's one coming behind! Conductor, give up the tickets before you leave.'

I must not pay attention to them. If I gave them one glance, they would take it as a come-on. They would shout further and with more gusto. I remained mute. I pulled down the passenger who was half-way into the bus but with his body still hanging outside. I did not even look at him, just heard him pleading, 'I have urgent business!'

'Urgent? Everybody's got urgent business to return home to.' From anxiety and fatigue, I was rash and shoved him off. Instantly I took his place on the bus and with my two feet firmly planted in the door frame I continued to push in forcefully. But a greater backlash forced me down again.

At that moment I discovered the person whom I had pushed down. He looked thirtyish; he was lighting a cigarette and staring at me. Why was he looking at me? Once again I forced myself up. 'Comrade, I'll help you to push in. I really have some urgent matters.'

'Don't bother!'

I applied my full weight, my shoulder, my waist, my hands, my legs, and my mouth. . . . The awful woollen scarf was being twisted around my head. My hair was falling over my eyes, yet I had no free hand to brush it off with. The boys were still roaring; the other passengers were sitting like deaf-mutes, apathetic, motionless. I felt I was being badly wronged. I'm only a girl, but I had to push with all my might, shouting at the same time. I had no chance to measure the weight of the crowd against me. I only knew that I had to shove myself in.

Suddenly, behind me, someone had pushed up into the bus. I felt a strong and firm force thrusting me forward. It was he. This fellow was persistent all right. I had no chance to utter a protest; he was forcing me continuously forward. The bus door gave a shake as if giving out a signal and finally shut.

The bus started to move. I wriggled around a few times, but I could not make out his face. I only got a glimpse of the cigarette in his fingers. I felt grateful to him, and ashamed. Yet I still said rudely, 'Extinguish your cigarette.'

It was you then! How could I know? You tell me what I should have done! Should I have pleaded gently? Sat down on the sidewalk and cried? Now I wish very much to treat you gently; without words or action just let me stare at you gently. But even if it should happen again, I can't guarantee what kind of reaction I would have.

It was a very normal and yet a very special Saturday evening. I remember every moment of it. . . .

I was late at the rehearsal because of unexpected extra work, and I hadn't had a chance beforehand to call them first. Not many of my colleagues knew I was writing a play on the side. I did not want to brag in front of them, yet if I did not make my absence clear, they would think up some interesting reason. I did not want to feed their imaginations.

As I was climbing the squeaking stairway, I heard a male voice. I realized the reading of my play was already approaching the end.

I did not enter immediately; I was standing at the door alone, listening. I felt that this baritone was very familiar. I was moved at once. Maybe I felt this way because the play was the result of my lonely struggles against defeat. What had been crafted with great concentration had often been demolished, what had been written word by word had been torn up page by page. This play had absorbed many of my wretched evenings and now, here were my lines being uttered by a stranger. I suddenly felt a new comfort, a relieved consolation. I had pushed through a whole day of work, my entire body was sore and exhausted and my stomach empty, but within an instant of hearing that voice I forgot everything. . . .

The voice stopped, and I shoved open the door.

It was a large rehearsal room. Facing me was a large wall mirror with the mercury fading out. A group of people were sitting in a circle. Judging from the voice, it was the man who had just read from the play who was talking with his back to me.

'I repeat, don't ever be late again. If you come and go at random, then please resign. Art is not for amateurs!'

So stern, so succinct. I was startled. I stepped forward softly, hurriedly thinking up some fine excuse. . . . Suddenly I stopped. I wanted to run away. When I came near the mirror, I realized at once—how could it be?

But he got up, turned around, and extended his hand.

It was you! How could it be you? The director? Oh, spare me!

Holding my hand, you introduced yourself to me. I also muttered some greeting, quite unintelligible, and stared numbly at you.

Stoutly built, wide shoulders, short-cropped hair, a face full of wrinkles. Any person who can eat, sleep, and work often has such a face. It is not unusual, but for you it is not appropriate. Among the pretty girls and handsome lads around you, you look like a roughneck who usually takes temporary jobs. An image of earthenware situated inside a fine gold-rimmed porcelain vase flashed into my mind. I thought of this analogy. At any rate, it's no big deal to face you squarely. I gathered up Ah Q-like courage[4] whenever I confronted an awkward situation. I kept my head high and stared straight at you. I met your eyes. For whatever reason, I was instantly mesmerized. Your eyes are not particularly beautiful but challenging and self-confident.

While talking, your eyes were flashing as if in surprise to find me standing in front of you. You gave me a look and smiled. The people surrounding us were not aware of this at all. Perhaps your smile was only a friendly sign, but I felt there was sudden humour in your eyes, as if you had discovered a joke. I have often tried to cover myself up in front of people, have tried to pretend to be fearless, yet from the very beginning you had by chance discovered me in a most awkward position, embarrassing too. At first I did not care what impression you had of me. I am no mannequin in a shop window, holding up two arms, speechless and motionless. Yet I did feel a little lost. . . .

All these were fleeting thoughts. I felt that we stood there facing each other for too long. I withdrew my hand from your grasp and immediately touched my face as if there were dirt on my skin or my cheeks were beginning to burn. I then said simply, 'Don't worry, I won't hassle you again.'

'Thank you. Suppose I refuse to buy a bus fare?' You smiled.

We stared at each other and burst out laughing. The actors surrounding us also laughed, without knowing why.

When we first met, I had no clear impression of the star actress Liu Jie. She was quiet and seemed to have some depth of character. My leading actor was fiery but resourceful. It was what I had intended. I had great hope and enthusiasm for Liu Jie, but as she played the part she only blinked her large beautiful eyes and muttered her words. I was disappointed, for she was only using a quiet, gentle appearance to cover up an inner emptiness. Her beautiful eyes expressed more than she really was. But I did not think it convenient to say so.

You were busy casting, going over the script with the actors, and discussing the costumes and sets with the designers. I sat quietly and casually looked around. All the props, doors, windows, and whatever you had were lined along the wall. The old-fashioned rural lamps and the dueling swords were placed together. There were all kinds of tables, chairs, materials, alike in their worn-out state. My original excitement was over, and I began to wonder. . . . What kind of picture, what kind of profound emotion did this depiction of the lives of young people give? But with this semi-professional local drama-workshop, with these conditions and these actors, there was no way of knowing whether the play would or would not end up a noisy, pretentious spectacle on stage.

What I am searching for may always be different from the reality. No matter how much hard work I have really accepted, I remain powerless against reality. My ideas and my demands are unfulfilled.

As I became uneasy, I was immediately soothed. Your voice—so calm, so rich—aroused my attention.

Ah, you were expressing your thoughts as director. As soon as I had turned my head to quietly observe you, I began to feel an unknown agitation. Strange! Your face, not an outstanding one, was transforming. It was imbued with a certain but unconscious confidence, a passion, too, which caused the taut expression to change. It was captivating. I saw from the actors' eyes that they were affected by your passion. I also was influenced. Such may be the director's power? I confess your analysis was correct. In some points you were more correct than I when writing them. You were more profound, more moving. Not only this, I felt creepingly that what I had waited for for so long, searched for for so long. . . . Heavens! I was losing my mind! I knew so little of you. Apart from your appearance, your profession, and your manner, I knew nothing about you. Yet, instinctively, I felt I had known you all along.

You finally turned around and said to me, 'I really like your play, and find it very moving, but there are places which need more work. Sometimes a literary script doesn't suit the requirements of actual performance.'

Of course I was altogether open to suggestions, especially yours, but I already felt like letting you know what was on my mind.

'You're very impatient, aren't you? Please let me finish!'

I remained quiet for a while, undeterred from thinking in my own way. Suddenly I noticed that when you were in deep thought your eyes beamed with a curious smile. I realized then that my voice was too loud, that there were only the two of us left in the rehearsal room; I was talking as if we were on a bus full of people.

We followed each other down the stairs. You stopped at the corner under the light. You examined me critically from head to toe.

'I did not expect this. Your play is written so beautifully, so bright! Yet you look like this.'

'What do I look like?' I was thinking that you were remembering my appearance in the streetcar, rude and helpless.

'You're strong-minded. That's rare!'

This description surprised me. I wanted to express humility as protocol demanded, but I could not help laughing.

'While reading the play I thought you were a gentle, quiet girl, yet you're like a boy!'

Really, you were a director! Always analyzing people's character, even mine. I could recite a whole list of virtues for females—gentility, compassion, patience, quietness, resourcefulness. . . . Yet I was not unhappy at your description of me. I'd rather be this way. Your words and the fresh stimulation tonight made me feel argumentative. I quickened my descent down the stairway to stand on the same step as you, and attempted an explanation of my muddled thoughts.

'I think that society demands more from women today; family duties and social functions fall more upon our shoulders. We must be as strong as men. I regret to think why there are so many men lacking manly qualities. . . .'

'Er, not easy. . . .' You did not openly say the words, but lowered your head and rubbed your arms as if there were bumps swelling up on them. Did it hurt you there? I wanted to ask you.

Then you raised your head. You were searching my face: 'Have you always been so self-confident?'

In your eyes, was I mad? Is it so obvious? Maybe, because I was used to speaking up and laughing aloud.

Really, deep in my heart, I am often wavering and lacking confidence, even timid, as when confronting you and after our first meeting.

When I encounter failure, when I am feeling despair, I become very quiet. . . .

I wandered off aimlessly and sat on a bench in a park to think quietly about the script. I had originally intended it to be a screenplay. It would not be my first failure. Really, I don't understand; no one has pointed out its deficiencies to me. I am searching and following my own feelings. I did not expect instant success, but when the characters who had constantly been in my imagination suddenly crumbled, those iridescent rainbow colours which had stimulated my imagined world vanished. I felt instantly empty.

My face and hands warmed under the soft sunlight. It was an unusually fine wintry day. I really hadn't noticed that the sky was so crisp, clear and blue.

A boy and a girl walked toward me, the boy's arms around the girl's waist. They sat down on the bench across from me. They were not much younger than I, yet they looked utterly happy and bright, completely unconscious of their surroundings. The girl leaned her head upon the boy's shoulder. The boy responded quietly, sometimes giving her a soft shake, as if he could not remain still too long. She squeezed her eyelids together under the sunlight, moving her lips slowly as if saying something. The boy patted her powdered face. She lifted her fingers to tweak his nose. Laughingly, they jumped up, hand in hand, and ran along the path leading to the woods.

I felt envious as I watched them. I could have had that innocent joy in first love, but it ended before it had fully begun. I have never rolled on the grass abandoned to happiness, or chased another uninhibitedly under the sun—this kind of feeling has vanished for me. I have relinquished some fleeting moments of joy and wasted many chances. I seem to have an uncertain mission in life for the living and dead of our generation; those who walk, crawl, stand, lie—life gives me so many deep impressions, but what I express is so shallow, so incomplete! Maybe I have no talent and no power.

I have assumed such a burdensome albatross. Perhaps I should quit writing. I ought to become a fool and a simpleton in order to experience happiness more. To tell the truth, every time I feel powerless in life and in work, I want to lean against someone's shoulder and shed a few tears, to let out some of the bitterness in my heart.

But whose shoulder? When I was small, a big boy once threw a rock at me. I ran away frightened. Father came. I hid behind his back. His wide back was the safest, the most secure shield. Now, father is no more. Even if he were still here, he couldn't help because we are not of the same generation. He would not be able to understand the pain in my heart, the sadness and the loneliness. Li Ke is a good person, but I can't lean against him. He is too weak.

Everything depends upon myself!

Yes, myself, this time too.

I could not sit quietly on the park bench any longer. I should not allow myself to be so sad, so wandering, because I understand myself too well. If I am in despair for one moment, three-quarters of an hour, ten days, half a month, it is all the same. I have to stand up alone. I can't help pushing, shoving, shouting each day on the bus. For my own career, I must, too. I must once again return to my failed manuscripts; I must continue to write, like a mule on a treadmill.

You! You must respect my struggle; yet you demand from me the customary female qualities. If I were not as strong as a man, I would not have known you.

Perhaps I always looked the same in your eyes, during our first meeting and our last parting. You will never know from the short distance we've walked together how much my heart has awakened. That episode is as fresh as if it had just happened.

We edited the play together under the lamp. I sat on the edge of the desk for a little while. Our experiences are totally dissimilar, but besides our upbringing, there must be some points in which we are alike. If not, why, when we worked together, did we never compromise? You have your directorial ideas. I have my creative ideas. Although I don't understand stagecraft, I can still disagree with you. One time we couldn't go on any longer. I threw down the pen and sat on the edge of the desk. You paced the floor, smoking silently.

I did not know how long you had been gesturing, reciting, acting out your ideas. You were acting out many roles, characterizing them and in this way rewriting the script. You were displaying your directorial talent. Your quick mind astonished me, made me admire you. In your impromptu acting, the small room was transformed into the divine realm of a creative spirit. I was fascinated by you. I was stirred to create again. I took up the pen and started to write. . . .

But I insisted that the long monologue of the main female role should remain uncut. Maybe it was too long. But if it were not so, it would not fully express my ideas. It is the gist of the play. You recognized that, too. Yet you insisted that to leave it uncut would make the play less lively and less expressive.

We argued for a while. Your old mother heard us and came out to see if under such tension there would be an outbreak of war.

'I find you rather stubborn.'

'Please take a closer look at me. I am only your mirror.'

We stared at each other and could not help laughing.

'Where did you learn directing? Which academy?' I asked. To tell the truth, I did admire you.

'It's my hobby. At first, when I was in college, I didn't know it would be my real profession.' Your dancing hands suddenly dropped down. You became very still and stared at an oil painting on the wall. It was a painting by Ivazhuvsky—'The Seven Grade Tide'. He specialized in painting the ocean.

I did not know what you were thinking. I walked to the bookcase. The first thing I noticed in your room were your books. I made up my mind to discover a few worthy of translation, but when I began to examine them, I realized there were only such books as *Oceanography, Naval Power, Astronomy and Ocean Engineering, English for the Seaman*. And there were several magazines, all relating to the art of sailing.

'You seem to like oceanography.'

'It was my major.'

I was amazed. You went out to get some boiled water. I began to arrange the manuscripts on the desk. I was wondering how a person so self-confident and so warm could also possess other unknown qualities. I wanted to find out.

There was a broadcasting programme on the desk. On the pages were items marked with red pencil. They were announcements of coming concerts. I didn't know that you were like me in this respect, seeking every possible opportunity to hear classical music and go to concerts. I put aside the programme. Perhaps through feminine sensitivity I noticed at a glance that there were photos under the desk glass. One was of a young woman.

Very beautiful, large dark eyes, gentle, soft. Yet the photo was very old. One could tell that the developing technique was not up to date. As a result the face lacked shades, showing whites, and the eyes were dull, somewhat sad. Who was she?

Immediately I felt ill at ease, as if I had intruded into your private world. I heard your footsteps approaching. I quickly slipped the photo back under the glass pane, and spread out the manuscripts over the desk top.

You sat down and picked up the manuscript, ready to get to work. Your face suddenly darkened. I gave a stealthy glance—oh, no! I had turned over the photo.

'It must be my mother again.' You frowned. You turned over the photo and put it back right.

I couldn't help making a hesitant confession. 'It was me. She . . . where does she work?'

'. . . She's dead, a long time ago, during the Cultural Revolution. The photo was torn off her student ID card.'

I was feeling very sorry. I hadn't meant to pry into your inner life, your hidden wound. I did not know it was like this, and that you, a tough hired hand, should be a sailor.

You were actually a graduate in oceanography. During the Cultural Revolution you were wrongly put in jail. You have experienced a great deal except seafaring. When the new policy was being implemented your case was still unresolved. You were looking for a job, seeking a way out of your troubles. You found my script through a friend. You became the director, a temporary job. You explained it so simply.

'You should be fighting the ocean, not directing a bunch of boys and girls or dreaming over magazines and books about the sea. It is funny, isn't it?'

No, no. It was not funny. I became silent. You were sitting against the lamplight in a dark corner. I could only see your statue-like body, motionless and strong. I understood you well, however, although we had just met. We are very different from each other; somehow our paths crossed. It must have been through destiny. I understand you, although you are often inclined to scoff. Also, I never endlessly discuss my problems with people. I prefer to give a shrug. How can I compare myself with you? You have suffered so much more, experienced so much more deeply. Who am I? At present, I can still write on the side, training myself. But you! You intensely wanted your own special career. Yet you hadn't had a single chance to step abroad.

I wanted to give a great sigh for your suffering. But I suppressed the urge. It would be too facile for me to do so.

What could I do for you? Even if it were just a little.

Suddenly I had a wish.

It was on just that day that Ozawa's China trip had become the latest topic in the news. The boys wanted to take a look at him. You also mentioned that you wanted to hear his Beethoven Symphony No. 9.

When tickets went on sale at the box office, I happened to have a day off. I went to stand in line early. But it was futile. I did not want to give up so I called Li Ke. His uncle was associated with the symphony and might be able to help. I tried phoning Li Ke all day long. I even went to look for him in the evening. I seldom asked him for a favour. He was very helpful. Yet when he brought me tickets for the second performance he gave me a questioning look. I realized that I was acting somewhat unusually. I was like someone in love for the first time, driven by an unknown passion, my effort to realize my wish increasing in geometric progression.

But he gave me the tickets. Of course he thought it his duty to accompany me to the concert, although he had no love for music.

I hurried to your house and handed you the ticket. I was trying to stop gasping for breath, to tell you lightly, 'I've already been to it.' I did this without any reluctance. You were happily surprised. I felt relieved. When you read the time of the performance on the face of the ticket, you frowned in disappointment. You had to rehearse the same evening. Your mother immediately snatched the ticket away.

I could picture Li Ke sitting beside an old woman, the goodhearted Li Ke! It might be funny. I was aching over the ticket, yet I dared not say a word.

For the last performance I went myself to wait in line to get a ticket.

I met you in front of the Red Tower auditorium.

You looked at my hand clasping a one-yuan bill.

You stared at me for a while. For the first time I turned away under your stare. I was afraid your sharp gaze would uncover the seedling growing deep in my heart. I was not sure yet.

People were hurriedly entering the theatre. We walked toward each other. Whenever we approached each other, we smiled. You were clasping a two-yuan bill.

I was smiling, not to attract any person who wanted to resell his ticket, but because my secret was uncovered by you. I was scoffing at myself, calling my own bluff.

A small bespectacled woman gave my arm a tug. She took out two tickets. It was I who was the lucky one.

When the concert was over, a throng of people waited in line for the bus.

'Let's walk for one stop?' you suggested. Of course I was used to a crowded bus, but I nodded my assent.

We walked on, exchanging our views on the concert and on the play we were rehearsing. I talked continually, but I felt that I was not saying what I wanted to say.

'Let's walk a little slower,' you said.

Oh, I was not aware I was walking any quicker than usual. In fact, I wanted very much to spend as much time with you as possible, and I wished the distance were longer. Perhaps because I was always rushing to work or doing errands, my body habitually leaned awkwardly forward with my chest and shoulders anxiously slanting ahead. You found such tomboyishness funny, too. I deliberately slowed down my steps and clamped my mouth shut.

'Why are you so quiet?'

'Nothing, it's all right.'

'If I go to sea, I shall remember tonight. . . .'

'Why don't you change your profession to the theatre? You're such an expert. Perhaps in your complex personality, the underlying element is pragmatism, like your surface appearance. . . . Oh, don't be angry!' I was saying too much again.

'Good, you're observing me! What you say is right. I love the arts; I'm lucky to be artistic. It makes one appreciate people, life, and nature with passion. Even in the most difficult situation, such as when I was escaping in the dark from the camp alone and wounded from abuse, I found the light of the lamps so soft, so wonderfully attractive in the woods. It gave one who was a castaway from normal life a feeling of the comfort of ordinary living; its fine and deep meaning. When I was lying down, worn out from hard work in the valley, a breeze blew over, a cloud passed by, the short grass quivered, the forest rippled like tidal waves. It made me forget my pain and sorrow. My heart became calm and peaceful. . . .'

When we came to the next bus stop, neither you nor I stopped. You kept talking. I listened. In this way, we continued along the wet sidewalk which had just been sprinkled with water. The street was quiet. We walked past another bus stop, and another.

'But I want to do something more concrete, especially now.'

'Your life is smoother now. Do you still want to wander at sea?'

'Yes. I've reached an age when I should settle down, but I don't feel that way.'

'Perhaps it's from a sixth sense that you've heard a calling from the lighthouse.' I was becoming more interested in oceanography.

'To tell the truth, when I visited my old schoolmates and saw their family life, I did feel envious. On the street I saw those innocent kids, really lovely, toddling along. I could have stopped and watched them for hours. But I'm very clear as to what I want to do, although I know I shall regret the loss of a normal life because of it. In making my choice, I felt uneasy, because I wanted to realise an unfulfilled dream. But our nation's maritime industry has only just started and it holds a tremendous future.'

I listened attentively, like a sponge absorbing every word. I wanted to find out all about you. But still I was not satisfied. I only sensed your entity. Once I felt like leaping up when suddenly my thoughts wandered to Li Ke. His personality assured his having a tranquil life; never could he be entangled in a whirlpool of crisis. But birds by nature want to fly high; they can never follow the path of slow amphibians.

And you, whatever fate befalls you, you would get up and press on, like salmon swimming over waterfalls and rivers—turning and twisting in the waterway to eventually reach the sea.

I was listening and not listening. I turned to watch you quietly. When I observed every line of your face, hoping to catch some glimpse of your true character and spirit, my analytic reasoning failed me. What remained was a pure, half-dreaming state that made me unwilling to shift my glance from you or to think any more. I only wanted to listen to your voice as I leaned close to your shoulder, following you forward. At moments I was curious, though also very depressed, because I wanted only to touch with the tip of my finger that strong and full form of yours . . . to see if it was actually true.

'If we continue to walk like this, it will be morning by the time we reach our destination. Are you tired?'

I wanted very much to walk on, but I found myself wordless.

As we crossed an intersection, a night truck plunged rapidly by. Instinctively I grabbed at you, and in doing so inadvertently touched your wrist which had a medicated patch on it.

'What's the matter?'

'Just a souvenir from our first meeting. It doesn't matter.'

It was when I shoved you on to the bus at our first meeting. I felt very sorry and looked sympathetically at your arm as I held it. I could feel your eyes on me.

'Why are you looking at me?'

'You look somewhat like her.'

'Her? . . . What was she like?'

'She was very gentle, but very strong. She majored in naval design. When we graduated, we were assigned to the same boat. . . . We had never had a chance to talk, but we both decided to dedicate ourselves to the seafaring industry. On that day, on the campus, she accidentally walked by me. I wanted to call out to her. Maybe I had some kind of premonition but I stopped. I felt embarrassed in public. She was quietly passing by, when there was a sudden skirmish between two rival factions and a stray bullet hit her.

'She was strong and yet gentle. . . .' I repeated in a low voice, feeling grieved for you, and somewhat lost for myself.

'You look something like her, no, not really. . . . I hope you will change your character. You can be powerful just by being feminine.' There was an unfamiliar light in your eyes; a profoundly gentle feeling flowed out of you, then vanished all too suddenly. I thought that your gentleness was not only because you were offering me sincere advice, but also because you were remembering her.

I did not know what to say. At that moment a bus came to a stop. I called out, 'Let's hurry. See you at the rehearsal on Wednesday.' I purposely behaved in an unsuitable way to cover my true feelings. It was my defence mechanism. It was regrettable. I did not explain to you at all.

After work, I followed the dimly lit alley home. A cyclist appeared coming toward me. At one glance I took in the profile. . . . Is it he. . . ? I wondered. But I was not yet home. No, no. It was not this at all. I had serious doubts, but instinctively I suppressed them. We had spent an hour together, but you, the outer you and the inner you, were melting into my own interior. The profile had even been a very similar one; when tracing it there was very little difference. Yet the style and the spirit could be greatly unalike.

'What's the matter with you?' I scoffed at myself. 'He is rehearsing, he has no time to come. And he doesn't know where I live, either. Nor does he know how I feel.' But I couldn't help thinking, 'Perhaps there is such thing as telepathy.'

You couldn't have known that after the concert I was hoping to encounter you, hoping that our eyes would meet. During the entire day this desire had been wheeling around. . . .

Later, at home, I sat at the desk, facing paper and pen. I had to write a short story, but I was in no humour to do so. I was restless.

Whenever I felt lost, life became monotonous and lonely. Whenever my heart was filled with some unknown emotion, I felt distracted. One missed out on both counts. When I was dealing with Li Ke, I felt I was being too strong, and was thus not content. But when I found myself emotionally led by a man and thought of him constantly, I would hope to adjust myself according to his wishes. I would suppress my own self, feeling in this way more dependent. Where was my self-confidence which had propelled me to go forward; or my unwillingness to show weakness? I became weaker, but I believed one must be dependent upon oneself only. This was my irrevocable conclusion.

I turned on the radio, hoping to be calmed by the music . . . it was Beethoven again, the F-major symphony. The feeling of spring was very easy to sense, at this moment especially obvious.

In the most beautiful passages I could no longer immerse myself in the music alone. I was distracted, thinking of you, wishing you could hear it too. . . .

I seemed to be walking beside a clear brook; in its reflection was a newly sprouted willow. At every step I took, amidst the branches, I was followed by the sun. You were always there, you never disappeared. How could it be! You were everywhere.

'Don't be enfeebled by love!' Maybe my feelings were too sensitive, larger than reality. What is reality for? A bubble had emerged through my own emotion. When the sun shone upon it, it became iridescent. I analysed myself coolly, scoffing at myself. But it was futile. How strange we all are! Just because of some lonely thoughts, the color and rhythm of life are all mysteriously transformed.

I was worried about you. You had no inkling of it as you rehearsed the play with the others. . . . I envied the female star Liu Jie, and those girls, they were listening to your words, looking at you and receiving revelations from you. Heavens! What has become of me? I can't tell anyone of this obsession. Let me be frank with myself. I am in love with you.

Do you really like me? I have no way of telling. I know men look upon the world differently, but in general they are alike as far as their demands and their ideas about women go. You also are the same. But me—you have classified me as a boyish woman. I wouldn't qualify as the Ideal. Strange, I knew it all along. I was even proud of being independent and cool. Now I feel a little sad. Why did I give you such an impression?

I was falling into a deep meditation. I was not innately this way. If it were not for dealing with the pressures of society or fending off other people's intrusions and jealousies, I would not assume the mask of neuter, sometimes even a manly mask. Could I transform myself into being more lovely? Yes, I could. I was not born masculine. Yet perhaps I was really being transformed. Since when? Into the memory of my life came many loose ends, unrelated vignettes: on a steep mountain track carrying a bucketful of water where a slight list would spill the water on to the parched yellow earth; or shouldering a pile of burlap bags and shoving them up a hill step by step with teeth gritted.

—The most beautiful ten years of my life were spent in changing several blue smocks, thinking about my gradually developing bosom, purposely hunching the shoulders. The first time I cursed was a put-on over inner timidity. Later, when angry I would scream, and when happy I would easily give a curse.

—Father was banished from the village. Mother could only weep. Wanting to console her, I would have to solve the problem faced by Father. I must go on living. Where to find work? Asking for help, giving presents, negotiating. . . . Weak and shy, thy name is woman. But when necessary, all was changed. I must make deals with society.

—Father went back to the city first. All was finished between us. To weep. So painful, one would want to die. Fool! I must bury my feelings with my own hands, must be calm and think what the next step should be. . . .

Thus, in feeling, I dare not let go. But once all is gone, it is only too tragic. In my career, on the bus, I must be like a man. I can depend upon no one in my career. When facing failure, I must try again. In politics, in living, in crisis, in making a choice, I must resolve my dilemmas by myself. You blame our separation on me? If there is God, God made me a woman, yet society demands that I be like a man. I have intentionally concealed my femininity for survival, for competition. Unwittingly I have entered my present state of being. Is it only me? If my feminine self were still living, after going through so much for so many years, what would she be like? Even though she had remained gentle, how about her inner qualities and her thoughts?

I have reflected too long. . . . If I were to confess all, no one would think I was a girl of twenty-eight. Life has made me realistic through constantly analyzing myself. I am not growing too fast, but getting old too soon. This kind of precocity is itself a tragedy. . . .

Nevertheless, you exist in my life. Everything is changed. For you I am willing to change, to become a real woman.

Before going to bed, I checked again the calendar on the wall. I would not be late this Wednesday, not even by one minute.

Everyone receiving a bus ticket from me, or passing me to get down from the bus, seemed to notice the light green woollen scarf around my neck. Is it too early to wear a scarf? I was self-consciously watching other people, hoping to see someone else with a similar scarf. If one's fashion is not in tune with the current mode, one arouses embarrassing attention, even if only through a scarf. . . . Before I left the house, I checked myself in the mirror: it was not too bad.

After work, I went to the headquarters' clinic.

'Turpentine oil? Where were you injured?' Elder Sister Wang, who was both doctor and nurse, gave me a closer look. She was guarding the stocks, which were stored in a medicine cabinet, its painted surface peeling. I wanted to take off my socks to show her, but finally she opened the cabinet lock, took out a clean empty bottle and poured in half a bottle of turpentine oil.

'Keep your foot still. . . .'

But I was gone.

I climbed up the steps two at a time. The stairway gave out a squeaking sound. As I approached the top of the staircase I heard the happy noise of laughter and talk in the rehearsal room. I slowed down gradually and took the steps one at a time.

The actors were all present and were being very noisy. Some were rehearsing, some were sitting staring at the script, some were giggling and chatting. I knew what was going on instinctively without close observation of the room.

I sat down in a corner beside a desk, took out the turpentine oil, and quietly slipped it into a drawer. I waited. Several of the actors and actresses came around and told me excitedly that there was to be a dancing party after the first performance.

'I'd step on people's feet, I don't know how to dance.' I explained.

'I'll teach you,' one actor said, sitting down on the desk and wriggling his body in a most friendly way.

Laughing, I thanked him. I was afraid his wriggling might spill the turpentine I had just put into the drawer. I must have had a strange expression on my face.

'It won't be you,' Liu Jie said to him calmly. 'The director must ask the playwright to dance. You fought and argued with him over this play. Was it worth it?'

'Am I really that fierce?' I sighed with regret, put on an embarrassed expression, lowered my head, and pretended to curtsey with an imaginary long gown. 'Sir, I am sorry,' I said coyly to the actor.

To my surprise, the actors were amused. They all burst out laughing. I also laughed. Suddenly there was a footstep on the stair, very light but very distinct. It was approaching in rhythm, the kind of rhythm I knew belonged to you. I stopped laughing at once, instinctively, and eyed the entrance. To borrow one of the phrases you often used when directing, I seemed to be judging my actions carefully, whether intentionally or unintentionally.

You walked in hurriedly, took off your coat, and apologized to us. I felt joy in hearing your apology and I was also excited by it. I noticed your every move. You did not bother to notice me at all, maybe because I was sitting in a corner. You arranged the actors and actresses and then sat down in their midst. The lights were turned on.

I sat in the dark corner, watching the performance, feeling your every smallest movement. There were some minor changes in the play, good changes. My emotion followed the passion of the main female role; its ebb and flow. At the same time I could not help wondering why you were late.

As the play neared my favourite section—Bah! . . . a bang on the table. You were reproaching her, telling her that her acting was not sincere enough, that her rhythm was all wrong.

Liu Jie blinked her beautiful eyes and muttered resentfully, 'The script was written that way. I really. . . .'

You were silent for a while, then you said, 'No matter, let's make a change.' You assembled the actors for a discussion before going on with the rehearsal.

What? Really changed! The character's actions and the range of the performance were changed. The dialogue was deleted in many places. It was not my play! I did not mean it this way. I was sitting there, yet you did not consult me. I grew very upset. I had meant to sit there quietly, even when I wanted to voice an opinion. I was going to do it appropriately, slowly, subtly. Now I had to restrain myself from speaking out. I heaved a great sigh.

You swivelled back and gave me a look. Immediately you pushed aside your chair, walked over to me and said, 'You're here? Sorry, I didn't get to talk to you. What do you think?'

I only wanted to say a few words, but you insisted on your own way so I had no choice but to speak. I really did not want to argue with you. Yet I had no choice, my characters must be as I had drawn them. As soon as I started to talk I got excited. My voice became louder and my words rolled out faster. I kept talking and talking. Suddenly, I realized that my insistence might be interpreted by you as stubbornness and aggression. You would never change your opinion of me. I stopped immediately, sat down, and stared at you. You were saying something but I had no heart to listen. I was suppressing myself.

'Is this all right?' I suddenly heard you say. 'Just let it be my way.'

'I . . . no way!' I became agitated, beside myself. I banged on the table. The actors all stopped, looked at us, and began whispering among themselves.

'You're so stubborn and unreasonable,' you said in a low, agitated voice, patting my hand, which lay on the table. Turning toward the actors you shouted, 'Who said you could stop? Continue!'

Nonsense! As if the understanding and trust which existed between us could be sacrificed. 'Stop this nonsense!' I replied.

You were stunned. You withdrew your hand and turned to walk away. You stood up and said, 'Calm down, we'll talk later.' Then you brushed me aside.

After the rehearsal, you went downstairs to answer a long-deferred phone call. The actors were walking away. I was still sitting there. You came upstairs again, picked up your coat and came over to say to me softly, 'You aren't angry?'

I wanted to explain myself, but I was upset. The words tumbled out of my mouth, 'why do you always give me trouble?'

You misunderstood. You gave me a stare, as if thinking I was wilful, unreceptive to suggestion. You sighed. 'Sorry, I have some urgent business. I'll have to talk with you later.' You turned away and walked out.

I was left alone.

This was awful. I was angry with myself. What was I doing? Was it for that imagined world of mine? For an unreal character's speech, for some small parts? Through all this I was damaging my image in your eyes. At that moment I was truly envious of Liu Jie and the other girls; no matter what they really were, they could always be gentle. Yet I, too, should be gentle and soft, mild in speech, yielding over such an insignificant matter. I should simply give you a smile. Then the difference would melt away. I had thought it was just because of the boyish coat I was wearing that I seemed masculine, but this coat had contaminated my style. I could not even take it off. I was bitterly disappointed in myself.

I discovered suddenly that I was standing in front of those fading mirrors. As I looked at myself, I began to work myself up into a rage; my hands in my pockets, muddy boots on my feet, my cotton-quilted coat with the first button missing. The pastel green scarf was such an eyesore. My thoughts were meticulous to the point of being pathetic, as if someone were laughing at me, yet my actions were rude to the point of being comical. I took off the scarf instantly and put it in my pocket.

I pulled out the drawer of the desk and saw the bottle of turpentine oil. I wanted to throw it out of the window, but finally I put it in my pocket.

Naturally I understand. Most of your suggested changes turned out to be correct. This was to be the first performance. After the curtains were drawn back I stood at the side watching the performance and observing the reaction of the audience. In the crosscurrent running directly between onstage and offstage I was moved by the power of the drama myself. I had not anticipated this. I wanted to confess to you that my own ideas had been wrong, but you were busy backstage so I planned to tell you during the dance-party. I had even quietly practised some waltz steps so that I could dance with you.

The reception of the play was more enthusiastic than I had expected. As I busily greeted the guests, I anxiously looked to see where you were. I only wished we could have a quiet moment by ourselves. Liu Jie was surrounded by people. She had acted better than I had expected. People were asking her about her perception of the role. She giggled but did not respond. She could not handle the situation any longer and came up to me for help. She grasped me and pushed me before the crowd. She said, 'I couldn't have acted out such a good role if it hadn't been for the director's instruction. He often told me to observe that she herself is that way, a tomboyish girl.'

I was standing in front of the crowd. Liu Jie's remark stunned me. I began to realise that you regarded me in this light. You put me in a category. You did not perceive the other side of me. The crowd was friendly and laughed in approval; I was smiling, too, just to follow their example. I was feeling very sad.

The music was rising. Some people came to ask me to dance. I refused them politely. I was sitting behind a column. My small success was remote from me. I felt weary. I wanted to close my eyes and just listen to the music.

'Do you want to dance?' someone asked.

'I have a headache,' I said.

But immediately I knew it was you who was sitting down at my side. Although I was feeling very sad, I was also naturally very nervous. I wanted to find a pretext with which to shield myself. 'This

. . . play.' I stopped. To let you think that I was a stubborn person was unthinkable; yet that was how you regarded me.

'Why is it that all we talk about is the play? Let's change the subject. We haven't really talked at all.'

Your voice was different. I raised my head. I was smiling, but I was sad. And I was speechless. I only stared at you gently, in silent promise. I met your eyes. They were no longer as sharp as usual, nor as self-confident, but thoughtful, concentrating. . . . With the happy rhythm of the music filling the hall and with the warm smiling faces passing by, I felt a sudden strange communication in our eyes.

I was about to lose control. I would be defeated soon. I turned away from your glance quickly.

'Shall we dance?' you asked again.

I stood up helplessly but just as I was putting my hand on your shoulder, the music stopped. I suddenly remembered your remark about me. The remembrance stirred my innately rebellious nature. In an intentionally sarcastic tone of voice I said, 'It seems we have no luck with each other.' I was laughing but trembling inside.

At this moment, Li Ke squeezed himself out of the dancing crowd and came up to me.

'My friend,' I introduced him vengefully.

The music was playing again, it was the Cuban song *La Paloma*. I escaped to Li Ke's shoulder. 'Let's dance,' I said. Without waiting for his answer I dragged him toward the centre of the hall and began dancing with him.

'I'm the one who should be leading,' Li Ke found himself saying.

At every turn, over his shoulder, over other dancing couples, I saw you standing beside the column. At every turn I saw you.

Li Ke was observing me with his clear, loving eyes. He blushed and muttered, 'You are wonderful. I . . . like you.'

Ah, heavens, he likes me, but I don't like him! I like the one who does not like me.

Liu Jie and her dancing partner turned around to us. 'Are you going to see him off?' she asked.

'Who?'

'Our director.' She kept turning around, sometimes farther, sometimes closer to us. 'He's going to sail, tomorrow morning at five o'clock. He's going to Guangzhou. Don't pretend that you don't know.'

Abruptly I dropped my hand from Li Ke's shoulder. I was standing in the middle of the hall. You had disappeared from the column.

I pulled myself away from the happy crowd. Scurrying everywhere, pushing my way through the crowd and stepping on other people's feet, I searched every corner but I could not find you anywhere.

The shadow of the dancing couples silently waltzed away from me. There was a sad baritone voice, singing along, as if very near, but remote:

When I left my lovely homeland,
You can't know how sad I was.
My loving heart wanted to sail away with you,
Like a dove flying free over the sea.

I don't know how I got to your house. The window of the small room was dark. I saw your parents. They told me you had to say goodbye to many people and wouldn't be back until very late.

'Is there anything for him? Or anything you want to give him?' Your mother kindly asked me. She reminded me that waiting too long would not be proper. I should have brought a present, but I had not brought anything. I was not able to think of it in time. Unconsciously I put my hand in my pocket. There was the bottle. I took it out.

It was empty! I don't know when the turpentine oil had leaked out.

What stop was this!

You were waiting under the yellow and blue bus stop sign. I could see your strong and stalwart build, and over your lips there seemed to flicker a red star. Under the street lamp, the profile . . . the image suddenly became intensely clear and strong. Many people were waiting under the bus stop sign, pressing down from the sidewalk. I could not find you again.

I got off the bus; after all the passengers had got off and others had got on, I got on the bus again.

At this very moment, were you sailing toward some distant land? Over the ebbing and flowing sea, golden lights flickering? What were you doing now? Standing on board, staring at the stars in the evening sky? What were you thinking?

Shadows from the street lights, waves of people, the traffic continually rolling on. The bells from bicycles rang through the everlasting honking of the cars like some sharply played nocturne. Then the nocturne vanished. My heart was full and heavy.

I longed to see you again. To see your eyes, your unforgettable eyes. I hoped my memory would hold fast, that I would preserve this momentous consolation and strength. . . . But as if through a dense fog, the more I wanted to capture the image, the harder it became for me to identify it. The eyes, the look, it was as if I were seeing them more clearly now, then suddenly the vision dimmed, becoming more and more remote.

I had found you, and then lost you. What had I done wrong? I sought bitterly in my memory for each encounter we had had, however brief.

The noisy dance party.
The argument at the rehearsal.
The long walk after the concert.
The only time I sat on your desk.
The squeaking stairway.
The overcrowded streetcar with the door which could not be shut.

Oh, what separated us was not mountains and rivers, or the wide expanse of the ocean, but myself.

The streetcar stopped, then started again.

She was still pushing among the passengers. Saying over and over again: 'Tickets, please. Give the seat to the ones who are carrying a child. The next stop is. . . .' Deep inside her heart sounded another voice, lamenting: 'Forgive me. . . .'

1980

NOTES

1 In northeast China.
2 Five is the highest mark.
3 Excellent ideology, excellent health, and excellent study.
4 The indomitable and funny hero in *The True Story of Ah Q* by Lu Xun.

15

Hints

By **FANG FANG**
Translated by Ling Yuan

Fang Fang 方方 *is the pen-name of Wang Fang* 汪芳 *(b. 1955), who was born in Nanjing. She comes from an elite family in China. She lived in Wuhan with her parents during her childhood. In 1978, she entered Wuhan University and graduated four years later with a degree in Chinese. She worked for the Hubei Television Station in 1982-89. She began her writing career as a member of the Hubei Writers' Association in 1989 and she is now vice-chairman of the Association. Fang Fang is a prolific short story writer and her works have been widely anthologized. To date, she has published eight collections of her stories, including* Where is Home? *(*He chu shi wo jiayuan 何處是我家園*, 1995) and* Black Hole *(*Hei dong 黑洞*, 1995). In 1982, she won the first prize of the 'Yangtze River Best Works' with her story 'Covered Truck' (Da feng che shang* 大蓬車上*). She is currently conducting research for a novel on the history of her family.*

I

When it occurred to Ye Sang that she had not done her laundry yet, dusk had already fallen, dyeing the air a pinkish-grey. Smiling inwardly, she told herself, 'I'm so stupid today!'

She began stuffing dirty clothes into the washing machine. Xing Zhiwei, her husband, was talking on the phone. As she dropped the last piece of laundry into the machine she noticed that he was modulating his tone.

The washing machine started humming. Ye Sang watched closely as the clothing and washing powder sank slowly into the swirling water. Outside, a feminine voice was singing: 'Let me move along, and find a home for my heart.' The voice was charged with such emotion that Ye Sang felt as if it came not from outside the window but from the heart of the tiny whirlpool in the washing machine. It sounded like someone in there was pleading. She smiled to herself, thinking how life was full of sentimental emotion. Ye Sang liked to listen to pop songs, but this did not change her opinion that most pop songs were nothing more than whines without good reason. They were like pickles: cheap and lacking nutrition, yet everybody liked them with their meals. Her husband's younger sister happened to be a pop singer; she had stopped dropping in to see her elder brother since she heard Ye Sang's remark.

The swirl of water in the washing machine churned up one of Xing's shirts, and it reminded her that she had forgotten to check that the pockets were empty. She frowned. 'I'm so scatterbrained today.'

The other day, a red cinema ticket had been left in the pocket, which stained Xing's cute 'Crocodile' shirt. He had hastened to explain he had been given the ticket by his office, and that the leading star in the movie had been such a flop that he hadn't mentioned it. Ye Sang now recalled that on that day, to her great discomfort, he had been unusually courteous. But she had declined to pursue the issue, thinking it beneath her to hold an apparently trivial incident against her man—only a woman with no dignity was capable of that. This thought had set her mind at ease in the days that followed.

As the sentimental song continued to waft in, she joked to herself about what Xing might say if another ticket turned up in a pocket. At that moment, her fingers touched something in one of the pockets, and she pulled out a slip of blue paper. As she unfolded it the unknown singer continued obstinately, 'Let me move along, and find a home for my heart.' The message on the paper said, 'Could I see you at the same place? Miss you so—Ding Xiang.' The handwriting was graceful to the point of being ambiguous. A jolt, like an electric shock, shot through Ye Sang, and she saw stars drift down like dust. Am I just going mad today? She asked herself.

With the slip of paper in her hand, Ye Sang walked softly over to her husband. Her heart ached faintly. Xing was talking to his boss on the phone. In between saying yes, he never forgot to slip in a fawning phrase or two. Ye Sang placed the slip of paper before him, then she sat herself down at the other end of the couch, eyeing him across the cold distance between them. Let's see how you account for this, she said to herself.

Xing replaced the telephone receiver and picked up the slip of paper. His face expressionless, he asked dryly, 'What do you mean? What are you driving at?'

The question left Ye Sang speechless. Indeed, what was she driving at? By now the singing, '. . . find a home for my heart,' had turned from murmuring to howling, echoing in agitation between Ye Sang and her husband. While Ye Sang was seized by sudden palpitations, Xing behaved as if nothing had happened. Grinning grimly, he sauntered away without so much as casting her a glance.

The door closed with a bang, shutting out the howling of the singer. Ye Sang let out a gasp of astonishment. She wanted to cry, but no tears came. She looked at the newly laid linoleum floor she had just cleaned with a mop, and thought, if tears fell on this floor they would look like clear crystals glittering under the ceiling lamp. Even this thought failed to move her to tears. The night deepened as Ye Sang sat dry-eyed on the couch. Outside, insects warbled faintly and made the night feel darker. Xing did not return. Did this mean he had gone to the 'same place' to see the woman named Ding Xiang, to hug and kiss her? Or to reach a hand to her breast, sliding it downward, just as she herself had experienced, while he said, as if he were delivering a speech, that he wanted to 'know more' about her? Ye Sang's scalp became numb at the thought. Her brain hummed, and she had difficulty breathing. Silently she asked herself, is my face flooded with a river of tears? But to her continued surprise, not a tear drop came to her eyes.

The alarm clock rang, as it did at this hour every morning, filling the otherwise empty room with some semblance of a homely atmosphere. Ye Sang passed a hand over her face as she stood up. Her tearless eyes felt parched. She went into the bathroom, washed with unusual fastidiousness, and tucked her shoulder-length hair into a bun at the back of her head. While she was doing this, her thoughts turned to the pop singer Wei Wei, who also wore her hair like this. She knew Wei Wei had married an American and borne him a child, and that her career was going downhill. Judging from what was said in the press, she led a happy life, but what lay on the other side of the coin was hard to tell. For breakfast, Ye Sang made herself a bowl of congee by soaking the previous night's rice in boiled water, and ate it with some Sichuan pickles. Picking up the bag she had often used for business trips, she went out of the door. She did not leave Xing a message—that did not occur to her at all.

The sun had just risen as she stepped out of the residential building. Its rays shone on her face, erasing all traces of the insomnia of the previous night as if melting ice. She hailed a taxi, and in an unhurried voice said to the driver, 'Just keep going.' Thus she left home, without so much as a glance back at the building in which she had lived for eight years.

The cab drove through the streets under boughs of green foliage. The glistening form of the imposing building in which Xing Zhiwei worked came into view, but she acted as if she did not see it at all.

'You want to stop here?' the driver asked.

'Why? For what?' she retorted.

'I just asked,' the driver said. 'Many of the people from that building of yours work here.'

Ye Sang sneered. 'So you know all about the people who live here, do you? I am not one of them.'

The driver sulked. 'That's your business, but you have to tell me where you want to go.'

It took her five minutes to come up with an answer. 'Perhaps, Xiaguan Dock is an appropriate place.'

II

Jiangshen, the ship Ye Sang boarded, set sail from Xiaguan Dock at half past six in the evening. The prolonged tooting of the steam horn startled her into reality. She realized she was running away. Where am I going? she asked. What am I doing?

She had thought of taking a second-class cabin, venting her spleen by squandering some of the money Xing, the family's chief bread-winner, had earned. But she ended up purchasing a ticket for a berth in fourth class, as if some divine force had changed her mind.

There was an offensive odour in the fourth-class cabin, which Ye Sang shared with a dozen or so passengers, most of them men from the countryside. She had sat on her bed for barely three minutes when the smell proved too much, and she left the cabin in disgust. Out on deck she leaned against the handrail, before her an unobstructed view of the landscape. She stared out, yet at the same time it was as if she saw nothing. She remained there, dazed, for what seemed like an eternity.

The ship negotiated its course, gently cleaving through the placid river like a sharp knife, and sending foamy, white waves rolling sideways towards its banks. In mere seconds, the scar left by the 'knife' disappeared without a trace, as if it had never been made. That is the essence of water, Ye Sang thought. This reminded her of the old saying that women are like water. She decided that the meaning was implied in this motion. Women had always taken the comparison as a compliment coined by men to refer to female innocence and tenderness, never perceiving the spitefulness that underlies it: that women have to endure the pain of having their wombs opened and closed while concealing the pain without a trace—because women are water.

Through her distracted thoughts Ye Sang was faintly conscious of the pitch dark surrounding her. The foamy, white waves had suddenly disappeared. Like an interminable black ribbon the river undulated alongside the boat, to the accompaniment of the noise and vibration of the engine underneath. As Ye Sang gazed raptly, the lights on both shores flickered as if about to be extinguished by the wind or abandoned by the boat. Whether blown out or abandoned, the result would be the same: they would finally disappear into the gigantic backdrop of the sky.

Ye Sang was carried away by the flow of this ribbon. How interesting! she thought. What is the driving force behind this perpetual flow? Is it noisy or silent in its depths? What would it feel to be at one with this flow of water? If people lived naked in this water, there would be no possibility of secrets between men and women. Sighing ever so softly, she sensed an aged voice ringing in her ears, 'Child, aren't you taking all this too seriously?'

The song she had heard the previous day came back to her mind in a soft, lingering tone: 'Let me move along, and find a home for my heart.' Ye Sang looked over her shoulder and imagined she could see an old man with silver beard and hair, and her smile froze at the sight of his eyes, the pupils so black against the whites. The aged voice rose once again, 'Give up all your foolish fancies, and go home where it's safe.' With these words the old man left. Ye Sang shuddered as she watched him drift away as if he was not governed by gravity at all.

It was near midnight when Ye Sang returned to her cabin. Her fellow passengers were snoring away and every seam and pore of the room was filled with the stench of their exhalations. On the upper berth opposite hers a man was reading in the dim light. When Ye Sang had eased into her bed she thought he asked her in a ghostly voice, 'Why don't you go?' This gave her a start. She raised her head and flashed her eyes at him, wondering what he was hinting at, but the man was flipping through his book, oblivious to her presence. Ye Sang was suspicious: If it wasn't him, then who else? Before she could get a clear answer, sleepiness got the better of her, and she succumbed to slumber.

Despite the sickening odour in the cabin, Ye Sang slept, and she dreamed. When she woke up in the morning, she had all but forgotten of what she dreamed, save a hand waving frenetically at her through a dense smog which was shattered by someone shrieking. She racked her brain but could not recollect what the shriek was all about.

That morning Ye Sang had instant noodles for breakfast. They came in a green package, spare ribs and chicken flavour, her husband's favourite. As soon as his image was summoned to her mind it dawned on her that the protruding hand in her dream was encircled by the cuff of his 'Crocodile' shirt, its blue stripes clearly visible. Ye Sang had bought the shirt for him on a business trip to Shenzhen. Her hands shook violently at the thought he was beckoning to her. She wondered if he would lose interest in Ding Xiang if she were flat-chested. He had said he liked Ye Sang because she had voluptuous breasts, that he was really turned off by a woman with a chest as flat as a runway. Ye Sang straightened her back and lowered her head to observe her own chest. As she stared into her cleavage she felt everyone else was, too. She hastened to bring her arms across to conceal it, and in so doing knocked the bowl of instant noodles to the floor. She was flustered as she looked about herself. Her fellow passengers gave her curious looks. Someone asked, 'Did you hurt your feet? There's a clinic on board the ship if you need it.' In a stupor she answered no. Her shoes were covered with noodles, and her feet were scorching hot.

By the time the boat had reached its destination Ye Sang's feet had become so swollen she had difficulty walking. The pain, however, distracted her from the endless torment of wild thoughts. See how weak I am now, she thought, even a bowl of noodles could cripple me like that.

Naturally no one was at the dock to greet her. Although the ticket she had bought covered the entire route, she had had no idea where she would disembark. The ship had pulled into Hankou Harbour without her realizing it. As she disembarked she was surprised to see the Turtle and Snake isles and the giant clock atop the tower of Jianghan Pass. Then excitement mounted when she realized she had returned to her hometown. Coming home never needs the guidance of the mind, for instinct is what counts.

Ye Sang hailed a taxi. In the local dialect she deftly told the driver, 'To Luojia Hill.'

The thought of her parents' home at the foot of the hill reminded her of a childhood spent picking acorns and playing hide-and-seek up on the hill with her two younger sisters. She even remembered the day when, in hushed silence, they watched a couple of college students emerge and kiss each other.

Ye Sang pushed the door open and stepped into the house. Her parents were not home. Only Second Sister was by the window, squinting at a tree leaf in her hand against the sun, all the while oblivious to Ye Sang, who plodded up and stopped by her. 'It's a hint,' Second Sister whispered to herself.

'Sister, I'm back,' Ye Sang said.

'Is that so?'

'I haven't been back for two years. Won't you even look at me?'

'You want me to look at you?'

Ye Sang sighed. She entered the room she had shared with her two younger sisters. Everything looked the same as she remembered. It was now five years since Second Sister had been diagnosed as schizophrenic. To Ye Sang, what the disease really affected was not her younger sister's mind but her age. She looked like a five-year-old girl, her expression full of childlike naivety as she listened uncomprehending to adults talking to each other. Whenever she lost her temper the best she could do was to whimper in the corner of the room. Yet Second Sister had a well filled-out figure. She was as buxom as Ye Sang. The third year into her college life she had become so smitten by a young man that her heart would arrest itself if she did not see him even for a single day.

The young man dated her twice, and on both occasions kissed her warmly. Their third tryst took place late one afternoon. Second Sister, her eyes sparkling with tender love, tore one leaf after another from a tree they were standing under. He took one leaf from her hand and told her that he did not love her but he was grateful to her for her attention. She could not believe her ears. Straining to avoid her gaze, he raised the leaf and eyed it against the sunlight. The leaf became transparent, with every vein visible. 'I have tried to hint to you, hinted repeatedly to you, but each time you refused to take it,' he said. Transfixed, she asked, 'You hinted?'

In the class the following day, she had stood up, and, ignoring the teacher and the roomful of classmates, said repeatedly, 'It's a hint. . . .' Her tone, serious and sad in a strange way, held the entire class in silence for minutes. She left college then and there, and had never returned.

Ye Sang lay down on Third Sister's bed. An old-fashioned wall clock, Father's favourite keepsake, rang a number of times. Ye Sang knew it was a gift her aunt had given her parents when she had returned home on a visit from Xinjiang. The clock was still ringing when Second Sister entered the room and sat down in a chair. Gazing raptly at Ye Sang, she said, 'It is a hint, haven't you realized it yet? It's a hint.' Ye Sang blinked blankly at the ceiling. She imagined she saw foamy, white waves rolling sideways; then a hand flicked across the ceiling, and in a few strokes tamed the river into an idyllic landscape painting. She replied, 'Yes, I have come to realize. It is a hint.' Second Sister said, 'Impossible. Nobody could have guessed it.'

III

Darkness fell. It seemed as if an entire century had elapsed when Ye Sang heard the door being unlocked.

Her parents entered together with Third Sister. Father was amazed at Ye Sang's unexpected return. 'What a great surprise,' was all he could say.

Mother, too, looked pleasantly surprised. She took Ye Sang by the hand and could not take her eyes from her. 'Your daughter has come home, what is there to be surprised about?' she retorted.

Third Sister threw herself at Ye Sang, crying, 'Marvellous, sister, it is high time you came to see us.'

Ye Sang smiled thinly. Pushing her sister away she said, 'My feet hurt.'

Only then did her parents see her swollen feet, which could no longer fit into her shoes. Both cried out in alarm.

Ye Sang was applying medicinal ointment to her burns when the telephone rang. Mother picked up the receiver, listened, and handed it to Ye Sang. 'It's for you,' she said. Ye Sang hesitated for a moment, then took the receiver. From the other end of the line came her husband's calm voice, 'What are you up to?' Without saying anything, she hung up.

'A hint?' Second Sister asked.

Ye Sang stared at her. 'Yes, that was a hint.'

In exasperation Mother shouted at Second Sister to go to her room. Watching Second Sister's retreating back, Ye Sang stood up, and took two tentative steps forward. 'I'm tired,' she said. 'I want to go to bed.' She followed Second Sister's shadow into the room. Behind her she could sense that Father and Mother were looking at each other in blank dismay. When she closed the door behind her she heard Mother murmur softly, 'My goodness!'

The next morning Ye Sang woke up to find Third Sister sitting by her bed, beaming. 'Good morning, Elder Sister, did you sleep well?'

Ye Sang smiled. 'Not bad.'

'Don't you want to hear my news?'

'What?'

'I'm going to be married.'

'Really?'

'Yes, I'm marrying Ning Ke, the postgraduate student Father tutored the year before last.'

This reminded Ye Sang of the tall young man she had seen at the dock a few years earlier when she arrived home for the summer holiday. He had come to meet her on behalf of her father, refined in bearing but looking rather solicitous. During the holiday, he had often come to seek Father about his studies. When Father happened to be away, he would sit on the couch in the sitting room and talk to Ye Sang. As he talked his eyes would bore into hers. Ye Sang said, 'Oh, him?'

'Elder Sister, you still remember him?'

'Certainly.'

Third Sister clapped her hands and giggled. 'Terrific! Our parents met yesterday. Today, his elder brother has invited me to dinner. Do go with me, please. He will have his elder brother while I have my elder sister to boost my courage. That puts us on an equal footing!'

Ye Sang recalled that when she had left Hankou at the end of the holiday, it was the same Ning Ke who had come to see her off at the dock. He had lingered with her until the departure time arrived, and Ye Sang had had to be the first to say goodbye. To her surprise he had suddenly blurted out, 'Had I come to know you a few years earlier I wouldn't have let you leave Luojia Hill—we shouldn't have let the opportunity slip through our fingers.' Ye Sang had smiled, and said, 'How silly of you to say something like that.' He simply said, 'You don't believe me?' At the time Ye Sang had thought a man behaving like that was rather lovable in a ridiculous way. But now, for no reason at all, a feeling of listlessness gripped her.

'Ning Ke will pick me up in a cab,' Third Sister said.

'I don't want to go. I can't walk,' Ye Sang replied.

'With the taxi you don't have to walk.'

'I said I don't want to go.'

Third Sister looked at her with startled eyes. After a pause, she said, 'Elder Sister, it's kind of odd, you coming home like this.'

Ye Sang answered dryly, 'Is it? There's nothing wrong with me. I just don't want to be forced to hear all about your happiness, that's all.'

'What did brother-in-law do to upset you? I won't let him off lightly!' Third Sister said.

'It has nothing to do with you,' was all Ye Sang said.

During breakfast the atmosphere was rather stifling. The silence was broken only when Second Sister repeated, 'It's a hint.' Third Sister tapped at her bowl with chopsticks and said, 'Sister, keep your mouth shut, or say something else! The way you say it makes me feel there are hints everywhere.' Ye Sang's heart missed a beat. She felt that hints and implications were indeed all-pervasive.

Their parents pulled long faces. Father remained silent, and Mother kept adding pickles to Ye Sang's bowl, something she usually only did for Second Sister. Mum is implying that I am the same as Second Sister, she thought.

Ye Sang had just put down her bowl when Father said seriously, 'Ye Sang, I want to talk to you.'

'About what?'

'About your frame of mind.'

'What is there to talk about?'

'Did you quarrel with Xing Zhiwei?'

'I wouldn't say it was a quarrel.'

'Then why did you return all of a sudden, and refuse to talk to him on the phone?'

'I just wanted to see my mum and dad, that's all. Is there anything wrong with that?' Ye Sang snapped.

'There is a reason for everything,' Father intoned. 'You wouldn't just come to see us on a whim.'

'But it was just a whim,' Ye Sang nodded.

'Did you ask for leave of absence?' Father persisted.

At a loss, Ye Sang blinked at Mother. It suddenly struck her that she had indeed forgotten to ask for leave of absence. Sighing, Mother said, 'Whatever happened, happened. Now let the child stay home and relax for a few days.'

Father became angry. 'They get this from you. None of the children can stand the test of things. One of them has already been ruined. I can't just sit here and watch another go to waste.'

Second Sister said, 'Dad's hinting at something?'

Ye Sang glanced at her, thinking how utterly perceptive it was of Second Sister to make this observation. 'I don't think I'll go that far,' she said. 'All I want is a rest. I feel so tired.'

'Why do you have to say such frightening things?' Mother said to her husband. 'The girl is just feeling tired and she wants to be home for a rest and see her parents at the same time. That's all!'

'I have a foreboding about all this. On our wedding night thirty years ago, I saw a hand flicking to and fro at the window curtain, and I knew that it meant I was to be punished. Now I feel it's about to happen.'

Ye Sang was stunned. 'A hand?' It reminded her of the waving hand in her dream. But what was the shriek all about?

'It's a hint.' This time it was Third Sister that said this. Father and Mother turned wide-eyed to look at her.

'Just be careful you don't become like Second Sister,' Third Sister said.

'That is exactly what I meant,' Father said.

And with these words breakfast came to an end.

Sunlight filtered through the window, and the air was filled with floating particles of dust—whether they were dancing nimbly or struggling on leaden legs depended on the mood of the spectator: the real manipulator of life.

Ye Sang was wearing a knee-length grey woollen sweater, and nothing else. She tried to walk around the sitting room, her feet looking better after medication. The skin on her thighs was so fair that light blue capillaries beneath it showed through. Second Sister was again sitting by the window perusing her tree leaf, her face as pale as white paper from long years of being indoors, her eyes darker than those of normal people. Her monotonous facial expression made her look like a paper puppet. As she observed the veins in the leaf, the sun tossed its beams on her hands and her attentive face. Her appearance, dainty and romantic, touched Ye Sang deeply. Second Sister's world must be very beautiful, she thought, or else how could she be so completely satisfied in herself, as if no one else existed in the world.

'Sister, can we go for a walk together on the hill?' Ye Sang said.

'A walk?'

'Yeah. It's a long time since I went there. Don't you remember, when you were small I often took you there?'

'When I was small?'

Ye Sang took her hand and said, 'Come on, come and give me some company.'

Thus the two of them went out of the house. The ground was hidden beneath a covering of autumn leaves that had fallen the previous night, and that snapped under their heels. 'What a beautiful sound,' Ye Sang said.

'It's a hint,' Second Sister said.

'Perhaps,' Ye Sang responded.

They rambled about with soft steps. Their shadows swept just as softly across the fallen leaves, causing, or so Ye Sang believed, a slight cracking sound of their own.

At that juncture Ning Ke happened to be passing in a cab on his way to pick up Third Sister. He had not expected to see the two sisters walking here, gingerly, on the fallen leaves. With their slow movement they instilled some life into the otherwise dreary-looking residential blocks surrounding them. Ning Ke's heart skipped a beat. What a strange couple of women! he thought. Recognizing Second Sister, he asked the driver to stop by them. As he got out, his eyes froze on Ye Sang's expressionless face. Then he cried out excitedly, 'Ye Sang!'

Ye Sang smiled. 'How are you?' she said. 'Third Sister is waiting for you.'

Without pausing she strolled past him. Ahead, a footpath came into view.

Autumn had set in, yet the trees still gleamed with a fresh greenness. The hill was no longer as deserted as it was in her teenage years. The road was too smooth, without the slightest suggestion of its former ruggedness. Thus the leaves were robbed of their sanctity and sequestered serenity. Second Sister began to cry out inarticulately. Ye Sang, her nerves stretched taunt by her sister's cries, wanted to restrain her, but Second Sister pulled free of her hand and began running and jumping along the tree-lined hill slope. Her clumsy actions struck Ye Sang as being rather congenial to the scenery, for it seemed to her that only with the commotion caused by Second Sister did the tiny hill gain motion and naturalness. In spite of herself she laughed loudly at the thought that here, on this hill, Second Sister was like a sprite. 'Sister, are you having fun?' she called at the top of her voice.

'Having fun?' Second Sister repeated.

As Second Sister's voice rose, Ye Sang felt as if she could see fragments of Second Sister's thoughts floating through the forests like so much gossamer in the wind. Some had risen to an unbelievable height, and now flew beyond the tops of the trees, where they dissolved into the clouds. Others were weighing down the green leaves. In the sunshine they glistened a dazzlingly purplish-blue. Stunned by what she imagined she had seen, Ye Sang cried, 'Ah! Ah, how beautiful this is.'

'Come over and have a look,' she said to Second Sister, and catching her younger sister's hand, pointed a finger at the sky full of her thoughts.

'Red, pinkish red. Lovely. . . . ' Second Sister said. Ye Sang watched fixated. Some red gossamer was indeed floating with those fragments of Second Sister's thoughts. The rosy threads were especially refreshing and intense, drifting merrily in the wind. Ye Sang was dazed. They could be mine, without a doubt, she thought.

IV

When dusk fell, Second Sister began to run a temperature. Then fever struck with a vengeance. Her face was flushed red, but all the time she was beaming.

'She caught cold on the hill today, that's for sure,' Father said. 'Give her some antipyretic, and see if she can stick it out until tomorrow.'

'I'd rather take her to hospital now,' Mother said.

'Why do you always make things difficult for me?'

'I am only thinking of what's good for our child.'

'I bet if I had suggested you take her to the hospital now, you would have offered to give her some medicine at home!' Mother paused for a moment. 'It's possible.'

Annoyed, Ye Sang said, 'Why do you always act this way? You're quite mad, both of you!'

'Ye Sang, what are you talking about!' Father demanded angrily.

Second Sister smiled demurely and said, 'It's a hint.'

It was very late when Ning Ke brought Third Sister home. At the sight of Ye Sang, with a mirthless grin on his face, he said, 'How are you?'

'You have no manners,' Third Sister interjected. 'You should have addressed her as elder sister.'

Embarrassed, Ning Ke became tongue-tied. Ye Sang smiled faintly and said, 'Second Sister is ill.'

The moment Third Sister went into the room to have a look, Ning Ke began to eye Ye Sang up and down without inhibition. 'You haven't acknowledged me as Elder Sister yet,' Ye Sang said.

Ning Ke said, 'Do you want me to?'

Then from inside the room they heard Third Sister shriek. 'She's running such a fever. We must get her to a hospital.' Aroused by her voice, Father and Mother scrambled from their bed and emerged with coats draped on their shoulders.

Third Sister came out of the room demanding, 'Dad, Mum, Second Sister is very ill. Were you intending to let her die?'

'How dare you!' Father shouted.

'You shouldn't say such things,' Mother chimed in.

Intervening, Ye Sang said, 'Let's not debate that now but decide whether we should get Second Sister to hospital or not.'

'That goes without saying,' Third Sister said. 'We cannot afford not to send her to hospital! Ning Ke, will you help me take my sister to hospital?'

'Don't you have an appointment early tomorrow morning?' Ning Ke asked.

'Then let me go to the hospital,' Father said.

'Don't you have two classes tomorrow morning?' Mother said, adding, 'I am afraid I can't go either, for the Provincial Education Commission people are coming on an inspection tour of our lab.'

'I have no plans. I'll take her,' Ye Sang said.

'In that case, it's best that Elder Sister and I take Second Sister to hospital,' Ning Ke said.

Under dim light the emergency room looked deserted. The night wind was not strong but it kept rattling the unhooked windows, pelting the silence of the room with single or repeated bangs.

Ning Ke moved awkwardly into the room, one hand shoring up Second Sister and the other holding high a transfusion bottle. Ye Sang was lost for words.

Second Sister was laid on a bed. She was so ill she allowed Ye Sang to edge her languid body into position. All the while, much to Ye Sang's surprise, she was saying, 'Funny.'

'You've stopped saying "it's a hint", haven't you?' Ye Sang said.

'Funny,' was all Second Sister said.

'She's being philosophical—there is an intrinsic relationship between "hint" and "funny",' Ning Ke intoned.

'Stop your glib talk!' Ye Sang snapped.

Ning Ke reddened in embarrassment and fell silent. Inwardly, Ye Sang found him rather ridiculous.

Second Sister gazed fixedly at the infusion dripping from the bottle into the tube. There was something peculiar about the look in her eyes, and in spite of herself, Ye Sang found her own eyes becoming glued to the infusion bottle as well. She fancied she could hear its pleasant metallic dripping sound in the tube, which hissed occasionally too. Ye Sang had trouble discerning the origin of the hiss; it took a while for her to realize that it was the infusion being sucked into Second Sister's vein. She thought she heard Second Sister say, 'Water is running hua-la-la, the nose is greeted by a sweet smell', and it seemed to Ye Sang she could see and smell the gurgling water. The scent was of roses, while the water flowed like a limpid brook. Ye Sang wondered if in the height of her fever Second Sister had sobered up. The thought jerked her back into reality. Rising to her feet, she asked, 'Sister, how do you feel?'

'She is quiet. Her condition seems rather stable. Don't you worry.' The voice was Ning Ke's. As he said this he placed both hands on Ye Sang's shoulders and pushed her ever so lightly down to her seat.

'Did you hear what Second Sister said?' Ye Sang asked.

'She said nothing,' Ning Ke answered.

'Yes, she did. She said the river was flowing hua-la-la,' Ye Sang said. 'And that she could smell a sweet scent.'

'I'm absolutely sure she didn't say anything,' Ning Ke replied. 'She is sound asleep.'

Ye Sang stared at him without seeing anything. Instead, she asked herself, 'Why didn't I see she was asleep? Was I hallucinating, or affected by Second Sister's illusions?' Seeing her stony expression,

Ning Ke laughed. 'Sometimes you look as naive as a little girl.'

This caused Ye Sang to lose her temper. 'Mind what you say!' As she said this that slip of blue paper came scudding out from a remote corner of her mind, and with it a bouquet of lilac. Recovering her composure, she said, 'Remember, I am your Elder Sister.'

Ning Ke looked at her and said, 'Have you heard the saying "Love for a house extends even to the bird on its roof"?'

Ye Sang's heart sank. 'Third Sister isn't a bird.'

'In my heart she is,' Ning Ke replied. 'I love the bird because I want to be near the house.'

'I really don't know whether you are being gallant or you just have no sense of shame,' Ye Sang said.

Ning Ke fell silent. In the dim light Ye Sang could not make out his countenance, but she surmised he must be blushing. This reminded her of her husband's unperturbed expression. If he still knows what shame is, that means he's not entirely bad. There are others who are not ashamed of anything.

Just as dawn was about to break, Second Sister woke up. The first words she said were, 'Very beautiful.'

'Can you imagine where her soul had gone when she was asleep?' Ye Sang asked Ning Ke.

Ning Ke answered, 'It must have been a place where birds sing and flowers have the sweetest fragrance.'

'That was quite a mouthful for you,' Ye Sang said. The thought of sweet scent and gurgling water drifted back to her mind.

V

It was about lunchtime when Father and Mother hurried over to the hospital. Second Sister's fever had gone. The doctor told them that she need not remain in the hospital another night but that it would be better to keep her in for observation for a few more hours. The parents stayed, allowing Ye Sang and Ning Ke to go home and get some sleep. Before Ning Ke left Father thanked him profusely. 'Don't stand on ceremony,' Ning Ke said. 'We'll soon be family.' Ye Sang was yawning sleepily, but out of the corner of her eye she caught his surreptitious glance.

They took a taxi together. Shortly after she got in Ye Sang dozed off. In her dream she could not decide if she was warm or cold. When she woke up she found they had arrived at their building. Ning Ke gave her a shove, and she realized she had been leaning on his arm. Raising her eyebrows, she saw him smile warmly, a smile she thought was tantamount to cunning. She scrambled out of the cab without so much as a goodbye or a thank-you, and made directly for the door. She flung herself to the bed, her heart throbbing rapidly, thoughts thronging to her mind as she mulled over the expression in Ning Ke's eyes. It was so easy to be entrapped, she thought, and self-control can be so fragile. How would she react if Ning Ke appeared at her bedside then and there? She decided it was quite possible that she'd say to him, 'Come here. I need you.'

But Ning Ke did not appear. Her sleep was a tangle of dreams until she was awakened by a noise. The sun was setting. Opening her eyes, she saw Second Sister lying in the bed opposite. Mother was tucking in the corner of her quilt, and Father was pouring water into a cup. Third Sister was talking loudly in the sitting room. 'Ning Ke,' she said, 'why didn't you sleep a little longer? See my elder sister—she's having a nice long sleep.' Ye Sang recalled that she had embraced a man in her dream, but that the man was definitely not her husband.

Ning Ke entered. At a glance he saw Ye Sang's sleepy eyes were wide open. 'Hi, did you sleep well?' he asked.

Ye Sang noticed the smell of his body was familiar, the same smell which had permeated her dream. 'Yeah, did you?' she asked.

'Yes, though not for very long,' Ning Ke said. Second Sister giggled and said, 'That's a hint.'

Most television programmes were boring and of bad taste, and every day it was the same, viewers had to put up with it. Ye Sang could have avoided watching television but seeing Third Sister enter the inner room with her hand around Ning Ke's waist, she had no choice but to lie languidly on the couch and stare at the television. 'Do you want to read a book?' Mother asked.

Ye Sang shook her head. She strained her ears in the direction of the inner room, feeling rather perturbed. 'Why don't you call Xing?' Mother suggested.

'Why?'

'He is, after all, your husband. And you are but a woman.'

'I don't know about other women, but I intend to follow my own ideas.'

'Do you mean to quit your job and stay home?'

'Certainly not.'

'Then what are you up to?'

'I am waiting.'

'Waiting for what?'

'I don't know. But I know what I am waiting for will come about soon.'

'You are talking exactly like Second Sister. I don't understand at all.'

'As a matter of fact, Second Sister is quite perfect in a simple and untouched way. I envy her greatly. In my whole life I may never find the same peaceful world that she inhabits. If I could enter such a realm, I would go farther, and let myself go completely.' As Ye Sang talked, she felt part of her being lifted into a vast sky so blue and pure as to be beyond expression. 'There I would have a place of my own.'

'Don't say such spooky things to me, Ye Sang,' Mother said. 'You used to have such a clear mind.'

'I still have a clear mind. In fact, it is getting clearer all the time,' Ye Sang said.

A few minutes later, Ye Sang watched Mother enter the study and say to Father, 'You've got to talk to Ye Sang. She's not quite herself.'

'That's ripe coming from someone who's not quite right in the head herself,' Father said. 'To me, Ye Sang seems rather normal. She's trying to teach that bastard a lesson, that's all.' She heard Mother say, 'Even so, she and Xing are husband and wife. We have to try and help them make a reconciliation.' And Father said, 'They may be reconciled for a time, but will they be reconciled for the rest of their lives?'

Ye Sang couldn't take this any more. A sense of frustration gripped her tightly, and in spite of herself she stopped her ears with both hands.

She realized Mother and Father were poles apart from where she was.

Understanding, she thought, is but a sign of self-deception and a means of getting around in the world. People's hearts are so far apart that no amount of 'understanding' can bridge the gap. Has anyone really ever understood someone else in this world?

Ning Ke and Third Sister were flirting with each other as they emerged from the room. They were startled to see Ye Sang with her hands over her ears, her face grimaced in a pained expression. 'Ye Sang, what's the matter with you?' Ning Ke asked.

Third Sister glared at him and said, 'Address her as Elder Sister. Be polite! Elder Sister, are you not feeling well?'

Their voices aroused the attention of Father and Mother, who hurried to the sitting room, their faces aged and worried, making Ye Sang feel even more perturbed. How could they behave like that? she thought. She felt as if myriad alien noises were tearing her inner world to pieces, and felt a desperate urge to throw all the pieces out. She wanted to shout loudly, to smash things in a frenzy, to tear at her hair, or burn herself. She was about to lose control when she heard Father's voice, which could not have been more amiable, 'Ye Sang, can you come with me tomorrow? I want to burn incense for your aunt.'

Ye Sang raised her head. In an instant the turmoil inside evaporated into thin air. In her mind's eye she saw the charming face of a woman. She used to sit beneath it on the woman's lap as a child and receive her gentle caresses. She could still imagine the warmth of her palm. Then came the day when Father went berserk, drinking and smashing things as if it were the end of the world. The commotion had caused Second Sister, still a toddler, to cry herself hoarse. Mother remained rooted to the spot, watching all this with cold eyes. Many days later Ye Sang had asked Mother what had happened. Mother had whispered, 'Aunt died.' Amongst her old memories, Ye Sang spied the ambiguous colours of bygone days, and it helped gather the fragments of her spirit together. 'All right,' she said, and in that instant she knew Mother's face had darkened.

VI

Many years earlier, Ye Sang and Mother had been on their way to Guanshan Hill when they had passed a tiny, run-down temple. With the air of a victor Mother had said that Aunt's remains were there.

Now, as Ye Sang stepped into the hall where the urns were kept, Mother's triumphant smile merged with the image of the crumbling temple. The interior of the hall came as a great surprise, for she had never expected a place for keeping the ashes of the deceased to be as large as an assembly hall.

Ye Sang followed behind Father, whose face had clouded over the moment he entered the building. He lumbered up towards an urn, and extended a hand to it. Ye Sang knew to whom it belonged. In silence he caressed the photograph attached to the urn the way a lover caresses his beloved. Tears trickled down his emaciated cheeks. Aunt's urn occupied a single slot on the shelf. It was painted with black lacquer, shiny and without a speck of dust despite the passage of twenty years. Father must have come often to caress it, Ye Sang thought, gazing at him demurely. But if the ashes were her Mother's, would he do the same? If that woman called Ding Xiang died, would Xing weep and grieve like this before her urn? The thought brought a malicious smile to her lips. Aunt's ashes had already lain in the hall for twenty years; they had yet to be buried. Was it Aunt that was waiting, or was it Father?

At last Father stopped weeping. He remembered the few sandalwood incense sticks he had brought along, and telling Ye Sang that this was Aunt's favourite incense, he carefully planted them in the burner in front of Aunt's urn and lit them. He did all this so softly and fastidiously that Ye Sang fled the hall in disgust. The smell of sandalwood followed her, enveloping her heart with its insidious charm. She felt the smell penetrating all the pores of her skin and flowing about inside her. Then the long-forgotten palm of the hand returned to her mind, caressing her with such warmth as to leave a lasting pleasant sensation. The feeling reminded Ye Sang of a song which went: 'The golden sun shines brightly; when the rooster has crowed three times, the flowers awake, and birds begin to preen their plumes.' . . . She wondered if Aunt now lived in such a place of enchanting beauty. She imagined she could see Aunt standing there looking like an angel, her face beaming with radiance, her breath violet blue. And as Ye Sang's mind wandered, Aunt's lips quivered as if she was saying, 'Ye Sang, how are you?' Ye Sang was torn between answering 'I'm unhappy' and 'I'm fine'. She said nothing, her jaw dropped open.

Ye Sang's mind was still swimming in the clouds when she felt a pat on her shoulder. 'Aunt!' she burst out.

But it was her father who patted her. As she collected her thoughts, Father stared at her with surprise in his eyes. 'Ye Sang, what's wrong with you?'

'Nothing,' she replied. 'I was remembering how Aunt was when she was alive, that's all.'

Father's eyes moistened. In a resonant voice he said, 'It is so touching to know you still care about your aunt. In this world almost everyone has forgotten her.'

'How come?' Ye Sang said sarcastically, 'You are still around. In my opinion there isn't a single day when you don't remember her.'

Father fell silent.

Ye Sang walked with Father for a long time. The bus came, but they let it go, and Father said, his tone resonant with all his years of experience in this world, 'Ye Sang, you are curious about Father's relationship with your aunt, aren't you?'

'No,' Ye Sang replied, 'I'm not. Everybody has his own private affairs.'

'But I want to tell you all about it.'

'How come?'

'It's not that I need your understanding and forgiveness, but that I want you to know the pain I have endured all these years. At the moment it is so great that I don't think I can bear it much longer. I chose this occasion because I know a person in pain is able to share the pain of others.'

'You think I'm in pain?' Ye Sang asked. 'If you think that way you are mistaken.'

'Ye Sang, I know you have been sensitive and proud of yourself since you were a little girl. But you needn't cover everything up before your father. If nothing else, I am your father.'

Ye Sang grinned coldly. 'Why would I be so foolish as to hide myself? All I want to do is to straighten myself out.'

'Straighten yourself out?'

'Yes, to rid myself of certain impurities, that's all.'

Father sighed a long sigh. 'What can I say to you? Let me tell you my story.'

Whether Ye Sang was willing to listen or not, Father began talking, perhaps because he could not wait any longer, because he wanted someone to share his past experience. Above the constant buzz of the fast-moving traffic on the road, Ye Sang listened as Father's story mixed in with its strange noise.

Father told her that the only woman he loved while a young man, and had loved all his life, was Aunt. They hit it off so well that they had decided to get married right after they finished college. They even went so far as to eat the forbidden fruit, the fulfilment and happiness of which Father could not forget even to this day. Aunt lived with her family in an old-fashioned red house by the riverside, a legacy bestowed on them by Aunt's ancestors. Rather dilapidated, the house was shared by Aunt and her parents, an elder sister, and two younger brothers. Aunt and her elder sister shared the same room, but because the sister was attending college in Sichuan, Aunt had it to herself. This offered good opportunities for the lovers' rendezvous. To avoid her parents' watchful eyes, Father would climb into the room through the window at midnight and out again before dawn broke. For this he suffered a great deal but he was never tired of it.

There came the day when Father was supposed to meet Aunt in her room as usual but it happened that her elder sister had just returned on leave of absence from college after falling ill for disappointment in love. Aunt, who was still busy rehearsing for her graduation ceremony, was not yet home and had not been able to tell him she had been delayed. Thus, as midnight came, he slipped into the room, which had long been the source of his pleasure and exhilaration. Without speaking a word, he flung himself on the woman in the bed. To his surprise she trembled as never before in her arousal. He thought it was all because they loved each other so much that a three-day separation was like three long years. This thought unleashed burning passion in him. Then, after their climax, he heard a strange voice that said, 'Who are you?' He all but slammed his head into the wall.

Aunt's trauma was palpable. 'She almost cried herself to death,' Father recalled in a plaintive tone. Her parents were outraged. They would have sent Father to prison had Aunt not implored them beseechingly not to. They finally swallowed their pride for the sake of their daughters' reputation. Aunt eventually forgave Father. Her elder sister agreed to let him go; she had much to thank him for, for oddly enough, that night's passionate love-making cured her of the psychological trauma which all but destroyed her. However, before Father could celebrate, it was discovered that Aunt's elder sister was pregnant. The only choice was for Father to marry her right away. 'That was your mother,' he said.

As Father recounted his story in a gloomy voice, Ye Sang had to fight the urge to laugh. How stupid of you, Father, she thought, to make love to the wrong woman without knowing it. Funny stories like this were such a rarity in this world. Yet the fact that Father had the guts to relate it to her made it impossible to laugh at him. Suddenly an important question came to her mind, and as it did, the streets quieted down and she felt she had received a blow on her head which caused such pain that she saw stars falling down like dust, reminding her of her ominous experience by the washing machine a few days earlier. The blood drained from her face. 'Was I the child?' she demanded. The question had her on tenterhooks, for if the answer was yes she would have been party to a death even before she was born.

She waited anxiously before Father replied, 'No, you are not.'

His answer was definite. Obviously he was not lying but Ye Sang refused to believe it.

'How come?' she asked.

He smiled bitterly. 'Good question. Because you were not the baby she conceived.'

'Then what happened to it?'

'It was aborted.'

'Why?'

'This was my only condition for marrying her,' Father said. 'I didn't want to have to live with the child that was the cause of my pain.'

Ye Sang fell silent. Her taut nerves relaxed. However, she felt, somewhat disappointed.

'You were born three years after our wedding.' Only after Aunt, who had gone to work in Xinjiang in a fit of pique, had written to say she had married, did Father begin life with Mother as husband and wife. The years thus wore on by. A year after Third Sister was born, Aunt returned from Xinjiang due to problems with her heart. Only then did Father learn that she had never married. The old passion was rekindled, and he began chasing Aunt as he had done before. He wanted to divorce Mother and compensate Aunt for her lost love. In loneliness Aunt responded to Father's passion, and in so doing she fell into the trap she had dodged so successfully thus far. In the old-fashioned red house, Father and Aunt renewed their love affair.

Aunt gradually regained her former beauty, and Father recovered his self-confidence. Then came the day when Mother suddenly descended on the scene. She stared at them as they lay together in bed before staggering away on enfeebled legs. Worried, Aunt told Father, 'Go home quickly, she will be unable to cope.' Father said these were the last words she said to him. As he returned home to talk to Mother about divorce, Aunt committed suicide by slitting her wrist. 'By the time I got to her, she had already bled to death, her face was as white as the wall, and there was a faint smile on her face. She lay there so calmly, my heart broke,' he said. 'After your aunt died, all your mother's insecurities were gone, but gone, too, was my happiness.'

Ye Sang broke into a cold sweat. Her legs were shaking. The smiling face of her aunt lying in a puddle of blood came rippling into her mind. Was she smiling at having severed her love and with it her torment? How, after this heart-breaking experience, could Father still live on peacefully in this world? In spite of herself Ye Sang turned to look at her father. What she saw was a face covered with a spider's web of wrinkles which had its centre between his eyebrows. He looked so old, and too emaciated to withstand a gust of wind.

'Ye Sang, how do you feel?' Father asked.

'Let me ask you: how do you feel?'

'I am pained to the extreme, but I can still manage to laugh.'

'Is that so?'

'That is what I wanted to tell you today,' Father answered. 'The durability of a person's life is rather strong, so strong that it's hard to fathom. For a time I thought I would die or go insane. But at the end of your aunt's funeral, I discovered I was still here, I had got through it. I hadn't gone insane, nor did I want to die, although I knew I would never for a moment forget her. What you should remember is this: Don't put life on a pedestal or expect too much from it. Human life is cheap and it can struggle on for a very long time. It can withstand anything, no matter how heavy the burden or how great the humiliation. To remain alive is our most fundamental instinct; the chain of life has to be carried on. In this world, you are just one link in the chain. Life turns you into its vehicle. You will overcome everything; so long as you are not unreasonable and don't lose sight of this, there is nothing in this world you cannot put up with. Your first cry is life's first hint to you that you should always keep your life as fresh and vital as your first cry. You have no right to desert life. You can only extend and substantiate your link in the chain, until the time comes for you to be detached from it, or until life deserts you.'

As Father presented his case, Ye Sang could see strands of his thought come wringing together. She felt the punch of his words as each additional strand was released. By the time Father finished his soliloquy she had been deeply moved, and all her worries were gone without a trace. Ye Sang distinctly heard the tooting of automobile horns and giggles of children. The river of life flowed by with a calm assurance that was teeming with fresh life. Laughter and cries were the light of life, but so were misery and happiness, enthusiasm and indifference, brightness and darkness.

VII

Ye Sang wanted to go back to Nanjing. She decided she had to face up to whatever was in store for her sooner or later. Her career was there, and she needed a normal life.

When she got up the next morning, Second Sister had drawn open the curtain and was surveying her leaf again. The bright sunshine showed the veins so clearly that Ye Sang could see them even from where she was, sitting on her bed. 'Sister, what did you see in the leaf?' she asked. Second Sister cocked her head and said confidently, 'A hint.'

At the breakfast table, Ye Sang asked Third Sister to buy her a boat ticket. 'Today I'm escorting a tourist group to Jingzhou,' Third Sister answered. 'I won't return until tomorrow. Can you wait till I'm back? I promise I'll get you a boat ticket then.'

Ye Sang looked at her for a lingering moment. 'All right.' She thought of the sentimental look in Ning Ke's eyes. In the back of her head she felt she had heard someone saying, 'This is the last day, and some story is going to unfold.'

That afternoon Ning Ke arrived with two pink tickets in his hand. Third Sister had gone to work. Disappointed, he said, 'Why didn't she tell me she was going to Jingzhou? I didn't come by these concert tickets easily.'

'Never mind, it's just a concert,' Mother said. 'You'll have plenty of opportunities in the future.' Ning Ke sighed and in a helpless tone said, 'You are right. Let's just throw them away. They only cost one hundred and twenty yuan after all.'

'How much?'

'One hundred and twenty yuan,' Ning Ke repeated. 'Sixty yuan apiece.'

Mother was unaware that the price of concert tickets had increased so quickly, and so much more than the price of chicken, eggs, and pork. 'Seems like so much money. You can't just throw the tickets away like that.'

'Let's do it this way,' Father said. 'Ye Sang hasn't been anywhere in the last few days. Why not let Ning Ke take Elder Sister to the concert. Ye Sang, what do you say?'

'I don't feel like going, Father. Ask Ning Ke to take you.' As she said this she glanced at Ning Ke. A chagrined Ning Ke stared back at her hard, then said, 'Why don't Mr and Mrs Professor go together?'

Mother, with a deadpan expression, said, 'That's for you young people to go and enjoy, not an old couple like us. It's better that Ye Sang go, so that Ning Ke's money won't be wasted. Ye Sang, it is time you went out and had a good time.'

Ye Sang raised her hands and said, 'All right. Now that everyone has persuaded me that I should accompany the gentleman, at the risk of my life, so be it.'

Ning Ke laughed. 'Elder Sister, it's so humorous of you to put it that way. Do you think I might produce a knife midway through and kill you?' Father and Mother laughed.

Ning Ke had dinner with the Ye's. Ye Sang wanted to dress herself carefully. In Nanjing, she had never gone to a concert without sprucing herself up, but this time, after thinking it over, she only draped a black coat over the dress she wore. However, she deliberately changed into a fine, sexy undergarment. As she followed Ning Ke out of the door she thought, 'Am I dressed like this for Ning Ke to seduce me?'

The concert hall was far from her home, with the Yangtse and Han rivers lying in between. Outside, Ning Ke hailed a cab. 'You are out to impress,' Ye Sang said.

'That depends on whom I am going out with and what we are going to do,' Ning Ke replied, opening the door for Ye Sang, and putting a protective hand to the door frame. The gesture changed her attitude in an instant. She sank down in the soft seat and gazed out the window at the urban scenery with the eyes of a dignified woman. Ning Ke hopped into the car from the other side. When he had seated himself comfortably he laid his hand softly on the back of hers.

Ye Sang did not move. She wondered if this was the beginning of the story. Next he took Ye Sang's hand into his and Ye Sang felt the palm of her hand begin to sweat. In her heart, desire mingled with refusal.

'You must have heard the phrase, "Give him an inch and he'll take a mile", haven't you?' she asked.

Ning Ke said nothing, simply withdrawing his hand. 'That's right.' After she had said this she fixed her eyes on the street scenes that flashed by. Remembering Ning Ke was a shy man, she wondered if he was still capable of blushing. Then she found she was somewhat disappointed at the removal of his hand from hers.

The concert turned out to be a flop. The singers sang distractedly. Half-way into the show at least three of them had obviously mimed to a pre-recorded voice track that was set a pitch too high. As the audience watched with rapt attention, an actress in red loose-fitting knickerbockers swung affectedly, while her belly remained absolutely taut flat as if she was not breathing at all. She finished to thunderous applause and had to answer three curtain calls before she was allowed to leave the stage. In her smile Ye Sang discerned craftiness and pride.

In a low voice Ning Ke said, 'Those who come here don't really have a love of music. They just like the atmosphere. They want to make themselves feel elegant by coming to a place like this, and it gives them something to talk about.'

'Are you one of them?' Ye Sang asked.

Ning Ke smiled. 'Certainly, but at least I'm aware of what I do, because I know they are the very people who spoil music. They are capable of mistaking dregs for cream and kicking cream into the dustbin of history.'

Ye Sang sneered. 'There are people even more disgusting—those who spoil language, who cannot speak like normal people, whose mouths contain nothing but high-brow language to impress people.'

Ning Ke laughed. 'Verbal abuse comes to you so easily! You want me to speak like a normal person, but if I do, I bet you won't listen to me. For example. . . .' He paused, then continued, 'I'll just stick to my high-brow language. Ye Sang, can we go back to nature and take a walk amidst flowers in the moonlight, so that the music here won't spoil us any more?' Ye Sang smirked, and stood up.

The moment they left the theatre Ning Ke slid his arm around Ye Sang's waist. Ye Sang wanted to wriggle herself free, but she ended up going limp in his arms.

In the same way they had come, Ning Ke ushered Ye Sang into the cab and he himself climbed in from the other side. The moment he had seated himself he had pulled Ye Sang onto his lap. The space was cramped, and Ye Sang felt rather uncomfortable, but she endured, wanting to know where the story would lead to. Ning Ke wrapped an arm around Ye Sang's neck. In this position he, too, was uncomfortable but his excitement quickly overwhelmed the discomfort. As he brushed Ye Sang's hair aside with his hand, he was stunned by her charm. What a unique woman, he thought, so very, very different! He placed his lips on Ye Sang's. Ye Sang kept her eyes shut, for she did not want to see his face. If I see his face, she thought, the spell would be broken. She felt scalded where Ning Ke's lips touched hers, as if a bundle of dry firewood had been thrown into the flames of her burning heart. The fire flamed, and then it raged.

In a trance she let herself be carried from the car and into a room. Her mind was spinning, while she herself was enveloped in the embrace of another man's arms. As her mind spun she saw a toy she used to play with as a young girl, a toy called 'Lotus Throne'. When the lotus was spun, the petals would flip open one after another until a throne emerged where the pistil should be. The throne was empty. Moaning and groaning now, she asked herself why the throne was unoccupied. If it was unoccupied, what was the point of opening up the flower in the first place? Did the flower open simply to display its emptiness? Did it mean that emptiness lay doggedly at the heart of everything? Ye Sang's thoughts roller-coastered. She was in turmoil. The force of life flowed and ebbed in her reverie. All the joints in her body seemed to crack. All her nerves were stretched taut. All her organs were competing with each other to make themselves felt. The air was filled with sound, which in mere seconds grew from a soft sizzling to a deafening thunder, as if a storm had swept her away from the mundane world which was so familiar to her, and set her down in an entirely new place where everything glittered like crystal and exuded a heady fragrance. She believed she had never been to this wonderland before. She was so struck by it that she all but screamed.

In anticipation she opened her mouth, and a strong current of hot air puffed unexpectedly into her mouth. When she heard the gasps which were unmistakably hers, her vision went black. Lightning flashed across her mind, and she found herself wondering if staying alive was the only alternative in life.

A tiny lamp was switched on and blue light illuminated the room. Ye Sang saw herself and Ning Ke, naked. She knew what she had done. I've become that woman named Ding Xiang, or my aunt herself. The thought induced peace to settle in her mind. She began to collect herself. 'Can't we stay this way for a while?' Ning Ke asked. 'I can still make love to you again in a moment,' Ning Ke said. Ye Sang thought it over and lay down again. Ning Ke lay beside her, his skin smooth like a fish against hers. When their skin moved against each other they felt no obstacle at all. 'Let's talk,' Ning Ke said.

'About what?' Ye Sang asked.

'Whatever.'

'May I tell you the story about my aunt?'

'You have an aunt?'

Ye Sang recounted all she had heard from her father about her aunt and about his theory about life. 'Father has sobered me up,' she said.

'The professor's story is contradicted by his conclusion,' Ning Ke pointed out. 'Life is cheap, and cheap things are more easily destroyed. In fact, every life has its weak links that come to light at different phases of life. Take your aunt for instance. She lived alone for many years in Xinjiang, which meant she was rather strong in coping with solitude and enduring hardship and pain. But there was one thing in life which she could not stand. That is why she committed suicide.'

'What do you think it was she could not stand?' Ye Sang asked.

'She couldn't stand sin.'

Ye Sang shuddered. She had a feeling that both her soul and body had been torn apart and smashed to pieces. Gazing at the eerie blue light, she felt as if she had seen Third Sister's face. 'You leave me lost for words,' she said.

'Don't you start imagining things. You are different from your aunt,' Ning Ke said.

'How so?' Ye Sang asked.

'You can endure both pain and sin, but you. . . .' He stopped short.

'Go on.'

'You cannot resist temptation.'

'So now you're mocking me for being unable to resist your seduction.'

'Don't you ever cast doubt on my feelings for you,' Ning Ke said. 'Tonight the two of us are cemented by love, aren't we? It happened so naturally and in such harmony, didn't it? We have feelings for each other in our hearts, haven't we? Our hearts have always been in communion, or we would not have felt so unlike strangers after all these years, would we? We have become one because we are a part of each other, one life corresponding with another. People are torn apart by unpredictable changes in this world, so that it's almost inevitable that they lose their ideal partner. Some never even find them, some lose their partner at close range. I always believed that you are my partner, otherwise how can I explain why you looked intimately familiar to me at first sight and why, after seeing you, I could not forget you? I don't believe in love at first sight, but that I am ordained by fate to be with you. I have always wanted to prove this to you, and to myself. Now that we have made love I know I am not mistaken.'

'Your wild thoughts are your weakness,' said Ye Sang coldly. 'You're starting to make me believe you are like my second sister.'

Ning Ke fell silent. Suddenly, imitating Second Sister's tone, he blurted out, 'It's a hint.' Then he laughed. Ye Sang did not laugh.

What rubbish he was talking, she thought, saying that Aunt could not stand sin. She could stand it about as much as me.

VIII

It was close to midnight when Ye Sang arrived home. The cab drove her right to the doorstep. Unexpectedly, Ning Ke didn't get out to say good night. He just blew a kiss goodbye. As Ye Sang watched, he pulled the door closed, and the car whizzed away. Presently the tail lamp disappeared into the night smog. Ye Sang knew that with the tail light gone, the story had come to an end. She felt relieved from head to toe. The depression which had been haunting her of late was utterly gone. Her heart was back on an even keel. As she opened the door she thought she had evened up the score with her husband. I simply did what he has been doing, and more beautifully at that, she thought. Now I can go home with an unburdened heart, live the way life should be lived, and spend the days as they should be spent, that is all.

The telephone rang the moment she stepped into the sitting room. Her heart gave a slight jump. Is it Third Sister wanting to know the whereabouts of her fiancé? The last thing Ye Sang expected was a call from her husband.

'Went to a concert?' he said. 'Your brother-in-law sounds like an interesting guy. This is the fifth time I have called.'

Ye Sang tried to keep her composure as she asked, 'Why seek me out tonight of all nights?'

'You sound like you're in a better mood, willing to talk to me,' he said.

'I have thought it through,' she answered. 'To stay alive means that so long as I don't care, everything will fall into place. From now on, I won't care who you sleep with, me or that Ding Xiang of yours.'

'So, in the space of a few days you have turned this vulgar,' he said. 'Let's put aside the question whether there is anyone called Ding Xiang for the time being. What I want to know first is, what has suddenly made you so open-minded? I wonder if you are yourself anymore. Or has your brother-in-law straightened you out?'

Ye Sang laughed. 'You are jealous.'

'Jealous or not, I have the feeling that while the voice is yours, nothing else is.'

'Amazing,' Ye Sang said.

'When will you come back?'

'I've bought a ticket for the boat tomorrow,' Ye Sang answered.

'Very good. I'll meet you at the dock. When you are back I think I can account for everything to you. It is not what you have imagined.'

'I wish I could believe that you were telling the truth.'

'All right. See you in Nanjing.'

He was about to hang up when Ye Sang cried out, 'Ah—what's the hurry? It's getting cold. Your thick woollen sweater is in a pink plastic bag on the second shelf of the walk-in closet. You can find your cotton trousers and jerseys in the third drawer of the wardrobe.'

Her husband laughed. 'Okay, Okay, I know. Bye.'

Ye Sang stood there numbly, telephone in hand. What does his laughter mean? she asked herself.

When she emerged from a shower, her body emanated a delicate fragrance. She paused by the bed in which Second Sister was sleeping. The moon shone through the window and laid its light on her pillow. The tiny hairs on her face reflected a radiance like that of an infant. The idea that Second Sister was bathed in moonlight as she slept every night made her pause. How did it make her feel? What was it like dreaming under the moon? Small wonder she acted so differently.

That night Ye Sang had a dream. She dreamed of boarding a boat on her journey home. The cabin smelled badly. She felt herself being vaguely caressed, while someone's hot breath brushed across her face. She lay there motionless, for she knew she was dreaming. The next moment she had a vision of herself walking in clouds that hovered over the Yangtse River, her steps nimble, her body free of gravity, and her skirt spreading as wide as the clouds themselves. She had never experienced anything like it, and she murmured to one of her fellow wayfarers that perhaps only in death could one move like this with the serenity of an angel. It flashed through her mind that her companion was none other than the old man she had come across on her way to Hankou.

The day Ye Sang left Hankou, her parents, Third Sister, and Ning Ke were at the harbour to see her off. They would have brought Second Sister along had Ye Sang not protested: 'Why should I need every one of you? Bidding farewell to my remains?'

At these words Father and Mother had just stared at each other. 'Elder Sister, what do you mean?' Third Sister had said. 'Elder Sister thinks differently,' Ning Ke had replied.

Ye Sang had smiled and said, 'Why are you so sensitive? I'll come back next year for Third Sister and Ning Ke's wedding. And I'll bring Father five pickled ducks, though I don't know why you should need this many ducks.'

As the boat began to move, Ye Sang's eyes moistened. Not having cried for so long, she had forgotten what it felt like. As the steam siren tooted in a prolonged whine, she could not tear her eyes from her loved ones on the shore. In spite of herself tears spilled down her cheeks. 'Why am I crying like this?' she asked. All this was not lost on Mother, who, choked with sobs, said loudly, 'Ye Sang, give me a call to let me know you arrived safely.'

Melancholy clouded Ning Ke's face. Standing behind Third Sister, he put a hand to his lips. Ye Sang knew what he meant, but she acted as if she had seen nothing. All the while Third Sister waved at her frantically. As Ye Sang waved back she asked herself, 'How can I repay you, sister? What shall you do to punish me?'

The ship sped away in a hubbub of voices. When all the well-wishers on shore had vanished, a sense of loss mixed with relief flooded Ye Sang. Returning to her cabin, third-class with a washroom, she saw her three roommates, two women and one man, chatting like a family in Shanghai dialect, which was unintelligible to Ye Sang. When people from Shanghai travel together, they keep to themselves without talking to others. Soon she felt bored, left out, and she went back on deck. When she returned to the cabin after night had fallen, her roommates were asleep. The man was snoring away like a droning machine, causing Ye Sang to toss and turn sleeplessly in her bed. Before dawn broke, she pulled on her coat and went out once again, having not slept a wink.

The moment she stepped out of the cabin she was enveloped by the wind, moist and chilly from the morning fog. The moon still hung in the sky. The wind, sweeping across the width of the river, penetrated her clothing, her skin, and her bones. Ye Sang shivered, yet she didn't feel the cold. The engine's monotonous churn made the river seem emptier and more deserted. Beyond the horizon on the other side of the river, two or three oscillating columns of searchlights occasionally flicked across the river. Ye Sang wondered if the fog would still be there in the morning. If it is, she thought, what will it look like? Will it obliterate the entire Yangtze River? The question reminded her of her previous walk in the clouds—at the time she was actually walking on the resilient and rubber-like surface of the Yangtse, and the fog mixed with her skirt like a drape of wings, making her believe that when the fog rose she herself would soar into the sky as well. Where would I touch down after I became air-borne? she wondered. There must be a destination somewhere, for living on earth is not the only form of, or place for, life. The problem is that none of us has been to the other places, and those who have are never heard from again. In her dream Ye Sang saw shadowy human forms moving in the distance. One of them looked familiar—it was Aunt.

When Aunt's face became visible, her voice took form as well. 'I can't stand sin,' she said. Ye Sang felt a jolt of shock. Blood rushed to her scalp.

A white streak appeared above the horizon. All was quiet on the river. The streak expanded into a sheet, which mingled with splotches of red. The ship continued to cleave a path through the river the way ships always do, and, as the beholder watched with a broken heart, the water opened and closed repeatedly as it always does. Ye Sang trudged drunkenly around the deck, round and round, not knowing where she should stop, nor what she was doing. Finally she halted at the bow because she had seen that the east had turned red.

As she watched, the red gradually unfurled, like a drop of red ink diffusing in water. As if affected by the colour, the river flowed more dynamically. The red kept spreading, and the water continued to sparkle, as merrily as a handful of pearls bobbing on water—Ye Sang could even hear them tinkling. The sun shot out its first beam with a bang so deafening as to send a shudder down Ye Sang's spine. More bangs ensued until in a riot of shimmering rays the golden-red arc of the sun popped up above the horizon. The Yangtze flowed on towards the sun as if a precipice awaited them where the river could empty itself lock, stock, and barrel in the heroic manner of a furious waterfall. In spite of herself Ye Sang was carried away by all this; in her heart she felt someone beckoning her. Second Sister's baby-like face emerged in the moonshine, and she said, 'Water is running hua-la-la; the nose is greeted by a sweet smell.' When she said this her naive face beamed a dainty and enchanting smile. It suddenly dawned on Ye Sang that the beckoning came from another realm, that had long been hinted at in her life prior to this moment.

By now the golden sun had half risen above the horizon in a dazzling blaze, setting half the river on fire. As Ye Sang contemplated the scene, she felt herself burning, and she could feel something tugging at her from the air. Yet she found she could not face the sky squarely for fear of being reduced to ashes.

When the huge crimson ball of the sun rolled off the surface of the river, and when the red flush spread from a distance to right before her eyes, Ye Sang's desire to take to the air got the better of her. I'm one with this turbulent current; I'm as blazing as the sky, she told herself. The thought persuaded her that she could tread on air, her body as light as a swallow on the wing. Before very long, she felt herself being borne away by the clouds, adrenaline pumping her high.

The next thing she heard was a loud thud, and the startled 'Ahh . . .' uttered simultaneously by many mouths in the vicinity. That was the last sound Ye Sang heard.

Shortly, peace settled on the river. The red flush above the horizon and on the surface of the water faded. All this was not lost on Ye Sang, for the glory of the morning would have been impossible without her elevation into the sky.

Falling down is just another approach to going up. This was the last thought that flashed across Ye Sang's mind.

1995

16

Curvaceous Dolls

By **Li Ang**
Translated by Howard Goldblatt

Li Ang 李昂 *is the pen-name of Shi Shuduan* 施淑端 *(b. 1952). She was born in Taiwan and received her university education (in philosophy) from the Culture University of Taiwan. She also received her MA in drama from the University of Oregon. Her novel,* The Butcher's Wife (Shafu 殺夫), *won a literary award from the* United Daily News (Lianhe bao 聯合報) *in 1987. Her works of short fiction include* Flower Season (Huaji 花季, *1984),* A Test of Love (Aiqing shiyan 愛情試驗, *1983),* Their Tears (Tamen de yanlei 她們的眼淚, *1984),* Sweet Life (Tianmei shenghuo 甜美生活, *1991), and* A Love Letter Never Sent (Yifeng weiji de qingshu 一封未寄的情書, *1986). Li Ang has recently published two novels, entitled* Everyone Uses the Incense Burner in Beigang (Beigang xianglu renren cha 北港香爐人人插, *1997) and* The Maze (Mi yuan 迷園, *1998), which caught the attention of many critics on the island.*

I

She had yearned for a doll—a curvaceous doll—ever since she was a little girl. But because her mother had died and her father, a poor man, hadn't even considered it, she never got one. Back then she had stood behind a wall every day secretly watching a girl who lived in the neighbourhood carrying a doll in her arms. The way the girl left her doll lying around surprised and confused her; if she had a doll of her own, she reasoned dimly, she would treat it lovingly, never letting it out of her sight.

One night as she lay in bed clutching the sheet to her chest, obsessed with the idea of a doll, she figured out a way to get one that she could hug as tightly as she wished. After digging out some old clothes, she twisted them into a bundle, then cinched it up with some string about a quarter of the way down. She now had her very first doll.

The ridicule this first doll brought down upon her was something she would never forget. She recalled it years later as she lay in the warmth and comfort of her husband's embrace. She sobbed until he gently turned her face toward him and said in an even tone of voice that was forced and revealed a hint of impatience:

'It's that rag doll again, isn't it!'

Just when it had become the 'rag doll' she couldn't recall with certainty, but it must have been when she told him about it. One night, not terribly late, he lay beside her after they had finished, still somewhat breathless, while she lay staring at the moon's rays streaming in through the open window and casting a fine net of light at the foot of the bed. She had a sudden impulse to reveal everything, to tell him about her first doll; and so she told him, haltingly, blushing with embarrassment, how she had made it, how she had embraced it at night in bed, and how, even though her playmates ridiculed her, she had refused to give it up. When she finished, he laughed.

'Your very own rag doll!'

Maybe that wasn't the first time anyone had called it a 'rag doll', but he had certainly used the word that night, and his laughter had hurt her deeply. She failed to see the humour in it, and telling him had not been easy. He could be pretty inconsiderate sometimes.

She never mentioned the doll again, probably because of his mocking laughter, and from that night on she began sleeping with her back to him, unable to bear facing his broad, hairy chest. Although it was the same chest that had once brought her solace and warmth, she now found it repulsive. It seemed to be missing something, although she couldn't say just what that something was.

Later on, her nightly dreams were invaded by many peculiar transparent objects floating randomly in a vast greyness, totally divorced from reality yet invested with a powerful life force. She seldom recalled such dreams, and even when she knew she had been dreaming, they vanished when she awoke.

It was a familiar feeling, the realization that she had obtained something without knowing what it was, and it worried her and drove her to tears. She often wept as she lay in her husband's arms, and he invariably blamed the rag doll. But it's not the rag doll! She felt like shouting. The rag doll had disappeared that night, never to return.

But she couldn't tell him, maybe to avoid a lot of meaningless explanations.

The dreams continued, troubling her more than ever. She would sit quietly for hours trying to figure out what the floating objects were, but with no success. Occasionally she felt she was getting close, but in the end the answer always eluded her. Her preoccupation took its toll on her husband; after being casually rebuffed in bed a few times, he grew impatient, and when he realized that things were not going to get better, he decided to take her to see a doctor. By now she was fed up with his bossiness and the protector's role in which he prided himself, but her dreams had such a strong grip on her that she finally gave in.

On the way, the oppressive closeness inside the bus made her regret going. She had no desire to open up to a doctor, nor did she think a doctor was the answer. As she looked over at her husband, a single glance from him convinced her that it would be useless to argue. Slowly she turned away.

Someone brushed against her. Glancing up, she saw a pair of full breasts whose drooping outline she could make out under the woman's blouse. Her interest aroused, she began to paint a series of mental pictures, imagining the breasts as having nipples like overripe strawberries oozing liquid, as though waiting for the greedy mouth of a child. Suddenly she felt a powerful urge to lean up against those full breasts, which were sure to be warm and comforting, and could offer her the sanctuary she needed. She closed her eyes and recalled the time she had seen a child playing with its mother's breasts. If only she could be those hands, enjoying the innocent pleasure of fondling a mother's soft, smooth breasts. Her palms were sweaty, and she wondered what her hands might do if she kept this up much longer.

Feeling a strong arm around her shoulders, she opened her eyes and found herself looking into the anxious face of her husband.

'You're so pale,' he said.

She never learned how she had been taken off the bus, recalling only the extraordinary comfort and warmth of her husband's arm. She leaned up against him in the taxi all the way home, gradually reacquainting herself with his muscular chest. But she couldn't stop thinking about those breasts, so soft and smooth, there for her to play with. If only her husband could grow breasts like that on his chest, with drooping nipples for her to suck on! In a flash she realized what was missing from his chest—of course, a pair of breasts to lean on and provide her with sanctuary.

Later on, to her amazement, the objects in her dreams began to coalesce. Those unreal and disorderly, bright yet transparent objects took on concrete form with curves and twists: two oversized, swollen objects like resplendent, drooping breasts; beneath the translucent surface she could see thick flowing milk. It's a woman's body, a curvaceous woman's body! She wanted to shout as the astonishing realization set in.

When she awoke, she experienced an unprecedented warmth that spread slowly from her breasts to the rest of her body, as though she were being baptized by the endless flow of her own milk as it coursed placidly through her body. Overwhelmed by such bountiful pleasure, she began to moan.

When she opened her eyes and glanced around her she saw that her husband was sound asleep. In the still of the night the moon's rays swayed silently on the floor beneath the window like a pool of spilled mother's milk. She began to think of her second doll, the one made of clay. Since her first doll was called the rag doll, this one ought to be known as the clay doll.

The idea of making a clay doll occurred to her one day when she had felt a sudden desire to hold the neighbour girl's doll. She had approached her, not knowing how to make her desire known, and after they had stared at each other for a few moments, she reached out and tugged at the doll's arm. The other girl yanked it back and pushed her so hard she fell down. Her cries brought the girl's mother out of the house, who picked her up gently and cradled her against her breasts to comfort her.

She had never touched anything so soft and comfortable before. She didn't know what those things were called, but she was instinctively drawn to them and wanted to touch them. After that, she lost interest in her rag doll, since it lacked those protruding, springy objects on its chest and could no longer afford her any solace. She thought about her mother. It was the first time in years that she had truly missed her mother, who had left no impression on her otherwise, but whose bosom must have offered safety, warmth, and a place to rest.

The feeling returned: she longed to tell her husband about her clay doll, but then she recalled how he had laughed before, a humiliating laugh without a trace of sympathy, the sound coming from the depths of his broad chest, ugly and filled with evil. As she turned slightly to look at her sleeping husband, from whom she felt alienated and distant, a vague yet profound loneliness came over her, and she desperately missed her clay doll.

It had been raining then, and the water was streaming down the sides of a mound of clay near where she lived. She regularly went there with the other children to make clay dolls, but hers were always different from theirs. She moulded small lumps of clay onto their chests, then worked them into mounds that jutted out. Most of the time she rubbed their bodies with water until they took on a silky, bronze sheen, glistening like gold. She fondled them, wishing that someday she could rub real skin as soft and glowing as that.

In fact, her husband's skin, which also had a bronze sheen, was as lustrous as that of her clay dolls. When she reached out to caress his body her hand recoiled slightly when she touched his hairy chest, and she wished fervently that a pair of soft breasts were growing there instead! Moved by a strange impulse, she unbuttoned her pajama top and exposed her breasts, full like a married woman's, and let them rest on her husband's chest, praying with unprecedented devotion that her breasts could be transplanted onto his body.

The weight of her heavy breasts on his chest woke him, and with an apologetic look in his eyes, he embraced her tightly.

Whenever she did something like this she had no desire to explain herself, so he would just look at her apologetically and she would calmly accept what he did. But each time his chest touched her breasts, she felt a strange uneasiness, and a peculiar shudder, tinged with revulsion, welled up from the hidden depths of her body. At times like this she felt that the man on top of her was nothing but an onerous burden, and she was reminded of old cows in her hometown, which stumbled along pulling their heavy carts, swaying helplessly back and forth.

She couldn't imagine that she would ever be like an old cow, wearily and dispiritedly bearing a heavy burden that could never be abandoned. Her husband's body had become a pile of bones and rotting flesh that made a mockery of his robust health, although it was slightly warm and exuded an animal stench. It was an instrument of torture that made her feel like she had been thrown into a wholesale meat market.

She began to experience a mild terror; the concept of 'husband' had never seemed so distant and fragmented. Before they were married, she had often stroked his shoulders through his shirt with something approaching reverence. Though powerful, they retained some of the modesty and stiffness characteristic of virgin men. They could be called young man's shoulders, not those of a grown man; yet despite the stiffness, the masculine smoothness of his well-developed muscles intoxicated her. After they were married, whenever she stroked his shoulders, she noticed how all the roughness and sharp edges had disappeared; they had become a soft place where all her cares and doubts melted away. She then sank into a new kind of indulgence, a feeling of nearly total security that became purely physical.

Her mild terror helped her renew her love for her husband's body, and although she was partially successful in this regard, she knew that this renewal would not last for long, and that someday a new weariness would set in to make him repulsive again. The only foolproof way to avoid that was for him to grow a pair of breasts to restore the novelty and security she needed so desperately.

The following days were spent in constant prayer and anticipation of the time when breasts would grow on her husband's chest, there to await the hungry mouth of a child.

How she wished she could be that child's mouth, sucking contentedly on her mother's breasts just as she had once rubbed her lips against the breasts of her clay doll, a form of pleasure so satisfying it made her tremble. She still remembered the times she had hidden in an underground air-raid shelter and covered her clay doll's lustrous skin with kisses. She was like a mole wallowing in the pleasure of living in an underground burrow that never sees the light of day. She derived more gratification from this activity than any father, any neighbour girl's doll, or any neighbour girl's mother could ever have provided.

One question remained unanswered: had there been a struggle the first time she kissed the clay doll? She recalled the time she had raised one of her clay dolls to her lips, then flung it to the floor and shattered it, leaving only the two bumps that had been on the chest looking up at her haughtily.

But she never had to worry about being discovered in her underground shelter; she felt safe in that dark, empty space deep underground. Besides, kissing her clay doll like that was perfectly proper; there was nothing to be ashamed of.

How she wished that her home had a cellar, a room unknown to anyone else, or some dark place where she could hide. But there was none—the place was neat, the waxed floors shone, and there were no out-of-the-way corners. She was suddenly gripped by an extraordinary longing for her hometown, where the vast open country and sugarcane patches provided an infinite number of hiding places where no one could ever find her. She missed it so badly and so often that the thought brought tears to her eyes.

She finally decided to tell her husband that she had to go back home. He lay there holding his head in his hands, frowning.

'I can't for the life of me figure out where you get such ideas. Didn't you say you'd never go back to that god-forsaken home of yours, no matter what?' he said contemptuously.

'That was before, things were different then,' she said earnestly, ignoring the impatience in his voice. 'Now all I want is to go home, really, I just want to go home.'

'Why?'

'No reason.'

'Do you think you can?'

'I don't know,' she answered, suddenly losing interest and feeling that defending herself was both meaningless and futile. It was all so ridiculous that she turned away.

'Are you angry?' He gently put his arm around her.

'Not at all,' she said.

She was genuinely not angry. She let him draw her close, but when her back touched his flat chest, the image of those vast sugarcane patches flashed before her, until the bed seemed surrounded by them, as far as the eye could see. 'He has to grow a pair of breasts, he just has to!' she thought to herself, in fact, said it very softly, although he was so intent upon unbuttoning her pajama top that he failed to notice.

As in the past, his hands made her feel unclean. She had always believed, although somewhat vaguely, that the hands fondling her breasts ought to be her own and not his. The weak light in the room barely illuminated the outline of his hands, which she allowed to continue fondling her breasts. It was funny that she was aware of his hands only when they were in bed together.

But it hadn't always been like that. When she first met him, his hands had represented success and achievement; like his chest, they had brought her contentment and security. Then, once they were married, his hands had brought her unimaginable pleasure. And now all she could think of was how to escape them. The foolishness of it all made her laugh.

She knew that this was inevitable, that all she could do was pray for him to grow a pair of breasts. For the sake of domestic tranquillity and happiness, she had to pray with increased devotion.

From the beginning she knew that in a unique situation like this simply kneeling in prayer was hopeless. A more primitive kind of supplication was called for; a thoroughly liberating form of prayer. And so, after her husband left for work in the morning, she locked herself in the bedroom and pulled down the shades, stood in front of the full-length mirror and slowly undressed herself. As she looked at her reflection in the slightly clouded mirror she fantasized that she was being undressed by an unknown force. She knelt naked on the cold hardwood floor, which was warmed by no living creature, put her palms together in front of her, and began to pray. Invoking the names of all the gods she had ever heard of, she prayed that a pair of breasts like her own would grow on her husband's chest. She even prayed for her own breasts to be transplanted onto his body. If the gods would only answer her prayers, she was willing to pay any price.

She derived immense pleasure from her prayers, and wherever her limbs touched the icy floor she got a tingling sensation like a mild electric shock. She looked forward to these sensations, for they made her feel more clean and pure than when she lay in bed with her husband, their limbs entwined. She began to pray in different postures, sometimes that of a snake wriggling on the floor, at other times a pregnant spider, but always praying for the same thing.

Her husband remained ignorant of what was going on, so everything proceeded smoothly, except that now a strange creature began to creep into her prayers; at first it was only a pair of eyes, two long ovals, their colour the dense pale green of autumn leaves that have withered and fallen. In the dim light of the room they gazed fixedly at every part of her naked body with absolute composure and familiarity. She took no notice and remained on the floor, where she laid bare her womanly limbs. Those eyes, expressionless and filled with a peculiar incomprehension, watched her, but since the creature's very existence was dubious, it had no effect on the fervour of her performance. She embraced the icy floor and kissed it with the vague sense that she was embracing a lover sculpted out of marble.

The pale-green eyes continued to keep watch, although now they were filled with cruelty and the destructive lust of a wild animal. At some point she discovered with alarm that she had fallen under the spell of the frightful sexual passion in those eyes, which she now believed belonged to a half-man, half-animal shepherd spirit sent down by the gods in answer to her prayers; moved to the point that she felt compelled to offer up her body in exchange for what she sought, she opened up her limbs to receive that mysterious man-beast. Under the gaze of those eyes, she lay back and exposed herself to their enshrouding vision. She had completed a new rite of baptism.

This may have been the moment she had been waiting for all along, for it surpassed her marble lover and her obsession with the hoped-for breasts on her husband's chest. She was rocked and pounded by the waves of a profound, unfathomable happiness, which also turned the pale-green eyes into a placid lake, on the surface of which they rose and fell in a regular cadence. Her happiness was compressed into a single drop of water, which fell without warning into the pale-green lake and spread out until every atom of her being had taken on a pale-green cast. After that she felt herself re-emerging whole from the bottom of the lake. When she reached the surface she discovered that she was a pale-green mermaid with hair like dried seaweed blown about by the pale-green winds. The water of the pale-green lake suddenly and swiftly receded, as darkness fell over everything and blotted out the pale-green eyes.

When she regained consciousness her first thought was that she had been defiled. Emerging from the chaotic spell of sexual passion, she slowly opened her eyes and was struck by the knowledge that her body, which she had always thought of as incomparably alluring, was in fact just another body; for the first time in a long while she realized that she was merely woman, no different from any other woman, with neither more nor fewer womanly attributes. She lay on the floor, sobbing heavily and recalling the breasts she had hoped would appear on her husband's chest. An inexplicable sadness made her sob even more pitifully. She was living in a dream, an illusion containing vast, hazy, transparent, and mysterious things, with no way to bring them all together. She knew there was no way, even though she had tried before, and even though she once believed she had succeeded; there was no way, she knew that, no way she could ever bring them all together.

She stopped sobbing. Numbly, vacantly, and reluctantly she got to her feet and slowly, aimlessly got dressed, as she knew she must.

II

She lay there, her arm gently wrapped around her husband's neck as he slept on his side. She felt safe, for the darkness around her was free of all objects; it revealed nothing but its own sweet self—boundless, profound, and bottomless. She gazed at her husband's dark, contented eyes and smiled. She had known that sort of happiness before, and was consoled by the knowledge that it would soon be hers again. Feeling like a wandering child returning to its mother's warm embrace, she believed that any child who had come home was entitled to return to its mother's breast. Gladdened by the thought of the pleasure awaiting her and her husband, she continued to smile.

She couldn't say how long the smile remained on her face, but it must have been a very long time. Since emerging from the vast emptiness of her dream, she had begun to love her husband's flat, manly chest with an uncustomary enthusiasm. She gave herself over to enjoying it and caring for it tenderly, for now she was relieved of her burden of uncleanliness and evil. When her husband perceived this change in her attitude, he started to treat her with increased tenderness. And in order to assure her husband of her purity and rebirth, she began to want a child.

Her image of the child was indistinct. She had always avoided thinking of children, for they reminded her of her own childhood and caused her to experience overwhelming waves of pain. But in order to prove her ability as a mother and show that she no longer required a pair of mother's breasts for herself, she needed a child, whose only qualification was that it be a child, with no special talents nor any particular appearance; as long as it had a mouth to suck on her breasts and two tiny hands to fondle them, that was enough for her. Her only requirement for a child was that it be a child.

She told her husband of her decision. As he lay beside her he heard her out, then laughed derisively.

'You sure have some strange ideas!' he said.

His remark amused her. She could—in fact, she should—have a child. Which meant that he was the strange one. She realized for the first time that her husband could be unreasonable and think illogically. The idealized vision of her husband, who had always been the epitome of correctness and reason, began to dissolve, and she knew she could now dismiss that irrational inferiority she had once felt; all she needed now was to await the birth of her child.

Her husband did not share her enthusiasm and was, in fact, decidedly cool to the idea. But she took no notice, intoxicated with the happy prospect of becoming a mother. She enjoyed standing naked on the icy bathroom floor and playing with her swelling, full breasts, pretending that it was her child's hands fondling the objects that represented absolute security—its mother's breasts. Her pleasure brought her fantasies that the tiny hands of the child were actually her own and that the mother, mysterious yet great, was actually an endless plain whose protruding breasts were a pair of mountains poised there for her to lay her head upon and rest for as long as she wanted.

Oh, how she yearned for rest; she was so weary she felt like lying down and never getting up again. Although the nightmares no longer disturbed her in their many forms, they still made indirect appearances. Late one night her husband shook her awake while she was crying and screaming in her sleep; her cheeks were wet with tears as he took her gently into his arms and comforted her. Deeply touched, she decided to reveal everything to him. More than anything else she wanted peace, complete and unconditional. So in a low voice she began to tell him about her clay doll, how she had made it and how she had played with its symbolic breasts. When she finished, he looked at her for a moment with extraordinary calmness, then reached out and held her icy, sweaty, trembling hands tightly in his warm grip.

A great weariness spread slowly throughout her body, and she closed her eyes from exhaustion. Her husband's attitude took her by surprise, for she had expected the same mocking laughter as before. But all he did was look at her with a strange expression on his face, a mixture of indifference and loathing, as though he were observing a crippled animal. She felt the urge to cry, but knew that the tears would not come; she felt like someone who had done a very foolish thing.

Maybe she had actually been hoping for her husband to react by mocking her again, for she remembered how he had laughed so cruelly when she told him about the rag doll; the rag doll had suddenly vanished from her dreams, and for the first time in her life she had known peace of mind. Now she was hoping he would laugh like that again to rid her of the clay doll, like amputating an unwanted limb to regain one's health.

She rolled over on her side, turning her back to the awkward look frozen on her husband's face, then closed her eyes and waited wearily for sleep to come.

In the haziness of her dream she was running on a broad plain, devoid of trees and shrubs, an unbroken stretch of flat grassland. She was running in search of far-off solace when she spotted two mountains rising before her, two full, rounded mounds standing erect in the distance. She ran toward them, for she knew that the solace she sought could be found there. But whenever she felt she had drawn near to them, they faded beyond her reach, even though she kept running.

She awoke and saw the moonlight at the foot of the bed, looking like a pool of mother's milk, and her heart was moved in a peculiar way. She yearned for those mountain-like breasts, and as her eyes began to fill with tears, she clutched a corner of the comforter and cried bitterly.

Suddenly, through her tears she saw something stirring in the surrounding darkness, rocking restlessly in the motion of her tears. Then, slowly it became visible in the form of a flickering thin ray of pale-green light. She sat up in alarm, shutting her eyes tightly and squeezing the tears out and down her cheeks, cold, as though she had just emerged from underwater. Then she opened her eyes again, and there lurking in the darkness were those eyes again, pale-green, cunningly long slits that were laughing with self-assured mockery. Oh, no! she wanted to shout, but she couldn't move. They stared at each other in the two-dimensional darkness, although she was sure that the eyes were slowly drawing closer to her. The pale greenness was growing crueller and becoming an approaching presence of overwhelming power. There was no way she could back off, nowhere for her to turn, and nothing with which she could ward off the attack. And all this time her husband slept soundly beside her.

She had no idea how long the confrontation lasted. The pale-green eyes stood their ground as they kept watch over her, sometimes revolving around her. The milky light of the moon grew denser, slowly creeping farther into the room. During one of the pale-green eyes' circuits around her, something else was revealed in the moonlight—the tail of an animal, covered with long silky black hairs, suspended lightly and noiselessly in the air. She knew what to do: she reached over to the table lamp beside the bed. The pale-green eyes did not stir; they kept watching her, smiling with consummate evil, as though they were looking at her with a slight cock of the head. She touched the light switch with her finger, but she knew she lacked the courage to press it.

The pale-green eyes knew it too, and wilfully remained where they were, watching her calmly with a mocking viciousness. All she had to do was press the light switch to win the battle, but she knew she couldn't do it, she simply couldn't. The pale-green eyes also sensed that the game was over. They blinked several times, then started to retreat. And as they gazed into her eyes for the last time, there was an unmistakable hint that they would be back, that she would never escape them—for her there would be no escape.

From then on she often awoke from disturbing dreams late at night, only to discover those pale-green eyes keeping watch over her quietly from afar or floating past her; they seemed to be evil incarnate, and every time they appeared, her own past reappeared before her with a stabbing pain. Needing a liberating force, she began to wish even more fervently for a child.

She sought the sucking mouth of a child, for she knew that the only time the pale-green eyes would not appear was when a mouth was vigorously sucking at her breasts. She wanted the consoling feeling of rebirth that comes with a child's greedy mouth chewing on her nipples, knowing that it would be more wonderful than her husband's light, playful nibbling during their lovemaking. She wanted a child, one that could show the pale-green eyes that she had become a mother. In order to achieve her goal, she felt a need to turn to a supernatural power for help, and that was when she thought of her wooden doll.

She no longer derived any stimulation from stroking her husband's body or from the imaginary breasts that had once preoccupied her. The chest that had filled her with such longing was now nothing more than a mass of muscle, flat and completely ordinary. As she recalled the breasts she had once hoped to find on his chest, she was struck by how comical and meaningless it had all been. She knew that no one could help her, that she had to find her own way out.

She had searched, ardently and with an ambition rooted in confidence, for a pair of breasts that belonged to her alone, not distant and unattainable like those of the neighbour girl's mother. Finally, in an abandoned military bunker, she had found a wooden figurine of a naked woman with pointed breasts, two even, curvaceous mounds on the doll's upper torso. This was the first time she had truly appreciated the form of those breasts she loved so dearly. Her clay doll's chest had been adorned only with shapeless bumps. As she fondled the exquisitely proportioned curves of the wooden doll she felt a heightened sense of beauty and a reluctance to stop.

Standing in front of the full-length mirror bare to the waist she examined her own full breasts, finding them so alluring that she had a sudden yearning for them. Crossing her arms she fondled them until they ached. She longed for them, she longed for those soft and lovely, yet dark and shadowy lines, she longed to rest her head on them, she longed to chew on those delightful nipples. She bent her head down toward them, only to discover that they were forever beyond her reach.

She would never forget the first time her lips had touched the nipples of the wooden doll and how much pleasure that had brought her. Those tiny nipples seemed to exist only for her to suck on, and since she could fit an entire breast into her mouth she could thus possess it completely. She prayed to the wooden doll for a pair of real nipples to suck on or for a tiny child's mouth to replace her own and suck on her breasts.

She wanted a mouth that was devoid of sexual passion, and her husband did not fit the bill. So when the pale-green eyes reappeared late one night, she climbed gently out of bed and began deftly unbuttoning her pajama top. As they watched her the pale-green eyes appeared puzzled for the first time. She unfastened her bra and began to fondle her breasts. The pale-green eyes, quickly falling under her spell, moved toward her. Two long, gleaming fangs shone through the darkness. The taste of imminent victory was wonderfully sweet to her.

As the pale-green eyes drew nearer, the gleaming fangs grew brighter. She dropped her hands to her sides, exposing her breasts to the approaching eyes. She imagined those fangs biting on her nipples and bringing her the same pleasure as a child's tiny sucking mouth. Overcome by this exquisite pleasure, she began to moan.

The pale-green eyes were startled out of their trance. They quickly recovered their mocking attitude and retreated nimbly after a long stare that betrayed the remnants of sexual passion.

She believed that the pale-green eyes, with their primitive lust, were capable of bringing her happiness and release. She craved them, and in order to have them she had to do as they dictated.

The vast sugarcane fields of her hometown spread out around her in all directions, layer upon layer, dark and unfathomable. She knew that there would be countless pale-green eyes staring at her in the heart of the sugarcane fields, that there would be countless tails stroking her limbs, that there would be white feathers filling her vagina, and that there would be gleaming white fangs biting down on her nipples. But it was a sweet, dark place, boundless and eternally dark, a place where she could rest peacefully, a place where she could hide. She longed for all of this, she longed to possess it all, and nothing else mattered. She yearned for her hometown and for the sugarcane fields where she could hide. She shook her husband awake.

'I want to go back,' she said with uncharacteristic agitation. 'I want to go home.'

The sleepiness in her husband's eyes was quickly replaced by a totally wakeful coldness. 'Why?'

'Just because.'

'You have to give me a reason.'

'You wouldn't understand.'

'Is it because of those damned dolls of yours?' he asked in an intentionally mocking tone.

'Since you already know, yes, that's it.'

Her frigid indifference enraged him.

'Haven't you had enough?' he said angrily. 'I forbid you from going.'

'Do you think I really want to go back? I'm telling you, I have no choice, there's nothing I can do. I have to return.'

She shut her eyes slowly, wishing she hadn't brought up the subject in the first place. Dimly she sensed that somewhere in the illusory, distant dreamscape the little girl's mother's breasts had exploded for some unknown reason, and a thick white liquid began to seep slowly out of them like spreading claws, snaking its way toward her. In her bewilderment, her first thought was to run away, but she discovered that she was drawn toward the thick white liquid, which was trying to detach her limbs from her body and suck them up into its cavernous mouth. Her feet were frozen to the spot. The meandering liquid drew closer and closer to her, until it was at her feet. It began to creep up her body, and she could feel the snake-like clamminess and springy round objects wriggling on her skin, as though two dead breasts were rubbing up against her. The liquid climbed higher and higher, until it reached her lips, and just as it was about to enter her mouth it suddenly coiled itself tightly around her like a snake. The feelings of suffocation and pain she experienced were eclipsed by an immense sense of joy.

She knew that the stream of white liquid would never enter her mouth, and that she would always be searching and waiting. Yet she wanted to seize it, for she believed that it offered her the only hope of attaining a kind of solace, a truth that would allow her to offer up everything in tribute. In the dim light, she set off on a search, not concerned that her husband might oppose her, for she was convinced that this was her only way out.

When she opened her eyes he was gazing at her, his eyes filled with remorse.

'Work hard at it, no matter how long it takes, and someday it will happen to you.'

'Maybe,' she thought. 'But not if I go about it your way. I have to do it my own way.' But that was a long way off. She leaned gently against his chest, recalling a naked mannequin she had once seen in a display window. 'I'll possess her someday, and maybe I'll call her my wax doll!' she said to herself softly.

1969

17

A Place of One's Own

By **YUEN CHIUNG-CHIUNG**
Translated by Jane Parish Yang

Yuen Chiung-chiung 袁瓊瓊 (Yuan Qiongqiong, b. 1950) was born and educated in Taiwan. She is a prolific writer of fiction and essays, who has also published poetry under the pen-name Zhu Ling 朱陵. Her short story 'A Place of One's Own' (Ziji de tiankong 自己的天空) won her a literary award from the United Daily News *(Lianhe bao 聯合報) in 1980, and she received another award for her short fiction from* The China Times *(Zhongguo shibao 中國時報) in 1984. Her collected works of short fiction have been published in several volumes, namely,* A Place of One's Own *(Ziji de tiankong 自己的天空, 1981),* As You Like *(Suiyi 隨意, 1983),* Spring Water Boat *(Chunshui chuan 春水船, 1985),* Vicissitudes of Life *(Cangsang 滄桑, 1985),* Two Persons' Affair *(Liangeren de shi 兩個人的事, 1983), and* Love in the Human World *(Fengchen qing'ai 風塵情愛, 1990). Yuen Chiung-chiung also published a novel entitled* Apple Can Smile *(Pingguo hui weixiao 蘋果會微笑) in 1989.*

She suddenly began to cry.

Lips pressed tightly shut, Liangsan sat there in silence and said nothing more. Tears streamed down her face as she looked at him, and her cheeks burned. She didn't know why, but all she could think about was that burning, itching sensation. She didn't know how Liangsan[1] felt facing a crying woman, or how Liangsi and Liangqi felt. The three large men sat around the table watching her cry. Tears blurred her vision. All she saw before her were three heads held high, but she couldn't make out their expressions.

'Sister-in-law,' Liangqi said. The blur in his direction moved. Jingmin looked down and tried to find her handkerchief in her purse. She heard Liangqi repeat 'Sister-in-law' as she dried her eyes.

'Uh,' she answered. Her vision cleared. Liangsan and Liangsi both looked down to avoid her eyes, their faces expressionless. Liangqi was still a youth and unable to control his feelings. He sat there red-faced.

Jingmin looked at him and he suddenly stood up. 'Why'd you make me come here anyway!' His voice broke.

Liangsi tugged at him. 'Sit down.'

Liangqi sat down. Jingmin saw that his eyes were red. When she first married, he was still in elementary school. Up until he entered high school, he had gotten along best with her, his sister-in-law. Now it seemed that he was the only one sympathetic to her. Heartbroken, she began to cry again.

'Didn't you already agree that you wouldn't cry?' Liangsan said slowly. He paused, then continued speaking in the tone of a superior to an inferior. 'This isn't home, you know.'

Jingmin wiped her eyes.

Liangsi played the role of mediator between them. He chimed in, 'Don't cry, Sister-in-law. Liangsan didn't say he didn't want you.'

Liangsan said, 'That's right.' He spoke without a trace of shame. 'It's only a temporary arrangement. She's making a big fuss right now. It's just a cover-up to calm her down.' 'She' referred to that dance hall girl.

When he mentioned that woman, a faint smile crept over his face, but just for an instant. Jingmin saw it clearly but couldn't understand how he could be so heartless. After all, they had been husband and wife for seven years. If other men had mistresses, their wives would have raised the roof. Only he could have arranged everything so neatly. He didn't take her seriously at all. And now he even wanted her to move out so that the other woman could move in. He took it for granted that she'd obey.

Liangsi said, 'That apartment Liangsan's rented for you is efficient. It's a bit small, but it's got everything.'

Liangsan said, 'It's a nice place to stay.' He frowned, but not out of vexation. It was an expression of solemnity and resolution. 'I'll visit you every week.'

Silence. Jingmin wiped her eyes with facial tissue, the slight rustling sound blended with her breathing. She kept sniffling, as if having caught a cold.

Liangqi folded his arms in front of his body and stared at her gloomily, as if he had suddenly turned into her enemy. Liangsi was the slickest operator in the family, and now his face was arranged in a solemn expression. Liangsan's face was a blank, as if about to doze off. He rarely looked so friendly. Perhaps he, too, had a conscience and felt he might be going a bit too far.

Jingmin finally spoke up. 'Why?'

The three men stared at her. She fell silent, bowing her head to think. Strangely, she discovered her mind was a blank.

This was an important matter for a woman. Her husband was having an affair and now wanted to separate. But she couldn't think of anything else, not even of crying. Then why had she just cried? Maybe because she had always cried easily, or because she had been taken by surprise. She hadn't thought this kind of thing could happen to her. Perhaps it was because she felt unhappy that they hadn't talked it over at home but had brought her here, the four of them sitting around a large round table like they were waiting to be served. It was absurd. By coincidence all the booths were full, so the brothers sat at one side of the table and she sat alone across from them as if they had nothing to do with each other.

She ought to have given a more appropriate response, such as rebuking Liangsan's ingratitude: What have I done wrong that you'd treat me this way? There was a lot of that shown on television. The least I should do is faint, she thought. But she merely sat there, painlessly healthy, her hands gripping her handkerchief under the table. She crumpled it up then released it. She noticed a cigarette burn in the carpet. The carpet was a deep red with a black pattern. Unless one looked closely, the hole didn't show. She wiped her face with the handkerchief again, guessing that her face looked terrible. She was afraid her nose was all puffy. She suddenly felt ashamed to appear this ugly at the time he wanted to leave her.

Liangsan said, 'She'll give birth in June. She needs a bigger place.'

Jingmin became despondent. She replied, 'Oh.' She felt stricken when he mentioned the child. She and Liangsan didn't have any children, but she hadn't known he wanted a child so badly. He had never said anything about it. She suddenly felt like crying again, and the tears came flowing down her cheeks. The men were silent. She clearly saw a tear drop onto her skirt, the sound seeming horribly loud, like rain beating on the pavement.

The door to the elegant private dining room opened. The waiter had finally shown up. The restaurant was very busy. Jingmin sat with her head bowed.

Liangsan said, 'Let's eat something! This place is famous.' He looked over the menu quietly, calmly soliciting the others' opinions. 'How about an order of shrimp balls?'

The waiter scribbled it down on his notepad.

Liangsi said, 'Let's order something a little less rich. Liangsan, this won't do. You'd better be careful about high blood pressure.'

'This dish is their specialty, understand?' Liangsan ordered four dishes and a soup.

The waiter went off.

'I think I'll go to the ladies' room,' Jingmin said, her head still bowed.

'Okay, go,' Liangsan said.

Getting up, Jingmin fumbled in her purse for something, then finally decided to take it along. The three men sat there politely in silence. Liangsi even smiled faintly.

Jingmin closed the door. On the other side was that family of three brothers who called her wife and sister-in-law. But at this moment she was shut out and felt at a loss for what to do. She just stood there in a daze. Warm, pungent aromas from the restaurant kitchen came floating over to her as she walked along the hall. At the end was the kitchen where she could see the chef's white hat and apron and the stainless steel cabinets. Around the corner was the dining hall, and beyond the many tables and chairs crowded with people was the automatic door. It was of brown glass, which made the outside seem dark like evening. Jingmin looked, wanting to walk right out. The hum of voices buzzed in her ears. But if she left, what would she do next? She felt frustrated. For all seven years of her marriage she had always depended on Liangsan. She'd never even gone out alone on her own. She didn't even know where this place was. Besides, she hadn't brought much money because she was always with him. And now he had brought her here to tell her this. She had believed in him, but he didn't take her seriously at all.

She was angry at herself for not being more competent. Why hadn't she even brought some money? There were too many things she wasn't up to doing. Before, when she went out, it had always been Liangsan who picked her up and took her home. She doubted whether she could even direct a taxi in the right direction. She was really incompetent. No wonder he wanted to get rid of her. To him it was just as easy as throwing out an old newspaper.

All she could do was head for the ladies' room. She looked in the mirror and saw in fact that her face was a mess. She washed her face and looked in the mirror to put on her make-up. After crying, her eyes sparkled. She looked closely at her reflection in the mirror, feeling she looked quite spirited, not like a woman who had just received a crushing blow. But why take this as a crushing blow, anyway? She didn't feel she loved Liangsan that much. They had been introduced to each other by a matchmaker. It was a quiet marriage that hadn't required any effort. Perhaps Liangsan felt deeper toward that other woman. When he mentioned her, his whole expression changed.

But she had cried so much just now. Liangsan probably thought she had had a mental breakdown. His whole idea had been first to shock her, then pacify her. He didn't want her to entangle herself around him and make a fool of herself. He didn't know she didn't care one way or the other. She had kept on crying because she was scared. Besides, she remembered she was almost thirty years old and was suddenly an outcast woman. If this had happened several years earlier, she would still have been considered young. She couldn't quite think how being a bit younger when cast out was an advantage, but everything seemed better when one was young. She began to hate Liangsan, as if he had dumped a bucket of cold water over her as she lay soaking in a hot bath. She began to make her face up very carefully. It was for Liangsan. She had always made herself up on account of him. But, having just put her eyeliner on, she wiped it off again. This too, was on account of Liangsan. If she looked too stunning, he'd probably feel unhappy. He had always thought that he was everything to her.

When she returned to the private dining room, the three had already begun to eat. Liangsan looked up at her and said, 'How about eating a little something!'

This was just like at home, the family sitting around and eating. Liangqi didn't look at her at all. Jingmin didn't know why, but she sensed a strong sense of shame in him, as if he were the only one here in the family who had done something wrong. She knew he sympathized with her. Maybe Liangsi did, too, but he didn't have such a strong moral sense. He picked out a lotus-leaf-wrapped steamed meat and gingerly spread the leaf apart with his chopsticks. Liangsan was always in a good mood when he ate. He slowly related how he had discovered this restaurant and directed Jingmin's attention to the dishes as he always had done in the past. 'Jingmin, you should really study how they did this. They really know how to cook here.'

Liangsi asked, 'She's not very good at things like that, is she?' He didn't look at Jingmin. He wasn't referring to her. 'With her background.'

Liangsan looked a bit regretful. 'That's true!'

Jingmin sat in silence, a bit unhappy that they would talk about that woman right in front of her like this.

Liangsan seemed to want to pacify her. 'Jingmin really is a good cook. That's really hard to find.'

His praise for her was probably limited to just these words. Liangsan was a real connoisseur. Actually, all the men in his family were. She sympathized with him at the thought that that woman of his didn't know how to cook. In that instant she thought of him as just another man and sympathized with him that his wife was no good. She forgot he was her own husband.

Jingmin said, 'Too bad you won't get to taste it anymore.'

Liangsan laid his chopsticks down and looked at her. 'What?'

'My cooking!' Jingmin replied slowly. She suddenly felt a sense of release. 'I don't want to separate.'

Liangsan looked up and blanched. 'Didn't we just agree to it?'

'Let's get a divorce.'

Jingmin felt a sense of satisfaction when the three brothers all stared at her at once. Their expressions differed, though. Besides, Liangqi was thin and Liangsan had a round face. But all the men in the family looked a lot alike.

This was how Jingmin got divorced. When she told people, they reprimanded her: 'How could you have been so stupid?'

Liu Fen reprimanded her as well: 'How could anybody be so foolish? Why'd you lay it out so clearly? No one will ever sympathize with you.'

Liu Fen was two years younger than she was and a divorcée as well. Hers was another kind of marriage. She had gotten pregnant in high school. Forced to get married, she never adjusted to married life and had gotten a divorce. Before turning twenty, all the important events in a woman's life had already happened to her. Her mother raised the child. She took good care of herself, not looking at all as if she had had a child already. She saw her former husband often, too. She said, 'As long as he's not my husband, I think he's really adorable.'

Jingmin used the money Liangsan gave her when they divorced to open a handicraft shop. It was small and she didn't hire any help so it usually had more business than she could attend to. Liu Fen would come over at those times to help out. She was a seamstress in a shop across the street. When not busy, she liked to go over and chat with Jingmin. The two would sit on the step in front of the store like grade school kids. In the afternoon when there was a breeze, it was a cool spot.

Liu Fen was used to plopping right down and crossing her legs. When it was hot out, she'd even wear shorts. She leaned over and patted Jingmin. 'How come you're so ladylike? At first I thought you were some cultured lady!'

Jingmin sat with her legs together and feet tucked under her. She was used to sitting in a constrained manner and couldn't loosen up all at once.

Liu Fen looked absently toward the entrance to the lane. Her son would be getting out of school soon. He was in fourth grade and already grown tall and sturdy. Liu Fen went on chatting about the news in the paper about Cui Taiqing.[2] 'You're already divorced, so why hate him so much? As soon as Xiaobing and I were divorced I didn't hate him anymore. We weren't fighting or hitting each other anymore.'

Xiaobing was only a year older than she was. They both had fiery tempers. They were no longer husband and wife, but when Xiaobing came to stay overnight they'd still quarrel with each other upstairs. The next day the garbage pail would be full of broken objects. 'Xiaobing is coming today,' she said slowly, thinking of something.

'Really?' Jingmin replied. 'You haven't been fighting much lately.'

'Eh?' Liu Fen said, startled. 'That's not fighting. You don't know what it was like before. It was as if I were a guy. He'd beat me up!' She concluded, 'Xiaobing has matured a lot.'

Someone came into the lane. Liu Fen had sharp eyes. 'Hey, Little Brother Xie's here again.' She mocked Liangqi by calling him 'Little'. She raised her voice listlessly from the step in front of the store. 'Hey, Little . . . Brother . . . Xie!'

Liangqi came over to them, his face rigid. Liu Fen didn't pay any attention. She grabbed him and made him sit down on the step. 'You haven't been here for a long time. '

Liangqi looked past Liu Fen to greet Jingmin. 'Big Sister Jingmin.' She had forgotten when he had begun calling her 'Big Sister Jingmin.'

Jingmin replied, 'I'll get you a glass of cold water.'

She brought out two glasses of cold water. She looked at Liangqi from behind. He had lost weight. His shirt hung on him.

She sat down and asked, 'How come you've lost so much weight?'

Liu Fen answered for him. 'He's been writing exams and staying up late.' She finished off the cold water and went back to her store.

Jingmin sat on the steps with Liangqi. Between them was the empty space where Liu Fen had been sitting. She had a funny feeling when the wind blew. It was as if they were sitting so close but there was still a distance between them.

Liangqi often came to see her. He was the only one in the Xie family to feel bad. He always had something on his mind. He sounded like he was angry with himself. 'The baby's going to be one month old.'

Liangsan had had a daughter. Liangqi looked down at his feet. 'Liangsan wanted a son.'

'Oh,' Jingmin answered gently. 'Men are always like that.'

Liangqi protested, 'I'm not.' He looked away from her as he spoke.

'Well, it's too early for you anyway.' Jingmin smiled at him. She looked over at the back of his head. His hair was growing fast—thick and dishevelled. She reached over as she spoke and tugged at his hair. 'Your hair's really long.'

Liangqi was startled and replied recklessly, 'Who's to cut it for me?'

'Let me do it, all right? I'm not bad with my hands.' She had learnt how from a magazine, but she had actually done it only on Liu Fen and herself. She turned her head to show Liangqi. 'Look at my hair. I did it myself.'

Liangqi turned around and stared at her awkwardly, his eyes soft and liquid. Jingmin couldn't help flirting with him. She leaned closer. 'Well, how about it?' She felt astonished when she blurted it out. Liangqi had always been a younger brother-in-law to her. She had watched him grow up. But just then she treated him just like any ordinary man.

She looked around for a sheet and wrapped him up in it. He didn't like the heat so she placed an electric fan in front of him. She first dampened his hair with a water sprayer. His wet hair plastered against his skull made his head look a lot smaller. Liangqi sat there obediently, his whole body encased in the sheet, only his head sticking out for her to work on. Jingmin first pinned his hair up and said to him, 'You look like a coed.' She smiled down on him. Liangqi looked up at her without moving his head.

She said, 'Do you remember I used to wash your hair for you when you were little?'

Liangqi said, 'Yes.' She didn't know why he answered so formally. Jingmin felt like laughing. When she had contact with him before, he had been a mischievous little boy. Now he was really grown up. He hadn't even shaved his mustache, probably because he'd been busy with finals. A visible dark streak lined his upper lip. Young men's skin was smooth and looked so clean. Liangqi sat with his lips pursed. He always looked like that.

The hair she cut off smelled of tobacco smoke. Jingmin sighed, 'How long has it been since you washed your hair?'

Liangqi replied, 'No one to wash it for me! '

'How about your own hands?'

'You've got them tied up.' He moved his hands under the sheet.

They were silent for a moment, then Jingmin said, 'Well, I'm not going to do it for you.' She added, 'Lazy.'

School had just let out, and the lane gradually filled with students. Some of them came to buy thread. Some girl students crowded around the counter. Jingmin went over to wait on them. Her business was always like this. It came in spurts. The girls knew her well. They burst out laughing.

'Mistress, you can cut hair!'

Liangqi sat stonily on the counter, the clips still in his hair. He shut his eyes as if angry. He was probably embarrassed. Jingmin ordered him, 'Liangqi, go sit inside.' Inside was her bedroom. Liangqi went inside the back room. She explained to the others, 'My little brother.' She turned to another girl and said, 'That's my younger brother.' Actually, no one paid any attention to what she was saying. She taught several of them some embroidery stitches. She took out the colours and background with printed borders to show them. She finally finished waiting on them and hurriedly went into the back room. The store and back room were separated only by a curtain.

She pushed it aside and went in, calling out, 'Liangqi.'

He had already taken off the sheet. He was sitting on the bed leafing through the *TV Weekly*. The curtain clacked together behind her. She had made it herself out of wooden beads. Bits and pieces of the world outside were visible between the beads.

In the room were a vanity table, a single bed, and a chair, with cardboard boxes and materials in the corner. With Liangqi in the room, she suddenly felt it had gotten a lot smaller. She stood awkwardly with her back against the curtain.

'Liangqi, are you angry?'

'No.' He put the magazine down. 'Big Sister Jingmin, you've changed. You're so capable.' He gestured and added mischievously, 'I don't mean you weren't capable before, though.'

'Let me cut your hair again.'

This time she had him sit in front of the vanity table. After cutting for a while, she discovered that Liangqi was watching her in the mirror. She stopped and asked, 'What's the matter?'

'What do you mean, what's the matter?'

'You keep staring at me.' She made a face like a shrew. She had watched him grow up. She wasn't embarrassed in front of him.

He said, 'Then who should I watch?'

'Look at yourself!'

Liangqi replied, 'All right,' and the two of them burst into laughter. Jingmin asked cautiously, 'Do you have a girlfriend?'

'Not yet.' He pursed his lips when he laughed, and looked even more mischievous. Jingmin looked at him in the mirror and suddenly felt a bit shaky. Perhaps Liangqi's clean-cut features seemed especially bright in the mirror's reflection. His face narrowed to his chin, its smooth outline very handsome. The clumps of hair in her hand were wet and glossy as silk. She felt as if she couldn't stop herself from sinking into his arms. Her head felt heavy. Body odour from Liangqi floated up toward her, the faint smell of cigarette smoke and perspiration. She had never had a man in here before.

Jingmin was afraid of herself.

She said, 'I'm going to watch the store for a minute.' She lifted the curtain and went out.

Liangqi followed her, taking the sheet off as he went. The hair clips were still in his hair. Jingmin felt like laughing. She lifted the curtain and went back inside. Liangqi followed again.

He suddenly spoke up. 'Big Sister Jingmin. I really like you.' He stood with his back to the curtain, the world shut away beyond him. On his crazy, damp, unfinished hair, the grey hair clips rested on his head like giant moths. He was scared, too, and having spoken, pursed his lips tightly as he stood there. He was a grown-up, but his slender, frail frame seemed to invite one to embrace him like a child.

Perhaps he had been thinking about this too long. Having spoken up, he was like a taut string that suddenly snapped. He wasn't smiling. His expression was determined.

They didn't know what to do. They just stood there. At last Jingmin said, 'Come over and let me finish cutting your hair.' Liangqi went over and sat quietly in front of the mirror.

She began to cry. She'd probably never be able to change this part of her. Liangqi tried to get up but she pushed him down. Tears fell onto his hair as she proceeded to cut it. She wiped the tears away as she cut. Liangqi anxiously apologized, 'Big Sister Jingmin, I'm sorry.'

'Never mind. I just like to cry.'

Liangqi was dumbstruck. Jingmin sensed something frightening in herself. She wasn't weeping hysterically, just sobbing silently, her eyes welling with tears as if she were finding release from daily injustices. Actually, that wasn't true. Having left Liangsan, she felt she had gotten along quite well on her own. Men just weren't that important. Whenever she was in a foul mood she'd cry. She'd cry when she read novels or watched movies on TV, too. Thinking of this, she laughed again and Liangqi, watching her in the mirror, was reassured. He smiled back sheepishly.

Jingmin said, 'It's just that I like to cry. It has nothing to do with you.'

She cut his hair with care. She did like Liangqi somewhat but not to that degree. He was still young; just look at the way he stopped worrying right away. She was angry with herself. She had been divorced less than a year but still cried when a man said he liked her!

'Liangqi, that's nonsense.' Jingmin said, but sensed her tone wasn't quite right. She took the scissors and rapped him on the head. 'I'm your Third Sister-in-law!'

Having finished cutting his hair, she washed his hair for him. The two squeezed into the narrow little bathroom. Liangqi bent over and lowered his head into the sink. Jingmin reached over and gripped his head with her left hand. A man this intimate with her was like a younger brother, lover, or son.

The cool water splashed out of the faucet and flowed over her fingers. Between her fingers were his long locks, like small black snakes curled on the back of her hand. The hair in the water floated up like strands of silk, in an orderly and beautiful fashion. She'd probably remember this for the rest of her life. In the afternoon there wasn't a sound outside. The old electric fan buzzed noisily in the front room, sputtering from right to left as it turned back and forth. The apartment was not new, and the bathroom smelled of mildew. The fragrant scent of the shampoo seemed to cover the mildew smell as well as the acrid perspiration from Liangqi. He lowered his head to let the water wet his hair. The parts she touched were all cool. He was quiet and obedient but breathed heavily. She knew he was in an awkward position. She felt the same way. She breathed carefully, inhaling only a little each time, then when she could no longer hold back, she exhaled deeply as if sighing. The two of them were pressed tightly together. Liangqi's breathing came rapidly as if they were committing an indiscretion, but they weren't.

After this she became restless and was always on edge. She finally got rid of the store and began selling policies for an insurance company. This was the only work she could find.

She carried big packets of information wherever she went and greeted people wreathed in smiles. She couldn't believe that she could do this. She wasn't particularly eloquent, but she looked sincere. She didn't force the policies on people. She just sat there and spread the information out for them to see and read the pertinent portions to the prospective customers in a candid manner. Whatever they said she'd only reply slowly with a 'yes'. Her stretching the word out over several seconds made people think she had something to say but didn't dare. Prospective customers found it hard not to sympathize with her. If they turned her down, they would always call her back sometime later. Her sales record was excellent, and she began to move up in the organization, becoming section manager.

She was darker and thinner now. She wore jeans because they were convenient. She wasn't as shy as before. Her eyes sparkled, and she had learnt to cross her legs up high when she sat down. Her smile was warm and bright without any trace of slyness. When people saw her this way, they let down most of their defences.

She met Qu Shaojie when she was out selling insurance. They began living together soon afterward. This time it was she who was the 'other woman'. She knew he was married, but she liked that tough-guy appearance of his. A spoiled man over forty, he hadn't yet learnt how to live. He was manager of an import-export company when Jingmin came bursting into his luminous office all of glass, stainless steel, acrylic, plastic, and aluminum.

Qu Shaojie sat behind his desk, clean face and hair, wearing a freshly pressed suit. He listened to her impatiently, his face in a scowl, tough and stubborn looking. He had insurance. He didn't need to take out any more. He didn't want to discuss it. Sorry. He had other things to take care of.

He was still polite and escorted her to the door. He wore aftershave lotion, the scent of green olives.

Jingmin decided she wanted him. She was thirty-three then, having been out on her own in society for four years. She had begun changing into a confident woman. Besides learning how to dress and make herself up, she had learnt how to use people, learnt how to deal with different kinds of people, and what words were most effective to get what she wanted. She paid attention to detail and was willing to sit quietly listening to others talk, with the result that she learnt how to sympathize with others' feelings and imagine their way of thinking.

She understood what kind of person Qu Shaojie was.

The second time she went, she dressed in a very feminine manner—a thin silk dress, her hair neatly combed close to her face. She only took up ten minutes of his time and didn't talk about insurance.

After that she went there often, and her visits increased in length. Sometimes they went out to eat together. She fell in love with him then, and it was as if her mind was suddenly a blank and she didn't take anything into consideration. All she could think of was him. Her confidence disappeared. She dressed up every day and went floating gracefully into his office. She would sit in a very dignified manner, her legs tucked underneath the chair, and watch him closely. Her whole person was fluent and elegant. Anyone could tell she was brimming over like a vase filled with water. Anyone except him, that is. He would knit his thick handsome brows obstinately. He was intractable. Whenever she came he'd raise his eyebrows. 'You're back to sell insurance?'

Jingmin couldn't stand it anymore. She was frightened when she discovered she was in love. She couldn't take this kind of seriousness. She loved him so much she felt her whole body was transparent. In front of him she was as sensitive as a fragile grass that retracted at the slightest touch. She was already grown up. Wasn't she a little too old to play this game? She stopped going to see him, as if she had forgotten all about him. But she couldn't give him up. She finally went back again and decided to come to terms with this affair. She didn't even know how he felt about her.

Qu Shaojie hadn't changed a bit, as if after all this time he had been nailed to his chair at his office desk without having left once. He looked up and arched his thick black eyebrows. 'You're back to sell insurance?'

He hadn't even changed those words.

Jingmin cried once more.

She finally got him to buy some insurance. Shortly afterward, they began living together.

When she told Liu Fen about all of these happenings, it sounded relatively simple. She recounted it in two or three sentences: 'I tried to get him to buy insurance, but he kept on refusing. I went there every day to pester him.' She held Liu Fen's new son in one arm. He was plump and heavy, and holding him made her arm ache. She switched arms. Lui Fen reached over. 'Let me hold him! '

'And then?'

Jingmin said, 'Later we got acquainted, and he finally bought some insurance!'

Liu Fen looked at her and passed judgement, 'It looks to me like you're doing OK.' She explained, 'You really look beautiful.'

'Oh,' Jingmin giggled.

Liu Fen married Xiaobing again. They opened a restaurant in the city with Liu Fen as cashier behind the counter. She had grown heavier. Sitting at the counter, she looked plump and white like a roll of steamed bread just out of the bamboo steamer. She put the baby on the counter and wiped the saliva from his mouth.

Jingmin played with him: 'Let's not eat anything but this little piglet!' She nipped at him. 'Take a bite. Take a bite.'

Some customers entered. The waitresses were busy, so Liu Fen went over to wait on them herself. She called out, 'Sit over here! What can I bring you?'

Jingmin had become the child's godmother the moment he was born, and they got along famously. She wondered if she really could get pregnant or not. Maybe she was just too old. She really wanted a child—by Shaojie.

Liu Fen came over and patted her on the back. 'Jingmin, the people at that table asked about you.'

'Which table?' This happened a lot. She had met many people while selling insurance.

'Come with me.' Jingmin smiled, picked the child up, and squeezed past the tables. A couple was sitting at the table with two children. The wife stared at her from afar, very cautiously. The man was wiping one of the children's hands, his face to one side. When Jingmin came closer, he finally looked up.

It was Liangsan.

Jingmin called out, 'Why it's Liangsan.' She really was a little pleased. Both sides introduced themselves. Liu Fen took the child back with her. Jingmin said enthusiastically, 'I haven't seen you in ages!'

All these years of experience had trained her in this kind of greeting. Liangsan looked startled, then smiled and said politely, 'You've changed a lot.' The two at this moment had no common past. Liangsan seemed like a new acquaintance. Jingmin felt that though she had forgotten many things, she didn't think he had been like this. She couldn't remember what he had been like, though.

She stood holding onto the back of a chair. Their family of four filled the four chairs at the table and didn't make any move to let her sit down. Jingmin therefore squeezed into the seat with the older daughter. This was something she wouldn't have done in the past. She saw Liangsan's strange expression. He repeated, 'You've changed a lot!'

'Everyone changes!' She smiled. She had a strange feeling that she had become two different persons. She rarely thought about what she had been like in the past, but facing Liangsan, her former self reappeared. She suddenly experienced a powerful realization of the great change between her past and present self. She smiled, holding her chin lazily in her hand. She knew she was making that woman uneasy.

'Liangsan, you've changed a lot, too!'

'No, I haven't.' Liangsan denied hurriedly.

'You're fatter.'

'I'm not either!' He still denied it. He suddenly seemed so pitifully disingenuous.

They chatted a bit about what they were doing now. Liangqi had gone to study abroad. And his little sister was married. Jingmin lied and said she was married too in order to save face.

Liangsan stared at her and asked, 'That's your son?'

'Yes,' replied Jingmin, half in jest.

Liangsan looked pained and, after a struggle, said regretfully, 'Who'd have thought you could give birth to a son!'

The three other women at the table, Liangsan's wife and daughters, sat there quietly in a daze. Jingmin understood what it was like to be Liangsan's wife. She felt sorry for that woman. Wearing a plain, neutral-coloured dress, she sat there quietly and obediently. When she met Liangsan she had been the most popular taxi dancer in the music hall. One could still tell she was beautiful, but she looked a bit faded. It was as if that woman had taken Jingmin's place at Liangsan's side and gone on living in a quiet, faded, contented manner. Maybe she was also happy that way. Jingmin hadn't had such a bad life before. But because of that woman she was now living a different kind of life. She felt she was better off now than before. She smiled at his wife good-naturedly but couldn't help joking, 'Does he still hate to brush his teeth before going to bed?'

Liangsan and his wife blanched. He laughed, but she became angry. Maybe she wasn't as gentle as she seemed on the surface. This time she was herself, not like the former Jingmin. And she didn't feel like she was going to cry. Maybe his wife would pick a fight with Liangsan when they went back home.

Jingmin went back to Liu Fen at the counter and had the kitchen make a special dish for Liangsan and his wife. As she headed for the kitchen, a cloud of steam came floating toward her. The chef in his white apron, the shiny stainless steel cabinets—perhaps this was the same impression from many years ago. Why were restaurant kitchens always the same? But she was not the same. She was an independent, confident woman.

1980

NOTES

1 The three brothers in the story are given names by seniority: Liangsan is third; Liangsi fourth; and Liangqi seventh.
2 A Taiwanese singer of the 1970s.

18

Rain

By **CHAN PO CHUN**

Translated by Linda P. L. Wong, with A. T. L. Parkin

Chan Po Chun 陳寶珍 *(Chen Baozhen, b. 1953) was born and educated in Hong Kong. She received her BA and MPhil in Chinese from the Chinese University of Hong Kong in the 1970s. Most of her works of fiction and prose found their first appearance in newspapers and magazines, such as* Sing Tao Daily *(*Xingdao ribao 星島日報*), and* Hong Kong Literature *(*Xianggang wenxue 香港文學*). Her major short stories were later published in a collection entitled* Looking for a House *(*Zhao fangzi 找房子*), which won for her the First Hong Kong Urban Council's Biennial Award for Literature (Fiction Section) in 1991. Her works of prose can be found in the collection* Crazy Friends *(*Kuang peng guai you 狂朋怪友*, 1994). Her first novel, entitled* The Square *(*Guangchang 廣場*) was published in 1997. She currently teaches creative writing in the Department of Chinese Language and Literature at Hong Kong Baptist University.*

In many of her stories, Chan Po Chun explores the moral dilemma confronting women in contemporary society and points out that women's desire for autonomy is not universal. Chan shows a type of woman whose desire for love and companionship may prove to be stronger than the desire for independence.

PA! A ball of heavy black shadow flashed across my eyes. I fell on the bed in spite of myself. My right cheek was seared by pain. I wanted to get up. I wasn't on my guard and another heavy blow landed on my right thigh. Tears were streaming down my cheeks as if waters had burst through a dam. I dabbed gingerly with the back of my hand. Feeling grossly wronged, I raised my head and looked at him. He was also staring at me. His face was full of anger. Afterwards, he grabbed a bathing towel from the bed and walked into the bathroom without looking back. I heard a bang and then the sound of running water.

I got up, put on my jacket, and took my leather bag. I opened the door and the gate, then walked out with no hesitation whatsoever.

It wasn't cold in the streets. It was drizzling though. Neon lights were reflected on the wet streets. Asphalt roads, generally monotonous and dull, decorated like some mysterious abstract painting—on the black background a patch of blue here, a patch of red there. My face was probably still red! Strange: my heart didn't feel anything. It was as if the whole world, including my own body, had already cut off any relationship with me! I was just like a girl who had lost her way, walking bewildered in the concrete jungle. One car. Two cars. Three cars. They slowly drove past. Tyres swept by on the roads with only a sudden squeak. These steel monsters seemed filled with life and knew how to soften their footsteps, so as not to disturb this slumbering city. . . .

I gazed fixedly at the drizzle. One by one the fragments of fine raindrops slowly appeared before my eyes. . . .

'I thought you wouldn't come!' In the distance I saw him in a sky-blue track suit emerging from the thin morning mist. I couldn't help turning my disappointment into joy. I had shouted it out even before I came near him.

'What?'

'I thought you wouldn't come,' I said. He was already walking towards me.

'Why not? I had an appointment with you.'

'I thought we couldn't run when it rained.'

'Rain or shine! It is only drizzly rain. What have I to fear?' He smiled. His natural curly hair was drenched with very, very tiny water drops.

'Let's warm up.'

How good looking he was when smiling!

My ears were again ringing with teases of jealousy or envy:

'Your elder sister's boyfriend really is gentle and beautiful!'

'I saw you run that day. One wore red and the other blue. What a lovely couple!'

'Hey! When you get married, you won't need to go to a church. Just run around the school once and treat it as a wedding ceremony!'

'And the guests will line both sides of the street.'

One by one these fragments floated across my mind. I couldn't help smiling. So sweet, my heart.

'What are you smiling at? Why don't you start your warm up? Lazy girl!' Smiling, he lightly patted the back of my head.

I walked out of the cinema while it was drizzling. In the streets of Mongkok, the people who had left the cinema converged with the flow of crowds. Those who forgot to bring umbrellas covered their heads with their hands or held newspapers over their heads. They scurried between cars.

'Dustin Hoffman played really well!' Certain scenes of the movie I just saw still lingered in my mind.

'He acts any role as if it were for real. I also like watching him very much!' he said, smiling. With one hand he put an automatic umbrella up. He put his other hand across my shoulders.

'In fact I can act too. Look at me and see if I can play a lame person just like him.' As I spoke, I lifted my left foot lightly off the ground. My sole turned inward and I limped.

'What are you doing?'

'Playing lame! Do I or don't I look lame?'

'You certainly do! That's enough!'

I ignored him. I continued to go ahead, limping more seriously!

'Hey! That's enough! You can twist your foot easily by walking like this. Be careful not to go really lame. . . . Stop that! Hey! If you do this again, I'll break your leg!' And so saying, he laughed again!

I made a wry face. My left foot returned to normal.

'You! So grown up yet so child-like!' His hand, which was resting on my shoulders, pinched my arm. Ouch! But sweet smiles rose up from my heart and stayed on my lips.

'You don't need to take me home. You go study! I'll go by bus!'

'H'm! O.K. I need to have more time to study. The day after tomorrow I'll see you after the exam.'

I walked out of the door of his house. Unexpectedly it was drizzling. The yellow light of the street lamps shone on the surface of the asphalt road and made it gleam golden. I set out across the gilded road and slowly walked towards the terminus. Suddenly I heard rapid steps behind me. I turned my head and looked. He was already standing right next me. The big black umbrella softly cut off the rain above my head. I looked up, pleasantly surprised—

'It is raining! I'd better take you home!'

The bus came just as I got to the stop. I got on and immediately picked a window seat. He was still waving at me outside the bus. The bus slowly drove away. He started to run in big strides as if he wanted to race the bus. After the bus accelerated, he just spread out his hands, smiling, and stopped running. All along I turned round to look at him until I couldn't see him. The corners of my mouth still stayed upwards. My eyes, involuntarily, had filled with tears.

All that was a few years ago! How could it end up being like today in so short a time. . . .

'How many times have I told you? It isn't that I don't love you the way I did. It is the circumstances that have been changed. Understand?' He often said this smilingly. But all these changes seemed to begin after he had been promoted.

Dully I stood in front of the window. The clock seemed reluctant to strike eleven and was dragging its hands slowly. But I saw it would soon be eleven. My heartbeat quickened with excitement. Very soon I would see him! I walked into the kitchen and again put the pot of soup on the gas stove. I turned it on and once again walked towards the window . . . the soup was boiling. How come he wasn't back yet? I turned off the stove. I went back to the window. He couldn't be in any accident! Night after night he worked to the point of dizziness and then walked unsteadily through the streets. In fact it worried me to death! The soup had gone cold. I really didn't know what was going on.

'Wait, wait, wait. Every night I wait like this. Even if you don't get sick of it, I do!'

'Who asks you to wait? Can't you just take a nap first?'

'You said you'd be back at eleven o'clock. I waited till twelve and you still didn't come back. Can't you see I worry? Look, what time is it?'

'I'm not an alarm clock! Oh honey! I wanted to come back to you at eleven o'clock. But how could I leave when the work wasn't finished?'

'In that case you should have called me. It would set my mind at rest!'

'When I get busy, I don't remember anything!'

'You men are all like this. Once you're married, you don't remember anything! Why did you remember everything in the past?'

'The circumstances have changed! Young lady! I'm not a student still! I have to work, earn money, raise a family. I can't possibly remember even very simple things like birthdays and Valentine's like I used to. Today we'll stroll in Stanley and tomorrow I'll take you to the Peak. . . . Can you learn to adapt to circumstances? How come you are in your twenties yet act like a kindergarten girl? Why don't you consider how busy my work is?'

'Right! I almost forgot you are a big busy person. But this kind of waiting for somebody, I really hate!'

'So, do you think I don't hate it? Day after day I work very hard and I'm busy from morning till night, only to come home to see that look in your eyes!'

'I know you hate it. You hate it even though we haven't yet been married for three years. You should be only too glad to stay outside for twenty-four hours a day so you wouldn't have to look at me, your sallow-faced wife. . . .'

'That's enough! Will you stop being so savage?'

'I really am this savage!'

'PA!'

My tears finally rolled down again! I shouldn't have quarrelled with him over something so trivial. In fact, though I scolded him, it wasn't what I really wanted in my heart. Surely it didn't mean that I was actually too lonely and was attempting deliberately to catch his attention. But he shouldn't have hit me! How it would make my mother's heart ache when she discovered he hit me! All the time I was growing up, my dad and mom never hit me! Was I really a very bad wife? Did he still love me? I was so selfish, so—nagging! Tonight where should I go? I could go back to my mom and ask her to tell him I wasn't there if he called. Would that make him anxious? But would that be going too far? Surely he hadn't really meant to hit me? Had he really reached the end of his tether? Maybe he started to regret it once he walked into the bathroom! Good Heavens! What should I do?

My thoughts were like a ball of messed-up silk, tightly netting my heart. I leaned on a lamppost and cried. Suddenly, a hand rested lightly upon my shoulder. The sensation was so familiar. Wiping my eyes with my hand, I slowly turned my head. There, beneath the dim yellow lamplight, was that delicate and friendly face. My anger instantly and completely vanished. In his eyes complicated feelings were intertwined: guilt, shame, and a little anxiety. He looked as if the heaviness inside had been lifted away. His lips moved a bit. He didn't say anything, just gently wiped the tears from my face.

Rain fell softly on our heads. . . .

1982

From: A Place of One's Own.

19

She's Woman; I'm Woman

By **Wong Bik Wan**

Translated by Yuet May Ching[1]

Wong Bik Wan 黃碧雲 (Huang Biyun, b. 1961) received her BSc in Journalism and Communication from the Chinese University of Hong Kong in 1984. She has worked as a journalist, a scriptwriter, and a freelance writer for newspapers and magazines since her graduation, and she spent time studying French and French culture in Paris. She also worked as a reporter for the Hong Kong Standard *for some time before taking up her current post in a law firm in London. Her works of prose have been collected in* Brave Women *(*Yangmei nuzi 揚眉女子*, 1987). Her first collection of short stories, entitled* Thereafter *(*Qihou 其後*) was published in 1994, to be followed by* Gentleness and Violence *(*Wenrou yu baolie 溫柔與暴烈*, 1994),* She's Woman; I'm Woman *(*Ta shi nuzi, wo ye shi nuzi 她是女子，我也是女子*, 1994), and* Seven Types of Silence *(*Qizhong jingmo 七種靜默*, 1997). She won the Hong Kong Arts Development Council's Award for Young Writers in 1997. Wong's tales are often controversial, for she speaks in a distinctly different voice, a voice that relates the absurdity of contemporary life.*

I thought Zhiheng and I could have stayed together for the rest of our lives.

Her name was Xu Zhiheng. When we first met, we were first year university students in a required course, 'The Art of Thinking'.

She was the only female student I knew who wore cheongsams and embroidered shoes to classes. What a stagy outfit, but she looked smart in it anyway. I remember that the colour of her shoes was vermilion. Her haircut, however, was short. Lowering her eyes and bending her head to take notes most of the time, she appeared to be a well-behaved student. But she was wearing peach red nail polish—only bad women would wear nail polish. And to seduce so quietly and subtly was downright bad. I didn't know that I would fall for a bad woman.

Really, her reputation had spread far and wide. My male classmates told me what her name was, that she was a student from the Chinese Department, that she had graduated from Jiangsu-Chekiang College, and that her family lived on Blue Pool Road.[2] When we were studying Plato in class, the male students gossiped about her in small clusters here and there in the hostel. I folded my arms and smiled, and a slight contempt for them arose from my heart. But they still liked to talk about her, calling her the 'Little Phoenix Courtesan'.

Zhiheng had been absent from class for a long time. Once I came across her at the train station. She just walked on, bowing her head, and following her in awkward steps was a male student.

A year later we met again in the class 'Introduction to Sociology'. Not wanting to bother himself with the trouble of calling the roll, the old lecturer required us to sit in the same place every time. I took the opportunity to sit next to Zhiheng. I remember that on that day she was wearing a loose-fitting cheongsam made of white and dark purple silk gloss. Very fine hair grew on her arms, and she had a certain scent about her—a mixture of cosmetics, perfume, milk, and ink—which later I called the 'Scent of the Phoenix Courtesan'. Her hands were so clear, smooth, and cool that I really wanted to touch them. But I didn't, for she wasn't even aware of my existence.

She skipped class again and showed up only when the lectures on Karl Marx's surplus value started. She wanted to borrow notes from me, which I showed her. 'It's no use even if I lend these to you. Only I can understand my notes,' I chuckled. Raising her eyebrows, she answered, 'Oh, maybe not.' As I was lazy, my notes were extremely short. My classmates called them 'telegraphic notes', and nobody ever wanted to borrow them. Anyhow, I saw her just breeze through the job and decode my notes neatly. Well, you'd better be clever if you skip class for a whole month! I liked clever, bright people, and perhaps that's why I took up with her.

I said, 'Let me buy you a coffee.' She replied, 'Fine.' That type of conversation was also telegraphic.

We were sitting in the sunset, speechless, both of us. I took a close look at her. Returning my scrutiny, she said, 'I've seen you before, Ye Xixi. You play the bamboo flute at night in a classroom all by yourself. I heard it.' She was wearing silver bangles, which jingled as she gestured. 'I know that last week you lost a pink Maidenform bra. I read about it in a poster in the hostel common room. It was you, right?' She laughed. 'Everyone in our hostel knew about it, even the guys in the men's hostel. You lost a 32B pink Maidenform bra! How vulgar.' I said, 'No, my size is actually 32A. I'm skinny.' Seeing the curves of her bosom, I joked: 'I bet you wear at least a 34B. After you get married you'll wear size 38.' Zhiheng lightly covered her breasts with her hands and sighed, 'Aiya, I'm afraid so.' Our mutual understanding began with a Maidenform bra.

Since then she came to class every time, and we chatted. We joked about the old shrivelled lecturer who wore skin-coloured nylon socks. I wondered where she bought her cheongsams, but she said it was a trade secret. I asked her to movies on campus. We went to see Lau Shing-hon's *House of the Lute*. That movie made us shriek with laughter. I dragged her to watch Eisenstein's *October*, during which we both fell asleep, waking up only when everybody had left. We went out for night snacks. At times she wore jeans, like when we had stir-fried clams. But she insisted on wearing her embroidered shoes.

In the second term of our third year, her roommate moved out without telling the warden. So I moved in. It was only then that we really began to develop a relationship.

Frankly speaking, I was impressed by Zhiheng's charms and I felt she was somewhat clever and easy-going, but I didn't really know her character. In this we were most like other men and women in love, as our initial attraction for each other was based on looks. Even though I wasn't a beauty, nor did I have her charms, I knew how to sell myself in a sly way. I was the type of person Zhiheng would like, I thought. My art of seduction was subtle—so was hers, with her cheongsams and embroidered shoes.

So, our residence became the 'Smoky Red District', for we both smoked. She smoked Double Happiness while I smoked Dunhill Menthol—Yes, we were putting on airs, wickedly. And we both adored Tom Waits. We danced in our room, her body extremely supple. We both were women. At times I read de Beauvoir, but later I thought her not classy enough, so I switched to Kristeva. Zhiheng liked reading I Shu.[3] Upon my objection, she started to read Sagin, then upon my further objection she read Angela Carter. Gradually we both made progress. I got a scholarship. She applied for one but she didn't get it—because she lost it to me.

On the day I got my scholarship money and got my photo taken for the University Bulletin, I thought of something. I remembered that when we went shopping together before, Zhiheng had wanted a flaming red cashmere top priced at $950, but she couldn't afford it. So I bought it for her that day, intending to give her the present at dinner. She didn't come back. I waited and waited till it got dark. Alone in the room, I didn't turn on the lights. In that late autumn night, seeing the fishing lights scattered here and there on the dark sea beyond the windows, I suddenly felt how heartless she was. I had had boyfriends before, but I had never missed them so much. She didn't make her bed today; she didn't wear her embroidered shoes today; she had only a little toothpaste left—I'd better buy another tube for her; her Phoenix Courtesan Scent lingered in the room; her powder and rouge; her tears. . . . Quietly I leaned against the window. Quietly I shed some tears, which dried quickly. Oh, Zhiheng.

I woke up, ate some bread, and I suddenly realized that the bread was stale, like animal feed. I had eaten bread for over ten years, but I could distinguish this taste and this smell only just then. There was an old saying: 'Don't gloat over your ability when you find out the truth—be grieved and have pity'.[4] This saying had become a cliché. But at that moment I was really grief-stricken, my grief intermingled with the stale taste I had encountered just now. Oh, how could I describe the sorrows of a worldly existence.

It was one o'clock in the morning. Leaning against the window, I heard the engine of a car and I saw Zhiheng getting off a taxi. She was wearing black clothes, and her flat shoes were also black. Poor me! There and then I still paid attention to what she was wearing. I realized that I noticed her clothes and her scent more than her character. Perhaps she didn't have any character. Suddenly I felt ashamed of myself. Am I any different from other men? I was also impressed by appearance. But I had never really touched her. Perhaps because we were never explicit about what we felt, so we had never done anything like kissing or hugging. We didn't even feel there was the need. The business of so-called fondling and kissing among lesbians is something invented by men so that they can feast their eyes on such spectacles. Zhiheng and I never did those things. I didn't even say 'I love you' to her. But I knew at that moment that I was deeply in love with her, so much so that I wanted to find out if she had character.

Leaning against the window, I felt my heart was aflame and beating fast. Here she comes. Here she comes.

As soon as she had opened the door, she slumped onto her bed, her face red and her whole body exuding the sour, stale smell of wine. I didn't know why but she was wearing heavy make-up that day, and her make-up was all smeared. I was reminded of the smell of bread. I became quiet, and swallowed the words I was going to say.

'You must be happy today. I'm very happy, too,' she smiled. CRASH—suddenly a battery of coins flew at me. 'Let me tell you, Ye Xixi, I'm just plain vulgar.' I didn't say one word in return. I just covered my face with my hands and the coins kept on flying at me—it hurt. After she became exhausted from throwing coins at me, she sat on one side of her bed, leaned against the wall, and rested. The room suddenly became dead quiet. The light was blinding.

'Zhiheng,' I ventured to call her.

She didn't reply, having fallen asleep. I wiped her face, removed her clothes and shoes, and kissed her feet.

I packed a few things, and left a note on the desk: 'Dear Zhiheng: If one day we were lost in the crowd, our lives wasted and meaningless, that's because we had not tried our best to live a full life.' Actually I had no ambition then. But she had.

That night I knocked on a man's door, a man who had wanted me for a long time. Oh, he looked so impatient. How could I be blind to that? But I didn't care because I didn't have a heart, nor did I possess my own body. Perhaps that was my revenge against Zhiheng and the man and myself. All day I was numb. I asked that man to rent a room for me. He left, and then I just continued with my classes, concentrating even more, unlike my usual self.

Whenever I passed by the hostel I always looked around. Was she in? Was she brushing her hair, doing her homework, or reading the newspapers? Would she miss me? After her sudden disappearance from my life, my life seemed extremely quiet and peaceful. No one knew and no one cared how I felt any more. Oh, Zhiheng.

One late autumn night I dined with that man. His conversation was utterly boring, so I just kept on drinking wine. I drank so much that I was totally flushed when the meal was over. Walking in the night wind, I threw up, and tears rolled down my cheeks and my body. He gave me his handkerchief, then I clutched at his arm tightly. At that moment, any man with a handkerchief would be good enough for me. So my contempt for him subsided a little. Really, if I had entered into a relationship with him there and then and had forgotten all about Zhiheng, it would have been a good thing. But as soon as he got into his small Japanese car, he hugged me tight and put his face right in front of mine. I teased him, saying, 'You could have been all right for me. But I really doubt your taste because you don't mind kissing a woman who smells so bad.' He was driving me back, disgruntled, when I said, 'Wait, I want to go back to the hostel and get something.'

It was 3am. Her desk lamp was on, yet I couldn't see her. In the dark night air, I craned my neck and looked. There she was, under the light. I don't mean to outshine you, Zhiheng. I have no ambition. I just want to develop a simple relationship with you. Why can't the world tolerate this?

Suddenly her shadow flitted past the window, and the light was switched off. That glimpse made me wonder if her hair had grown longer, if someone clipped and painted her toenails. After I was gone, who would button up her clothes at the back? At night, who would come to see her? Who would miss her and think of her? Who would know whether she was happy or not? Who would compete for trifles with her? Who would be her beloved? Who would be deemed her threat?

I wanted to see her very badly, just a glance.

I rushed upstairs, found the door locked, but I had the key. Zhiheng was asleep, her bosom rising and falling, rising and falling, and her figure still full. After a few weeks, she hadn't lost any weight, nor had she languished. On closer look, her toenails appeared to be well clipped and her nail polish bright red as usual. I also discovered a few stuffed toys in her bed. She was holding a bunny in her arms and sleeping like a baby. How peaceful! She lived well even after I left. The sun still climbed up the sky, the curtain of night still fell, and in the dead hours of the night, someone was still asleep while the other was still wide awake. Somebody next door was still tapping away on the typewriter, still doing the homework, still minding the business of the mundane world. All at once tears gushed from my eyes. I choked. Someone was strangling me. Who was it? I grabbed my throat, thinking that tonight stars would fall like rain. Zhiheng, my tender feelings for you had been totally wasted.

My tears fell on her face. I squeezed my throat till my face turned red and my breathing became difficult. Roused from her sleep, she took hold of both my hands firmly, and asked, 'Why are you doing this?'

She embraced me. Breathing in her scent, I fell asleep peacefully. Vaguely I heard a car honking downstairs. Who cared? That man had fulfilled his mission in my life and I would have nothing to do with him anymore. I had Zhiheng.

Zhiheng held my face with her hands, saying, 'You're so silly.'

No answer came from me, for I only wanted to sleep. Sure the sun would rise tomorrow.

After this Zhiheng was nicer to me. At night we studied till late and she always made ginseng tea for me. She was usually quite lazy in her studies, so why did she change her ways? I vaguely felt that she was different. She was even using the perfume 'Opium'. I felt suffocated.

She started going out at night again. At midnight, she would invariably wear her flaming red oversized woollen sweater and black boots, and she prowled around like a panther. Waiting for her downstairs was a sapphire blue sports car. When she came back, her cheeks were invariably flushed. She would even bring back warm, sweet dumplings for me. But I had no appetite. Those dumplings made of glutinous rice powder should be eaten while hot; otherwise they turn hard. The following morning I did not know what to do with the hard dumplings. Zhiheng was never there. We were fourth year students already, but she was taking only eleven credits.

During Christmas I wanted to go back home for a night. When I saw Zhiheng packing, I asked how long she was staying with her family. Shaking her head, she replied, 'I'm going to Beijing.'

I paused, not saying anything for a long while. The Christmas before during our trip to Japan, we had agreed that the destination for our next trip was Beijing.

Quietly I hid my face in my hands. 'Zhiheng, don't you remember?'

She pulled away both my hands and looked into my eyes: 'Yes, I remember, but that was before. Now I have my big chance. When you know how to plan for your future, it doesn't mean that my life has to be ordinary and dull.' She kissed my forehead, and then she left.

I sank down in the middle of the half-empty room, thinking that I could sit motionless like that forever. Then I lay prostrate on the floor, and found that the carpet had become dirty. Zhiheng and I bought this after running around in Central for one whole afternoon. She insisted on buying a Persian carpet, while I, thinking a Persian carpet impractical, suggested an Indian one. Finally we compromised and settled on a Belgian one. Still holding our carpet, we had a Dutch meal. Zhiheng even ordered a dozen fresh oysters. All our money was spent. . . . When did all that happen?

That Christmas I was depressed and I stayed inside the library all the time. One day when I was flipping through the pages of a magazine, suddenly I saw a fat man. His face was sallow, and he was wearing a pair of ski goggles. I was stunned. To my further surprise, I found out that he was accompanied by Zhiheng! I closed my magazine and went to the canteen to eat, pretending as if nothing had happened. But it just turned out that I sat in the same seat I had when I first came here with Zhiheng. I felt dizzy and almost cried. Biting my lip, I returned to the library and actually started to concentrate on my books.

When she returned I was dozing off at my desk, where a magazine containing her pictures lay open. I didn't look at her, nor did she move. She sat still, took a puff of her cigarette, and said, 'All is lost.'

I made weak tea for her. She held my hand tightly; gently I stroked her hair.

I didn't ask her any more questions, neither did she mention this episode again. Even now I still don't know what had happened to her. She didn't go out at night any more, and she started practicing how to carry herself gracefully, proudly turning her head this way and that way.

As graduation drew near, I kept my so-called seductive behaviour in check. After all, I wasn't a social butterfly or a dance hostess, so that kind of behaviour wouldn't help me earn a living. I wanted to become an academic instead, so I applied for graduate school. Frankly speaking, you don't need great courage or great wisdom to become an academic. Just look at me. With some packaging, a nonentity like me could become an intellectual. So I buried myself in studying contemporary Western philosophy because that subject, being totally opaque to the lecturers and me, was a short cut to a higher degree. Well, when I finished my thesis, everyone got a few good laughs from it, and everyone was happy and relieved.

In the meantime, Zhiheng and I became rather distant from each other. She looked more beautiful and attractive than ever. She was flashily dressed even during examinations. My classmates told me that she was having an affair with a teacher. Then someone told me that she modeled for a magazine. Why did everybody else know more about Zhiheng than I? I realized that this couldn't go on and we didn't have much time left. I wanted us to rent an apartment together. She could continue with her social life while I would go on with my studies. We could keep a cat, own a Persian hand woven carpet, and eat soft sweet dumplings together in the middle of the night. I asked but little from life.

Wrapped in these thoughts, I brought back to our room a bouquet of flowers. I wanted to spend some time together with Zhiheng. In the afternoon, the hostel was very quiet and peaceful.

A tie was hung on our door. Holding a bouquet of gerberas, standing in front of the door, I didn't know what to do. Following an old British custom, Zhiheng was giving the signal that a man was in the room. How could that be? In our room? They would even make love in my bed, leaving me the dirty bed sheet to wash. Then I couldn't sleep in that bed the rest of my life. To me, men's semen was the most ridiculous thing in the world, more disgusting than liquid detergent, snot, or sputum. How could you do this, Zhiheng?

The president of the hostel's student committee living just across the corridor was coming back to her room. 'What? Forgot your keys? Want me to open it for you?' she asked.

'No, thanks,' I replied hurriedly, taking out my keys.

There they were in my bed, Zhiheng and a man, threshing and thrusting. I simply felt that the gerberas in my hand were drooping. I was even afraid that the petals might be strewn all over the floor. Ignoring me, Zhiheng still had her eyes half closed. The man stopped, but he didn't even try to throw some clothes on. His face was full of pimples, his hair unkempt, his age around thirty. I stared straight at him: 'Sir, this is the women's hostel. Please put your clothes back on.' Zhiheng glanced sideways at him and said, 'Forget her.' I grabbed the clothes on the floor and threw the lot at them, shouting, 'Put on your clothes now! I don't talk to animals.'

That man did hasten to slip on his clothes, but Zhiheng just turned in the bed and smoked. She didn't say one word. I picked up the condoms scattered on the floor and told the man, 'Sir, take these back with you. Show some respect.'

'Sorry. . . .' Hurriedly he thrust the condoms into the pockets of his pants. I opened the door for him and told him, 'Sir, I have a special relationship with Zhiheng. Please respect us and don't do this anymore.' He didn't react at first. He got alarmed only after a long pause; then he cried out in a low voice: 'You two! You two are abnormal!'

I slapped him on the face and slammed the door.

Zhiheng glared at me, her face crimson. The cigarette end was going to burn her fingers, but she still glared at me, motionless. I leaned against the door, and I didn't move either. What was time after all? When everything was destroyed, who cared about time? I didn't know how long we kept on with this stalemate, but her cigarette was burnt out, and the winter outside cold and leaden.

The sky was darkening, and the darkness deepened.

Suddenly Zhiheng gave a light laugh, and then two drops of tears rolled down her cheeks.

'No matter what, we can go on as before,' I said.

'No, we can't. You're too naive. One day I will win and you will lose—to me!'

I buried my face in my hands. 'But I've never wanted to compete with you! Why do you try to get advantages from everyone?'

'He can help me to get my pictures in the magazines, or even to become another Isabella Rossellini. Can you do that for me?'

'Still why do you want to get advantages from men? We aren't prostitutes.'

'Haven't you got advantages from men before? In this there is no difference between the good student and the bad student.'

I sank slowly into my seat, remembering certain men. I had breakfast with them, I dined with them, I drank wine with them. I thought of that man, to whom I almost entrusted my whole life, just because he happened to have a handkerchief ready when I was drunk.

We all have our weaknesses.

'I'm hungry.' She got up, threw some clothes on her naked body, and said, 'Excuse me, I have to go out.' I made way for her, and I heard her heavy footsteps fade away. The gerberas wilted noiselessly in the dark. Closing my eyes, I suddenly realized what was meant by an 'empty show'. Henceforward everything would merely be an empty show.

That night I slept early. When I woke up the following day, Zhiheng was asleep like a baby, cuddling a toy bunny. I left a note, saying that

I wanted to meet her for dinner at the canteen. Then I went to class. I didn't think that she would come.

I waited for her at a table near the door. The dusk of the wintry day hung like death. She did come, sporting a woollen sweater and pants and earrings studded with bright blue gemstones. Her hair was tied back loosely; a shawl was thrown lightly round her shoulders. A half smile flitted past her face when she saw me. I realized that she had grown up into a sophisticated woman. Even her smile was a calculated one. See, after all, she'd learned something from her books.

We ordered some food and beer. She ate very little but she drank so much that she was flushed even before the meal was over. We gossiped about our old Sociology lecturer who at long last was asked by the university to retire early, congratulated each other on that, and drank our toast to his retirement. She told me that she had got a contract for modeling, a feat we proclaimed to be great. I told her that I had completed my thesis, had applied for a scholarship to go to Britain, and had been granted an interview. We laughed happily together. When she saw me shivering, for I drank too much beer, she gave me her shawl. When we walked in that windy night, I pressed against her body, complaining that it was cold. She put her arm round me, and we continued our walk on campus just like that. The night was beautiful, the sky deep blue. 'Let us move somewhere else after we graduate, a place where you go out and work, while I stay home and read,' I said. She became quiet, and then she said, ' I'm afraid that you'll fool around.' I laughed, 'I don't fool around. I'm so skinny. How can I fool around?' She gently pressed her breasts, saying, 'Well, then, I'm afraid it's me who'll be fooling around.'

We remained silent for a while. Suddenly she hugged me, surprising me with her show of affection. When she let go of me, she said, 'It's getting late. You get your things in the library. I'll go back first.'

Briskly I waved, then I turned to leave. She waved back to me, saying goodbye. 'You're crazy,' I chided, 'I'm not leaving you for good.' I left without looking back.

At the hostel I met the student president. She heaved a sigh of relief when she saw me. Then she started to drag me to see the warden. I had to put down my books first! What's the hurry? She said it was urgent, and she dragged and pushed all the way to the warden's.

Finally I sat down on the sofa in the warden's residence and began turning the pages of *Breakthrough* listlessly. A reader wrote, 'Dear Counsellor: I'm so confused, I don't know what to do. He left me. . . .' The warden was Taiwanese, but she could speak Cantonese with a strong nasal accent. She made piping hot Oolong tea for me. I put my hands over the teacup to warm them, and waited for her to speak.

The TV was muted. Only images flitted past the screen, casting flickering shadows and colours on her face. It was scary. Amidst the play of light and shadow she held back for a while. Then she started, uttering the following, word by word and phrase by phrase: 'I have received a complaint saying that you and Zhiheng have an abnormal relationship.'

The hot Oolong tea burnt the tip of my tongue. I raised my head to look at her. I didn't know why, but I smiled.

'In addition to being learned, university students should also have a good character.'

'I don't think what we do is a base, immoral thing. Lots of men and women are much worse,' I looked straight into her eyes. She didn't budge. She stared straight back at me.

'What you're doing is—abnormal, and it hinders the progress of civilization. How a society can form a stable system depends wholly on the natural relationships among humans.' Her words came intermittently to me. I couldn't hear her clearly. Not looking at her anymore, I turned the pages of *Breakthrough*. The Counsellor replied, 'Dear Ling: It is wrong for you to ruin the relationship of another couple. But Almighty God will forgive you. . . .' Terrified, I closed the magazine hurriedly. I stared at the silent screen. A long time elapsed before I said in a low voice, 'Why do you impose your moral standards on us? We don't create any trouble for other people.' I didn't know if she heard it. I only felt that since my voice was so wavering and low, it seemed that someone else was whispering these words in my ears. I started, and looked around, but there was no one.

Putting down my cup, I said, 'If Zhiheng doesn't leave me, I won't leave her.' Then I went to the door and opened it myself.

'But this afternoon she promised me that she would move out. And I also promised her that I would not make this public. I'm only seeing you for formality's sake.' She spoke from a distance. I stood at the door, pressing the handle, the cold handle. 'Thank you,' I said. Quietly and gently I closed the door and left.

I didn't know how I struggled back to my room. The long, long stairway was no Jacob's Ladder, leading me to eternal truth. I walked with difficulty. My limbs felt like they were being torn to pieces and my eyes hurt with every movement that I made. I covered my eyes. So let it be, let me go blind, let me see only darkness.

The door was not locked; somebody was in the corridor. I straightened my back, bit my lip, and went in. Well, she could pack up and clear out so efficiently in one afternoon. She left only a new pair of vermilion embroidered shoes and a pink Maidenform bra on my bed. I turned the bra over and checked the label. Size 32B. She got it wrong again. I smiled to myself, 'It's 32A, Zhiheng, 32A! I'm skinny!'

So I also moved out after her departure and rented a small dark room near the university. My life was even darker. I became more shortsighted than before, but I stuck to my old rimmed glasses. I started to wear only blue, purple, and black. I quit smoking, drank only water and switched to vegetarian food. People wail aloud when they are jilted, but I was incredibly quiet, my heart and mind like the landscape paintings of the Song and Ming dynasties. In the dark night I listened to Kunshan[5] melodies. Lonely like a shadow, often I stepped on the broken sounds of my footsteps. Embracing myself, I told myself: 'I still have this.' Biting my lip, I told myself: 'Don't cry and don't complain.' I wished to become a rational being—there was a reason to everything. She had her difficulties.

Later, on the cover of a magazine I saw her picture, her full lips and smile. I didn't turn the pages of the magazine. That beautiful woman was just one of thousands of beautiful women, but she was not the Zhiheng that I knew. Then I saw her at the graduation ceremony. Her gown was fluttering in the wind and she was smiling in the sunlight. She looked in my direction, shading her eyes with her hand. I couldn't see her clearly enough to know if her smiling face looked any different. I only stood motionless, embracing myself. A man who looked familiar stood beside her. I tried to think back, and then realized that he was one of those whose pictures we saw in the magazines. She had her choices. She left me because I wasn't good enough. But the Zhiheng that I remembered. . . . We didn't care about being good enough or not.

. . . I remember her cheongsams, her embroidered shoes, her indomitable air when she copied my notes, her smile when she lightly pressed her breasts, her lazy look when she lay in bed reading a romance. . . . I remember that when I was cold she gave me a shawl to warm me up, when I was triumphant she threw coins at me, when I was reserved and distant she clutched my hand and said, 'All is lost.' I remember, yes I remember, I tied her hair, clipped her toenails, and bought a bouquet of gerberas for her. I remember that when my eyes filled with tears, when my hands squeezed my throat, she took hold of both my hands and asked: 'Why are you doing this?'

Why? I thought Zhiheng and I could have stayed together for the rest of our lives.

1986

NOTES

1 The author would like to thank Louise Ho for her comments on the translation.
2 The College is a famous traditional school in Hong Kong, and Blue Pool Road is situated in a rich neighbourhood.
3 Popular writer of romances in Hong Kong.
4 *Confucian Analects.* Book 19, Chapter 19.
5 In Jiangsu Province, China.

20

The Flower Spirit

By **Wong Oi Kuan**

Translated by Terry Siu-han Yip and Kwok-kan Tam, with Jason Gleckman

Wong Oi Kuan 黃愛群 (Huang Aiqun, b. 1958) won a Gold Lion award for her story, 'The Flower Spirit' (Hua hun 花魂, 1985), in a short story competition jointly sponsored by the two influential Singapore Chinese newspapers Lianhe zaobao 聯合早報 *and* Lianhe wanbao 聯合晚報 *in 1985. She attended Chung Cheng High School, a Chinese middle school in Singapore, and graduated from Nanyang University with a degree in commerce and accountancy. She writes with an elegant style typical of Singapore Chinese residents. She is currently editor of* 'I'-Weekly.

Written in the form of an interior monologue, 'The Flower Spirit' is a frightening tale of a young, dumb woman who was involved in a lesbian relationship with her female boss. The practice of lesbianism is not typical of the Chinese tradition, but is becoming more and more common in the twentieth century with more women having acquired economic autonomy in a male dominated society. Although the relationship described in the story is primarily that of lesbianism, it can be seen as a cultural by-product of the revolt against male dominance.

I still remember the story a little girl sitting next to me told me when I was in primary three: her mother said that a butterfly was a spirit transformed from a withered flower. That was why a butterfly could never live away from flowers, for it had to fly amidst them, searching and re-searching in order to reclaim its body.

Why didn't the Creator make me a flower instead of a person? Rather than live as an abnormal human being, I could be a colourful butterfly which knows that the meaning of its life is to look for its lost body. But what about me?

I took a seat near the window. The waitress, as usual, let down the Venetian blinds for me, but the glare of the setting sun in June still managed to get in through the slats to scorch my face.

Rose Restaurant was situated at the centre of the city. At dusk the streets were flooded with people; some hurried through after shopping, others rushed to the cinemas. Today, as usual, the passageway outside my window was packed with moving shadows, gliding back and forth. The shadows of these busy people occasionally cast shades on the blinds, which were deflected into my eyes.

Through the slats of the blinds, I saw clearly that the pedestrians outside were going from the left to the right, yet the setting sun played a trick by pulling back their shadows so that they seemed to be passing from the right to the left. And for those who walked from the right to the left, the slanting rays of the setting sun performed the same trick, making their shadows seemingly go in the opposite direction.

The waitress handed me the menu. I randomly pointed my finger at 'lamb chop' and then ordered an iced lemon tea under the 'Drinks' column. This done, the waitress was smart to leave me alone.

Every day after work I would hop on a taxi on Thomson Road and spend more than five dollars to get to this restaurant to have my dinner. A little calculation upon my fingers showed that I had been frequenting this restaurant for three months; no one could be more familiar with the waitresses here than I was. I did not come because the chefs in this restaurant were particularly good or because their food suited my taste, but because there was a very nice bar inside the restaurant where one could listen to songs after six every evening. So I often rushed through my dinner in order to move to the bar inside so that I could listen to the songs while I was drinking.

There were two singers, a young man and a young woman. Certainly I would not come for the woman singer. Not only did I dislike her, I can say I hated her. She had an unpleasant voice, but she did dress up fashionably and the make-up on her face was filled with sharply contrasting colours. Her crimson red lips looked like ripened fruit, heavy and ready to fall. When she sang, she would cast her seductive glances at the males in the audience. And whenever she performed with the male singer, she would take the opportunity to lean her body against his. Although she wore four-inch high-heel shoes, her head didn't even reach the shoulder of the male singer. Her English name was Louisa. To tell the truth, a singer like Louisa was only suitable for night clubs, or the road show during the Ghost Festival, but never for such an elegant bar as this. Her style was too crass for the atmosphere of the bar.

The male singer was of an entirely different type. To tell the truth, I began to come to this Rose Restaurant every day after I listened to him singing 'The End of the World'. Whenever he finished singing, he would step down from the platform and stay for a while, chatting with the bartenders and waitresses before he left. Everybody in the lounge called him Angus.

Angus was no more than twenty-five, or twenty-six at most, a young man with a light brown complexion and a handsome face. Tall and lean, he had thick black hair as dark as ink. When he sang, he would swing his hair back in a seemingly carefree way. He was charming and good looking and had straight sword-like dark bushy eyebrows to match his sharply defined eyes—which were as bright as the winter stars. His high nose resembled the bulb of a water-green onion, under which were two finely-curved thin lips. When he sang, he showed his snow-white and uniform teeth. He was so handsome. I subconsciously felt that he was a man of sentiments and nostalgia because the songs he chose to sing were all old popular English lyrics, such as 'Butterfly', 'Young World', 'Rhythm of the Rain', 'Johnny Come Lately', 'The Young Ones', 'He'll Have to Go', 'Smoke Gets In Your Eyes', 'Devil Woman', 'My Sentimental Friend', 'Sealed With a Kiss', 'Love Story', etc. All these were the songs I loved.

Disco songs and break dancing do not suit my taste. Although I will only be twenty-three next month, I am a full supporter of nostalgia. I always think of my past, especially the days of my childhood.

As I sat down at a corner table in the lounge, the band had already begun to play the prelude. Angus stood in a relaxed way before the microphone. As usual, his partner, Louisa, was dressed up in a sexy and exaggerated fashion. She was such an eyesore; my patience for her had reached its limit.

I subconsciously felt for the letter in my pocket. It was still there. I spent one whole night writing it for Angus, while Eve was playing mahjong at Mrs Mo's home. Although I repeatedly reminded myself that this was a very stupid thing to do, I really could not withhold my feelings any longer. I was deeply impressed by Angus and I had lost control of myself in my infatuation for him. Moreover, I felt very lonely and needed someone to talk to. I thought Angus would be the best choice of a listener.

I am not a considerate person. But, in fact, who in this world has been considerate to me? It was after I had mustered up courage and left my family to move to Eve's apartment that I was shocked to realize that the world could be even worse than I had thought it to be. Thus I have become more and more self-centred, for I feel that the world owes me too much. Would Angus accept a person like me, especially after he had learnt about my secret? My mind was in complete confusion.

When I sobered myself up a bit, I found that Angus was already singing the last part of 'Butterfly'. This song had been sung at least twelve times in the past three months. In the midst of scattered applause, he stepped down from the slightly raised platform. Contrary to his usual practice, he did not chat with his friends. He simply greeted them with a nonchalant hello and left. I wondered why he had to leave in such a hurry tonight.

I paid the bill immediately and followed him outside.

I saw him rush out of the restaurant toward a white Mercedes, which apparently had been parked at the roadside for quite some time. A fat woman clumsily crawled out of the car to greet him instantly. She put her arms around Angus's waist in an intimate way and they disappeared into the car.

I couldn't believe my eyes. Oh, Angus, how could you do that? How could you? My heart was shattered as if struck by thunder, and my hands were trembling. The letter I clasped in my hands slipped out and fell to the ground. . . .

I don't know how I returned safely to Eve's place. I only know that I got on a bus listlessly. The bus passed by the Katong Community Centre, which was fenced on all sides. A group of people were doing Taijiquan exercises there in the basketball field. Their movements were so slow, while my heart and stomach were boiling and turning inside me. I felt dizzy and exhausted and my mind was completely blank. I suddenly felt that I was out of harmony with the rhythm of the world.

I took the keys out of my handbag, opened the steel security door, and then the wooden door, only to greet stark darkness. Eve has not come home yet, I concluded.

I turned the knob of the bedroom door and was startled by the sight of Eve puffing heavily at her cigarette with her back to me, the dim light from the cigarette flickering in the dark. Frightened by this unexpected scene, I immediately switched on the light.

Eve bent her body forward and put the cigarette in the ashtray on the end-table, and then turned round to look at me.

'So you have come back at last!'

She spoke in a cold voice.

I flung my handbag on the dressing table, and threw myself heavily on the soft bed.

Eve raised her head, a wicked smile hung around the corner of her mouth. Her eyes were filled with crazy burning passions. She walked slowly toward me, sat on the bedside, took off her nightgown, and stretched her hands to unbutton my shirt.

This behaviour was already familiar to me. I knew what would follow next, yet I began to feel restless and disturbed again.

When Eve put her cheek against mine, I could smell the strong fragrance from her hair. This was the privilege of being the owner of a beauty parlour and a hair salon. Eve's hair was always done by the 'sisters' in the salon.

I could also feel her heart, pounding fiercely against mine, the perfume from her body, and the softness of her breasts.

The thing I feared finally happened.

She caressed me on the nape of my neck and armpit with her hands. I felt extremely uncomfortable. My face was burning hot. I really wanted to slip away, but my legs had become watery and would not follow my orders. One moment Eve ruffled my hair, the next she bit my entire ear. I wanted to throw up and I turned my face away. Suddenly she turned my head toward her and kissed me full on the lips. I clenched my teeth, yet I felt Eve's tongue trying hard to pry open my incisors.

This moment Eve's face was all crimson red and her hair looked untidy. She began to stick out her tongue to lick my face and my body. I felt dampness and stickiness all over. It was extremely unbearable. I wanted to cry out loudly, but I couldn't even whimper.

Peeling an apple, Eve turned her back to me. Her nightgown, as thin as cicada wings, could not conceal the beautiful curves of her body.

Truly, I had never thought that two women could do something like that until I met Eve.

No one would dispute that Eve was still a beautiful woman at the age of thirty-two. Besides being beautiful, she was also successful. She possessed the best things in life; I couldn't understand why she came to like such a disgusting game. I only knew that she was my boss and I was one of her five employees. Apart from that, I knew nothing about her. She, on the other hand, could read me like a book. Perhaps it was exactly because I had exposed all my weaknesses to her that I found myself under her control. After all, I was still too young to know much about life.

When she turned toward me, she had already peeled off half of the apple's skin. The spiral-shaped red apple skin dangled to the movements of her knife, and the sheen of the knife flashed brightly before my eyes.

Perhaps she saw the pain on my face, for her soft and tender complexion suddenly turned devilish and wicked looking.

'Thinking of that young guy singing at Rose Restaurant again?' she uttered through her gnashing teeth.

Neither did I nod nor shake my head.

The last bit of skin fell from the fleshy apple, forming complete rings of red on the floor. Eve's face had turned pale with anger. The knife slipped from her hand and dropped on the end-table, making a clinking sound.

'You think men are really wonderful, don't you? When their wives talk to other men, they suspect them of infidelity. But they consider it natural to hang around with two women at the same time!'

Eve made a self-mocking chuckle through her teeth, and then bit the apple in big mouthfuls, munching it to pieces.

She had never grumbled in such a way before. I crossed my arms before my chest, but I still trembled all over. Even my teeth clattered with emotion.

'What is it? Broken-hearted? Let me tell you, men ain't no damn good, especially someone who sings in a bar and possesses such handsome looks; God knows if he is not some wealthy woman's beau!'

My heart jumped as if pricked by a needle, cramping fiercely.

The plump and clumsy figure of a woman flashed into my mind again: she threw her arm around Angus's waist and they climbed into the milky white Mercedes.

Eve stopped her munching, looked askance at me and said: 'As a matter of fact, you yourself have some good qualifications—a beautiful face and a fine figure. But you have no chance. He is a singer! How the hell would he give a girl like you even a glance? Ha! A singer marrying you would certainly be the biggest joke in the world.'

The knife was sending out tempting flashes of light on the small end-table.

. . . Eve was holding my hands affectionately. Her smile was full of kindness and tenderness. Ever since I first met her in the beauty parlour, I felt that I had finally found the only person in the world who understood me. I was then very grateful, very grateful to her. I was often moved to tears, when I was moving my pen fast to pour out my story and troubles to her, and when she was patting me gently on my shoulder to comfort me.

The Eve before my eyes now looked so ugly without her make-up. The muscles in her face were contracting intensely. The sly smile which spread to the corners of her eyes looked detestable. I could hardly imagine that the woman before me was the woman who once moved me so deeply. I clenched my fists, like a small, wounded animal ready to seek vengeance against an enemy which dared to attack it.

'What's the matter? You can't even take in a few words from me? You shouldn't blame me! Blame your dead mother who didn't take good care of you when you were sick in primary three. . . .'

She began to recount one by one the things she knew about me and my past until I saw only her mouth open and shut, without hearing a word.

The day I came home from the hospital, Dad blamed Mom for not having sent me there early enough. Mom then took hold of my hair and threw me heavily to the corner of the bed, shouting angrily:

'You short-lived dead thing! Star of bad luck!'

I felt a sharp pain on my forehead, and then realized that some cold liquid was flowing slowly down my head to the corner of my mouth. I opened my mouth and licked it. It tasted salty and smelt fishy. Dad was so awe-struck that he only stood there horrified, without knowing what to do. . . .

I felt a piercing pain in my heart. I forced myself to stand up from the bed with the support of my arms. The shining knife on the end-table again flashed into sight, against the shadow of Eve, rocking in ferocious laughter, like the branch of a tree shaken by gusts of wind. At this moment I again seemed like an animal whose sore spot was being scratched by the enemy. The intense pain drove me to make some gurgling sound in my throat. Was I crying or giggling?

I moved slowly, step by step, towards the end-table. Eve was standing right next to it. She would never dream of what I would do. Perhaps in her eyes I was always a weakling, a tiny ant that could be crushed to death at any moment with the flick of a finger.

I fixed my stare on her, looking at her from her snowy white neck to her heart and chest. My eyes were full of spiteful hatred, and my face hid behind the darkness of my heart. I could feel my right hand trembling all the while.

Eve looked attentively at the apple in her hand. Perhaps in her eyes I was like the apple, which she had bitten and devoured to leave nothing but the seeds.

'Dare curse me if you have the guts! Point at my nose and curse. . . .'

Without waiting for her to finish her words, I grabbed the knife in my right hand with thunder-quick speed, and threw myself on her body. . . .

1985

Stories of (Dis/)Location

21

Ah, Fragrant Snow

By **Tie Ning**

Translated by Zha Jianying

Tie Ning 鐵凝 (b. 1957) was born in Beijing. She started her writing career in 1975 and has published short stories, novellas, novels, film scripts, and prose work since then. Her long works of fiction include The Rose Gate *(*Meigui men 玫瑰門*, 1987) and* A City of No Rain *(*Wuyu zhi cheng 無雨之城*). Her short stories, such as 'A Pile of Cotton' (Mianhua duo 棉花垛), 'Ah, Fragrant Snow' (A! Xiangxue 哦！香雪) and 'The Pregnant Woman and the Cow' (Yunfu he niu 孕婦和牛) were very well-received and have won for her a number of literary awards in China. In 1996, she published the five-volume* Tie Ning's Collected Works *(*Tie Ning wenji 鐵凝文集*). Her film script 'The Woman in Red' (Hongyi shaonu 紅衣少女, 1985) won the 'Golden Rooster' Award in 1985, and her short story 'Ah, Fragrant Snow' was made into a film that received an award at the 41st International Film Festival in Berlin.*

If trains had not been invented, if nobody had laid railway tracks into remote mountains, small villages like Terrace Gully would never have been found. The village and its villagers, in a dozen houses, hid in the deep wrinkles of an old mountain, silently accepting the wilful mountain's tender caress and brutal temper.

But now, two slim, glittering railway tracks stretched over the mountain. They bravely spiralled halfway up, then quietly felt their way further, winding and turning, turning and winding until they reached the foot of Terrace Gully. Then they made their way into the gloomy tunnel, dashed ahead to another mountain, and hurried away into the mysterious distance.

The villagers jostled to watch the green dragon whistling past, bringing with it a fresh breeze from the strange world beyond the mountains. It hurried along the back of poor Terrace Gully. It went at such a pace that the sound of the wheels rolling on the tracks was like an eager voice: can't stop, can't stop! It had no reason to stop at Terrace Gully. Did anyone in the village need to go on a long journey? Did someone from beyond the mountains want to visit relatives or friends at Terrace Gully? Or were there oil fields or gold mines? Terrace Gully had nothing to attract the train's attention.

Nevertheless, a new stop was added to the railway timetable: 'Terrace Gully'. Perhaps some passengers had made a suggestion, and one of them who had some influence was related to the village. Perhaps the train attendant, a jolly young fellow, had noticed the pretty girls of Terrace Gully. Every time the train passed, they would come in groups, stick out their chins, and stare at the train with greedy eyes. Some pointed at the train, and occasionally you could hear coy screams when they poked each other.

Perhaps none of these was the real reason. Perhaps Terrace Gully was just too small—so small it made your heart ache, so small that even the gigantic dragon couldn't bear to stride proudly ahead without stopping. Whatever the reason, Terrace Gully was on the railway's timetable now. Every evening at seven o'clock, the train from Beijing to Shanxi would stop here for one minute.

One minute—so fleeting—yet it threw Terrace Gully's peaceful evenings into disorder. It had been the custom in the village for everyone to go to bed right after dinner, as though everyone heard the old mountain's mute order at the same time. The small stretch of stone houses would suddenly become completely noiseless—so quiet that it seemed the village was silently confiding its piety to the old mountain. But now, the girls of Terrace Gully served dinner in a flurry, absent-mindedly grabbed a quick bite, put down their bowls, and went straight to their dressers. They washed off the dust and stains of the day, revealing their rough and ruddy complexions, combed their hair, and then vied with one another in wearing their best outfits. Some girls put on new shoes, which they were supposed to wear only for Spring Festival; others even secretly put a little rouge on their cheeks. Then they ran to the railway, where the train passed. Fragrant Snow was always first; her next-door neighbour, Frail Phoenix, followed right behind.

At seven o'clock, the train slowed down as it approached Terrace Gully, gave a loud crash and a shake, then stopped. The girls rushed toward it, their hearts thumping violently. As if watching a movie, they looked into the cars through the windows. Fragrant Snow hid behind her friends and covered her ears. She was the first to come out of her house to watch the train, but retreated when it arrived. She was a bit scared by its gigantic head. The monster spurted out magnificent white smoke, as though it could suck Terrace Gully into its stomach in one breath.

'Fragrant Snow, come here!' Frail Phoenix dragged Fragrant Snow to her side. 'Look at those golden rings in that lady's hair. What do you call them? It's the lady in the back seat with that big round face. Look at her watch, it's smaller than my nail!'

Fragrant Snow nodded. At last she saw the golden rings in the woman's hair and the tiny watch on her wrist. But soon she noticed something else. 'A leather schoolbag!' She pointed to a brown leather satchel on the luggage rack.

Fragrant Snow's discoveries usually did not excite the other girls, but they still rushed up around her.

'You stepped on my toes!' Frail Phoenix cried out and complained to another girl who was pushing to the front.

'What a loud voice! You want to show off so that white-faced man[1] will talk to you, don't you?'

'I'll tear your mouth off if you repeat that!' Frail Phoenix cried, but couldn't help looking over to the door of the third car.

The fair-skinned young attendant stepped down from the train. He was tall and had jet-black hair, and spoke with a beautiful Beijing accent. Perhaps this was why the girls called him 'The Beijinger' behind his back. 'The Beijinger' crossed his arms on his chest, keeping a distance neither too close to or too far from the girls: 'Say, young ladies, don't hold onto the windows, it's dangerous!'

'Oh, so we're young; are you so old?' the bold Frail Phoenix retorted. The girls broke into laughter. Somebody gave Frail Phoenix a shove, and it made her almost bump into him. Instead of being embarrassed, this boosted her courage.

'Hey, don't you feel dizzy staying in that train all day long?' she asked.

'What do you do with that thing hanging on the ceiling? It looks like a broadsword,' another girl asked. She was referring to the electric fan in the railway car.

'Where do you heat the water?'

'What if you run into some place that got no roads?'

'How many meals do you city people eat every day?' Fragrant Snow asked in a low voice, hiding behind other girls.

'Bah, I'm at the end of my rope,' grumbled 'The Beijinger'.

They wouldn't let him go till the train was about to start. He glanced at his watch as he ran toward the train, and shouted back, 'Next time, I'll answer all your questions next time.' He had long, nimble legs, allowing him to jump onto the train agilely. Then, the green door shut with a bang. The train dashed into the darkness, leaving the girls beside the ice-cold tracks. For a long time they could still feel the slight quiver of the tracks.

Everything became quiet again. On the way home, the girls always quarrelled about something trifle.

'She's got to bind the nine golden rings together first, then stick them in.'

'No. She didn't do it that way.'

'Sure she did.'

'Frail Phoenix, why don't you speak up? Still thinking about that Beijinger?'

'Get lost. You talk because it's you who's thinking about him.'

Fragrant Snow didn't say a word. She just flushed with embarrassment for her friend. She was only seventeen and had not yet learnt how to rescue someone from this sort of talk.

The same girl kept teasing Frail Phoenix, 'I know, you like him but haven't got the nerve to admit it. He's got such nice skin!'

'Nice skin? That's from staying in that big green house all year long. Let him try Terrace Gully for a few days,' someone in the shadows said.

'There you go. Those city folks all hide in rooms from the sun. They should see our Fragrant Snow. Our Fragrant Snow was born with this pretty skin. If she only did her hair into a bunch of curls like those girls on the train.'

Frail Phoenix had no response except to let go of Fragrant Snow's hand. Frail Phoenix couldn't help feeling defensive about the fellow, as if the girls had belittled someone related to her. She firmly believed that his fair skin was not from hiding in rooms. It was natural.

Fragrant Snow put her hand back into Frail Phoenix's. It seemed to her that she had somehow wronged her friend, and she was asking forgiveness.

'Frail Phoenix, have you lost your tongue?' the same girl attacked again.

'Who's lost whose tongue! You girls look at nothing but whether a fellow's got nice or ugly skin. You like him, why don't you go with him?'

'We aren't the right match.'

'Don't you think he's got his own girl?'

No matter how heated these quarrels were, the girls would always part amicably because an exciting idea would arise in everyone's mind: tomorrow, the train would pass again and they would have another wonderful minute. Compared to this, a little quarrel was nothing.

Ah, that colourful minute was filled with the joy, anger, grief, and happiness of the girls from Terrace Gully.

As the days went by, the girls added a new dimension to this precious minute. They began to carry rectangular wicker baskets full of walnuts, eggs, and dates to the railway station, and stood under the train's windows to quickly strike up bargains with the passengers. They tiptoed and stretched their arms all the way up to raise baskets full of eggs and dates to their customers, taking in exchange things that were rare in Terrace Gully: fine dried noodles, matches, or, the girls' favourites, bobby pins, gauze handkerchiefs, sometimes even richly coloured nylon socks. Of course it was risky to take the latter items back home, for they might get scolded for making decisions based purely on their own fancy.

The girls seemed to have a tacit agreement to assign Frail Phoenix to 'The Beijinger'. Nobody else but Frail Phoenix, basket in hand, would ever go to him. It was amusing to see how she made a deal with him. She always dawdled on purpose, putting a full basket into his hands just when the train was about to start. The train began to move before he had time to pay for her eggs. He put the basket on the train, and made gestures to explain something to her, while she stood by the train feeling happy. She was glad that he took her eggs without paying. Of course the fellow would bring money to her the next time, and would bring a bundle of noodles, gauze handkerchiefs, or something else. If the noodles weighed ten catties, Frail Phoenix would insist on taking out one catty to give back to him. She felt this was only fair. She wanted their contact to be a little different from a regular business sale. Sometimes she would remember the girls' remark: 'Don't you think he's got his own girl?' As a matter of fact, whether or not he had his own girl was of no concern to Frail Phoenix, because she never thought of going away with him. But she wanted to be nice to him. Did she have to be his girl to treat him nicely?

Fragrant Snow was taciturn and timid, but her sales were the most successful of all the girls. Passengers loved to buy from her because she looked at them so trustingly with her pure, innocent eyes. She had not learnt how to haggle over the price; she simply said, 'You offer as you think fit.' They looked at her face that was as pure as a new-born baby's, with her lips as soft as red satin, and a beautiful feeling would come over them. They couldn't bear to trick this little girl.

Sometimes she would seize an opportunity to ask passengers things about the outside world. She asked if the universities in Beijing would want students from Terrace Gully, and what 'musical poetry' was (she happened to see this term in a book a classmate brought to school). One time she asked a middle-aged woman with glasses about a pencil-case that could close automatically, and how much it would cost. But the train started moving before the woman could answer. She ran quite a while after the train. The autumn wind and the whistling wheels rang in her ears; then she stopped and realized how ridiculous she was being.

The train was soon out of sight. The girls surrounded Fragrant Snow. When they found out the reason for this train chasing, everybody laughed.

'Silly girl!'

'It's not worth it.'

They tapped her mockingly on the shoulder like the venerable elders would do.

'It was my fault. I should have asked her earlier.' Fragrant Snow would never think that this was not worthwhile; she only blamed herself for acting too slowly.

'Bah, you might as well ask about something better,' said Frail Phoenix, carrying the basket for Fragrant Snow.

'No wonder she asked that. Our Fragrant Snow is a student,' said someone else.

Perhaps this explained everything. Fragrant Snow was the only one in Terrace Gully who had passed the entrance examination for middle school.

Terrace Gully had no school. Fragrant Snow had to walk five miles every day to the commune school. Although she had a quiet disposition, with the Terrace Gully girls she always had things to talk about. However, at the commune middle school she did not have many friends. There were a lot of girls, but the way they acted, the expression in their eyes, and their soft laughter made it seem that they wanted Fragrant Snow to realize she was from a small village, a poor place. They asked her over and over: 'How many meals do you eat every day at home?' She was ignorant of their intention, so she always answered innocently, 'Two meals.' Then she would ask, 'What about in your village?'

'Three meals,' they would always answer proudly. Afterwards, they felt pity and anger for Fragrant Snow being so slow.

'Why don't you bring your pencil box to school?' they asked again.

'There it is.' Fragrant Snow pointed to the corner of her desk.

Actually, everybody knew that the little wooden box was Fragrant Snow's pencil box, but they all looked shocked. The girl sitting next to Fragrant Snow started fiddling with her big plastic pencil box, closing it with a click. This was an 'automatic' pencil box, and only long afterward did Fragrant Snow learn the secret of how it shut automatically. It was because there was a small magnet hidden inside. The little wooden box was a special present made by Fragrant Snow's father, who was a carpenter, to celebrate her success in the entrance examination. It was unmatched in Terrace Gully, but here in the school it looked awkward and outmoded. The little box shrank back timidly in the corner of the desk.

Fragrant Snow's mind was no longer at peace. The meaning of her classmates' repeated questions suddenly dawned on her. She realized how poor Terrace Gully was. Her eyes were fixed on her classmate's pencil box now. She guessed that it must be from a big city, and the price must be quite outrageous. Would thirty eggs buy it? Or forty? Fifty? Her heart sank.

What am I thinking about? Did Mother collect eggs so I could go off on wild flights of fancy? Why is that inviting click always ringing in my ears?

Late autumn came to the mountains. The wind grew colder and the days got shorter, but Fragrant Snow and the other girls never missed the seven o'clock train. Now they could wear their colourful cotton-padded jackets. Frail Phoenix wore two pink barrettes, and some girls tied their plaits with braided elastic bands. They had traded eggs and walnuts for these things with passengers from the train. They carefully dressed up from head to toe, imitating the city girls on the train. Then they lined up by the railway tracks, as if they were waiting to be reviewed.

The train stopped and heaved a deep sigh, as if it were complaining about the cold weather in Terrace Gully. Today the train showed an unusual indifference towards Terrace Gully. All of its windows were tightly closed, and passengers were sipping tea and reading newspapers in the dim light. Nobody glanced out of the windows. Even those familiar passengers seemed to have forgotten the Terrace Gully girls.

As usual, Frail Phoenix ran to the third car to look for her 'Beijinger'. Fragrant Snow tightened her red scarf, switched her basket from her right hand to her left, and walked by the train. She tiptoed so that the passengers might see her face. Nobody noticed her, but on a table, something among the food caught her eyes. She put down her basket and held onto the window frame, her heart violently pounding against her chest. She assured herself that it was a pencil box with a magnet. It was so close she could have touched it if the window had been open.

A middle-aged woman attendant dragged Fragrant Snow away, but Fragrant Snow kept watching the pencil box from a distance. When she had assured herself that it belonged to the girl by the window who looked like a student, she ran over and knocked on the window. The girl turned round and looked at her. Seeing the basket in Fragrant Snow's arms, she waved her hand apologetically and showed no intention of opening the window. Fragrant Snow ran toward the door and when she reached it, she grabbed the handrail. If she had been a little hesitant when she was running toward the door, the warm air from the car had strengthened her confidence. She leaped onto the footboard with agility. She intended to run into the carriage as fast as she could and in the shortest time trade her eggs for the pencil box. She had so many eggs. She had forty today.

At last Fragrant Snow stood on the train. She held her basket tightly, and stepped cautiously into the car. Just then, the train gave a lurch, and the door closed. The train began to move. She threw herself at the door only to see Frail Phoenix's face flashing past the window. It did not seem like a dream; everything was real. She had left her friends, and was standing in this familiar yet strange train.

The train gained speed, carrying Fragrant Snow with it, leaving Terrace Gully behind. The next stop was West Pass, ten miles away from Terrace Gully.

Ten miles in a train or a car was nothing. Passengers chatted for a while and soon reached the West Pass stop. Many got on, but only one got off. It was Fragrant Snow. She had no basket in her arms, for she had quietly put it under the girl's seat.

On the train, she had told the girl that she wanted to trade the eggs for the pencil box. The girl had insisted that she would give the pencil box to Fragrant Snow. She had also said that she didn't want the eggs because she lived in a dormitory and ate in a dining hall. She had pointed to the 'Mining College' school badge on her coat to convince Fragrant Snow. Fragrant Snow had taken the pencil box but had left her eggs on the train after all. No matter how poor Terrace Gully was, Fragrant Snow never took anything without paying for it.

Earlier, when the passengers had learnt that Fragrant Snow was getting off at West Pass, what could they say to her? They had tried to persuade her to stay overnight at West Pass, and the warm-hearted 'Beijinger' had even told her that his wife had a relative living at that train station. Fragrant Snow did not want to find his wife's relative. His suggestion made her a little sad, for Frail Phoenix, for Terrace Gully. Thinking of this sorrow, how could she stay on the train? Hurry away, hurry home, and hurry to school tomorrow. Then she could open her schoolbag proudly and put the pencil box on the desk. So she reassured those who were still trying to talk her out of returning home, 'Don't worry, I'm used to walking.' Perhaps they believed her. They had no idea what mountain girls were like. They believed that mountain people were not afraid of walking at night.

Now Fragrant Snow stood alone at West Pass Station, gazing after the departing train. Finally, it was completely out of sight and a wild emptiness surrounded her. A chilly gust of wind blew on her and drained the warmth from her body. Her shawl had slipped down to her shoulders. She wrapped it closer about her head, then sat on the railway tracks curled up with cold. Fragrant Snow had experienced all kinds of fear. When she was a young girl she used to fear hair. If a hair stuck to her shoulder and she couldn't remove it, she would cry in terror. When she grew older she was afraid to go to the front yard alone at night. She was afraid of caterpillars and being tickled. Now she feared this strange West Pass, feared the gloomy mountains, and the dead silence all around. When the wind blew through the nearby grove, she was afraid of the rustling sound. In ten miles, there were many groves and thickets she would have to walk through.

A full moon was rising. It bathed the silent valley and the greyish-white trails. It bathed the withered autumn leaves and the rough tree trunks. It lit up the overgrown brambles and queer-looking stones as well as the troops of trees rolling over the hills and meadows. It lit up the glittering small box in Fragrant Snow's hand.

Only then did she remember it and hold it up to take a closer look. She had not even looked at it on the train. Now, under bright moonlight, she found it to be light green with a pair of white lotuses. She opened it cautiously, then closed it the way her classmate had done. It closed tightly with a click. She opened it again, and felt that she should put something into it right away. She fished a little cold cream case out of her pocket and put that in. Then she closed it once more. Only now did she feel that this pencil box really belonged to her. She thought of tomorrow. How she hoped that they would question her over and over again at school tomorrow.

She stood up. All of a sudden her heart was full and the wind felt much milder. The moon was bright and clear, and the mountains, shrouded in the moonlight, reminded her of a mother's breast. The leaves of walnut trees had been blown by the autumn wind, and curled up into golden bells. For the first time, she heard clearly their nocturnal singing in the wind. Her fear was gone and she walked forward on the ties with vigorous strides. So this is how the mountains are. This is how the moon is. And the walnut trees. Fragrant Snow seemed to recognize for the first time the mountains and the valleys in which she had been reared. Was this how Terrace Gully had been? Not knowing why, she walked faster. She was eager to see Terrace Gully and she was curious about it as if she had never seen it before. Surely, some day the girls of Terrace Gully would no longer beg from anyone. All the handsome fellows on the train would come to the village to court, and the train would stop longer—maybe three or four minutes, maybe eight or ten minutes. It would open all its windows and doors, and anyone could get on or off easily.

But it was still tonight that Fragrant Snow had to face: the train had carried her away from Terrace Gully. Forty eggs were gone. What would Mother say? Father worked day and night, stripped to the waist, his back the colour of red copper, making chests, cupboards, and trunks. This was how he earned money to pay Fragrant Snow's tuition. This thought made Fragrant Snow stop. The moonlight seemed to have turned dim, and the ties unclear. What was she going to say to her mother and father? She looked around at the mountains. The mountains were silent. She looked around at the nearby poplar groves.

The poplar groves rustled but refused to give an answer. Where was this sound of running water coming from? She saw a shallow brook some metres away. She went over and squatted by the brook. She remembered a story from her younger days. One day when she and Frail Phoenix were washing clothes by a river, an old man selling sesame candy came over. Frail Phoenix advised her to trade an old shirt for some candies. Frail Phoenix had also suggested that she tell her mother that the shirt had been accidentally washed away by the running water. Fragrant Snow wanted the sesame candies very much, but she hadn't traded the shirt for them after all. She still remembered how the old man had waited patiently for her to make a decision. Why was she thinking of this small incident now? Perhaps she should fool Mother this time? The pencil box is far more important than sesame candy. She would tell her mother that it was a magical case and whoever used it would have luck in everything he did: go to college, take trains, and travel everywhere, have whatever he wanted, and not be scorned. Mother would believe all these because Fragrant Snow had never lied.

The singing of the brook shifted into an elated tone. It ran forward happily, dashed on the stones, and occasionally splashed up in small sprays. Fragrant Snow wanted to resume her journey now. She washed her face with the river water and smoothed her tangled hair with her wet hands. The water was chilly but she felt refreshed. She left the brook and went back to the long railway track.

What was that ahead? It was the tunnel. It stared blankly like an eye of the mountain. Fragrant Snow stopped but did not step back. She remembered the pencil box in her hand and imagined her classmates' bewildered and envious gazes. Their eyes seemed to glimmer in the tunnel. She bent over to pull up a weathered weed, then stuck it in her braid. Her mother had told her that this way one could ward off evil spirits. Then she ran toward the tunnel.

Fragrant Snow began to feel hot from walking. She untied her shawl and let it hang around her neck. How many miles had she walked? She did not know. She only heard small, unknown insects chirping in the bushes, and she felt loose soft weeds caressing her trouser legs. Her plaits had been blown loose by the wind, so she stopped to braid them neatly. Where was Terrace Gully? She looked ahead and saw many dark spots wriggling on the tracks. They became clearer as they moved closer. They were people. It was a crowd walking toward her. The first was Frail Phoenix. Behind her were the girls of Terrace Gully.

When they saw Fragrant Snow, they stopped.

Fragrant Snow guessed that they were waiting. She wanted to run to them but her legs became heavy. She stood on the ties and looked back at the straight tracks. The tracks were suffused with a dull glow under the moonlight, recording Fragrant Snow's journey. She suddenly felt her heart tighten, she began to cry. They were tears of joy, and of satisfaction. In front of that stern, good-natured mountain, a pride she had never felt arose in her heart. She wiped away the tears, took the weed out of her plait, then, holding up the pencil box, ran toward the crowd ahead.

On the opposite side, the motionless troop began to flow as well. At the same time the girls' joyful cheers burst out in the silent valley. They called Fragrant Snow's name, their voices so warm and spontaneous. They were laughing; that kind of bold, hearty laugh that had no restraint. Finally the ancient mountains were moved and trembled. They echoed in a sonorous, low, and deep voice, cheering together with the girls.

Ah, Fragrant Snow! Fragrant Snow!

1982

NOTES

1 A colloquial expression used to refer to any fair-looking young chap who likes to mingle or flirt with girls.

22

Distant Journey at Eighteen

By **Yu Hua**

Translated by Eric K. W. Yu and Kwok-kan Tam, with Peter G. Crisp

Yu Hua 余華 (b. 1960) was born in Haiyan, a small town near Shanghai. A year after he graduated from middle school in 1977, he worked as a dentist for five years. In 1992 he graduated from the postgraduate programme at Lu Xun Literary Institute. Besides short stories, he has also written novels. His novel, To Live *(*Huo zhe 活着, *1994), was made into an award-winning film directed by Zhang Yimou. His works of short fiction can be found in the collections,* Summer Typhoon *(*Xiaji taifeng 夏季颱風, *1993) and* The Past and the Punishments *(in English translation, 1996). He has published three volumes of his stories in* Collected Works by Yu Hua *(*Yu Hua zuopin ji 余華作品集, *1994). He is currently a member of the Guangdong Writers' Association. Many critics consider Yu Hua as one of the foremost, provocative writers in China. In his works, as he has admitted, there is the shadow of Kawabata, Kafka, Chekhov, and Tolstoy.*

The asphalt road rose up and down incessantly, as if pasted onto the surface of a heaving sea. Walking on this road through the mountains was like being in a boat. It was the year I reached eighteen. A few yellow strands of hair fluttered from my chin in the wind. They were the first to settle there and I cherished them especially. I had walked on this road a whole day. I'd seen many hills and clouds that reminded me of close friends, so I called these hills and clouds by my friends' nicknames. None of this tired me out, despite the long day's walk. I walked like that. Having passed through the morning, close now to the afternoon's last hours, I could even see the first streaks, like hair, of the dusk. But I hadn't come upon an inn.

I met many people on the road. None of them knew what lay ahead or whether there was an inn. 'Why don't you go there and see?' That's what they said. Very well put, I thought; after all, I really was going there to see. Still unable to find an inn, though, I felt I ought to begin to worry.

I was surprised at having seen a car only once in all my day's walk. I saw the car at noon, just exactly when I wanted a ride. I just happened to want a ride then, I hadn't begun to worry about an inn, I was just thinking that a ride would be terrific. Standing by the roadside I waved my hands. I tried hard to wave them in a casual and elegant manner. But the driver didn't look at me. The driver and the car were both alike in ignoring me, they passed before my eyes like a flash out of a fucking gun. I ran after the car for a while, just for fun; I wasn't worrying about an inn then. I ran and ran till the car disappeared, and then laughed hard, to myself. Laughing so hard hurt me when I breathed, though, so I stopped immediately. And then I went on walking in a good mood, though with some regret. I regretted that I hadn't held in my elegant waving hands a great, heavy stone.

Now I really wanted a ride, because the dusk was advancing, and the inn had still not come out of the belly of its fucking mother, the road. I'd seen no car the whole afternoon. If I were to try to stop a car again now, I could certainly manage it, I thought. I would lie down in the middle of the road and for sure any car would brake sharply enough to stop right by my ears. But still I heard no sound of a car engine. I could only go and see. Well put, 'go and see'.

The road rose up and down. Its high peaks always tempting me. Tempting me to run up them, desperately, to see if there was an inn on the other side. But every time I reached a peak I saw only yet another higher peak, and lying between it and me, always, a great despairing arc. And yet I ran up and up again and again, always running desperately. Now I was again running up a peak, and this time I saw it. Not an inn but a truck. Parked in a dip of the road, facing me. I could see the driver's raised buttocks, on which the sunset cast its glow. I couldn't see his head, it was buried under the truck's hood. The hood was lifted at an angle, like a lip turned back. In the back of the truck bamboo baskets were piled high. I thought to myself, bananas with any luck. I thought there'd probably be some fruit in the driver's cab as well, once inside I could get hold of some to eat. The truck was facing the way I was coming from, but I was past caring about which way I went. I wanted an inn. Failing that, I wanted a car or something like it. And there, right in front of me, was the truck.

I ran over excitedly to the truck, greeting the driver with: 'How are you, my fellow countryman?'

The driver didn't seem to hear me, he was still busy fiddling about with something under the hood.

'My fellow countryman, do you want a cigarette?'

Only then did he make any effort to look around, sticking out a black greasy hand to grab the cigarette I was offering. I hurriedly lit it for him. He took a few drags and put his head back under the hood.

I felt at ease, he'd taken my cigarette and so was obliged to give me a ride. I strolled round the truck, trying to find out what was inside the bamboo baskets. I couldn't see, so I used my nose and smelt apples. Apples aren't bad, I thought.

Before long he'd fixed the truck. He lowered the hood and jumped down off the front of the truck. I rushed forward and said: 'Could you give me a ride, my fellow countryman?' Unexpectedly, he shoved me with his black hands, rudely yelling: 'Fuck off!'

I was speechless with anger. He slowly opened the door and the engine started roaring. I knew this was my last chance. I had to take the risk. So I went round the other side, climbed up and opened the door and got in. I was ready for a big fight, there in the cab with him. As I got in I roared at him, 'You've still got my cigarette in your mouth!' Then the lorry was already moving.

He just smiled and looked at me, vaguely amiable, as if lost. He asked, 'Where are you going?'

I said, 'Anywhere, it doesn't matter.'

He asked kindly, 'Do you want an apple?' He was still looking at me.

'You bet!'

'Then climb into the back and get one.'

He was driving so fast there was no way I could climb out of the cab and into the back. So I said, 'Forget it!'

'Go get one,' he insisted, still looking at me.

I said, 'Don't stare at me, you won't find the road on my face.'

Only then did he turn his head and look at the road.

The truck was going back the way I'd come. I sat in my seat comfortably, looking out of the window and chatting with the driver. We soon became friends. He was a self-employed furniture remover. The truck was his and so were the apples. I even heard coins chinking in his pocket. I asked him, 'Where are you going?'

He said, 'Come along and you'll see.'

He spoke so intimately it was like one of my brothers speaking to me. I felt much closer to him. Outside the window, the scenes ought to be ones I was familiar with. Those hills and clouds reminded me of yet another group of friends, and so I called out another set of nicknames.

I simply didn't care any longer about an inn. This truck, this driver and this seat—I was at ease and happy. I didn't know where the truck was going, neither did he. Anyway, it didn't much matter what was ahead. So long as the truck moved, we could go and see.

But the truck broke down when we'd become really close friends. My hand was on his shoulder and his on mine. When he was about to tell the feeling of hugging a woman for the first time, all of a sudden the truck broke down. It broke down climbing up a slope. It ceased roaring and stopped like a stuck pig. So he got out and climbed back up to the engine, turning up the lip-like hood and ducking his head beneath it. Sitting in the cab, I knew his buttocks must be stuck up in the air again, but the truck's lip blocked my sight and I couldn't see. Still, I could hear he was trying to fix the truck.

After a while he pulled his head out and closed the hood. His hands were even blacker. He rubbed his dirty hands on his clothes, and then jumped down onto the ground and walked towards me.

'Fixed?' I asked.

'No, it's done for, can't fix it,' he said.

I thought this had to be the end of the world, and then I asked, 'Then what are we going to do?'

'Just wait and see,' he answered, unconcerned.

I stayed inside the cab, not knowing what to do. I started to think about an inn. Just then the sun was setting, rosy clouds or banks of fog were rising like vapours. The idea of an inn came back naturally to my mind, expanded gradually, and within a minute filled my brain completely. My brain was gone, leaving only an empty space filled with the growing inn.

Now the driver was doing aerobic exercises in the middle of the road. He went right through the sequence seriously, from beginning to end. Afterwards he jogged round the truck a few times. Maybe he'd been confined to his cab for too long and needed some exercise. Seeing him move about outside, I couldn't remain in the cab, so I opened the door and jumped down. I didn't do any aerobic exercises or jog. I just kept thinking about an inn, and nothing more.

Then I saw five men coming down the slope towards us on bicycles. On the rack of each bicycle there was a pole with two large bamboo baskets, one tied on at each end. I thought they were probably peasants who lived nearby, coming home after selling vegetables. Seeing some people coming, I was very happy. I went towards them and shouted, 'How are you, my fellow countrymen?'

The five men jumped off their bicycles when they got to me and I leaned forward, asking, 'Is there an inn nearby?'

They didn't answer, but asked me, 'What's in the truck?'

'Apples,' I said.

They pushed their bicycles towards the truck. Two of them climbed up and handed down ten baskets of apples. The other three remained below, removing the covers and loading the apples into their own baskets. Amazed, I didn't understand at once what was happening. Then I grabbed hold of the hand of one of them and shouted, 'These guys are robbing the apples!' Right at that moment someone's fist punched heavily into my nose and I fell to the ground. Getting to my feet, I found my nose, limp and flattened, hanging as if flapping from my face, blood running down from it like sad tears. By the time I was able to see the big guy who hit me clearly, all five were already on their bicycles and well away.

The driver was strolling about, taking deep breaths. I guessed he was exhausted after all that jogging. He didn't seem to know what had just happened. I shouted to him, 'Your apples are gone!' Only then did he turn towards me. I found him getting more and more cheerful. He was looking at my nose.

Just then many more people came down the slope on bicycles. At the back of every bicycle were two big baskets. Mixed in amongst all these people were children. They all rushed forward together, surrounding the truck in no time. Some of them jumped up onto the truck, and the baskets containing the apples were taken down one by one. The apples from some of the baskets that were broken dropped out of them like the blood running down from my nose. The people were all madly putting apples in their own baskets. In just a few seconds, all the apples in the truck had been moved onto the ground.

Some tractors came roaring down the slope and stopped alongside the truck. A bunch of big guys jumped down and started loading apples up onto their tractors. The empty baskets were thrown down one after another. By then apples were rolling all over the ground and everybody was squatting down like frogs, picking them up.

That was when I dashed forward, forgetting about any danger. Throwing myself at them, I shouted, 'Robbers!' I was greeted with kicks and punches, every inch of my body was struck almost simultaneously. As I helped myself up from the ground, a few kids threw apples at me. Some hit my head and broke. Fortunately, my head did not break. As I was going at the kids to thrash them, someone suddenly kicked me savagely from behind, in the kidneys. I wanted to cry out, but when I opened my mouth no sound came. Down on the ground again, this time I could no longer get up. In my confusion, I could only watch them grabbing apples. I began to look about for the driver. He was standing away at a distance guffawing at me. Then I knew I must be looking even more fantastic than when my nose was bleeding.

At that moment I didn't even have enough strength for anger. I could only watch all these outrageous acts, staring wide eyed. I was most angry at the driver.

More tractors and bicycles came down the slope. The new comers joined in the havoc. I found there were fewer and fewer apples on the ground. I watched some people leaving while others were still arriving. The late comers began to get to work on the truck. I saw them remove the windowpanes and tyres. They even prised open the planks. Without tyres the truck looked even more miserable, lying defenceless on the ground. Some kids were picking up the baskets thrown from the truck. I found the ground was getting cleaner and cleaner and there were fewer and fewer people. But all I could do was watch, I didn't have enough strength to get angry. I sat on the ground. Unable to get up, I could only let my eyes wander about.

Eventually it was all empty, except for one tractor next to the truck. Some people were looking around the truck for whatever could still be taken away. After searching for a while, they got back up onto the tractor one by one, and the tractor started moving off.

I found the driver had also jumped up onto the tractor. Having taken a seat in the cab, he guffawed at me. I saw my red knapsack in his hands. He'd taken my knapsack. My clothes and money, some food and books, were all inside it. And he'd taken it.

I saw the tractor move up the slope and disappear. I could still hear its sound. But very soon even that sound vanished. Things quieted down, it grew dark. I was still sitting on the ground, feeling cold and hungry. I'd lost everything.

I sat there for a long time, and then I got up slowly. It was very difficult to get up, every time I moved pain shot through my body. But I managed to get up, and limped towards the truck. The truck looked pathetic, lying there, damaged, scratched and dented all over. I knew I, too, was hurt all over.

It'd grown completely dark. Emptiness all around, except for the badly damaged truck, my companion in pain. Looking at the truck, I was extremely sad. It seemed to look back at me, just as sad as me. I touched it with my hand. It felt cold all over. I felt the wind beginning to blow, gathering strength. The leaves up the hill shook and rustled, sounding like the sea. This sound frightened me, I felt cold all over like the truck.

I opened the door and climbed into the truck. I found some comfort in the seats still being intact; they hadn't been ripped out by those people. I lay down inside the cab. I detected the odour of petrol leaking slowly out, and it smelt like the blood dripping out of my body. The wind grew stronger and stronger outside, but lying on the seat I began to feel a bit warmer. I felt that though the truck had been scratched and buffeted all over, its heart was still there, sound and warm. I knew my heart was warm too. All the time I'd been looking for an inn, only to find it was right here.

Lying in the heart of the truck, I thought of one sun-filled afternoon. The sunlight was very beautiful then. I remembered I'd played cheerfully outside for half the day and returned home. Outside my window I looked in and saw my father inside, packing a red knapsack. I leaned on the window ledge and asked him, 'Dad, are you going on a journey?'

Dad turned toward me and said affectionately, 'No, I'll let you go on a journey.'

'Let me go?'

'Yes, you're already eighteen. It's time you learnt about the outside world.'

Later on I put that beautiful red knapsack on my back. Dad patted me on the head, like patting the rump of a horse. So I went out of the house happily, trotting like a horse in high spirits.

1987

23

Earth

By **CHANG SHI-KUO**
Translated by John Kwan-Terry

Chang Shi-kuo 張系國 (Zhang Xiguo, b. 1944) was born in Chongqing, China, but received his secondary and tertiary education in Taiwan. He obtained his PhD from the University of California, Berkeley in 1969. He is currently professor of information engineering at the University of Pittsburgh and also a research fellow of the Institute of Mathematics, Academia Sinica, Taiwan. Chang Shi-kuo's fiction is particularly noted for its varied style and themes. Among his published works are the novels Pastor Pi *(*Pi mushi zhengzhuan 皮牧師正傳*, 1963) and* Waters from the Yellow River *(*Huanghe zhi shui 黃河之水*, 1979), and the collections of short stories,* Earth *(*Di 地*, 1970), and* Banana Freighter *(*Xiangjiao chuan 香蕉船*, 1976). Chang Shi-kuo is also noted for his works of science fiction, such as* Nebula Suite *(*Xingyun zuqu 星雲組曲*, 1980) and* Nocturne *(*Ye qu 夜曲*, 1985).*

1

The stone slabs on the threshing floor still glowed yellow in the light of the sun, but standing in the breeze one could already feel a cold nip in the air. At the bottom of the valley stood a cluster of single-storey houses, from whose chimneys ascended thin columns of grey-white smoke; whiffs of smoke were also rising from the roof of Kid Stone's[1] thatched hut that stood on the other side of the slope. It was time for supper, but the three Chen brothers were still gathered outside, engaged in some interminable argument. Dressed in a cheap suit and dangling a pair of leather shoes in his hand, Lao-da was sitting on the doorstep. Lao-er had a singlet thrown over his shoulder, and was puffing away at his cigarette, gesticulating at Lao-da and muttering an endless stream of reproaches. Lao-san[2] was pacing up and down the threshing floor, his hands behind his back, pursued by a handful of young chickens which were running excitedly round and round.

'Father has just died and here we are talking about selling the land! This is a heartless thing to do. This piece of land came down from our ancestors, we can't sell it just like that,' Lao-er said.

'That's not a fair way of putting it. True, it's not a good thing to sell one's land. But if we don't sell, who is going to farm it? Huowang[3] doesn't want to stay and I can't come back either. I have my shop in Taipei to look after, and that just leaves me no time at all. Will *you* come back to farm the land?'

Lao-er puckered up his brow and took a few furious puffs at his cigarette.

'There you are! You don't want to come back either. No one wants to come back, so there's no one to look after the land. If we don't sell it, what are we going to do with it?'

'This is ancestral land. So the only question is: are we going to lease it out or are we going to hire someone to farm it?'

'This is hilly country; the ground is stony and there's not enough water. Who is going to rent it? To hire someone to farm the land is a sure loss. I'm a businessman, I ought to know. Every year, we end up with only a few dozen baskets of kumquats and two hundred catties of low-grade tea. If we did the farming and picking ourselves, we might be able to make a little profit, but it wouldn't be much. It wouldn't even cover the cost of labour if we hired someone to look after the land for us. I'm a businessman, I know these things.'

Lao-da took up his shoes, tapped them on the ground a few times, turned them over, and peered inside to see if they were free of sand. Lao-er threw away the end of his cigarette and fixed his gaze on Lao-san, who was still pacing up and down the threshing floor.

'You're still the best man to stay, Huowang. How about it, eh? You and Father have been taking care of the land all this time, so you should keep up the good work, okay?'

'Oh no, I won't do it. You fellows are leaving me in the hills to dig the ground so you can go off to your jobs in the city and earn tons of money. I already wanted to move into the city the year before last when I left the army. But Father was living, and you said I ought to take care of him, so I didn't have much choice. I've suffered enough here these two years. I'm not going to be the fool again. I don't care which of you stays behind. I'm moving into town to make money and find a wife. Don't expect me to grind away my life in this dump.'

'If you want a wife, we'll give you all the help we can. As for farming, there's nothing wrong with it really, is there?'

'If there's nothing wrong with it, why don't you come back then? This is ancestral land, it is heartless to sell it—it is so easy for you to talk. You know that farming is a hard life; that's why you ran off to find work. And you expect me to like it here?'

'All right, all right!' Lao-er interrupted angrily. 'If you two want to sell the land, sell it and let's be done with it. There'll be money to share, so why should I care? In any case, this family will not be farmers any more.'

'It's not that we won't be farmers.' Lao-da pushed a foot into one of the shoes. 'Frankly, this piece of land is just no good for farming. To make it pay, we must be ready to sweat our hearts out like Kid Stone. If we can work like that, we can earn our fill of money outside. I suggest we do just that. When we have earned enough money, we can come back and buy another piece of land—good farm land this time, and Father will surely be happy down under.'

'Since we've made up our minds to sell, let's find ways to sell it. This plot of land is not that easy to sell, I tell you!'

'What about selling it to Kid Stone?'

'He isn't that rich. Anyway, he was Father's rival all his life. If we sell the land to Kid Stone, Father won't be able to rest in peace.'

'The best thing is to go to town and have a look around to see if there's anyone who wants to buy land. . . .'

'Better spend some money to take out a small advertisement in the newspaper then. To do business, you must know a thing or two about advertising. . . .'

'Let's go tomorrow. . . .'

As the evening wore on, the voices of the three brothers subsided into a distant murmur. The sun, hovering uncertainly for a while over the tree-tops on the crest of the hill opposite, suddenly disappeared behind the dark curtain of the woods. Darkness crept rapidly through the valley. From time to time, the houses at the foot of the hills sent out faint glimmers of light, but no light came from Kid Stone's hut. The autumn insects broke into song, a monotonous sleep-inducing chorus. The creek higher up shimmered white in the distance, reflecting from the sky the last rays of the now invisible sun. Further downstream, the area around East Bamboo Town was one broad filament of twinkling brightness.

The night market in the town was just beginning to come to life, but in the valley, one by one the lights went out in the houses. Long before the stream itself became engulfed in darkness, Kid Stone, the Chen brothers, and the occupants of the other houses had entered into the land of dreams. Night, then, enveloped the entire valley.

2

It was past twelve. At Pockmark Zhao's noodle stall set up at one end of the bridge, customers trickled away one by one, and now it was almost deserted. On the other side of the bridge, in the plainly furnished quarters built for enlisted men, people who had been sitting outside enjoying the evening breeze were dragging their rattan chairs into the houses, yawning repeatedly as they struggled lazily to shut the doors behind them. The billiard parlour adjoining the bridge was also closing up for the night. A few army recruits were laughing raucously with the lady markers and helping them to put up the door planks: strip by strip the dull yellow light that spilled from the room was pasted over. In the distance came the sound of a dog barking, and the crisp, resonant tap-tapping of the wooden clapper of a vendor of wonton noodles. The regular sound came on and off, and could be heard winding its way along the alley, growing more and more distinct. Pockmark Zhao cut up the last pieces of chicken wings and pig's-head meat, sprinkled a few drops of sesame oil on them, and served them up in a dish to his last two customers.

'Captain, try some more, try some of this cold snack.'

'Thank you, thank you.' The one who was addressed as captain raised his cup. He was middle-aged, tall, and of sturdy build.

'Come on, Lao Zhao,[4] stop running about. Sit down and have a drink with us.'

'Oh, thank you. I'll go get a dish of shelled peanuts.' Pockmark Zhao deftly flipped some shelled peanuts from the food cupboard onto a dish and brought a chair over beside them.

'I'm so sorry about tonight. There was slightly more business today, so I've only tiny bits of everything left.'

'Oh, what does that matter? We're old friends.' The other man, who had a swarthy complexion, spoke up. 'Come, Lao Zhao. Here's to you. I hope that in this trip to the south, you'll get the wife you want as soon as you arrive there!'

Pockmark Zhao broke into a broad smile and chuckled. Under the flickering light of the oil-lamp, the pockmarks on his face seemed to stand out even more sharply. 'I'll drink to that.'

The captain also raised his cup. 'Come, Lao Zhao. Here's to you too. May the flowers bloom and the moon shine full on you and your bride. May you have an early marriage and a happy union.'

Pockmark Zhao chuckled again, 'May . . . may the land the captain has bought make him a millionaire at once, may everything go the way he likes.'

'Well said, well said, let's all drink up.'

'Bottoms up, bottoms up!'

Afterwards, the three men flicked the bottoms of their cups toward each other. Swarthy Face took a single wipe at his mouth and said, 'Well, frankly, Captain, your luck is not bad either, not bad at all. What a stretch of land you've got, for only forty-five thousand, almost half a hill and a house to go with it, too! It's like picking it up for nothing.'

The captain laughed quietly. 'My wife felt differently, though. She didn't like the idea of spending all our money at one go. What are we going to eat in the future, she said. We'll have half a hill and you worry about what we are going to eat, I said. Even if we can't grow anything but sweet potatoes, we won't have to go on empty stomachs.'

'Da-sao[5] worries too much, but women tend to be more cautious over these things; that's how they are. If I had such money, I too would have bought land and a house. With land of one's own, what need one worry about anything? It is certainly better than pedaling a pedicab for a living here.'

'Lao Dong, I'll tell you what. Why not get rid of the pedicab and go with me to the country to help me start the farm? Think of this piece of land as your own. If the venture brings in money in the future, we'll split the profits. We're sure to make something. What do you say?'

'Mm . . . well. . . .' Lao Dong poured himself a cup of Red Dew wine. 'I got my pedicab after I'd almost worn my knuckles to the bone, you know. These Resettlement Quarters that I work are not exactly a gold mine, but still, as such areas go, they are not bad.

Frankly, I don't think I can bear selling my pedicab and changing jobs.'

'I hope you don't mind my saying this, Lao Dong. Look at Lao Zhao's noodle stall. It doesn't make big money, but it's a steady job. And if the business is well-managed and the customers keep coming in, it may even be possible to open a small restaurant in the future. That's why I won't try to persuade him to come along with me. But you are different. Though you are just past forty, though you can still pedal your pedicab and earn just enough to feed yourself now, what are you going to do in a few years' time, without any savings to speak of, and still having to pedal for a living? Life can be pretty bleak then. A man who does not worry for the future will live to regret it very soon. Isn't that so? And as the saying goes, of the three ways to be unfilial, the most damnable is not to leave behind a son. You ought to do what Lao Zhao here is doing, save up some money and make plans to get a wife. Things will be much better that way, don't you think?'

Pockmark Zhao, usually a man of few words, chuckled in agreement. 'What the captain says is true, you know.'

Lao Dong sighed and said, 'I appreciate your kind thoughts, Captain. But at a time like ours, how can a man of my kind talk about plans for the future? Better do as the monks do: say my prayers today and let tomorrow take care of itself. If I have money today, I'll have my fill of food and wine and go for some fun at the pleasure-house. If tomorrow I'm without a cent, well, I'll just stay in my room and idle away the time. Just muddling through, you might say. If I can muddle my way through till the day we fight our way back to the mainland and everyone is able to return to his old home, all is well then. But if I don't live long enough to see it, well, it must be that I didn't do well in my last incarnation and I am fated to the kind of life I have. I wouldn't bear any grudge against anyone.'

'Everyone has his idea of what he wants from life. If that's how you feel, I have nothing more to say,' said the captain. 'As for me, I have been a soldier for the greater part of my life, and although I have a family, my wife and children have been on the move with me everywhere, so all this time we've never really known a settled, peaceful life. And it is I, Li Zhenzhi, whose ancestors, for generations, had farmed the land. Farming is a hard life, but after a while, a person seems to grow roots which bind him to the very earth itself. And that's what makes him feel that he belongs, and is also secure. I have been drudging away these many years, so now I really want to have a piece of land where I can settle down, even if it means extra work and extra sacrifice.'

Lao Dong emptied another cup of wine. The drink was having its effect on his dark complexion, which had now turned a deep purple. 'I still remember the time we were living in Shanghai when I was a child. In those days, my father was a businessman and our family was rather well off. I had an attendant who followed me everywhere I went, and my little sister had a nurse-maid to look after her. So you see, Captain, I come from a good family! One day, my father called me to his room and, giving me a copper coin, said to me: "Son, spend as much of my fortune as you like. I won't say a word even if you spend all of it. Only keep this copper coin for me, and keep it well. Take the coin out when you turn twenty and promise yourself that from then onwards you'll double it every year. By the time you are forty, you'll have such a sum that you won't be able to use it up for the rest of your life." Captain, my father built the family's fortune with a pair of empty hands. All these years, my father's words have stayed firmly in my mind. I have made a point of remembering them. Captain, those words of my father make a lot of sense, don't they? I'm forty-three this year. If, from twenty onwards, I had done what my father told me and doubled the number of coins every year, the first year two coins, the second year four, and so on, I would have collected several million coins by now! Captain, what my father said really makes sense. It's a pity I am no good. I didn't do what my father said.

'Captain, I was a boy scout, you know, the year little Japan invaded Shanghai and the 19th Infantry was locked in battle with the Japanese there. Dressed in a boy scout uniform, equipped with rope, whistle, and a tremendously long dagger—the kind that boy scouts wear—I was scurrying backwards and forwards exposed to the direct line of fire every day, carrying messages, reports, and food for our side. Oh, I was a promising young man then, Captain, one of the select few, you might say. The papers were filled with news stories of how brave we boy scouts were. Yes, we did manage to do quite a bit.

'And then, I don't know how it happened, the 19th Infantry began withdrawing from Shanghai, and quite a few boy scouts started to run with them, without knowing what they were doing. I also followed the Infantry in their retreat, and as a result was cut off from my family for several years. And that, Captain, is how I became a soldier. When at last I returned home, my father had died, the business had gone, the family was in ruins, and I had become a soldier.

'Still, Captain, what my father said does make a lot of sense. If I had followed his words and from twenty onwards doubled the number of coins every year, it would have been fantastic now, wouldn't it? The first year two coins, the second year four coins, the third year eight. . . .'

Lao Dong sounded more and more like someone talking in a dream. His words became increasingly incoherent until, his body bent over the table, he fell asleep. Shaking his head gently, the captain stood up, helped Pockmark Zhao close up his stall, and got Lao Dong on his feet. Then, with Lao Dong leaning heavily on his arm and followed by Pockmark Zhao pushing his stall, the whole party shuffled slowly across the bridge, guided by the unsteady, swaying light of the oil lamp.

'Lao Zhao, if you aren't leaving tomorrow, come over to my place for dinner. My son Li Ming is coming back and he said in his letter that he was bringing something for you and Lao Dong.'

Lao Zhao chuckled with delight. 'Thank you, Captain, thank you.'

3

Up on the stage, the four Raymond Brothers were playing their special Beatles number. The young men and women were rock-and-rolling on the dance floor, their bodies writhing in all directions, up, down, backwards, forwards, encouraged by the resonant twanging of an electric guitar. Li Ming was twisting his hips and nodding his head uncontrollably, his eyes fixed on his partner, a dainty, attractive girl with long black hair spread over her shoulders, who was munching a piece of chewing gum as she danced and was speeding up her movements as the beat of the music quickened. She wore a contented smile on her face. As the music reached a pitch of frenzy, the youngsters on the dance floor, as if compelled by some primitive instinct, gave out a yell; the girl's movements became even more frantic, her smile more alluring. There was something infectious about the music and the jerky sharp cries. Li Ming, with sweat dripping down his face, was groaning involuntarily and shaking himself with abandon, as if all the primitive, animal impulses that had been contained in him were shooting off his arms, neck, hips, cranium, and every other part of his body, a sensation which gave him an indescribable feeling of pleasure. The Raymond Brothers finally brought a stop to the primeval din; only the electric guitar remained playing, strumming out a low, ponderous tune. The couples on the dance floor dispersed in different directions to their tables. Slightly dazed, as if just woken from a dream, Li Ming led his partner by the waist back to their seats.

'Hey, Mei, you seemed to enjoy the dance very much, didn't you?'

She gave him a smile. 'Sure, didn't you?'

'Actually, I was lost in admiring you, especially the way you danced, as if you didn't have a care in the world. I was watching you all through the dance, you know.'

'Cheeky!'

Back at their table, she picked up her glass of orange juice, drank a mouthful and frowned.

'Ming, order an ice cream soda for me, won't you?'

'Let's eat outside. Things in here are too expensive.'

'But I want one.'

Li Ming stood up reluctantly. The waiters were hanging about near the door at the other end of the room, so he squeezed his way through, placed his order, then made his way back. Meanwhile, the Raymond Brothers had struck up another number, and his partner was already on the dance floor with a boy, jerking and twisting her body like one possessed, hair tossing in the air, arms flailing up and down. Li Ming knew this was called the 'Monkey', one of the most popular dances of the day. He lit a cigarette and glanced at his watch: both hands were pointing at eleven. He was beginning to feel impatient and somewhat bored watching the wild shapes and postures on the floor. These faddish dances, it's fun while you are doing them yourself, but watching from the side-line, you can't help feeling how much they resemble epileptic attacks. The people on the floor began shrieking. A confused babble of sharp cries bombarded his eardrums. He had heard cries like these before, he remembered, several months back, in a cheap, filthy hotel in Yokohama.

It was the first time their ship docked at Yokohama. He and the other two apprentice hands on board had immediately vanished like wisps of smoke and turned up in Tokyo to sample those much-talked-about striptease acts. By the time they returned to Yokohama, it was too late for them to get back to the ship, so they put up in this dingy little hotel for the night. About midnight they heard someone entering the room next door; there was only a partition of very thin boards between the two rooms. The man sounded like a foreign sailor, obviously a very drunk one. Once inside the room, he began hollering that he wanted a woman. The woman arrived, and a moment later, from the other side of the thin boards came the sound of panting, punctuated by the woman's cries. They couldn't sleep; the three of them, sitting in the dark, listened the night away. About once every hour the indefatigable sailor would babble for a while, then the panting would start again, rising in volume until there were cries. . . .

'Shit!' Li Ming took a few quick nervous puffs at his cigarette. The Raymond Brothers went on playing number after number without stopping, the dancers went on twisting, shaking, and shrieking. He could no longer see where Zhou Mei was; a gentleman sporting a gay necktie and a huge potbelly was dancing at the side of his table and completely blocking his view. He couldn't help cursing again, 'Shit!'

At last the dancing stopped and the electric guitar subsided into a droning, ponderous tune. Zhou Mei emerged from the scattering crowd, her brow beaded with sweat.

'Gee, that was fun! Have you ordered the ice cream soda for me?'

'It's been here for ages.'

'Thanks.' She flopped into a chair, took hold of the long-stemmed glass, and threw him a smile. 'You aren't angry with me for dancing with someone else?'

'Of course not. I'm not that narrow-minded.'

'I saw you sitting here looking so bored. I thought you were angry with me.'

'I wasn't angry. . . . I was only thinking.'

'That's swell then.' She picked up the small spoon and scooped up a small lump of ice cream. 'What were you thinking about?'

'About us.'

'Aren't we doing fine? What's there to think about?'

Li Ming looked at her. He could never make up his mind whether she was really that innocent and naive or whether. . . . He leaned over and held her soft small hand in his.

'Mei, let's go. I've something to talk to you about.'

'But what's the hurry?' She drew back her hand gently. 'I want to dance again.'

'The Raymonds are going already. There will be floor shows only. You won't like them.'

'Do we have to go?' She cast a look at the stage. The musicians were just removing the guitar. 'What's the time now?'

'Past eleven.'

'Only eleven! The Raymonds will play again at one,' she said triumphantly. 'They always do, I know. If we leave now, we'll be missing the fun.'

'You really like to dance that much?'

'Sure. It's a drag going home this early. Anyway, Mom and Dad are out at their mahjong games and won't be home till past midnight.'

'But . . . I have a lot of things I want to talk to you about tonight. Let's go, please. We'll come again another time.'

'Spoilsport,' she pouted, but relaxed into a smile the next moment. 'All right, I'll listen to you this once, but only because you are back from a long trip.'

At the entrance to the restaurant, a number of taxis were queued up waiting for customers, and a few hippie-type young girls were hanging around, trying to pick up anyone willing to take them in for a free dance. Li Ming stumbled out through an opening in the taxi-line, followed closely behind by Zhou Mei. She turned her head quickly and said smiling, 'Do you know what I'll do if I become rich?'

'What'll you do? Buy more dolls?'

'Oh, no. If I were rich, I would send someone here every night to get tickets for every girl who wants to dance but can't afford it. How does that sound to you?'

'Great!' Li Ming smiled. 'You have the ambition of a Du Fu.'

'You think so? I thought people in ancient times were all long-bearded squares. Du Fu liked dancing too?'

'Don't be silly. He wanted to build houses for all the poor people of the world.'[6]

'Oh, then he *was* a square after all.'

'Are you cold? Would you like to have my jacket?' She shook her head. They were walking along East Nanking Road, and for a while they did not speak a word. It was getting windy. Night-time in Taipei could be rather chilly.

'Ming, you said you wanted to talk about something? I am listening.'

'Oh, yes. What do I want to talk about?' He slapped at his forehead lightly. 'I can't remember what I wanted to say just now.'

'You are really something. You pulled me out in such a hurry, here we are and now you have nothing to say.'

'Don't be impatient. Let me get into the right mood first.' He took a deep breath. 'Yes, I wanted to tell you that my family bought a piece of land.'

'Oh?'

'My family bought a piece of land. Father sold his grocery store and used the money plus the last installment from his pension to buy this large piece of land in the country.'

'That's swell. So this is what you wanted to talk to me about?'

'That's not all. I may not be able to work as a seaman anymore. I'll have to help my father get the farm started.'

'Why? Can you earn more from farming?'

'That isn't the main reason. I . . .' He hesitated. 'Let me put it this way. I must have been away for a good half year on this trip, and in that time, I visited many different countries and met many different people. But what was constantly in my mind was the small town I left behind and its people. It is an ordinary little town, which you can't even call pretty. And the townspeople, too, are common, humble folk; people that you can find anywhere. Still, I was always looking forward to coming back. The beautiful cities and ports that I'd been to did not strike me as places I could belong to, much less settle down in for the rest of my life. My real home is there, in that small ordinary town. Back there, I feel so comfortable, so completely relaxed. I can never feel like this in any other place. . . .'

'You were homesick. You're bound to feel homesick if you are away for so long. After a while back, you'll be itching to go away again.'

'Maybe you're right. I used to tell you how fed up I was with that place. It was the most monotonous town on earth, with only two cinema houses and not a single decent bookshop to speak of. Every time I went home to spend my vacation, there was absolutely nothing to do, except share some mindless chatter with friends and play an idle game of chess, or be cooped up at home with Mother and Father, staring at each other without anything to say. In the end, I would almost choke to death with boredom and would give anything to have a brief fling in cities like Taipei and Keelung.'

'I don't like living in the country, either. Last month, I stayed at my aunt's for a spell. The first few days weren't too bad, but afterwards I was just bored stiff. I prefer Taipei any time. It's such a gay place and so much fun.'

'But out at sea, faced with nothing more exciting than the blank walls of my cabin, I had plenty of time to think things over, and I guess I finally managed to work things out. What we describe as commonplace, for example, usually has an attractive side to it. During those months at sea, the things that I used to look back on with a sense of loss were not the wild, gay moments of my life. It was the small, trivial events that kept coming to mind, such as the time when a friend and I squatted on the bank of a small lake, trying to fish and play chess at the same time. When the game was over, we pulled in our rods to have a look; they were as clean as new. We thought we might as well let the fish have a good meal, so we threw all the bait into the lake. We had a good laugh that time. Then there was another time, a very hot day during the summer vacation it was, when I dropped in at my old school to pay my former teacher a visit. He had just written a poem, and in a loud and delightful voice he asked me in. He was bare-backed and was fanning himself with a rush-leaf fan. As soon as I was inside, he began chanting and explaining, character by character, the poem he had written, in classical metre, in praise of snow. Such simple, mundane incidents came to my mind so vividly that they seemed to be re-enacted before my very eyes. I think I am just an ordinary anybody, that's why I fall into such trivial recollections. And since I am but an ordinary man, why not lead an ordinary life? I'd be happier that way; don't you think so?'

'Sure,' she sighed. 'You may say what you like, but I still prefer living in the city. Life is pretty ordinary here, too, but at least there's more chance to have some fun.'

'I said just now I'd be going to the country to take up farming. How do you feel about that?'

'Do as you like. In any case, you always have plenty of excuses for doing what you want. But I was thinking . . . if you work as a seaman, you'll get your promotions after a few years; you'll be second mate, then first mate. Didn't you tell me last time that if all went well, you should become captain in ten years' time? That's not bad. As for farming, after ten years, twenty years, you'll still be farming. Right?'

Li Ming couldn't think of what to say in reply. After a long pause, he ventured lamely:

'What you say makes sense, I guess . . . I'll have to go back and think things over carefully.'

'This is what you've been wanting to talk to me about?'

'Eh, . . . let's forget it, it's not important.'

'Fine. I'm so tired from all this walking.' She waved her hand and shouted, 'Hey, taxi!'

4

Li Ming left his house and followed the lane that led to the school. On both sides of the lane lay paddy fields that, at this time of the year, already looked like a shimmering sea of yellow, undulating in the wind. It was near harvest time. Very soon, one would see the threshing machine set up, the busy comings and goings of men, women, and children, the neatly tied bundles of straw standing in the fields. The playground would be taken over by the farmers who would cover its concrete floor with heaps of rice grains, depriving the students, for those few weeks, of their usual game of basketball. But when the sparrows came in flocks to enjoy a feast, the schoolboys, with slingshots ready, would rush to the playground after school to chase the birds. On one weekend Li Ming knocked down more than a dozen sparrows that way. Then, if no teacher was around, they would light a fire by the side of the air-raid shelter at the far end of the playground and gorge themselves on barbecued sparrows. During the harvest there would be no reports or complaints of missing bag-lunches. . . .

At the extreme end of the paddy fields stood the low wall of the school house, which Li Ming jumped over easily. He had come this way every day when he was in junior high school. In those days he was a small boy, so he had a few bricks conveniently stacked up at one corner of the wall to help him over. The bricks were still there. Maybe other boys were using them now as he once did.

The students were struggling through the second class of the day. There was nobody in the school yard. Li Ming made his way to the front gate. Lao Jing was not at his usual place in the shed; probably it was his day to be cleaning guns at the armoury. The administration building was a single two storey structure painted a sombre grey, built not more than three years before, but already the plaster was peeling off in ugly patches. The school motto, 'Propriety, Righteousness, Integrity, Dignity', had obviously received countless coats of new paint: somewhere in the process, the character for *dignity* had lost a stroke. The main office was almost empty of people, all the teachers having gone to their classes. Li Ming quickened his steps as he walked past the principal's office. The room farthest back in the building had a black-coloured plate on the door with the designation of some section, town, and district. Ever since this section set up its office, it had taken over this corner of the school's administration building for its use. Li Ming went in. The two employees, sitting cross-legged in an ungentlemanly fashion and reading their newspapers, looked up at the same time.

'Hi, Rooster Kung, haven't seen you for a long time.'

'Li Ming! Hey, when did you get back?' Gong Jizhong got to his feet. He was a tall, thin, weedy-looking young man with a lethargic manner. 'Day before yesterday I was at your place. Your old man said you were back for a day and had left again. What's the itch this time?'

'I had to go to Taipei to take care of something.'

'You mean your girl, don't you?' Gong Jizhong laughed. 'I just can't believe it, an ordinary young girl has come to mean so much more to you than an old buddy of more than ten years' standing. Dear, dear, what are friends coming to nowadays? Oh, sit down, sit down!'

The other employee brought a chair over. Li Ming thanked him and sat down. Gong Jizhong offered him a cigarette. They lit their cigarettes, then looked at each other and smiled. Gong Jizhong leaned over and patted him on the knee. 'Hell, I thought you would look like a bamboo pole when you came back, but look how you've put on weight instead. You've really set about stuffing yourself. Boy, do you make me sick! The food on board must be good.'

'Not bad, meat and eggs every day, American standard. But what have you been doing to yourself? You look vegetable-green.'

'Oh, well. It's a long story.' Gong Jizhong gave the other employee a quick look. 'This position is not exactly a money-maker, you know. Right now, I'm stooping to get a mere two-and-a-half pecks of rice, not even five.'[7] The two of them laughed. Then Gong Jizhong gave himself a brisk tap on the side of the head.

'How stupid of me. Let me introduce you two. This is Li Ming. We were in grade school and high school together. A graduate of the Marine Institute—now upgraded to a university, I understand—pursuing his career on a merchant ship as fourth mate, otherwise designated as apprentice-trainee. And this is Jin Zhaonian, also from the Department of International Relations, National Cheng-chi University, but one year my junior. He is now installed in the august position of Deputy Director of this Office and concurrently Administrative Secretary plus

Three-days-a-week Handyman General. His official standing is just slightly below mine, so you might say "He sits above ten thousand but looks up to only one".'[8]

'I have heard of the other official titles, but "Three-days-a-week Handyman General" is a new one to me.'

'You dumb ass! Obviously, as Director of this Office, yours truly takes charge of the remaining three days.'

The three men burst out laughing. Li Ming looked at Jin Zhaonian.

'When I was undergoing training on Mount Success, there was a gentleman in the camp by the name of Jin Yinian, or "Hundred Thousand Years of Gold". Is he, by any chance. . . .'

'He's my elder brother.'

'Oh, he was a terrific basketball player. He played for the regiment's team.'

'That's him all right. He has always loved basketball. He must have an easy time of it in the army, spending his days playing basketball.'

'He must be abroad now?'

'No. He's returned to Zhongxing University[9] as a teaching assistant.'

'I see,' Li Ming paused. 'You two brothers have very uncommon names. Don't you have another older brother called Jin Wannian?'

Jin Zhaonian nodded.

Li Ming couldn't help smiling. 'Isn't there a Jin Yinian or Jin Yuannian as well?'[10]

'No. There are only three of us in the family.'

'They come from a family that believed in planned parenthood,' Gong Jizhong interrupted. 'Three is just the right number: ten thousand, a hundred thousand, a million, that is perfect calculation; one more will break the order, one less will make it meaningless.'

'How will one more break the order? What about "Jin Jingnian"?'

'What Jin Jinnian, Yin Yinnian? What are you talking about?'

'I said "*Jing*" as in "Bei*jing*". Ten million make a "jing".'[11]

'Oh well,' Gong Jizhong said. 'It doesn't have the ring of a name anyway. Three is just right.'

'By the way, when you were in the Marine Institute, did you know a Chen Qiren?' Jin Zhaonian asked.

'Oh yes. But we were in different departments. I was in Navigation, he was in Management, so we didn't know each other that well. You know him?'

'He is my cousin.'

'He has a very attractive girlfriend.'

'Yes. Her name is He Meiji, if I remember correctly. She was supposed to be campus beauty queen, too.'

'He Meihui?' Gong Jizhong interjected, eyebrows raised. 'I know He Meihui. Come to think of it, I had an interest in her at one time. Are you telling me that actually Jin's cousin had landed her already?'

'That was settled ages ago, so don't you start having ideas.'

'So one less eligible maiden for me. What rotten luck!'

'It just seems so incredible,' Li Ming said. 'In a place like Taiwan, no matter who you come across, if the fellow is about your age, you're bound to discover some connection between you before two words are out: if you are not relatives, then you must be mutual friends of some third person.'

'Right,' Gong Jizhong punctuated. The three broke out almost simultaneously, 'Taiwan is such a small place!'

'Taiwan is such a small place,' repeated Gong Jizhong. 'There's too little room and too many officials, so we end up the way we are. Distinguished graduates in International Relations from Zhengda[12]—mind you, Zhengda's Department of International Relations is no crummy joint—men with qualifications and ability like us, end up only division-nine officials, worth just ten piculs of rice a year. . . . And to get even this much,' he added, 'you have to have ways and means.'

Ever since he was in junior high, Gong Jizhong had demonstrated his literary and artistic talents. Thanks to him, Li Ming's class used to win every one of the school's display-board competitions. Likewise, in essay competitions, it was Gong Jizhong who took all the prizes. When he was attending senior high, his articles were already appearing in the literary supplement of the local papers. At one time, too, he actively participated in the editing of pamphlets and miscellaneous literature for the local branch of the Organization for the Recovery of the Motherland. He showed all the signs of becoming an outstanding writer. Who would have thought that in the end, all that this experience and competence would lead to was a division-nine post?

'Well, why don't you have a go at one of the special recruitment examinations for diplomatic personnel? If you make it, you can go abroad.'

'Why bother? Even if I made it, it would mean two monotonous years in the Ministry of Foreign Affairs before I could even have a chance to be sent abroad. And even if I were sent abroad, would I be better off? At best, it would just be an opportunity to go abroad.'

'Don't you even want to go abroad?'

'I am too lazy to move,' Gong Jizhong yawned. 'Anyway, when you have left the country, what then? Look at you. Haven't you been abroad often enough? What have you gained from it all?'

'My kind of going abroad and what we are talking about are two different things.'

'The way I see it, there isn't much difference. You go away to see more of the world, to add to your experience, that's all there is to it. But I am a *xiucai,*[13] you know, and I am supposed to know everything there is to know between heaven and earth without taking a step beyond the door of my house, so what can I get out of leaving the country? The ancients left home to seek knowledge, the moderns leave home to emigrate. As they said of old, you should attend to your filial obligations and move only when your parents are no longer alive. I have an aged mother to care for, a tender sister to protect. So I stay put.'

'Sounds reasonable. If what you say is true', Li Ming said, 'then I'd better give up my seaman's job and retire to the mountains.'

'That's a way, too! Anyway,' Gong Jizhong heaved a sigh, 'when all is said, no matter what your work is, the idea is the same: just to keep alive. What else could we do? If it weren't for this, I wouldn't have to break my back for a meagre two-and-a-half pecks of rice.'

Li Ming fell silent. After a brief pause Gong Jizhong said, 'Let's go see Jumbo.'

'I thought he'd been sent to teach in Taipei.'

'A man of his calibre? You must be joking! As it is, he's lucky after being sent to the south to have been able to get himself transferred here.'

'I suppose he got our old principal to help him.'

'Of course. As the saying goes, "A single day of discipleship will foster an everlasting bond between teacher and pupil".' Gong Jizhong stood up. 'He doesn't have classes in the morning. He'll be in his quarters, so let's go.'

Li Ming exchanged some small talk with Jin Zhaonian and then went out of the office with Gong Jizhong. On the playground a class of junior grade youngsters were doing their physical training exercises.

The instructor kept blowing his whistle, and the little urchins were vigorously standing up, bending down, standing up, bending down, without being given a moment's rest.

'Rooster, there are many things about this office of yours I won't try to flatter you about, but I must say, you have a highly qualified staff. Take the two of you, both university graduates.'

'I am here because I had no other way. Jin Zhaonian is here because he had his way.'

'How do you mean?'

'His father is a member of some government committee or other. If they don't have their way, who does?'

'Oh? . . . But then what's he here for, in this out-of-the-way backyard?'

'Well, he broke up with his girlfriend and became pretty down in spirit, I suppose,' Gong Jizhong explained in a casual tone of voice. 'So he came to this isolated "backyard" to recuperate. "Shutting himself off from the world to reflect upon his mistakes, and cultivating the health of his spirit", so to speak.'

Li Ming couldn't help laughing. 'He is quite an affable fellow, like some character from one of those pulp novels. The beginning of the tale is promising. Has it got a sequel?'

'Has it got one! The story goes that as soon as our handsome young hero arrived in this rustic desolation, he picked up a "blooming wild lily growing beside his path, a young and lovelorn creature, with dreamy eyes and cool, delicate hands". Our heroine, in the proper style of *The View From The Window*, was a grade-twelve student. Various scenes from *The Western Chamber* have been enacted already—"Transfixed on Encountering the Beauty", "Serenade for Seduction", "Secret Betrothal in the Rear Garden". The stage is set now, I suppose, for "The Cross-examination".'

'Anyway, this is really making the best of one's situation, and the story will have a happy ending this time, I expect.'

'The trouble is, it may not. When the girl gets knocked up, you may find it a bit difficult to see a happy ending.'

'Then he becomes a cad! Why didn't you talk to him before?'

'Why should I put my nose into other people's affairs?' Gong Jizhong shrugged his shoulders. 'I'm not sure at all he would have listened even if I had talked to him. As long as it's not my sister that's knocked up, why should I bother? If he had fooled around with my sister, then it would be different, of course; then I would have chopped him up into little pieces. Well, that is Gong Jizhong's philosophy, for what it's worth.'

'You are taking an increasingly cynical view of life.'

'If I don't amuse myself with playing cynic, how am I going to pass the long days?'

Jumbo's room was at the end of the second row of bachelor quarters for the teaching staff. Gong Jizhong knocked at the door. Jumbo poked his head out, gave a delighted laugh, and said, 'There you are! When I got up this morning, I broke my tea-cup for no apparent reason. Filled with apprehension, I cast a divination, and drew the Diagram of Earth which reads, "Friends gained in the south-west, lost in the north-east." That's how I knew that today I was going to receive friends from distant lands. Uncanny divination, don't you think?'

'There goes our street-corner Daoist with his mumbo-jumbo again,' Gong Jizhong scoffed. 'Even if you are right, you've got half of it straight. Friends gained in the south-west, that I can see. But what's the nonsense about friends lost in the north-east?'

'The loss of friends in the north-east has already come to pass. As for gaining friends in the south-west, isn't that materializing at this very moment? Furthermore it is said that the loss of friends in the north-east will bring much rejoicing, which is to say that the said loss is the ill luck that ushers in good fortune. Don't you remember the reports that Lao Cheng had stepped on a mine in Quemoy and killed himself? We were even making the funeral arrangements when out of the blue he dropped in on us, as lively as a cricket. That, in short, is the story of how a friend was lost in the north-east.' Jumbo guffawed.

'Quemoy is not in the north-east. Who are you fooling?'

Jumbo turned out both palms of his hands in a gesture of defeat: 'If everyone was as full of scruples as you, there would be no place for fortune tellers.'

'You have lost weight again, Jumbo,' Li Ming said. 'You don't look like an elephant anymore. You are beginning to look more like a scrawny mule.'

'You expect everyone to look like you—with fat head and floppy ears?' Jumbo patted Li Ming on the shoulder. 'My clothes are growing in size every day, but I don't waste tears over that.'

'Miss Chen is well, I gather?'

'Oh, that's over, for more than two months now.'

'No wonder you look thin. What happened? You two were on the point of being hitched for life.'

'That's where the trouble started. Anyway, this is what happened. We shilly-shallied for a long time. When it came to showing my hand, her parents asked me if I was able to go abroad. I asked them how they expected someone like me—a penniless schoolteacher who had only recently graduated from the Chinese Department of the National Taiwan Normal University—to be able to go abroad. Then they wanted to know if I was financially sound. I replied that I might be in the future. So they said if that was the case there was no point in pursuing the matter further. To make matters worse, she turned out to be a perfect daughter, not the kind who would argue with her parents. So we parted company. After a month or so, she contracted a long-distance engagement with someone abroad.'

'How vulgar,' Gong Jizhong said. 'Jumbo here can't even conduct his love affair without falling into the rut of the "Butterfly and Mandarin Duck" school of fiction. You people who dine on the classics every day haven't got the guts to blaze a path for yourselves.'

'Well, tease me as you like. I don't really blame her. What kind of a future would she have with a poor schoolmaster like me? To call it quits is the best possible thing to do. Even if it sounds corny, I still say with all my heart that I wish her all the happiness in the world.' There was a note of pain in Jumbo's voice. But being by nature optimistic, he immediately recovered his habitual good humour. 'Well, Li Ming, let's talk about you instead. How is Miss Zhou doing?'

'What a superfluous question!' Gong Jizhong cut in. 'He's just back from his tryst in Taipei, so what do you expect? Of course, things are fine.'

'Things are not exactly fine. She's quite good to me, that's true. I was in Taipei for two days and she went to a lot of trouble to get leave from her work so as to keep me company. But . . . somehow, most of the time she doesn't seem to understand how I feel about most things.'

'Tut, tut!' Gong Jizhong teased, screwing up his face. 'Just listen to him. Miss Zhou took two days off to keep him company, and he still says, "She doesn't understand me!" You'd better face the truth. It's you who are after her, so it's up to you to accommodate her. It's you who should try to understand her, and you have the nerve to be whimpering about her not understanding you! That's exactly how a booby like you would behave.'

'I also think you are being unreasonable, Li Ming,' Jumbo added. 'Your head is too stuffed with feudalistic rubbish. You may have hoodwinked others, but you can't hoodwink me. She's a high school graduate and isn't as well educated as you are, so you subconsciously feel that she doesn't measure up to you in anything. She can't understand you because you think you are superior to her in every way. Rooster is right, you are a booby to think like this. Actually, Miss Zhou Mei strikes me as a very fine girl. She's more than usually fun-loving, I know, but what young girls don't like to have a bit of fun? What really matters is that she is by nature candid and sincere, clear-headed and practical, and not woolly-headed like most girls. It is really not easy to find someone like her these days. What is all this nonsense about understanding and not understanding; what is it but poison spread by all these stupid stories that glut our bookstores? Too many of us now have been infected by this sickness! So long as a man and a woman can be on speaking terms with each other, are not separated by too wide a social gap, and can get along with each other well enough to live together, that's all that's needed. And still, here you are, demanding that one understand how the other's mind works. You'd better look for perfect understanding on the moon!'

'You fellows are forcing a cap on me that doesn't fit!' Li Ming protested. 'If I had ever looked down on Zhou Mei at all, may I be damned in Heaven's name, may I . . .'

'Don't try to trump up excuses,' said Gong Jizhong, cutting him short.

'I'm not trumping up excuses. She doesn't understand me, and I don't say this without having perfectly good reasons.'

'Well, I'm afraid you'll have to hold over your complaints for a little while.' Jumbo looked at his watch. 'I have to go to a staff meeting now, so if you'll excuse me. We'll have to postpone our conversation till we meet again.'

'It doesn't make any difference one way or the other whether you attend such meetings or not, does it? It's not often we can get together like this, so don't be a kill-joy,' Gong Jizhong said persuasively. 'Summon the courage you always had in skipping all the weekly school gatherings; be your old reckless self again, just this once.'

'The man of character does not look back on the brave deeds of his past,' Jumbo said, with a theatrical gesture of the hands. 'Talk, that's where my desire lies; meetings, that's where it does not lie. And yet, I forsake talking for meetings, why? Because I've got my rice-bowl to worry about!'

Smiling good-humouredly, Gong Jizhong stood up. 'Well, if you put it that way, let me not spoil your career for you.'

'I have an idea,' Li Ming said. 'My family has just bought a piece of farming land that has a house to go with it. We can get a few of us together and spend a couple of days there this Saturday. We can swim, play chess, or just talk. What do you think, eh?'

'Good idea,' Gong Jizhong said. 'I'm not a busy man, so it's no problem for me. What about you, Jumbo, can you get away for a couple of days?'

'I don't have any class on Saturday. I can make it. We can ask Lao Cheng to come along as well. He works in the Railway Administration and comes here to see his girl every week. Hank is in Taoyuan and most probably can't come. Oh, yes, there's also Xiao-Yu. He's going away next month and said he would make a trip back before leaving. I can drop him a note about this.'

'Then there are five of us already, just like that.' Li Ming was excited. 'Five old friends in one place for two whole days, swapping memories and old dreams before going on each other's way. Won't that be just great!'

'Ooo. . . .' Gong Jizhong stretched himself lazily. 'What a reliving of memories and old dreams. Amen.'

5

'I'm back, Captain.' Pockmark Zhao was standing outside the wire-netting door, a straw hat in one hand, beaming from ear to ear.

The captain took off his spectacles, put down the newspaper he was reading and stood up. 'Come in, Lao Zhao. The sun is so strong outside, what are you standing there for?'

At these words, Pockmark Zhao pushed open the door and stepped in; then he turned around and very carefully secured the door latch. Li Da-sao was just coming from the house, and, seeing her, he burst into a grin of greeting, 'Da-sao, I'm back.'

'Aiya, it's Lao Zhao! Have you had your lunch yet? If you haven't, I'll go make you some.'

'I've eaten, thank you, thank you. Don't trouble yourself, Da-sao.'

'Sure? With us, you don't have to stand on ceremony, you know.'

'Of course, of course.' Pockmark Zhao was still standing there, grinning foolishly. 'Da-sao, Xiao-wu[14] is back, isn't he?'

'He's been back for some time now. In fact, he came back the day you left; you left in the morning, he arrived in the afternoon. He asked about you, and he's brought back two bottles of foreign liquor for you and two for Lao Dong. I joked about it to him. It's the perfect gift for Lao Dong, I said, but you should have brought Lao Zhao something else. Lao Zhao isn't much of a drinker. But he smiled and said he didn't think of that when he bought it. Well, just take these small gifts as his way of saying that he still remembers old friends. We always thought he was such an awkward, muddle-headed child. But after a long trip from home, he has matured a lot and become very considerate. He brought his father a Jamaica-made cigarette holder and a good-quality lighter, an overcoat for me, plenty of cosmetics for his elder sister, and a Japanese doll for his little sister, besides things for you and relatives. As for himself, he didn't buy a single thing. I asked him why, and he said, "The next time, Mother, I'll buy something for myself, but this being my first trip abroad, I ought to get you people the things you like." He's put himself to so much trouble. . . .'

'Come, Lao Zhao, sit down. Don't just stand there as if you were glued to the ground.'

'Sure, sure.' Pockmark Zhao sat down, still gripping his straw hat in his hand. 'I must thank Xiao-wu properly. Is he home?'

'No, he's out again,' Li Da-sao said. 'He went to the country with those buddies of his early in the morning. Said they would be staying there for a few days. Last night, he kept pestering me to cook this and that for him. I said, in this hot weather, food can't keep and you will have to finish it in a hurry. He said there were quite a few of them, that the food was not enough to last them even a day, and the next day they would have to do their own cooking. Well, all his friends have big appetites, Xiao-wu too—they are young people after all. The day before, we made some three hundred dumplings for some guests that Xiao-wu had over, and the five or six of them cleaned up the lot at one sitting. It makes me happy to see the way they eat. I said, "Xiao-wu, when you are away. . . ."'

'Tai-tai,[15] go and make a cup of tea for Lao Zhao, will you? He must be very hot and thirsty having come all this way.'

'It . . . it's all right. Don't trouble yourself, Da-sao.'

'Let me get you a bowl of iced almond bean-curd. I made a pot of it for Xiao-wu yesterday, but he said it was too watery and troublesome to carry. You'll have a bowl too, Zhenzhi?'

'Yes, I think I'll have some. More sugar for me, please.'

Swaying this way and that, Li Da-sao went into the house. The captain looked at Lao Zhao, and his solemn face broke into a smile. 'How is it, Lao Zhao? Has everything gone smoothly with you? Judging from your looks, I'd say it has.'

Pockmark Zhao chuckled, 'Captain, you've guessed right. It's this I've come to see you about.' He looked quickly around to make sure they were alone, then leaned forward and said in a low voice, 'Thirty thousand for the one with two eyes, fifteen thousand for the one with one eye; which is the better, eh, Captain?'

'What're you talking about?'

'It's the betrothal money I mean. Captain.'

'Oh, the betrothal money. You said thirty thousand for the one with two eyes, fifteen thousand for the one with one eye?'

'Yes, yes,' Pockmark Zhao nodded with some vehemence. 'That's what I mean. I was in the south as you know, looking for someone suitable, and I met these two families that I like very much; there is this girl from one of the families, only eighteen or nineteen, not bad-looking at all, and she can read and write; it's not easy these days to find a girl like her. Her family wanted thirty thousand dollars before they would give the girl away. The girl from the other family is just over twenty, not bad-looking either; the only snag is that one of her eyes is damaged. Her family said that she got the damaged eye from playing with fire-crackers when she was small. She is a very able girl, can do heavy work as well as sew and embroider. Her family said that it's because she has a damaged eye and her looks are spoiled that they are asking for only fifteen thousand as betrothal money. I thought this over for a long, long time, you know. This family is asking for only fifteen thousand. That's a real bargain, but then the girl has only one eye. The girl from the other family is really not bad at all, but then the betrothal money is twice as much. If I marry her, it will mean spending every cent that I've saved all these years. That's a bit hard to take. I've been thinking of one girl, and then of the other, and the more I think the more mixed-up I am. I don't know what I should do. That's why I've come back to ask your advice, Captain. I hope Captain can make up my mind for me.'

'Oh, so that's the story.' The captain stroked his nose, but stopped talking as Li Da-sao came out carrying a tray.

'Come, Lao Zhao, try this bowl of almond bean-curd. It will cool you. Zhenzhi, there's sugar in it; if it's not sweet enough, you can add more.'

'Thank you, Da-sao.'

The two men took up their bowls. Li Da-sao sat down by herself.

'Lao Zhao, is it hot in the South?'

'It's hot, very hot. It's too hot even to wear singlets. It's much hotter than here. '

'How many days were you in the South?'

'Let me see.' Pockmark Zhao rolled up his eyes and began counting on his fingers. 'I left last Thursday and came back last night. One day, two days, three days . . . eight days altogether.'

'So you were around a great deal, weren't you? Found someone you like?'

'Hee, hee,' Pockmark Zhao chuckled.

'Look how happy you are. You must have found her. What's she like? Everything satisfactory? How much betrothal money did her family ask for?'

'Tai-tai,' the captain put down his bowl. 'I still have something to talk over with Lao Zhao, so could you please clear away the bowls?'

'So that's how it is,' Li Da-sao sounded displeased. 'You two want to keep me out of this, don't you? But this is exactly where I can be of help, can't you see? Zhenzhi is a man, what does he know about such things? Don't you agree with me, Lao Zhao?'

'Tai-tai!'

'All right, all right! I won't bother you, if that's what you want.' Li Da-sao snatched up the tray angrily. 'Don't forget that it was I who suggested the idea of going to the South. Now that everything has turned out well, you want to keep me out. What a way to thank people!'

As Pockmark Zhao watched Li Da-sao hurry into the house, his face assumed a look of uneasiness.

'I . . . I owe Li Da-sao an apology.'

'Don't you worry about her. She can't keep anything to herself. If she knows about this, then it won't be long before everyone else knows about it too, and that may not be what we want. We'll let her know when everything has been worked out. What's the hurry?' The captain took out his cigarette holder and inserted a 'Double Happiness'.

'Lao Zhao, I've been trying just now to analyze what you've told me, and I've come up with a few points which you might think over. As for deciding what to do, I'll leave that to you. Is that all right?'

'Sure! sure!' Pockmark Zhao nodded several times in agreement.

The captain took the lighter from the coffee table, lit his cigarette, and then handed the lighter to Pockmark Zhao.

'What do you think of this lighter and cigarette-holder? Not bad, eh? They're from Xiao-wu.'

'Oh yes, this is a really classy lighter. You have a very filial son in Xiao-wu, Captain.'

'Hm. . . .' The captain blew out a long stream of smoke, without adding any comment. After a pause, he spoke in a serious manner. 'Right, I'll go over what you've told me and what I make of it so you'll have a clearer picture of the situation.

'First . . . er, for the sake of convenience, let us call the family that asked for thirty thousand betrothal money Family A, and the other Family B. First, let's examine the question of the money. Family A asks you for thirty thousand dollars, while Family B asks you for fifteen thousand, that is, only half of what A wants. So from the point of view of the money alone, Family B is a much better bargain by far, right? So Side B—I mean, Family B—is one up on that score.

'Point two, the question of expenses. To get married, you have to take care of a number of things besides the betrothal money—decorating the bridal chamber, buying new furniture, the dinner party. These things cost quite a bit, you know. At a very conservative estimate, I would put these expenses at around twenty thousand. Oh, you would get back a decent sum in money-gifts, that's true, but don't forget, Lao Zhao, that all our friends are poor folk, and he would have to be a very close friend indeed who will come up with a gift of, say, eighty or one hundred dollars. So, even supposing you can get back fifteen thousand in money-gifts, you still need to have five or six thousand on hand. If your choice is Family A, you'll have to be prepared to spend thirty-five thousand for your marriage. Right? If your choice is Family B, then you might just scrape through with twenty thousand. It's been a hard life for you all these seven or eight years and it's not been easy to come by this kind of money. If, in order to contract this marriage, you not only spend all your money but end up brooding on a pile of debts, do you think it's worth it? So this is where Family B scores again.

'Point three, the question of the girls' looks. You said that the girl from Family A is good-looking, that the girl from Family B has a damaged eye. At first hearing this seems to indicate that Family B is not as good a bet as Family A. But think carefully. You, Lao Zhao, are a noodle-stall owner. What does a person like you want such a pretty wife for? I ask you, aren't you just inviting trouble? Take Gao Desheng, who married last year. He got himself a beautiful wife all right, a lady-marker at a billiard parlour. Everyone was green with envy at the wedding. And now, look what's happened. She's run away with some bum! Gao Desheng abandoned his restaurant to go after her in Taipei. But how is he going to get her to come back? And even if he manages to get her back, what does a woman like her know about contentment and duty? Sooner or later, she would run away again. If you marry this kind of woman, won't you be just asking for trouble?

'The girl from Family B has a damaged eye, but that is precisely what is good about her. It's a guarantee that once she's married to you, she won't have strange fancies in her head, but will stick with you through thick and thin. On top of that, she can do heavy work as well as sew and embroider; she'll be a very valuable helper. What do you need a wife who can read and write like a scholar for? So long as she can look after the family properly, bear your children, continue the line of your family and pay respects to your ancestors, you've got all you want. Doesn't that make sense?'

Pockmark Zhao was listening to this exposition with intense concentration, sitting motionless with mouth agape and eyes in a wide stare. As soon as the captain finished talking, he sprang up with alacrity and grabbed the captain's hand.

'Captain, what you've just said is so . . . so very true! Actually, I felt more or less the same way, but after you've explained everything, it's all become perfectly clear to me. I'll go to the South at once and deliver the betrothal money, just . . . just to make sure no one's gotten ahead of me. Hee, hee! Thank you, Captain. Thank you. . . .'

6

They were sitting or standing about lazily in the shade of the trees. Lao Cheng and Jumbo picked up a few small stones to keep the paper chess-board down; they were about to continue their mammoth battle of a hundred rounds. Gong Jizhong was on one side, acting as referee. Li Ming was lying on the grass with eyes closed. Xiao-Yu, seated some distance away, surveyed the distant view of the valley below. The air was heavy with silence. Occasionally, a stray breeze would set the leaves of the trees rustling gently. All of a sudden, Lao Cheng clapped his hands and burst into a triumphant crow of laughter.

'Aha! A double-rook check, you're done for!'

'Wait a minute, wait a minute.' There was a note of panic in Jumbo's voice. 'Where did that rook come from?'

'It was moved from the left flank. It's a straight game, and it's checkmate. Don't you try any tricks.'

'Rubbish! Your rook was sacrificed for my knight ages ago.'

'That was in the last game. My rook has been moving unchallenged throughout the game, very cleverly camouflaged. What sacrifice are you talking about? Checkmate, checkmate. Rooster, what's the score now?'

'Eighteen to five,' Gong Jizhong announced. 'Hey, Jumbo, do you still have the face to go on, after all this? Better get off the hook now and let me have a bash at it with Lao Cheng.'

'Can't be done. We agreed on one hundred games, so let's finish the hundred.'

'What a heel! You sit on the toilet without a single bowel movement, just so no one can use it!'

'It's all right with me,' said Lao Cheng, 'if he doesn't mind being thoroughly licked. Come on, let's set up the pieces once more.'

They became quiet again. In the silence Li Ming heard the strains of a folk song coming from the nearby woods. The tune came and went with the falling and rising of the breeze until, after some minutes, the voice of the singer trailed away into the distance, leaving behind the dull tap-tapping sound of a tree being cut down.

> Axe on wood tap-a-tapping,
> Birds in the air chirp-a-chirping,
> Out of the silence of the dark valley
> They move to the lofty trees.[16]

As Jumbo was thus chanting, he suddenly broke out, 'There! Watch my rook. Check!'

'What's the excitement? A move to the side, that will fix it.'

'A move to the side, eh? That won't help you. Check again.'

'What check?'

'With my knight of course. Have you gone blind all of a sudden?'

'No. Forward.'

'Once moved away from the palace, the king is either sick or dead.'

'No matter. "To brandish the sword one great pleasure brings: Do not fail the valiant dreams of youth"!'[17]

'Good. I'll grant your wish then. One more time, check. . . . Wait, that won't do, that won't do. I can't check like that.'

'You made a move, and that's it. A man of honour doesn't go back on his word.'

'But my hand is still on my piece!'

'You took your hand away just now. Don't make excuses. You've made your move, and that's that.'

'No, no, that won't do. A disastrous move. I can't make this check.'

'Cheat. Hey, referee!'

'Shit!' Gong Jizhong gave a big yawn. 'One point each: nineteen to six. What sort of a kiddy game do you think you guys are playing anyway? Yelling, fighting, and grabbing each other's pieces. . . . What! You dare beat the referee? Help, help!'

'We'll show you, you foreigner's lackey, you turncoat, you comprador, you running-dog!' Jumbo caught hold of one of Gong Jizhong's legs. 'Here, Lao Cheng, grab the other leg. Let's give him the treatment, let him taste his "tortoise straining to look at the moon".'

'With pleasure! Aha, Rooster, who would have known that your day would finally come?'

Gripping his legs at the ankles, they forced them backwards over his head until the feet touched the ground. Gong Jizhong was curled up like a dried shrimp, and hollering in pain. It was from some stories of the martial arts that Gong Jizhong first learnt of this form of punishment. And ever since, whenever they were in high spirits, 'tortoise straining to look at the moon' had been a favourite trick the old friends played on one another.

'Ai-ya! Ai-ya! Let me go, let me go. You're killing me.'

'All right, we'll ease up a bit. Recovering your breath now? Now, tell us, can you see the moon?'

'No, there's no moon.'

'No moon, eh? Partner, give him the works again!'

'Hold it, hold it. I can see the moon now, I really can!'

'What does it look like?'

'Round.'

'Round? Look again.'

'Crescent?'

'No. Take another peep.'

'Hold it! I can see it now. It's square, yes, it's square.'

'That's better. Okay, let's spare his dog life this time.'

The two of them released their hold. Gong Jizhong turned over and lay on the ground to catch his breath. Jumbo stood on one side looking down at him and shaking his head.

'You're slipping, Rooster. How come you give in so fast? You used to be able to stand at least five minutes.'

'Well, I'm no longer young now.' Gong Jizhong scrambled up. 'Even my joints are turning stiff. A few years from now, if we still play this game, you'll have to be ready to dig my grave.'

'Probably there's another reason,' Lao Cheng interrupted. 'You've lost your burning enthusiasm to uphold the truth.'

'Oh, well, what can I do? Even Copernicus can't face up to it, not to mention a weakling like me.' Gong Jizhong smiled. 'Come to think of it, the moon can be square, you know. That will make the poets mad with joy. Just think! Won't it be exquisite fun hunting for adjectives to describe a square moon?'

Xiao-Yu came over quickly from where he had been sitting.

'Hey, Li Ming, get up.'

'What's the matter?' Li Ming sat up.

'I have just been watching a farmer working on the hill-slope down below,' Xiao-Yu said with a note of excitement in his voice. 'You know what he did? First, he dug up the ground to about a metre deep. After that, he turned over the soil, carefully picked up the stones, which he carried to one side, and then he filled the ground up with the soil again. He worked like this all morning. Those large pieces of rock over there were dug up by him just now.'

'That's right,' Li Ming said. 'The land in these hills is dry and full of rocks. It is possible to plant trees, but grain just won't grow. You have to dig up all the rocks first, loosening up the earth, before you can start planting grain.'

'Such a clumsy way of doing things! How much soil can he turn over in one day? A few square metres. It'll take years before he's finished.'

'Look before you start criticizing. See that stretch of the slope further down covered with terrace after terrace of fields? He carved it all out by himself in that clumsy way you described just now.'

'You don't say!' Xiao-Yu stuck his tongue out in disbelief. 'He must be a truly remarkable fellow to have cleared such a vast piece of land! Like the legendary old man removing the mountain.'

'You see before you the fruit of thirty years' work. All these thirty years, he has lived in that thatched hut over there, every day digging up the rocks and carrying them away, and by sheer persistence clearing up this land for cultivation. People around here call him Kid Stone.'

'Kid Stone. A very fitting name,' Jumbo said. 'Are your folks planning on doing the same thing, Li Ming?'

'Oh, no. We're thinking of planting various types of fruit-trees. Fruit-trees will grow well in this kind of soil as the roots can develop firmly. They're no problem.'

'But what about fertilizers? How are you going to get them in?'

'Fertilizers. . . .' Li Ming scratched his head. 'I can't say, but there must be a way. I'll have to go back and find out more about that.'

'I don't understand you and your folks,' Jumbo said. 'I had the impression that you wanted to come here to start a farm. Now that you've got your land, you don't come to look after it. Won't the land go to waste like this?'

'What do you mean we don't look after the land?' Li Ming was annoyed. 'Hasn't Lao Dong been staying up here in the hills for the past two days? He's going down only today to meet my father. As for my father, he'll be here soon enough, when he's bought all the tools, seeds, and fertilizers he needs. And then they'll be living here in the hills all the time. In what way are we neglecting the land?'

'That's fine then, fine,' Jumbo said in a conciliatory tone. 'Don't be offended. I asked out of friendly concern, that's all. I feel . . . that farming is not like any other work. You can't take up farming just for fun. To be a farmer, you have to work really hard like Kid Stone, otherwise it'll be no use at all. If you go about it just for kicks you won't make it.'

'For kicks? My father's put everything he's got on this one throw; he's sold his grocery store even. Do you call this kicks?'

'No, of course not. I apologize for saying that, all right?'

'Li Ming,' Xiao-Yu said. 'I am very much with you for coming to these hills to start a farm. There's no doubt in my mind that we are rooted in the earth. If we are away from the soil, it is impossible for us to take roots. Modern man's constant feelings of loss, frustration, and anguish can, I think, be traced to his alienation from the soil.'

'That's the way my father feels. . . . Of course, he can't put it the way you do, but he has lived those experiences of confusion and rootlessness that you're referring to; that's exactly the way he feels.'

'I can believe that Li Ming's old man feels like that,' Gong Jizhong interrupted. 'But I don't believe that Xiao-Yu can feel like that. It is true that Xiao-Yu has dwelled long enough in his ivory tower, and he has read widely in philosophy. But does he have genuine feelings for the earth as he puts it? I don't believe he does.'

'You shouldn't doubt my sincerity. My feelings are genuine. Heaven is my witness.'

'If you really feel like that about the land, then why do you have to go abroad?'

'You think I want to go that much?' Xiao-Yu said. 'Then you've got me wrong. Of course, if I said that I don't want to go abroad at all, I wouldn't be honest with myself. All my friends have gone one after the other; you can't expect me to be different. Universities abroad are better equipped, have better facilities, and offer a healthier research environment. It wouldn't be true to say that I am not attracted at all. But if it is possible for me to remain here to do research, then I will absolutely not leave.'

'There is a graduate programme in your department. Why don't you study there?'

'It's not good enough.'

'So what are we talking about?' Gong Jizhong smiled. 'We've been talking nonsense all this time.'

'That's not true.' Xiao-Yu 's face flushed. 'When I have completed my studies, I will come back to help reorganize our graduate programme so that young people in the future can stay here for advanced studies without having to go through what I have to go through, far away from home.'

'Bravo! Everybody, get this. Xiao-Yu has signed a post-dated check. Let's see if it does cash twenty years from now.'

'That's enough. Let's stop this squabbling. Anyone who says another word will meet immediate execution!' Lao Cheng barked. 'Let's go back and have some lunch. In the afternoon, we can go to the creek for a dip; we need to stretch ourselves a bit.'

After a meal of fried noodles, they went down the hill in a group. Half way down the slope, they passed a pavilion in which were seated several strongly-built men sipping tea. Along the narrow lane outside the pavilion, a few wooden carts were lined up, each loaded with several large tree-trunks.

'Look at that!' Xiao-Yu stuck his tongue out again. 'Can you imagine the momentum of these vehicles moving down-hill with that huge load on them? What a time these poor men must have with those carts!'

'They work in the timber yard back there. Every day they have to travel up and down six or seven times and each round trip means five or six kilometres over hilly ground.'

'My! My! If I were to do it, I could at most manage a single trip.'

'Don't make me laugh,' Gong Jizhong put in. 'If you could manage to make a single trip with a load like that, Xiao-Yu, I'd drink up all the water in the creek.'

'Ah, yes, the aborigines in this area have a legend which tells of how a Frog Spirit once drank up all the water of the creek. In the end the aborigines became so thirsty they couldn't bear it any longer. So they sent their bravest man to kill the Frog Spirit. After the Frog Spirit was killed, his body lay as that hill facing us.'

They all looked up, and sure enough the hill they saw was roughly shaped like a frog.

'Phew! I take back my words. It would be no fun to be killed and changed into Mount Rooster.'

'You?' Lao Cheng teased. 'You'd be changed into a heap of mud at most. And as a gesture of our long-standing friendship, we'd formally name it the Fallen Phoenix Mound, offer libations and sacrificial notes.'

They reached the foot of the hill and continued on their way past a small paddy field, then across the pebble-strewn floor of a semi-parched river-bed until they came to a small beach, a sandy stretch formed by the curve that the creek made at this point in its course. They changed into swimming trunks and jumped into the creek. The water swirled in eddies around them. Li Ming let himself be carried by the current across to the other side of the creek. He lifted his head and saw a truck far off crawling on its way, like a ladybug, along the ribbon of road stitched around the waist of the mountain facing him. Looking up from the bottom of the valley, he saw the mountains rising to a more breathtaking height and the thick green underbrush seemed to extend to the very edge of the sky to merge with the azure blue of the heavens. He lay down on a sun-baked slab of stone, watched through narrowed eyes the drifting clouds, and listened to the rhythmic sound of running waters beside him. On the opposite shore, Jumbo could be heard softly chanting Li Bai's 'Early Departure from Baidi City':

> I left Baidi in the morning swathed in the coloured mists of dawn,
> Reaching Jiangling in but one day, journey of a thousand miles.
> On the two shores of the waterway gibbons cried ceaselessly,
> My boat sailed swiftly through the folds of ten thousand hills.

Li Ming closed his eyes. He felt happy.

7

As he stepped out of the station, a blast of yellow dust hit Li Ming in the face so that he had to shut his eyes tight. With knapsack on his back, and his shoulder turned against the wind, he waited till the dust and sand had blown over before he dared open them. Then he walked slowly towards the banyan tree in front of the station. The hot air came in waves. A thick layer of yellow dust had settled on the glass cupboards in the food-and-drink shops that lined both sides of the road. Flies remained glued to the glass without the least sign of movement, and one could just make out a few dim shapes inside the shops huddled up in the shadows. Two pedicabs were standing at the foot of the banyan tree. A man lay stretched across one of the pedicabs, snoring heavily, his shoulders bare, and a cap thrown over his face. The other driver was nowhere to be seen. Li Ming walked over to the occupied vehicle, put his knapsack down on the ground beside it and wiped the grimy sweat from his face.

'Hey, friend, mind taking me to Dongda New Village?'

Bare Shoulders stirred, then lifted his cap from his eyes and gave Li Ming a sidelong glance. Just as Li Ming was thinking that the face looked familiar, Bare Shoulders jumped up smiling.

'Xiao-wu! What brings you here at this time?'

'Lao Dong, it's you!' He cried in delight and shook the other man's hand vigorously. 'What a surprise. I thought you were with Father at the farm. How come you are back here pedalling?'

'Oh, I . . . a friend of mine had to go to Magong, so I offered to stand in for him for a couple of days, to earn a few extra dollars. Why are you here all of a sudden? You should have dropped us a line to let us know beforehand.'

'I decided to come back quite suddenly. Our ship was in Japan for some major repairs and we were supposed to be stuck there for a fortnight. Luckily our shipmate's banana boat was about to leave for Taiwan, so I got a passage from him. I landed at Kaohsiung and came up north by train the same night. That's why I didn't have time to write.'

'This will be a very happy surprise for Captain and Da-sao. No one expects you to be back so soon.'

'How are they?'

'Fine, they are fine. Let me take you to your place.'

So saying, Lao Dong picked up the knapsack and placed it in the pedicab. Li Ming jumped in. Lao Dong gave the brake-shaft a push and began to pedal along the only asphalt road in the small town. The surface of the road was as uneven as ever, and the pedicab staggered from side to side as it went rattling over the potholes and battled with the occasional gusts of sand-laden wind. Sometimes Lao Dong had to stand up on the pedals and push with all his strength, making the muscles on his tanned calves stand out like whip-cord.

'What a terrible wind. It's been such a long time since I've been through anything like this. Can't say I'm used to it!'

'You said it. Driving a pedicab for the last two days has been torture. Every day you finish up with hair and face caked with dust or mud. It's no bloody fun, I tell you!'

'Weren't you happy helping my father with the farm, Lao Dong? Why take on all this trouble?'

Just then, they reached a bad stretch of road, so Lao Dong pedalled over it standing up. When the vehicle had steadied, he sat down again.

'Well, Xiao-wu, to be very frank with you, Captain's farm has folded already.'

'What! Folded? Father did write to tell me that the yield was poor, but he didn't mention anything about folding.'

'It's folded. We didn't have the experience, and we didn't have enough help. Every time we had to do the picking, we couldn't finish the job, and of what we did manage to pick, half would have rotted before we were finished with the packing. This is for the kumquats. As for the tea, it was worse. We had to pay hired hands to help with the picking, and even then it was hopeless. The tea too, was of low quality and didn't fetch much in the market. We never made any profit. It was loss all the way. When I saw what was happening, I said to myself, well, this can't go on like this, I can't go on dining off Captain's table and living off his pocket. That's how you find me here, pedalling for a living again.'

'Where's Father now? Is he still on the hill?'

'No. He's moved down and has opened a grocery store. This time we were really lucky to have a friend like Pockmark Zhao. He lent us his savings so Captain could have the capital to open his store and I the money to pay for the deposit for my pedicab. It is in times like this that you know who your friends really are. None of my meat-and-wine friends would lend us a cent, only Pockmark Zhao came up with help.'

'And the land? Is it still ours?'

'No. It's sold, and a good thing it was. Captain didn't lose much, and the money he got was enough to pay off his debts and to take out a lease on the grocery store.'

'Who did he sell the land to?'

'To Kid Stone, the fellow on the other side of the hill who spends the whole day, from morning till night, turning up the soil. . . .'

'Yes, I know who you mean.'

Lao Dong gave the brake-shaft a pull as the pedicab negotiated a curve. They were now on a mud track.

'Xiao-wu, when you see Captain in a moment, please try your best not to ask too many questions. If he brings up the subject, just ask a couple of questions as a matter of course. As a result of this business he's been in very low spirits lately.'

'I know. Thank you, Lao Dong. I'm so sorry we brought you to this state, with all your money gone. . . .'

'Don't say that! I had a pedicab before, and I still have one now! Even if I did lose a bit, what is money after all but a paper game? I didn't have any with me when I came into the world, I can do without any when I leave it, so you can see, it's no great matter to cry over. When Captain asked me to go with him, he was in fact giving me the break of my life; it's I who couldn't thank him enough for his concern. The farm failed, it's true, but it's just our rotten luck that we got this damned piece of rock-land. Otherwise, who knows, we might have hit it rich by now.'

The vehicle came to a stop in front of the bamboo hedge of the house. Li Ming jumped down from his seat. Lao Dong was already pushing open the wooden door and shouting into the house.

'Da-sao, Xiao-wu is back!'

In a moment, Li Da-sao had hurried out, her hands still white with flour. After Li Ming's filial greetings, Li Da-sao held on to his arm, her eyes brimming and lips trembling until she suddenly burst into tears.

'You are thinner, Xiao-wu,' she said between her sobs. 'Did you have a hard time at sea?'

'You are imagining things. Every time I'm back, you say I'm thinner. But I've put on more muscle each time.'

'Who says Xiao-wu is thin!' Lao Dong added. 'He's darker, yes, but that makes him look ever tougher.'

'Where's Father?'

'He's at the shop, not very far from here. Xiao-wu, your father and I didn't manage to write you in time. Our land. . . .'

'Lao Dong told me about it already. You don't have to say anything, Mother.'

'Ai!' Tears began streaming down her face again. 'On account of this, your father has aged by the day, and more of his hair has turned white. It's all for nothing in the end. If he had listened to me at the start, then things wouldn't have ended up like this. Your father thought my opinions were only a woman's scruples. Actually, a farmer's life is not a steady kind of life. I saw that from the start.'

'Mother, let's not cry over this any more. Things didn't turn out too badly really, and we didn't lose that much. Though the money is gone, the good thing is that Father no longer has to wear his heart out over his piece of rocky land.'

'Xiao-wu is right,' put in Lao Dong. 'I'll have to go and make a couple of runs more, Da-sao. You two have a good talk.'

'Thank you for driving Xiao-wu here. You will come for dinner tonight, won't you? And, yes, since you people must have something to drink, can you bring back some cold snacks on your way here?'

'That's no trouble. No, don't worry about getting the money now, Da-sao, we'll settle that later. See you in a while, Xiao-wu!'

Li Ming went to the bathroom at the back of the house and turned on the tap: there wasn't a drop of water. He shrugged his shoulders, then took up a scoop and filled the wash-basin up to the brim with water from the bucket. Li Da-sao came in softly.

'There's been a drought for the past few days and the Water Department has started rationing.'

'Oh.' Li Ming jerked down his own towel from the rack. 'I haven't seen Little Sister around. Is she out playing?'

'She ran off to take part in some cavalry-fighting practice or other. She'll be gone for a few days.'

'That imp. Aren't you worried?'

'What can we do? She's so excited about it. She just won't listen to anyone.'

'Has Fourth Sister been back?'

'She was here last month. Your brother-in-law got a raise and promotion. They were very happy. Xiao-wu, there's still some dirt at the back of your ears. Come, let me clean it for you.'

'It's all right.' Li Ming wrung the towel dry. 'Have any of my friends been here?'

'Gong Jizhong and Xiang Siyi were here. There were probably others, but I don't remember their names. Gong and Xiang seem to be doing all right. They got together and started a tutorial class and now have quite a few students. Would you like to ask them over for dinner?'

'Not today, Mother. I don't feel too well. I'd like to have a rest.'

'The long journey's probably got you down. Do take a nap. I'll go get you a packet of *wufen* pills. You can take them with water. '

When Li Ming opened his eyes, the dizzy feeling was still there. It was dark already, and Li Da-sao came to ask him if he wanted to eat yet. He shook his head, then turned over and lay there, facing inside. Li Da-sao tiptoed out. He could hear his father's voice outside.

'. . . Let him sleep some more. Came all the way like that, he should sleep some more. Tai-tai, you go ahead and save some food for Xiao-wu.' He spoke with a thick drawl; he had probably had more than one or two swigs from the wine jug.

'Captain,' it was Lao Dong's voice. 'Don't take what happened between us and Wang Fulai last night too much to heart. He came to ask us to help him out with money. Naturally, as things look—you were, after all, his superior officer, and I a comrade-in-arms—we should give him whatever little help we can. But he came at the wrong time. We're just like the clay-molded Bodhisattva who couldn't even keep his own hands from falling apart in the torrent, so how could he expect us to lend him a hand? And it's not that he didn't know about your farm. He did, and yet he came to borrow money. That's not what I would call tactful. We did our best to help him, everything that is humanly possible. If he is still not satisfied, and wants to speak ill of you, then it is he who is in the wrong. I wouldn't trouble myself over him if I were you, Captain.'

'Ai . . . How can I hold any grudge against Wang Fulai? We've been like brothers all these years! That year our unit was cut off in Xuzhou and I was lying there wounded, he picked me up and carried me on his back for seventy, eighty miles, that's how I managed to get out alive. So, when all is said, I owe him my life. Now he needs help because his wife is going to have a baby and they have to move. If he can't depend on me at a time like this, who can he depend on? Ai . . . it's my cursed luck that things turn out this way. If our farm had been a success, or if the idea had never occurred to me in the first place, then we wouldn't have ended up like this now, and we wouldn't have soured our friendship over this matter of a mere thousand dollars.'

'Actually, the way I see it, Wang Fulai has no one to blame but himself. What does he want to move his family for? Why does he have to go to the south in order to open a shop? Isn't it all on account of his wife? At the very start, when he wanted to marry that woman, we told him what it would be like. Even if a woman of her profession could turn over a new leaf and stop monkeying around with men, marrying her kind would only invite ridicule, disrespect. Wang Fulai was very close to her at that time of course, so he wouldn't listen to anything we said.'

'I wouldn't blame Wang Fulai entirely. A woman who paid for her freedom from her own money in order to marry her man obviously wanted to make something better of her life. If people had talked less and let them live their life in peace, there wouldn't have been so much trouble. After all, from ancient times to the present, stories of prostitutes returning to an honourable way of life are not uncommon.'

'But Captain, just think. It's not as if she'd been plying her trade in Taoyuan for a day or two only. And the people who knew her, they're not just one or two either. So how do you expect everyone to keep his mouth shut? Whenever people began whispering, Wang Fulai would roll up his sleeves and threaten to beat them up. But the more you threaten, the more people will talk, and things can only get worse that way. And in the end, what happened? Even friends who'd known him for a long time refused to have anything more to do with him. I don't see how the two of them can go on living together in Taoyuan like this.'

'Wang Fulai has always been a hot-head. He was already like that when he was serving in my unit, and would talk back whenever I gave him orders. Now it looks as if he's become even more short-tempered. He came to see me last night and blew his top before we'd even managed to say two words to each other. Just imagine, if I really had the money, how could I not have let him have it? But since I didn't have the money, we could have at least talked things over. But no, he turned around at once and stormed out. I didn't have a chance to say another word.'

'It was the same thing at my place. He came barging in as if I'd owed him these hundred years the money he asked for. People don't usually go about borrowing money like that! Anyway, I turned over to him everything I had on me and I said, believe it or not, this is all I possess apart from this pedicab and the blanket. If you take it, you'll be doing me an honour, if you don't take it, I can't do anything more. He almost burst out crying, I tell you, and said that only Pockmark Zhao and I were real friends. So I said to him, you went to Captain's place demanding such an impossible sum. How do you expect him to promise you anything? And when he took a little time to answer, you flared up. Who is being a lousy friend? He didn't have anything to say and refused to stay a moment longer; he left that very night.'

'Ai . . . So money is driving him out of his mind too. Even heroes can be unmanned by a piece of silver! We've been through that all right. . . .' Bang! The captain struck the table with his fist. 'Shit! All my life I've worked hard, I've suffered, but not one lucky dollar came my way. Then after great difficulties we finally got a piece of land, but the bloody land turned out to be lined with rock. What rotten luck! Here, drink this, let's drink up!'

'Cap . . . Captain.' Lao Dong spoke with a heavy slur. 'I'll be frank with you. When the farm went broke and I moved down from the hill, a lot of things suddenly became clear to me. We are like, you know what, like the monkey who's learnt to play a lot of tricks. You teach the little monkey a trick and he won't take a minute to pick it up. He plays his tricks all his life, you can bet on that, but when you try to teach the old monkey—that's what he's become—a new bag of tricks, he can't, he just can't learn any more!'

'We're old, that's what we are, old.'

'Captain, I've fought in countless battles, died countless deaths, what have I not lived through? That I've managed to keep my skin is a miracle already. I should be thankful for that alone. I do not wish for anything more now, except to pay a visit to my ancestral home, to sweep my old man's grave just once before I die. Oh, if I can do that, I'll have lived a full life. I'll have lived without regrets.

'Captain, come to think of it, there's a lot of sense in what my father said. Supposing I had begun at twenty, and every year doubled the number of coins I had, I would have become rich by now instead of pushing a pedicab for a living here. Just try counting, the first year two coins, the second year four coins, the third year eight, the fourth year sixteen. . . .'

Li Ming couldn't bring himself to listen any more. He pulled the pillow tight over his ears. Tomorrow, he thought, tomorrow he must leave, come what may. He would not stay here. He would rather drift with the tides to the end of the world, and let loneliness and memories erode his heart away. . . .

8

'Your letters, San-fu.[18] The Company's forwarded them here.'

'Thank you.' As many as three. Who can they be from? He made out Zhou Mei's hand at a glance, deliberated for a moment, then put it to one side. He opened a large envelope first and took out a red card, a wedding invitation. So Lao Cheng is finally getting married. Who would have expected it? He looked at the date. It was a few days too late already. What a pity. It would have been fun to tease the bride or let Lao Cheng have a last taste of 'tortoise straining to look at the moon' on his wedding night. There was nothing much he could do now, except send Lao Cheng a belated present.

The remaining letter was an aerogramme, addressed in English. Li Ming looked at it for a long time, then it suddenly struck him that it must be from Xiao-Yu. He looked at the sender's address; it bore a post office box number of the California Institute of Technology. So dreamer-boy had finally made it and managed to get into one of the top schools in the world. He opened the letter. Yes, the tidy, printed appearance of the script had the unmistakable hallmark of Xiao-Yu's hand.

Li Ming,
You haven't expected to receive my letter, I am sure. I got the address of the shipping company you work for from Jumbo only

recently. Jumbo told me that your ship plies between the US and Japan and that you make a round trip every few months. If that is the case, you are bound to call at Los Angeles one of these days, and when that happens, I hope you will be able to come and see me. Just imagine, miles from home in a strange land, and able to have a heart-to-heart chat with an old friend. It will be just great.

It's been almost two semesters since I transferred here from a small college in the Midwest. Life during the first semester was simply hectic. I had to work at a feverish pace, under enormous pressure from the professors and almost overwhelmed by the avalanche of course work and assignments. Needless to say, the standard of the students here is high, so that in this respect the small college I came from is in a different league altogether. At the beginning, I felt I simply couldn't stand the strain, but now gradually I am getting used to life here.

The most dispiriting enemy that a foreign student faces here is loneliness. I am lucky enough to have a fellowship, which takes care of all my living expenses, so I am spared the grief of having to work in a restaurant to support myself. But loneliness is one thing I can't get away from. Usually I am busy with my work, and I don't feel it that much. But on Sundays and other holidays in particular, as I see my American friends rush out to their various activities, while I have nothing to do but pace between the four walls of my room, the feeling of loneliness becomes so unbearable that I have to force myself to go out, to find someone to pass the time with, or to join one of those God-knows-what parties. I used to think that these meaningless activities were a waste of time. Not any more. Now I am beginning to get used to them. Fear of loneliness is one factor that accounts for my change of attitude. Attraction towards the opposite sex is another. So it seems that man has not only his psychological needs but also his physiological needs to satisfy sooner or later. And as one gets older, one can only feel the more acutely the animal aspects of human nature.

In the past I considered reminiscence a sin, excusable only among the old for whom there is little hope of an active future. But lately I've found myself quite often lost in recollection, especially of my high school days with my old chums in the small town, in play or study. Those days were the happiest moments of my life. Do you still remember the weekend we spent at your place in the hills just before I left—you, Jumbo, Rooster, Lao Cheng, and myself? We didn't have anything planned for those few days, but we did have tremendous fun, with our dips in the rivers, our games of chess, our bantering, and, of course, our 'tortoise straining to look at the moon'! But, ha, how happy those days were in my memories! Since my arrival here, I have had my fair share of country hikes, long distance excursions, picnics. On every such occasion, nothing is left to chance; everything is planned in meticulous detail by the selfless organizers: the programme of activities has to be varied and inexhaustible, the food has to be rich and plentiful, the sexes have to be balanced in number . . . in a word, whatever is humanly possible is done to make the day a smashing success. But I have no relish for these mechanized picnics of a motorcar culture. Perhaps when we entertained ourselves, we did so spontaneously without forethought, that's why we were able to enjoy ourselves. But this other kind of entertainment is different, it is carefully programmed, that's why the fun is drained out of it.

How are you and your family faring with your land? Have the harvests been good? I really envy you for owning such a large tract of land. During the two years I've been here, I don't believe I have heard a cock crow once. American chickens, you see, are bred and reared under artificial light. From the time they hatch to the time they're dispatched—a matter of two to three weeks—they never see the sun. There is no better symbolization of America's modern technological civilization than these machine-cultured chickens. What is America, after all? It is an assemblage of mass-produced cars, artificially bred chickens, and some millions of miles of super-highways. How can people take root in such a place? Just think. How can a life spent locked up in a car, whirling the whole day along super-highways—how can such a life be rooted? To grow roots, to free yourself from the sense of estrangement and loss, you must live close to the earth.

When Li Ming finished reading the letter, he smiled in spite of himself. Xiao-Yu is Xiao-Yu after all, still surveying the world from his ivory tower. 'To grow roots', 'estrangement and loss', 'modern technological civilization'—so he still clings to his formulas. Perhaps it's time to shake him up a bit? Li Ming took out pen and paper and began scribbling:

> *Xiao-Yu, I am very happy to have received your letter. Unfortunately, I have this piece of bad news for you. We have sold our land already, to Kid Stone. The land can belong only to people like him. For people like us, a life of wandering and 'estrangement' is our lot, we are not worthy to inherit the earth.*

At this point, Li Ming put down his pen and glanced over what he had written. All at once the thought struck him—what is the point, what am I doing this for? Xiao-Yu dreams his dreams. Well, he is luckier than most of us then. Why must I go and shatter his visions for him? Would the world be a better place if everybody turned into a Xiao-Yu? Li Ming's face broke into a smile.

He opened the porthole, rolled the unfinished letter into a ball and threw it into the sea. Then he opened Zhou Mei's letter.

1967

NOTES

1. A nickname, presumably given long before, in Kid Stone's younger days.
2. Literally, Lao-da, Lao-er, and Lao-san denote respectively the first, second, and third oldest of the siblings in a family; here used as alternate proper names.
3. Name of the third brother, Lao-san.
4. *Lao* literally means 'old'; often used in conjunction with a surname in reference to a male person, indicating friendliness or mild affection.
5. Literally, the wife of one's eldest brother; often used as a polite form of direct address for, or reference to, a friend's wife.
6. An allusion is made to lines in a work by the compassionate and well-known poet Du Fu (AD 217–770).
7. The poet Tao Yuanming (AD 365–427), referring to the meaningless and unfulfilling life of a government official, once remarked that he was stooping for the meagre civil service salary of five pecks of rice.
8. Idiomatic expression referring to the position of a prime minister.
9. Chung-hsing University.
10. The two names mean, respectively, 'one year of gold' and 'the first year of the Golden reign'. Li Ming is teasing Jin Zhaonian, whose name denotes 'one million years of gold'. The names of his two brothers are Jin Yinian, meaning

'hundred million years of gold', and Jin Wannian, meaning 'ten thousand years of gold'. The Chinese characters for 'one' [yi 一] and 'hundred million' [yi 億] are homonyms.

11 Gong Jizhong feigns mistaking Li Ming to have said 'jin' [gold]; hence the joke 'Jin Jinnian, Yin Yinnian' literally means 'gold-gold-years, silver-silver-years'.

12 Short for 'Guoli *Zheng*zhi *Da*xue' National Zhengzhi [Cheng-chi] University.

13 *Xiucai* as used in this context is one type of traditional Chinese scholar.

14 Literally, 'Little Fifth', the fifth of the siblings in a family. It is an affectionate or familial form of address, referring here to Li Ming.

15 Form of direct address for one's wife.

16 From the *Book of Songs*.

17 The quotation is from a poem written by the political figure Wang Jingwei (1883–1944). The complete text, as translated by Anthony C. Yu is:

With ardor I sang through markets of Yen [yan];
Calmly I became the captive of Ts'u [Chu].
To brandish the sword one great pleasure brings:
Do not fail the valiant dreams of youth.

18 Third mate; direct address by the title is polite and established practice.

24

Ximi in the Metropolis

By **CHANG TA-CHUN**

Translated by Edith S. Y. Wong and Kwok-kan Tam, with Hardy C. Wilcoxon

Chang Ta-chun 張大春 (Zhang Dachun, b. 1957) comes from a family originating from Shandong, China. He received an MA in Chinese from Catholic Fu Jen University, Taiwan, in 1983, and is currently a lecturer in Chinese at Catholic Fu Jen University. He is a prolific writer, and his publications include collections of short stories, such as Portraits of Chicken Feathers *(*Jiling tu 雞翎圖*, 1980),* Selected Works by Zhang Dachun *(*Zhang Dachun zixuanji 張大春自選集*, 1981),* Apartment Tour Guide *(*Gongyu daoyou 公寓導遊*, 1986),* Axis of Time *(*Shijian zhou 時間軸*, 1986),* Sixi Worrying About the Country *(*Sixi youguo 四喜憂國*, 1988),* The Great Liars *(*Da shuohuangjia 大說謊家*, 1989), and* The Weekly Diary of Young Big-Head Chun *(*Shaonian datou Chun shenghuo zhouji 少年大頭春生活周記*, 1992). His works are popular among Chinese readers in Taiwan and overseas. He has been awarded the first prize for short stories and science fiction from both the* China Times *(*Zhongguo shibao 中國時報*) and* United Daily News *(*Lianhe bao 聯合報*) in Taiwan. He is regarded as one of the most talented young writers to deal with a variety of subjects that capture the satiric aspects of contemporary Taiwan society.*

Ximi walked out of the office building and looked around carefully for a moment. Then, as usual, he walked 500 feet towards the east along the mounted compressed air train rail. The rail reflected the sunset over him like a rainbow embroidered in gold. At the same time every day, he would raise his left hand, pretending he could touch the rainbow above him, and sing the song 'I love the Metropolis' while he was finishing the 500-foot walk. Then he would step in front of the telecommunicator and briskly say to the device, 'Composite man Ximi reports. Request to return to the dormitory. Everything follows the rules. I love the Metropolis.' Then he would walk 1000 feet towards the south where a regular carriage would transport him back to the dormitory along Highway No. 8.

But today was different. He forgot to sing. He forgot to raise his hand and pretend he could touch the golden rainbow. There was a little problem with his whole thinking system. He had remembered something he should not have remembered. But once that event had happened, he could not forget it. The worst thing was: he was afraid the symbols stored in his memory could be scanned by the surrounding electronic detective system. That would be disastrous. Ximi could not but stop walking. He looked up and saw a compressed air train pass by above the golden rainbow. The faces of the natural men's children in the compartment vanished in an instant. That was the school bus of the Eastern Kindergarten of the Education Headquarters. The kids were on their way back to the Western residential city. It was said that natural men were divided into families as their units. Each family consisted of two ranks. The parent rank supervised the children rank and the ranks would rotate every twenty years. When the children rank became the parent rank, the previous supervisors would give up their families and move to the satellite to 'undergo learning and leadership for the new rank'.

Ximi could not make sense of the what seemed the overly complex social system of these natural men and their thousands of terms, such as 'structure', 'occupational division', 'division of population', or 'information system'. His batch of composite men was manufactured for ten years and yet so far he had only seen one natural man, known as 'Supervisor', who had taken good care of this batch of composite men assigned to work in this tax unit. After the routine photo ceremony every morning, he said, 'Aye, very good, everything follows the rules. The Metropolis loves you.' He would often add after this polite remark, 'Your team of comrades had the best components. Remember, a new batch must be superior to the previous one. Only in this way can the Metropolis have a bright future. This is the progress of the "total man". The natural men are proud of your contributions; and you should also be proud of the contributions from natural men. Now let's take a photo to preserve the glory of today!' Usually, they would follow the previous practices in the manufacturing and training factory. Immediately after the word 'glory', they would turn to the east with their faces towards the sun, raise their left fists, and show their white teeth. Then, 'kacha', the huge camera at the central square of the office building would preserve the precious memory of today. Of course, each composite man would receive a copy of this photo before the end of the working day. They would type out what they had learnt during the day into their personal mini-computer and print it on the back of this photo.

Ximi touched the plastic bag that contained the photo in his pocket. He was worried that after he returned to the dormitory today, his writing would be interrupted. Should he honestly record this event into his diary as he had done in the past? If he did so, would the comrades in the Auditors' Division record a fault in his record? Maybe this was not only a fault. Usually 'knowing what you should not know' could be minor or serious. If his fault was considered serious, three faults or one mistake would be recorded and this would mean the end to his 'glory record' for this month. If his fault was considered to be still more serious, if he was accused of crimes like 'storing confidential events', or 'communicating confidential events', which would cost him two mistakes up to two blemishes, then the 'glory record' for the past year would be erased. The worst thing was: Ximi became conscious of fear for the future. This was beyond two blemishes and reached the degree of two big mistakes. The 'Supervisor' once said, 'Composite men have a precious future forever. This is because you have a glorious past and a glorious present. You must not investigate the future, doubt the future, nor fear the future. The existence of the future Metropolis depends on your concentrated efforts today. Everything follows the rules. The Metropolis loves you.' Ximi nodded eagerly while listening to this speech and remembered it by heart. The first thing he did after returning to the dormitory was to write down this speech on the back of the photo. As there was not a single fault in his writing, he even received a bonus as a reward.

But if he did not record that event into his writing, this might constitute the crime of 'hiding the truth' or 'cheating the comrades'. Then at least two blemishes would be recorded. Ximi shook his head and when he lifted his head again, the sun had already disappeared behind his back. The compressed air train rail turned into charcoal, which looked like a quake in the sky.

He quickened his steps and ran towards the electronic communicator, shouting, 'Composite man Ximi reports. Request to return to the dormitory. Everything follows the rules. I love the Metropolis.'

Ximi did not attach much importance to the fact that he had missed the carriage and returned to the dormitory late. He recorded this event in the computer and expressed his sincere regret. 'This should be the last paragraph. But how should I record the events that happened beforehand?' Mumbling to himself, Ximi did not forget to turn off the input button of the computer. He sighed deeply and lay back with a thrust. He liked lying down in this way, where the back of the seat was at an appropriate level. Many composite men envied Ximi's chair. Ximi used up 1.5 bonus in exchange for this multi-purpose chair, which could be used as a bed, a bathtub, a toilet, or a cradle. The design of the cradle, in particular, was extravagant. Every time the composite men mentioned this chair, they would say, 'We heard that natural men slept in this thing when they were small children.' Then everyone would shake their heads and laugh. Sometimes Ximi would imagine himself to be a tiny baby of natural men. He squatted in the cradle, closed his eyes, and let the rhythm of the music, which matched the tempo of the movement, bring him to a place where he had never been before. He imagined that place to be a honeycomb-shaped bedroom in the manufacturing factory and a large group of natural children in the compressed air train would protrude their heads from the honeycomb, and sing 'I love the Metropolis' with Ximi—

I love the Metropolis, I love the Metropolis!
I love new life, I love all mankind!
Everything requires discipline; everything follows the rules.
Everything in pursuit of perfection; everything is in order.
Natural men, composite men, all belong to one family.
Make efforts to concentrate; be sincere, be single-hearted.
Don't ask about the past; don't fear for the future.
Seize the era of the total man. Glory is now!

Every time when he sang up to this line, Ximi felt very excited and he wanted to defecate. Then he pressed a button and the cradle would transform itself into a toilet. At the same time, Ximi would open up his eyes and watch the pose of a natural child squatting in the cradle from the mirror of the computer screen.

But today Ximi obviously was not in the mood to play with the cradle. He simply lay down on the bed quietly and tried hard to make himself feel safe and peaceful. The dormitory was the only place without the installation of the electronic detective system. As long as he turned off the computer, he could reflect without worry on his faults, mistakes, and crimes. The 'Supervisor' had warned him before, 'New life is far more advanced than the past. You can now enjoy more privacy—ah, sorry, this word is too dirty; I mean, enjoy more freedom. Haven't you noticed that all the detective systems in the dormitory have been demolished? Remember, this is the glory of the modernization of the Metropolis! Each comrade of composite men should set a high standard for himself and always reflect about himself. For the sake of the peace and discipline of all mankind in the Metropolis, each comrade should treasure this freedom and take the initiative to devote his heart to this era. Don't hide and don't fear. Everything follows the rules. The Metropolis loves you.'

Yes, yes, Ximi thought. He stared at the hexagonal roof in his bedroom, which was far more spacious than the dormitory in the manufacturing and training factory. He could make love with TV stars through telecommunications any time he liked. He could mix the protein from his dinner leftovers and the vegetable pill from his breakfast, add alcohol to produce a swooning and anaesthetic ecstasy. The most important thing was that he could think freely about the rules he had broken that day. Most of the time, after he had thought about it freely, he would still be honest to the computer. As long as that event did not constitute a serious fault or mistake, Ximi found it relaxing to record all those events on the back of the photo.

Two years ago, for instance, there was a little problem with his television. While he was watching the midnight show, the antenna received the TV programmes of the natural men and a shadowy image of a naked woman appeared on the screen on the wall. Jumping up from the toilet, Ximi tensed up immediately. He secretly turned off the communication button of the computer to avoid the whole process being imported into the data filing system of the main frame. Then he returned to the toilet, turned it into a bed and pressed the button of the telecommunication lovemaking game. That was an amazing experience. Ximi recalled the experience of doing that thing with a natural woman. Although the image of the natural woman received through the stimulation of the brain waves was only a shadowy grey image, Ximi remained sleepless all through the night. As a result, he had mixed up a tax return the next day—he deducted a composite single man's tax allowance from the entertainment allowance of a natural man's wife. Eventually he recorded the cause and effect of the whole mistake into his record but surprisingly, he did not get one single weakness. The comments from the Audit Division were: 'The logic of self-reflection was sound. The event was contributory to the exploration of the potential sex crisis of the comrades of composite men. The Metropolis loves you.'

In the next two years, although Ximi intentionally failed to repair the visionary network, he had never seen the grey image of that natural woman. Sometimes the television channels would switch but the programmes received were mostly the educational programmes produced by the Metropolis. Ximi did not have any motivation to watch these programmes, as he would never be a natural man over the golden rainbow. The education of a composite man is incessantly conducted through his job. His educational goal is 'the pursuit of glory'. If he can attain sufficient 'glory records' within a specified period of time, maybe he could be approved to select a pretty, tender, and young TV star to be his companion. In this way he could immediately apply for a larger dormitory and achieve more bonuses with his companion in order to exchange them for a larger chair with more features and purposes. At that time he could ask his companion, who worked in the TV station and enjoyed a broader exposure to life, if the babies of the natural men had the same pose as the composite men when they were squatting in the cradle. How long would this intellectual question keep on torturing him?

Ximi returned to reality from his fantasy. The same question still hung on between his eyes and the hexagonal roof: should he be honest about what had happened today?

That was a pink tax return for March, with the signature printed 'R. No. 7321'. This was a composite comrade working in the Research Department in the Northern Industrial Headquarters. Ximi often liked to imagine the comrade's look and lifestyle from the colour and serial number of the tax return. This gave him great enjoyment in his simple and routine working life. If it so happened that the memory bank of the other side emitted certain waves at the same time, say, for instance, that man thought about completing the tax return while Ximi was processing it, then Ximi would feel elated as if he had incidentally lifted his head and found a natural man sitting in the compressed air train saying 'hello' to him. It was as if he could read the image of the comrade's room or his expression while the comrade was filling in the tax return.

Originally this kind of rare event was strictly prohibited in the old life. But the era of the Metropolis had progressed. In the new society of the 'total man', academia had once again promoted the 'possibilities and restrictions of the communication among composite men' through the public media. According to these experts in the theory of Metropolitan life, 'each new generation of the composite men possessed stronger communication abilities and desires than the previous one.' Communication through normal materials to achieve simple communication, such as through a tax return, a film or more than two things, would not constitute the so-called 'infringement of privacy'. Moreover, the academics among the natural men who subscribed to this view had emphasized incessantly that 'the composite men of today biologically possess a high degree of virtuous elements, such as purity and honesty. The term "privacy" has become a cliché in history. To open up this kind of "spiritual journey" through a kind of brain wave communication will not make men fall into the most despicable crimes such as "peeping". Relatively speaking, this kind of communication could promote the harmony among composite men as well as elevate the "careful consciousness" of an individual in his free behaviour.' Ximi agreed with these remarks and this is why he never felt that he was peeping while he received the message from the tax return. By the same token, he would not be conscious of any material which had been processed by him and which fell into the hands of his comrades. All his thoughts and behaviour had maintained a high degree of 'careful consciousness'.

However, the message communicated through this pink tax return with the serial number 'R. No. 7321' was a real exception. Ximi was shocked when he typed '14 distinctions' on the computer keyboard; 14 distinctions—are these not equivalent to a record of 42 bonuses,

136 fairs, and 408 strengths? His mind went totally blank for a few seconds. Ximi had not accumulated so much income in the past ten years, not even adding up all the income for each year. He immediately looked back at the items under '14 distinctions'. The tax return only recorded the wording, 'special operation reward'.

'Shit!' he uttered a dirty word. He closed his eyes and began to meditate. He must make this clear: What kind of composite man was this 'R. No. 7321'? Had he been manufactured in the same batch with Ximi? What did he look like? Where did he live?

In his meditation, Ximi did not think that he had responded out of jealousy—jealousy was a serious crime of at least one blemish. He was only curious. However, this pink tax return did not seem to cooperate. Or to put it in another way, that composite comrade did not cooperate. He had never attempted to remember the episode of filling in the tax return. Ximi sat still in his workstation, stopped working, and even forgot the lunch he loved most—vegetable texture made of additional sugar plus natural plant fibre.

Ximi remained stuck with this stranger for six hours in this way. An image suddenly appeared in his exhausted brain waves. It was 'R. No. 7321!'

He belonged to a new generation with a nice appearance. He might have been manufactured in the same batch as Ximi. Looking at the way he ran towards the laser mirror and, reviewing his face in a very detailed manner, Ximi decided he must be very confident of his body structure and his appearance. Sometimes Ximi would look down at the pink tax return in between his long fingers. Then he would look up at his own reflection from the laser mirror, during which he destroyed a pimple at the back of his neck. Then, a composite woman appeared in the mirror. 'Xisa, very happy face,' she said. This must be his companion. Xisa turned his face and looked at his companion. What a beauty! Ximi looked carefully and recalled that she was the main actress for a midnight series, which ran for two months several years ago. It was said that this was the most remarkable record in the history of television in the past few decades. Finally Xisa said, 'Just now while I was filling in the tax return, the computer told me that I had got 14 distinctions in the past month.'

'What?' the woman screamed and went straight to Xisa and held him tight. Xisa looked at her beautiful long blue hair. He stretched his long fingers to touch the hair ends as if he was tickling natural lake water. 'So we could change for a new dormitory with an independent traffic station and traffic network. Oh God! How wonderful! I love the Metropolis. Moreover, Xisa . . .' She pushed away her companion and looked at him with a direct stare, her eyeballs slightly inclined upwards, 'Could we . . . could we apply for an adoption of a composite child?'

'You are kidding,' Xisa's brain waves were a bit confused when he uttered this sentence. This produced something like a grey shadow. Ximi found that not important and continued to pay attention to what his companion said: 'I am speaking the truth. Xisa, didn't we always wish to play with a little baby as those natural men do? I heard that we need only three distinctions to rent one from the training factory for a year. Think of it! For the whole year!'

'This is impossible. This "violates the rules", don't you know? Composite men can't. . . .'

'Everyone knows that we can't, we can't bear our own children as the natural men do. But it's only for fun.'

'Xilu, listen to me. We can't even. . . .' Xisa shook her shoulders, 'Do you know?' Speaking to this point, he pulled Xilu to the other end of the room and turned off the button of the computer. He continued, 'Do you know how we got these 14 distinctions?'

Xilu shook her head, messing up her lake-like hair, with tears in her eyes.

Xisa helped her sit down on a flying carpet, which looked very expensive. 'Have a look at the video tape I have recorded.'

Ximi was stimulated by the grey images. Surprisingly, the video tape that Xisa had recorded was a programme of the natural men—a short educational programme. Maybe the big dormitory that Xisa lived in was an upper class one—usually an upper class dormitory was located on higher ground and closer to the natural men's residences. Maybe the transceiver system of his television was more precise. Although the entire performance had lost the normal three-dimensional effect and strong colours, the resolution was very clear and the contrast between black and white was stark.

A couple of the natural species appeared on the screen. They smiled to the audience and raised their left hands holding their fists. The man said, 'Everything follows the rules. I love the Metropolis.' The woman said, 'Everything follows the rules. I love the Metropolis.' They said together, 'Dear parent comrades, do you find it difficult to be family supervisors? Our child was considered the naughtiest in the Metropolis. Whenever he refused to receive supervision and education. . . .' The couple looked at each other, shook their heads and smiled bitterly. The man continued, 'I would feel ashamed towards the era of the new age.' The woman said, 'Me too.' The man said, 'But being ashamed was not proactive enough.' The woman said, 'Therefore we needed more effective methods of supervision.' The man nodded and turned his face towards the audience simultaneously with the woman. He opened up his knitted brows and smiled, showing his clean white teeth. They said happily together, 'We have found a new method.' The couple spread their arms and pointed towards the audience, 'Please take a look!'

A huge net appeared on the screen. Ximi could imagine the three-dimensional effect of spreading out the net, which could let people fall back 30 degrees under extreme fear and helplessness. The camera panned quickly towards the centre of the net. There stood a naked little boy aged around ten. At the earliest end of Ximi's memory in the training and manufacturing factory, this boy's size was similar to that of the other composite children in the honeycomb-like little bedroom. His silver and shiny soft hair lay on his shoulders and his dark black eyes expressed an extreme anger or fear, staring straight at the camera as he shouted, 'What are you looking at? You shit!'

'Don't use dirty words, kid!' the caption appeared, provided by the previous mother supervisor.

'Shit! Shit! Shit!' the boy ran towards the camera, made a face in front of it, and started to urinate. Ximi suddenly felt that a screen without three-dimensional effect had its advantages as well. Otherwise, he would really feel as if he were being dirtied by the boy. The boy said while he was peeing, 'Whoever sent me to school is shit.'

'You have only studied in a kindergarten for a few years. That would not be enough for being a natural man in the era of the new age. You have to go further, don't you know? (She began to sing.) Everything requires discipline; everything follows the rules. Everything is in pursuit for perfection; everything is in order—Kids! The Metropolis loves you.'

'Those are your rules, your discipline, your Metropolis!'

'Shut up,' the father supervisor's voice was heard to say.

The boy on the screen stopped speaking and returned to his angry and fearful expression.

'If you don't want to be a natural man, you can't be the future leader of the Metropolis. . . .'

'No, No! I only want to be a kid. I am myself. I don't want to be an adult,' the boy fell on the net disappointed, his body and his two short legs pressed against his breast. He put a thumb into his mouth and started weeping, 'No. I am only myself . . . I am . . . private.'

'There is nothing private in the Metropolis, kid,' uttered the woman supervisor in a tender voice. 'Natural men, composite man, as long as they are "total men", there is nothing private.'

At this moment, the father supervisor provided the caption slowly, 'If you refuse to be a real natural man, you can only be a composite man! This is your own choice, kid.'

The boy suddenly fell into an extreme fear. He screamed with a sharp and terrible voice. The scream lasted for a while but the voice became fainter and fainter as the camera zoomed in closer and closer. The boy's silver white hairs stood up one by one as if drawn by the endless darkness behind the net. Then, his hair was pulled, strand by strand, and the speed of pulling quickened. Before long, the boy had become totally bald. His crying and screaming continued but the voice vanished. Instead, the song 'I love the Metropolis' slowly rose. That boy then lost his eyebrows, which flew towards the dark hole of the net one by one. Then. . . .

Xilu screamed and hid her face. Xisa turned his head and looked at her, spreading his fingers to touch her blue hair. When Xisa turned again towards the screen on the wall, the boy had lost his angry eyes and was left with only two empty sockets. The music had not ceased. As the kid lost one more organ, a new electronic organ and harmonics were added to the music. This short song was repeated many times and finally the boy's little genitals disappeared from the screen. The images received from Xisa's screen had become shadowy, as if sprayed by some foggy substance. Xilu was still weeping and could not speak. At this moment, Xisa wiped his eyes and the huge net on the screen was segregated into thousands of screens, some with hair, some with pieces of eyeballs, some with tiny hands and tiny legs. The screen changed and the smiling faces of the previous couple re-appeared.

'Although we lost the boy in this family,' the man said, 'this,' the woman continued, 'is the consequence of the failure in our supervision and education.' 'But the boy was resurrected. Under the strict selection, analysis, restructuring and adaptation of the new era of the Metropolis,' the man said, and the woman continued, 'a new composite man joined the Metropolis and the team of the total men. Everything follows the rules. I love the Metropolis.' As she finished she turned her face to look at her companion. The man continued and said to her, 'Everything follows the rules. The Metropolis loves you.'

Xilu's body was shaking and she could not speak for a long time. Xisa turned his hands once again and said, 'We composite men did not know our genealogy because actually we don't have a "self". Xilu, do you understand now? You always said my pair of hands did not balance with other parts of my body. These are not my hands! My eyes, my nose, my teeth . . . they are not "mine". Your hair, ha ha ha,' Xisa picked up her companion and smelled her hair. 'This is not "yours" either!'

'Miserable! Miserable!' Xilu's voice became dumb. She squeezed her fat arms as if they were not part of her body.

'Are you and I miserable, or are those children of the natural men miserable?' Xisa straightened up and at the same time snatched the tax return on the carpet. 'That was why I began this new research.'

'I . . . .' Xisa was walking in the room and finally stopped in front of the laser mirror. He pointed at his three-dimensional image in the mirror, 'This man had to stop all this! Xilu, you know what to do?'

Xilu blinked, her eyes filling with tears, and shook her head.

'Only if the composite men manufactured this year became the last batch of composite men could we stop the horrible things you have just seen and our horrible births from happening. I have injected two kinds of medicine into the brains of this new batch of composite men. One will stop their ageing such that they can remain at twenty years old forever. They can maintain a high level of physical capability and intelligence and their anti-biotic system is more perfect than that of our generation. It simulates the "immortality" of the Metropolis. They can really be considered as natural men. I saved all these human resources and capital for the Metropolis and maybe all these savings can be transferred to the development of the new satellite. But the second medicine . . . well . . . I don't know if this is right. . . .'

Xisa looked at Xilu and Xilu looked at him. Xisa turned again to the laser mirror. The expression in the mirror was extremely complex: he was happy, but he was disappointed; he showed pity, but contained some anger. 'At least I hope I am a composite man injected with this medicine.'

'What?'

'This medicine will help the new generation of composite men forget themselves, forget who their "I's" are! Or put it in another way: they only know that everything in Metropolis is "me".' Xisa pointed at the laser mirror, 'The laser mirror is "me"! Then he pointed at the computer, 'The computer is "me", the dormitory is "me"! And all the things outside as well. . . .' Xisa ran across the room and pointed everywhere and shouted, 'The road is "me", the research building is "me", the satellite is "me", the Metropolis is "me", and thousands and millions of composite men, natural men, and total men, all are "me"!'

Xisa obviously was a bit exhausted. He lay down on the carpet and said with a sigh, 'Composite men have no selves at birth. Why do they need to know "me"?'

'Xisa!' Xilu gave out her hand and touched Xisa's neck. A piece of her finger nail destroyed the pimple, 'Xisa!'

'The supervisor said that the second medicine was more amazing. From now on all detective systems in the area of composite men could be abolished.' Then Xisa imitated the tone of natural men: 'Xisa, you have created a new life for composite men. Maybe we could transfer you to the area of natural men to undergo a new phase of learning! Now we only need to do one thing, and that is to alter the lyrics of the song "I love the Metropolis".'

Xisa began to sing again and again, 'I "am" the Metropolis, I "am" the Metropolis. I "am" new life. I "am" total men. . . . Don't ask about the past. Don't fear for the future. Seize the age of the total men. Glory is now.'

When Ximi received the last brain wave from Xisa saying for the ninth time, 'I love the Metropolis,' Xisa shouted, 'Who am I . . . Oh?'

Ximi looked at the pink tax return and tried to catch Xisa's shadow, but to no avail. He could only guess: Xisa's systematic memory could be interrupted by an accident somewhere. But why did Xisa recall this scene, such that Ximi could have this opportunity to learn the truth of the whole event? Was he undergoing some kind of detection or revelation? Ximi did not want to continue thinking. He glanced at the sunset which was going to vanish outside the house and stretched his legs which had been frozen for six hours. He went to the scanner at the entrance of the office to get back the photo of this morning and asked himself, 'Why should I know all these things?' Then he became very careful.

Ximi reviewed the whole process once again and his body, lying down, could not help shaking. Except for Xisa and Xilu, he was the only composite man in the area who knew where he came from. He was afraid. He did not want himself to be so special. He could only utter continuously, 'I won't believe. I won't believe. I, I, Ximi won't believe, Ximi won't believe. . . .' Speaking like this would make him purer, more honest, and more competent to face his own writing today.

Then, Ximi's legs slowly pressed against his breast until he felt that he no longer shivered. He pressed the button in the cradle and the music 'I love the Metropolis' arose. He did not know whether he should sing 'I love' or 'I am'. He simply put his finger into his mouth and hummed the song.

1984

25

Transcendence and the Fax Machine

By **YE SI**

Translated by Terry Siu-han Yip, with Hardy C. Wilcoxon, Jr.

Ye Si 也斯 *is the pen-name of Leung Ping Kwan* 梁秉鈞 *(Liang Bingjun, b. 1949), a poet and novelist. He received a Diploma in English from Hong Kong Baptist College and his PhD in literature from the University of California, San Diego. He has taught comparative literature and translation at Hong Kong Baptist College and the University of Hong Kong and is now a professor at Lingnan College. He is a prolific writer; his works of fiction have been collected in* Shimen the Dragon-keeper *(*Yang long ren Shimen 養龍人師門*, 1979),* Paper Cutting *(*Jianzhi 剪紙*, 1982),* Island and Mainland *(*Dao he dalu 島和大陸*, 1987),* Three Fish (San yu ji 三魚集*, 1988), and* Postcards from Prague *(*Bulaige de mingxinpian 布拉格的明信片*, 1990). His prose writings have been collected in* Morning Greetings from the Grey Pigeon *(*Huige zaochen de hua 灰鴿早晨的話*, 1972),* Miracle Lunch *(*Shenhua wucan 神話午餐*, 1978),* Water-Coloured Figures *(*Shanshui renwu 山水人物*, 1981),* Landscape *(*Shanguang shuiying 山光水影*, 1985), and* The Flamingo in Kunming *(*Kunming de hongju'ou 昆明的紅嘴鷗*, 1991). He has published a number of collections of his poetry, namely,* Thunder Rumbles and Cicada Chirps *(*Lei sheng yu chen ming 雷聲與蟬鳴*, 1979),* Journeys *(*You shi 游詩*, 1985),* Cities of Memory; Cities of Fabrication 記憶的城市，虛構的城市 *(1992) and* Poems in Flux *(*Youli de shi 游離的詩*, 1994). He won the Hong Kong Urban Council's Biennial Award for Literature in 1991. The title of this story appeared in English in the original.*

I turned thirty-seven this year. Single. I work as an assistant research fellow in a cultural studies institute. After my full-time work, I also work part-time for a finance company. My main hobby is reading—reading the Buddhist classics, the Bible, and the Koran. I used to specialize in Anglo-American literature. But ever since the local scholars set up a 'Chinese School' and bibliographic studies became very popular, I have not been on friendly terms with them. Every time they compiled a bibliography or published a volume of selected papers, they would exclude my name. Gradually, I felt the presence of these bibliographies everywhere. It seemed that there was an invisible Chinese brush moving above my head, brushing me off to non-existence. Since then I have started reading all sorts of books. I subscribe to French magazines and journals which discuss special topics in religion and literature. Perhaps people studying religion are more tolerant and inclusive. When I've sent them my manuscripts from time to time, I've actually received replies.

There is only one reason I have remained single: I am not very good at interpersonal communication. Before I was thirty-five, I could see different virtues and merits in every single girl I met. I idealized them and could find reasons for loving them all. Of course I suffered a lot as a consequence. To compensate, after the age of thirty-five, I began looking for and discovering many faults in the girls I knew. And so I no longer loved anyone, which gave me peace of mind and contentment.

But there is always an exception.

One drizzly evening I was having a couple of drinks with my photographer friend Li Bianshing when I happened to mention a conference on 'literature and transcendence' that was going to take place in France several months later. I told my friend that I had been invited to compile some data and write a paper for the conference, but correspondence with the conference organizers in France took up a lot of my time and I found the whole communication process very troublesome. Ah-Sheng urged me to buy myself a fax machine. Later, as we were walking along the streets of Causeway Bay, feeling a little light-headed, Ah-Sheng suddenly said, 'Didn't you want a fax machine?' propelling me into a nearby shop full of telephones and fax machines. I was proving true what the girls I knew used to say: walk aimlessly in the streets of Causeway Bay, and you'll wind up shopping. Since Ah-Sheng knew the manager of the shop, it did not even matter that I had no money with me. When I later left the shop,

I was no longer single. I was taking a fax machine home with me.

Her appearance was ordinary, but somehow I found her more and more pleasant to my eyes. Perhaps this was why people often said that love grows with time. A fax machine is used only to fax writings, which is not something one thinks of as especially important. But when I got mine, I no longer had to run all over the streets with my writings, trying to decide if the toy-like post-boxes were real or not. I did not have to stamp my feet before a closed post office. I did not have to walk along the busy tram lines looking for a place to deposit the written words in my hands—words that were fresh from my heart—very personal and confidential. I did not have to drift about like a lonely wandering spirit, visiting some communication centres or lingering at the clubs for expatriate journalists. I did not have to feel sad over the seemingly long-lasting Saturdays or Sundays. Even when the world outside was filled with bullies and deception, when interpersonal communication was full of traps and pitfalls, I was still certain that, on returning home, she would always be there, faithfully receiving and sending out information. She was my reliable link with the faraway.

Place a sheet of paper in the fax machine and its spirit would appear at the other end of the world. That was a comforting thought. It was not necessary for me, with my love for words, to give in to the ever-changing and ever-fading speech. My personal and private thoughts could be covered up secretly and poured out only to a 'black-coloured ear'. Even the most rude, rough customs officer would not be able to inspect the electronic waves in the air. I could actually leave a material record of my communication with the intellectual and spiritual world. It allowed me to secure a facsimile, a true copy, a true record of my spiritual journey. When my memory fails me in future years, I may still be able to recall traces of my heart and my feelings with certainty. What was more, I could avoid the troubles in the human world. I no longer had to listen to people's sighs on the other end of the telephone line, or watch tears running down people's faces. It was also not so easy to catch meanness and jealousy on paper as it was from people's voices. I no longer had to receive phone calls from my bad-tempered friends and let my ears suffer the shock when they slammed down the receiver. Really, the fax machine allowed me to readjust my position in the world. I could sleep with abandonment, vaguely hearing her murmuring voice in my dreams; like music which put my heart at peace. I felt carefree at last.

Gradually I began to rely on her. I was no longer used to expressing my feelings. And yet she seemed so innocent and uncalculating that it was only natural for her to become my only confidante. I could not help thinking of her during the day when I was caught up in the power politics of the office. I thought of her happy face, thinking that she seemed to represent a more substantial kind of communication. I wanted to stay with only her after work. I would prepare a bowl of spaghetti or salad, pour myself a glass of red wine, sit before her and feel relaxed and relieved. Together we would listen to music or lie in the sun. She alone supported me in my communication beyond this world. On the days when there were no messages, I would place my written words in the machine and naturally the words would be copied out. She would reprint phrases like '*The Concept of Transcendence in Romantic Poetry*' and '*Kant's View on the Concept of the Sublime*' on sheets of paper that bore her unique scent. It was like hearing her agreement and receiving her praise and approval. That gave me great confidence.

It was exactly because of this blissful state that the first tension between us came as an extremely painful experience. The sudden silence in the middle of a fax transmission appeared like a silent protest to the abstract of my essay. Was it a gesture of complaint when only a few sheets of paper were allowed to pass through the machine? Hastily I picked up my original script from the floor and read it again from another angle. Yes, perhaps I should combine points two and three. Perhaps the middle section on page two should be deleted. Were some of the issues too abstract? The conclusion . . . Yes, perhaps the conclusion was a bit too ambiguous for the younger generation—I have not forgotten that my fax machine was a product of the new generation and she inevitably would carry with her the values and standards of her generation—perhaps it was too positive, or was it too remote for them? So I sat down and went through the whole script one more time. The length of the script was reduced in the final version from the original four pages to three. I placed the script in the fax machine again and the first page passed through it smoothly. But the second page was half way through when the machine stopped. I waited for a long time. Finally I had to redial the number and send the script all over again. The same thing happened. The machine stopped again when it came to the middle of the third page. I could do nothing but re-fax the third page again. Although the two letters *O.K.* also appeared later, I was still unsure whether the script had actually reached the other end. Was the fax machine's silence and strike today a protest against something? With a drumming heart and a disturbed mind, I came up with many reasons.

Then everything seemed fine again as if nothing had happened—until three or four weeks later. The same problem occurred again when I tried to fax a letter and a bibliography overseas. It stopped again in the middle of the second page. And when I pulled the original script out and thought of re-faxing it, the paper roller began to move, receiving new messages from outside. This interrupted my devoted efforts. As the paper slowly rolled out, I could read messages of all kinds: furniture sales by emigrants, second-hand cars, do you need a reliable part-time maid? Japanese *udon* noodles, long grain rice, and taxi surcharges. They were like characters in a novel, narrating another story. I read the messages carefully to make sure that they were not replies from overseas religious associations for me, rather than promised blessings from certain advertising companies and information agencies which had my number.

A practical joke? Perhaps it was not a practical joke. The second time I received such messages, I thought: is there any special meaning in their selection of me? I spent more time reading through the codes and signs. Their messages seemed to have no connection with the script I had sent out and yet they also seemed not unrelated. But what kind of relationship was it? I read the messages again and again, and as these advertising messages were faxed in continuously, I had no opportunity to send my messages to those faraway.

The murmuring sound finally stopped and the in-coming messages were completed. I picked up the letter I had put aside and tried to place it back on the fax machine. But somehow I felt worried and wanted to re-read it once more. Having read the messages I had just received, I could not help wishing to revise the plan of the academic paper I had mentioned in the letter I was holding in my hand. I thought that it was still not brief enough; it still carried too many heavy thoughts and was touched by too much idealism so that it sounded a bit lofty and unreal. So I began to revise the whole script once again.

But when I sent the letter to the priest, I carelessly picked up the ad on drainage repair and faxed that as well. The matter was not yet over. I decided to follow up the number on the ads and fax a message to each one of them, demanding them not to fax in so much junk mail everyday. But in doing so, by mistake I faxed out my letter to the priest as well. Like most people, I worked under great pressure and could only complete my task at the last minute. In a hurry I finished faxing my message only to find that I had made an irrevocable mistake. The response from the two sides were more or less opposite. The lofty critics thought that the inclusion of a worldly edge to my transcendental thoughts showed an inclination toward the 'frivolous' and the 'shallow' on my part, and expressed their concern and worry. The replies from the advertising companies were, as usual, short and de-humanizing. However, they were certainly annoyed to find themselves entangled in the intellectual consideration of an entirely different world. The over-heavy seriousness of the other party—me—seemed to embarrass them. I knew not where to begin, but there were no words in the advertising world for such things. I could draw from their cold expressions that they thought I must be a religious fanatic who had lost touch with reality.

The writing of my conference paper was more difficult than I had imagined. It was not only because academic papers were usually very difficult to write, but also because I was so preoccupied by my present problems that it was hard to find a space in my mind to reconstruct my remote intellectual thoughts. Things like office politics, my mother's rheumatism, and rushing to come up with a budget proposal for the next financial year all weighed upon me so I could not breathe. Both the priest and the professor wrote to find out what had happened to me since the deadline for the paper submission was near and yet they had heard nothing from me. I squeezed my mind to come up with a humble letter, explaining my situation. I dialled the long-distance number and the fax machine sent back a loud signal. It did not get through the line. It was like sending out signals to the distant stars in the universe, lost in the flow of light and sound.

I stayed up several nights in a row working on my paper, but I still missed the deadline by one day. When I eventually managed to get my first draft out, there were still a few footnotes missing and a few points left for further elaboration. But I was already totally exhausted. I crawled toward my fax machine and when I looked up, I saw the time on the clock hanging on the wall. It was 4.30am.

Slowly and gently I placed the fresh, warm manuscript in the fax machine, trying hard not to hurt her. I moved the sheets softly, and caressed the small buttons. Then I leaned over on top of her, waiting quietly because this was the only communication I had with the distant world of the soul faraway. I devotedly hoped that everything would go well and the message would be transmitted and the response properly received. I waited for the call tone to be changed, with the connection made, to an answering tone, clear and smooth in its melody. I moved the script, adjusted its position, trying to find a better connection. And yet the calling tone knocked on and on at a door that stayed shut, reverberating like a call to the far distance, or floating in the universe without a home. Some sensitive and mysterious things remained unconnected; the sacred door did not open to admit me.

It did not matter. We would try again. I thought of the respectable French priests and professors who were enjoying the beautiful sunset in the scenic south of France and singing psalms, free from the troubles of ordinary people like us. The songs of the psalms echoed and re-echoed in the air. I was really too tired. I dozed off, but woke up again. Fragrance of wine. Colours of Impressionist paintings. I woke up and dozed off and woke again. My script on literature and transcendence still could not be faxed, could not be sent to the land faraway. Gradually the red light on my fax machine began to blink. The red light followed by the green light, and then another red light. She was making all sorts of funny and strange sounds; then she gave off a fume of white smoke. She was sick.

I was in a terrible fluster. The deadline had passed. Certainly I wanted to catch up, to make a connection with that world of transcendence, which I believed to be good and beautiful, and to share my ideals. On the other hand, I had a strong feeling that the most important thing to do was to take care of this worldly fax machine before me. At a time when she needed me most, I should help her get over her troubles, to make her recover from her illness. I tried to massage her and press her with my fingers; I tried to feed her with all kinds of mild paper medicine; I checked her pulse and heartbeat. I used all my paper to test the machine, helping to keep her stomach and intestinal movement smooth and normal. My text on transcendence was mixed with the food remedy and the instructions of the plumber. I checked her pulse and pressed her acupoint, and the mixed sheets were faxed out smoothly. I had no idea where they would end up, or what the response of the receiver would be. I no longer cared so much. Being caught between transcendence and the fax machine, I could only do this much. I could only try my best and take care of the most urgent matters within my limits, hoping that that would let me find a way out.

1990

26

The Poem of Spring

By **Cai Shuqing**

Rewritten in English by the author

Cai Shuqing 蔡淑卿 (b. 1939), better known as Chua Seok Keng in Singapore, obtained a BA from Nanyang University in 1963. She studied library science in Australia, and later worked as a librarian in the National University of Singapore Library. In 1985 she joined the Singapore Ministry of Broadcasting as a script reviewer. She likes to publish under her pen-names, of which the two most often used are Qing Qing Cao 青青草 and Xie Yue 謝羽. In the 1980 short story competition organized by the People's Association, she won third prize. Besides short stories, she has published a novel, A Thousand Miles of Willows *(*Qian li liu lu *千里柳綠, 1986).*

A gap left by the window curtains, which had not been drawn properly the night before, allowed the golden sunlight to seep through. The million blinding rays showered on the floor and touched her cheeks with glowing sensations. She turned over angrily, trying to find a corner where the sun could not reach, so that she could go back to sleep. It was useless. Irritated, she got up to draw the curtains shut. The room was suddenly dimmed. But the illusory dream could not be continued.

She had been dreaming of Sibai again. What was the dream? She vaguely remembered that she was hurriedly touching her face, which was still covered with the night cream put on before she went to bed, and arranging her messy hair. He was talking to her spiritedly. The same rosy face, shining with youthful enthusiasm. Why did she look so old in the dream? What was he talking about? She could not remember. Probably she was trying to excuse herself so that she could run into the room to touch up her face. At the same time, she could not bear to leave him, so afraid that the slightest movement she made would make him disappear. Or was it because of those deep penetrating eyes, which still overwhelmed her? It had been quite some time since she saw those eyes, even in her dreams.

The telephone was ringing downstairs. She sprang from the bed, and remembered immediately that Amei was on duty today. Lazily she lay back on the bed.

'Madam, the call is for the Master,' Amei called out as she came upstairs.

'Tell him the Master has gone out.'

She said this with some anger. How could he be at home! Every Sunday morning he was either out jogging or lining up to buy 4-D tickets[1]. When had he become such a common man? The more common he became, the more disgusted she felt. Why must one go through the same routine and start behaving like everyone else once one is tied by the marriage bond? As for her, when did she start playing mahjong? How she had despised the game in her younger days! Now she would always mumble the same thing, 'I am a beginner, I have just learnt the game', as though this would lessen the guilt of her addiction to the game. It could never mend that hollow feeling inside, as if she had lost something and could not feel free and easy again. The other day, when she had been in the midst of a game and could not attend to her son's request, she felt ashamed when he retorted by calling her 'you gambler'. She was no longer the good housewife and mother she had once been.

Reluctantly she got up from bed. The image in the mirror reflected a greasy face, dark and stiff. She had always blamed the room for its poor lighting and subsequently for the dark blemishes on her face. But would she dare expose her face to the sun? She had tried to get sunglasses with bigger and bigger frames; how else was she to hide those increasing lines around her eyes? Damn that optician. He had told her:

'Madam! This frame is too big. It doesn't suit a person of your standing!'

She had gone to the same optician for years. That was why the man knew she was a teacher. What she could not stand was the understanding and sympathy in his tone. But alas! In trying to hide her years, could she blame him for pointing it out bluntly, with good intentions?

And when had those thin lines on her forehead become more and more obvious? Once, she was inspired by the Wonder Woman hairstyle on TV, and thought of leaving a fringe on her forehead so that she could hide those lines. But she lacked the courage for the experiment.

Dismayed, her face showed a natural frown where all lines gathered. The dull eyes were filled with melancholy. On seeing this image in the mirror, she was suddenly alarmed, and quickly put on a smile so that she could look better with the artificial contortion.

The thought of the reunion dinner struck her. Was it this that had been troubling her? It must be. That was why she had dreamt of him again.

Xiuyin's husband, Yongming, was an active committee member in their alumni association. There was always this or that activity, be it ping-pong or badminton. Over the last few years, whenever they got together, Xiuyin would always try to drag her into some activity. She had always declined with all sorts of excuses. The main reason was that she knew Sibai was also an active member of the association and was always with them. She did not want to meet him. Was it due to a lingering hatred, or was it because she did not want him to see how haggard she had become? She could not say which reason was the stronger. Perhaps there was an element of both!

However, when Xiuyin had telephoned her the other day, she was tempted and finally agreed to join them. Did she want to see him again, at this age when her heart should be serene?

'Tomorrow night we have an alumni reunion dinner. Xiuyin has asked you to attend,' she had told her husband, Yichao, at the dinner table the night before.

'I am not going. It is your alumni association. I am not familiar with them. What would I do there?' He not only refused outright but also asked the question with irritation.

'My classmates have always asked about you; they would like to meet you too!' She said earnestly, hoping that his attendance would make her feel easier, especially if Sibai were to bring his wife along.

'There is no need for them to make my acquaintance. Besides, I have already promised Wang that I will go over to his place for mahjong.'

There was absolutely no room for compromise. *Is he like this to his customers too?* Every time he had to attend a function, it was taken for granted that she would dress well and accompany him. He would then introduce her to his friends and clients as 'My Wife', and she would have to force herself to engage in small talk, saying things that she did not mean or replying without giving much thought to her answers. If she did not wish to go, he would surely say 'How come?' without asking whether she was feeling well. When it came to her own social functions, nine times out of ten he would refuse to go. He never wanted to give it a try, to do it once, for her sake.

She changed into a casual dress. On second thought, she changed again, this time into a blouse and pants. She had to do something to while away the time. *Why not spend the entire morning at the beauty parlour and in the afternoon go to the hairdresser's for a hair set?* This would also boost her confidence. Yes! It surely would, and this was what she needed. She might not believe that the beauty parlour would give her back her youth, but she had to do it just to be good to herself. Also, it would put her into an awkward position when friends asked her whether she was getting facial treatment. Whenever she said 'no', her friends would exclaim:

'Oh dear! If you don't, it may be too late.'

And so she had started to go for facial treatments and hair setting. In her heart, however, she was always an advocate of the soul. She believed more in inner beauty than in outward appearance. Sometimes, to please Yichao and to pamper herself, she would doll herself up and admire herself in the mirror. And Yichao, who would be dressing next to her, would ignore her completely, treating her like the wedding photograph on the wall. It hung there, neglected and unnoticed for years.

If you don't care, then I will make myself pretty for others, she thought to herself in retaliation. The girl she knew at the parlour, Shirley, was not there. Another girl, Lily, attended to her. If it had been Shirley, she could have easily chatted with her and the hours would not have seemed so long. Today, she was not in the mood. It wasn't poor Lily's fault. Her heart felt so heavy, as though something was stuck inside. She could not relax. When the ice-cold cream was applied to her face, it even caused her to have goose pimples. Perhaps the air-conditioner was turned on too high; she was feeling cold and she asked Lily for a thick towel to cover herself.

Under the rhythmical movement of the fingers and listening to the hissing sound of the massage machine, she felt hypnotized and pictured herself performing on a blurred TV screen, with episodes of the past flashing across the screen. One moment she was cycling round the lake with Sibai and the next moment they were eating ice-cream under the mushroom-shaped shelter. Then there was the cold and fierce look on her father's face, followed by Sibai's expression of anger and resentment. The episodes followed one after another in a disorderly manner.

'Madam, could you relax a little? You are frowning and it is difficult for me to massage.'

Lily's voice echoed in the room. The flow of thoughts stopped, all the pictures disappeared. It always happened like this, even here, lying on the couch with her eyes closed. Recently, these dreamy thoughts had been attacking her mind. Sometimes, sitting in the car, looking at the blue sky and white clouds outside the window, she would be lulled into this dreamland of the past, or, when awakened in the middle of the night, her mind would be drifting into bits and pieces of past memories. Insomnia had come back to her now that her two children were grown up.

'Madam, you can get up now. Shall I pluck your eyebrows, too?'

Lily's inverted face suddenly appeared large before her.

'It is not necessary. I will be setting my hair this afternoon. Could you please call Miss Li of the hairdressing department and book an appointment for me after lunch? Tell her I will be there at two.'

Passing by a hawker stall selling sour plum juice, she was tempted to stop and have a drink. However, on seeing the hawker dipping a used glass casually into a pail of dirty water and refilling it with the juice, she decided against it, and walked into a coffee shop. It was easy to find just one seat. She did not want to miss the beef-intestine noodles here. She had tried the same thing at many other places; this was the only stall comparable to those in Kuala Lumpur.

Beef-intestine noodles were always Sibai's favourite. She remembered the first time when he had dragged her along to try it, she had almost vomited. Later, when she got used to seeing it and had tried a bit from his bowl a few times, she had begun to acquire a taste for it. *Are hobbies infectious, too? And once you have been infected, is it so difficult to give them up?*

She could not help looking around. When Sibai first came down to Singapore to look for her, they came to this coffee shop all the way from the campus just to have the same thing. The weather was so hot that perspiration oozed from his forehead and his two bushy eyebrows were locked together.

'Why is it so hot?' He wiped his neck briskly with a large handkerchief, and then pulled at his shirt collar. He looked very displeased. It was not entirely due to the weather, she knew, for he was always like that, full of grouses, even though he was joyous for a short moment when he first appeared outside her hostel room, seeing her for the first time after a long separation.

'At least I have stepped physically into a university. Those who study here are really the gods' favoured ones.'

He said this sarcastically and stretched himself in the rattan chair.

'Is it convenient for you to stay with Wende?' she tried to change the subject.

'How can it be convenient? The three beds almost take up the entire room. And to lay a mattress on the floor, you still have to wait until all of them are in bed. If I had known, I would not have come.'

When he realized that she looked hurt, he quickly sat up and said: 'Jieying, I did not mean it. Not that I don't think about you. I had to wait for the vacation and, even then, I still had to have money. Damn it! It was so hard to find the money. I dared not ask Uncle as he was already against my going to the Teacher's Training College. The allowances given by the college are paltry, although I could eat and stay there. My pocket money was hardly enough.' He was complaining again.

'Didn't I tell you I could pay for your transport fee first? Wende also assures us that there is no problem staying with him as his roommate is always out.'

She really wanted to help.

'Do you think I would want to use your money? I rejected Wende's offer of fifty dollars this morning.'

A strange feeling came over her. *Could this be Sibai? When had he become so hostile and cynical?* She wanted to cry but there were no tears. She said awkwardly, 'Friends should help each other. Although I help you sometimes, I never said I did not want you to return the money. You know I can't come up to Kuala Lumpur to look for you. I can only anxiously wait for you to come and see me. I didn't know you did not miss me.'

'Who said that I don't? During those first days after you left, I could do nothing but roam the Lake Gardens at night and think of your gentle words.'

'Me too,' she lowered her heard shyly and continued, 'Whenever I attend lectures I can't help but think of you. How nice it would be if you could attend the same lectures.'

'You are always dreaming. I don't think I can ever be at the university. I don't even dare to dream about our future.'

It irritated her to hear him going back to such talk again, but she could never clear the thin barrier existing between them. When she thought about it today, it still seemed strange to her. *Girls are always making their own dreams and will not face practical problems.* She remembered telling him, 'Why must you think so far ahead? When you finish your course, you will become a qualified teacher. I am in the arts stream and when I graduate, I will be a teacher too. We can be in the same line and, by then, I don't have to listen to what my family says. I can go to K.L. and find a teaching job.'

'Can you really not pay attention to your father? And without a university degree, how can I match you? Without a good background or a degree, what can I offer you in marriage?'

He was getting louder and louder.

'I don't ask for anything in marriage, as long as you are nice to me and so long as you love me.'

She was filled with self-pity and her voice was choking.

'Ai!'

Sitting opposite her, he stretched out both his hands across the table and grabbed hers. Pulling her hands to his face, he caressed her fingers with his lips.

'You little devil, I don't know whether heaven is good or bad to me. If it is bad to me, it would not let me meet you, fall in love with you. And if it is good to me, why doesn't it let you be born into a poor family, or I into a rich family, a Dato[2] family perhaps, so that I can drive you around in a car, and not have to worry about your cousin going after you, or your father's objection?'

Those tightly closed eyes, those interlocked eyebrows, the warm breath from his nose tickling her hands—all these seemed to be lingering on in her dreams, refusing to go away.

'Jieying! Why are you eating here alone?'

She felt somebody's hand on her shoulder. There was no need to guess who it was. Those rings set with diamonds and jade told her that it could be none other than Yuhua.

'I just had a facial and will be going back for a hair wash and set later. Why is Cousin Robert not with you?'

Without much enthusiasm, she watched Yuhua pull up a chair and sit down opposite her, with no regard whatsoever for a couple who were already waiting and standing nearby.

'Don't ever mention your cousin to me; when did he ever accompany me shopping? Don't you remember the time when he left us at Pearl Centre, and made us wait for him with all those bags and parcels? And when he came, he even had the cheek to complain about parking. It is even worse now, I can't even get a lift from him.'

'Didn't you like his ways in the beginning? You said he was unlike other thick-skinned suitors, that he was unusual. Now you complain,' she purposely reminded her.

'You have the cheek to tell me this! Wasn't it you who wanted me to help you—to say that you were not in, and to ask me to go out with him? It was all because of you that he finally became my boyfriend. Who else can I blame but you?'

It sounded like complaints, but it was obvious that she was quite pleased—just look at all those lines caused by the broad smiles. Her whole body was glittering like a Christmas tree, with all that jewellery. *Can't blame her. Her father was a taxi driver; there were eight of them in the family and she was the eldest. She had to support herself through university. To meet someone like her cousin, rich and capable, what a find!* Each time Jieying asked Yuhua to entertain her cousin, she would grumble, but her heart was only too willing. Each time, she would come back happy and satisfied. *How did she do it, was it her talkative ways?* Anyway, she could dance, she could socialize, everything was just right for Cousin Robert, unlike Jieying—she was always being teased by her cousin who called her a nun just out of the nunnery.

Soon after Yuhua graduated, she was whisked away by Cousin Robert in a bridal car. Jieying's father was sore about it. For some time he nagged at her.

'I've never seen such a stupid girl. Your cousin is such a nice man, and a graduate from Australia. He is good for you in every respect. Yet you gave him away to someone else. You think a husband is so easy to find? Besides, your Auntie does not like this girl; unrefined, she said. She is blaming you for introducing him to the wrong girl!'

Actually, she wanted to tell her father, her cousin had never loved her. She could have given him a chance. But she had disliked him right from the beginning; she always felt that the English-educated were too shallow. Take her liking of poetry, for example. He knew nothing about it. How could she live with someone like that? And there was, of course, that wonderful Sibai. But she would not tell all this to her father; she was quite glad to see him feel the loss. She derived some sense of satisfaction out of it. He deserved it; who asked him to object to her relationship with Sibai? Were it not for him, Sibai would not have been made to feel so inferior, and would not have married someone else as a result.

'Hey! What are you thinking about? No wonder your cousin always says you are so enigmatic. Your head is full of ideas. Oh! I remember now. You wanted to push me on to Robert because of a guy called . . . what . . . Bai? Come to think of it, he was not worth it. He only came over twice in four years. How could you call that going steady? Each time he came, there were quarrels, and didn't it all come to nothing in the end?'

Yuhua's words hurt.

Jieying looked at her sideways. She had noticed Yuhua's way of hitting others' soft spots. *That boastful look of hers!* She never dreamt that, married to a rich man and bearing him two sons, and with the business doing well, Yuhua would have become so overbearing. *How could she describe Sibai in that way? What did she know about love? How could she understand that Sibai was afraid that he was not good enough for her? If Sibai were to be like her, and be servile to everyone, he would have succeeded, too.* When she turned twenty-eight and still had no plans for marriage, hadn't Father hinted to her through Mother, 'Didn't you have a boyfriend in K. L. before? How is he now? Is he married? Is he still teaching?'

If only Sibai had been like Yuhua! But Sibai could never be like that. He could never be as immature, shallow and overbearing as Yuhua.

'What spell have you come under today? Why are you not answering me? Will you be free later? Would you like to come with me to Metro? I am taking a few Indonesians there shopping.'

'No, didn't I tell you I have to go back for my hair wash? We have an alumni reunion dinner tonight.'

When they arrived at the hotel restaurant for the reunion dinner, Jieying walked in nervously, closely following Xiuyin. Usually, when she accompanied Yichao to dinners, she behaved naturally and calmly. What had happened to her tonight? Was it those familiar faces at the door? Why was everyone changed in their looks? All the youthful spirit of their younger days was greatly reduced.

How will Sibai look? Has he come? Has he seen me? Jieying suddenly became very conscious of herself. Having been a mother for several years, she had lost her shyness. Sometimes, when she stood outside Yaohan,[3] she would feel perfectly at ease, knowing that eyes would not be set on her because she was no longer young. But now, if it were not for Xiuyin, she would never be able to walk in!

Many greeted Xiuyin; one or two who had met Jieying before also acknowledged her with a 'Long time no see!' or a 'You've come too!' It was merely words. Actually, who would really notice her? No one would think, 'Why is she here this year?' Everyone was stretching his or her neck to see which female classmates had aged, and which male classmates had become prosperous. Only one person, Sibai, would think much of her coming.

When they were finally seated, Xiuyin was like a butterfly, flying from table to table. Probably she was carrying out a mission for Yongming to organize meetings. Jieying felt a bit left out. She was the only one at the table; the others had not yet arrived. She did not dare turn her head. She surveyed the whole room with a quick glance. *No. No sign of him.* She wished he would not appear. The hairdresser, Miss Li, had piled up her hair, knowing that she was attending a dinner. When she finally saw herself, looking like a stiff geisha girl in the mirror, it was already too late. And after Miss Li had tried to rearrange it, it had become a mess. Her carefully powdered face was now marred by grease and sweat. Having forgotten her face blotters, she had to use her handkerchief, which became smudged with the pink and red of rouge and powder. She was quite sure she looked a wreck now, but she would never powder her nose in public.

And if he came, would he bring his wife along? To tell the truth, she did not want to see his wife. Subconsciously, she did not want to associate him with a woman. To her, Sibai was Sibai, a single entity. When she had heard about his marriage from Xiuyin, she had been completing her university course. She had not heard from him for two years by then. She suffered, she hated, but gradually she forgave him. She knew it was only a matter of time before Sibai married someone else. It was like worrying about cancer. Finally confirmed by a doctor, it would bring pain to the heart. It was something you had to go through. She could still feel his pain at not being able to have her, those sighs choked with tears still seemed to vibrate in her hands. He would never forget her. He still loved her; she was confident of that. Her Sibai still belonged to her, even at this moment.

Those sharing the same table with Xiuyin had arrived. They had met Jieying before, and went into the same routine conversation with her: 'How many children have you got? How many boys and girls?' followed by 'Are you still working? And where?' No matter how seriously she answered, she knew that the other would not really listen. Conversation was a tool to break the ice, the more irrelevant the better. The enthusiasm, the ideals, and ambitions that had shone on everyone's face during school days had disappeared with age and maturity. What had taken their place was a sense of contentment, contentment over the possession of children, over well-paid jobs, cars, and houses. *Who cared about ambitions and ideals?* Armed with the mortarboard, she had tried to carry out her mission of education in her early years of teaching. After some time, she slackened in her preparation of lessons, and teaching became meaningless after she had a family. After the day's work, she could not wait to rush home and lie down for a rest. When Yichao's business became more and more established, he had nagged at her to stop work many times. And she did, finally. It was mainly for the children. As soon as she stopped work, the world suddenly became smaller. Confined to activities within the four walls of home, time became abundant. She always thought secretly: if she had married Sibai, life would not be like this. Sibai was at least a person who knew how to appreciate life.

When Xiuyin finally came back to the table, it was time for the first course. It was the cold plate, of course, followed by shark's fins, roast chicken, and the usual dishes. *Chinese food is supposed to be rich in variety, but why does every restaurant serve the same dishes? There is hardly ever anything new.*

It was not Xiuyin who had told her about Sibai's venture into business, but Yongming. Yongming and Sibai had been classmates. When Sibai later moved his business to Singapore, Xiuyin once asked her whether she would like to go to their welcoming dinner for him. She had declined. She did not want to welcome his wife. Tonight, she came for him. And Xiuyin? She sat there as though she knew nothing.

The singer was singing 'Love Thoughts by the Riverside', 'We Together', and even the song 'Dreams of Yesterday', made famous by Baiguang.[4] But of course she was lacking in that special appeal, that husky and lazy tone. And her overly made-up face ruined the melancholy mood that was supposed to accompany the songs.

Suddenly, some busybody requested the song 'If Only We Had Met Before My Wedding'. Her heart missed a beat. In those days in K. L., even before Sibai, she had fallen in love with the beautiful lyrics and the sadness in the song. The song had been made famous by Li

Xianglan. Her songs had always been so captivating, and lingered in one's thoughts. None could compare with her.

You left me a sweet poem in lovely spring,
But let me pass my days alone through every spring,
Till the day I did a bride become,
When your name I ceased to bid welcome.

The chords in her heart began to strum. How could she have become a bride that year? That 'Poem of Spring' still played inside her heart year after year. It was not because there had been a lack of suitable men; rather, there was no room in her heart for another Poem of Spring. *No, nobody could write another 'Poem of Spring'*. With the years, factors such as a high position with a good salary and a good life came into consideration. Those lacking in such qualifications would bow out, while those able could, of course, easily turn to others. The ability to dream had gone away with the disappearance of Sibai. Those sheets of poems and prose on the desk had gathered dust for a long time. The dream woven by Spring had gone with Sibai.

After her graduation, her father had used his influence in their hometown to secure a teaching post for her. The pay, however, was extremely low. To tell the truth, she did not mind the salary of two hundred dollars a month, since she could save on accommodation and food provided at home. It was a small town, anyway, where one did not need to spend much money. Feeling rebellious against her father, however, she did not want to stay in her hometown. She applied for a teaching job in Singapore. The pay was double and Father could say nothing against it. Another reason why she chose to stay in Singapore was because of the facilities it offered. She could take up courses such as music, painting, and flower-arrangement in her spare time. Why should she leave Singapore, a place many had wanted to come to? As for Kuala Lumpur, with Sibai marrying another woman it would only add to her misery if she stayed anywhere near the place.

A few times when she went home on vacation, Father had introduced a few men to her, but in retaliation she turned them away. She was conceited, too. Why should she be assessed by others as if she were a piece of property? With her looks and capabilities, even though she was going on thirty, she was confident that she could find someone to marry. Take Yichao for example, hadn't he quietly waited for her for a number of years?

She had always felt that Yichao was too worldly. There was nothing romantic about him. They had met at a dinner party, a school board gathering. They discovered that they had attended the same university, and naturally found it easier to talk to each other. It was his father who dealt with the school board matters, but had passed on the work as well as his hardware business to his son. And he was doing very well.

When he first called on her for a date, she had just come back from her hometown. Her parents' anxious words were still ringing in her ears: 'Jieying, we are not nagging you. You've had your education, but every time we make arrangements for you when you come home, you refuse to accept. And in Singapore you are not doing anything about it. What will happen if you keep delaying; you are already twenty-seven or twenty-eight. . . . '

Why should I go out and find men? Someone has come for me. So with only the intention of trying it out for fun, she accepted Yichao's date. He was unlike other suitors who would take her to a movie or a nightclub on the first date. Instead, he took her to a seaside restaurant. After going out with him a few times, she found that he was not an expressive person. Perhaps he let her feel that he admired her, but he would never say so. What she could not stand about him was that he was always so careful about money. Each time he called for a bill, he would study it item by item before paying. Never could he just pay graciously. Although he was not really a miser, she always felt he looked so niggardly. Sometimes she would grab the bill and pay first. And Yichao let her do so without the slightest discomfort. At first she was quite put off by his behaviour, but later, she thought, 'It is better this way. I don't owe you anything and will not have to feel bad if we part.' It was later, at a charitable function where Yichao made a donation, that she changed her mind about him. She realized that on important issues he might be a thinking person after all.

If it had not been for her father's over-eagerness, she would have agreed to marry Yichao sooner. When Father came to know about Yichao and his family background, he could not hide his pleasure. 'My hat off to you, Jieying. Why, you let your father worry for so many years when all along you have already found a fine candidate. Come to think of it, his father has business connections with us. This time, don't you miss this golden opportunity, like the last time, your cousin. . . . '

Were it not for Mother who stopped him and changed the subject, he would have gone on further about the cousin and her. 'It was all because of that stupid cousin; if not for him, I would not have become what I am today. But don't you be too happy too soon,' she grumbled to herself, and decided not to accept Yichao's proposal too early. She had never really had the urge to marry him.

Yichao was good to her. All the necessities, he gave her. They had a home, specially-designed furniture to go with it, a car, air-conditioned too, and a servant to look after the children. Compared with her colleagues, she was certainly better off. But she always felt there was a barrier between her and Yichao. It was a form of communication she needed from the heart, but she could never have it with Yichao. Hearing her talk about it sometimes, he would laugh at her for day-dreaming. He never tried to enter her heart or to take a look at the world inside her. He felt that he had done his duty by giving her a comfortable life, by buying her expensive jewellery and dresses, and making her look as good, if not better than his friends' wives, and that was enough. He could devote the rest of his attention to his business. Sometimes, he would find her strange—she would be deep in her thoughts and refuse to answer him, or she would just snap back: 'You wouldn't understand!' and make him so angry. On such instances, he would grumble at her:

'What are you really thinking about? You seem to lose interest in everything. Reading books and even love novels! You women are really dreamers.'

Perhaps that was it. He had never liked to dream! He had become more and more practical. After striking small sums of money a few times, he had become a 4-D addict. Whenever he saw a car booked by a policeman, a receipt number, the number of a new telephone installed by a friend, he would be engrossed in buying numbers. *Isn't that as bad as day-dreaming? He doesn't play mahjong very often, but once he is at it, he can stay up all night and not return.*

What? Dessert already? People were streaming by her table, but she did not see Sibai. This was an anti-climax. Wasted plans and effort—the trouble she had gone through at the beauty parlour, the nervousness she had felt. Well, at least she could laugh away all this by herself. Feeling quite lost and leaning back in her chair, she waited for Xiuyin who was busy circulating.

'Is that you, Xiuyin, why didn't I see you just now?'

It was Sibai's voice. She looked in its direction, and saw a tall, fat man with a bald head. The side view revealed a large paunch. But the voice sounded like Sibai's, the same low and manly voice which had lingered on in her mind.

'Jieying is here too. Jieying, look! Sibai's here.' She felt Xiuyin pushing her shoulders.

'Hey! Is that really Jieying? I didn't expect you. I've never seen you here. What brought you here tonight?'

It was the same man, the body slightly bent, the face coming nearer. Is that Sibai? She hesitated, as though she had been rudely awakened in a train and could not find herself amidst the roaring sounds. *How could Sibai look like this? His forehead had receded, his cheeks become puffed up and fleshy. Bulging fat around the eyes pressed them into tiny slits. Hadn't he had double eye-lids before? And those burning eyes which still shone in her dream last night, what had happened to them? The high lean nose that I loved, why had it expanded both ways as though only then could the flesh support the bridge? Only the mouth, the curved mouth, remained the same as before. It was Sibai's mouth all right.* Xiuyin was not pulling her leg.

'Why, don't you remember me? Is your husband here too? Hey, Susie, this is Mrs Lin Yichao, the one I mentioned to you before.'

As though the words 'twenty years later' were flashing across a movie screen, the scene that appeared before her became confusing, with unfamiliar faces and props. She didn't quite know how to react. And the new character called Susie, so loving by his side, almost leaning on him, must be his wife. What was her Sibai up to? What a drastic change in these twenty years, so drastic that one does not know how to relate to it. 'Oh!' She managed to utter a sound from the throat, and pulled the muscles in her face with some effort so that she could put on a smile. Her hand was immediately grabbed by a woman covered in glittering jewellery.

'So! This is Mrs Lin! They were talking about you at the table just now. They say your husband is a developer and that he has recently built some houses for sale in Katong. Sibai says he knows you very well, and we were just thinking of meeting you to discuss the matter! We didn't realize you were here too.'

The make-up on her face was thick. A pair of eyes slightly larger than melon seeds was neatly drawn with eyeliner behind a spectacle frame. But the nose, it rose from the lower point and spread out on both sides! This was what you call a lion's nose. Women with this type of nose made husbands prosperous. The clear and crisp voice slipped out from a mouthful of snow white teeth under the nose. Every word she said was like a missile firing into Jieying's ears. *What a woman! And she, Sibai's wife?*

'I . . . I don't quite know, I never interfere in his business. . . . I will have to ask him first.'

She had to stop several times. She realized that her reply did not reveal much concern for Yichao, so she had to add a few more words, here and there, as though she were making a jig-saw puzzle, trying to piece together the past and the present. In her hurried movements, she did not know where to start. She couldn't help looking at Sibai again. The dashing hero that lived in her heart, where had he gone to?

'I understand Mr Lin's Phase I at Katong has been sold out. Has the second phase started? We are thinking of buying a house there. Furthermore, I am in real estate brokerage, and would very much like to meet your husband. I am sure he has much that could be of benefit to me. Here, this is my calling card with my telephone number on it. We would like to invite you both for lunch or dinner, whenever you are free.'

It is Sibai, the oil and grease secreted after a meal still glittering on his forehead, and perspiration streaming down his face. The same old way of perspiring. In a daze, she accepted his calling card and put it on the table without thinking.

'Yes, you two are old friends after all. You should keep in touch. If I had known earlier that Sibai knew you, we would have called on you.'

The powder was peeling off as a result of her vigorous smile, which also pushed up her glasses.

'Susie used to teach at an English school in the Federation. Since we came to Singapore, she has stopped teaching and switched over to the insurance business. She is now working for an insurance company and if you ever need any insurance in business, you can contact her.'

What a broker, even recommending his wife's business. Looking at him making such a great show, she felt terrible, as though she had just swallowed a bowl of worms and it made her want to vomit, and yet she couldn't. It was stuck inside her, churning in confusion.

'Yes, I will look into that!' She made a great effort to suppress the sickness and impatience in her voice, for the conversation had made it difficult for her to breathe. She looked at the smiling Xiuyin who was by her side, and, as though begging for help, said:

'Can we go now? Where is Yongming?' Her tone was almost breathless.

'Yongming is at the door; let's go.'

Xiuyin is an understanding friend after all. Just look at her sympathetic eyes; she must have encountered such a display before.

'Where are you staying Mrs Lin? Can we give you a lift?' Sibai's wife rushed forward.

'It is not necessary. Xiuyin will take me home, good bye!' She started to walk away.

'Mrs Lin, have you bought insurance?' She followed her.

'Yes, I bought it a long time ago,' she replied without hesitation.

'Would you like to buy another policy? I can deduct all my commission for you. I don't aim to make a profit. All I want is to fill a certain quota so that I can win a free ticket to Europe. Mrs Lin, if you have any friends interested in insurance policies, you must recommend them to me!' She followed closely behind till they reached the door.

'Yes, certainly, I will.'

Yongming and a crowd of people were seen going in the opposite direction. She was moving forward quickly when suddenly a card was stuffed into her right hand.

'This is the card you left behind on the table. My office address and number are written on it too. I am usually out of the office during the day. It is best that you call me at home at night. If you wish to call me in the morning, do it before nine for I will not be out yet.'

The woman's voice rang again.

'Jieying! Don't forget! We will have lunch with you and your husband some day. Please don't forget to tell him about it. I will call you another day. Good bye.'

The same low voice, so enchanting, which used to echo in her mind before, had now faded with the breeze. She did not have to think about it anymore. It was as easy as shrugging off dust. Cold as it was outside, it brought her a sense of relief. Yichao's voice always sounded honest and sincere, he never smiled in such a servile manner.

Alas, fate on purpose played us out,
By chance a meeting brought about,
For us to swap indifferent greetings,
With sweetness and despair in silent sufferings.

No wonder the singer could smile while singing those words. She must have seen many comical incidents in her career. How many times had she dreamt of her meeting with Sibai? In her imagination their meetings were not without joy and laughter, but there was more sadness. Never could she have dreamt it would happen this way, without any preparation. It was like being pushed on stage, looking so silly and wishing to get off immediately. Well, she couldn't say that there was not the slightest bitterness or pain. It was like a scab on a sore, almost healed, and the act of suddenly pulling it off only made it hurt a little. Afterwards, there was only a feeling of relief. At least there wouldn't be much of a scar left.

It was really cold sitting in the back seat. She rolled up the window. *I wonder whether the children have gone to bed. That stupid Amei always sleeps like a pig, she will not go and cover them with blankets. I hope Yichao will not catch a chill coming home this late.*

1980

NOTES

1 Lottery tickets.
2 'Dato' is an honorific title given to people who have made a great contribution to society.
3 A Japanese-owned department store.
4 Famous Chinese singers of the 1940s.

About the Editors

KWOK-KAN TAM is Professor in the Department of English at the Chinese University of Hong Kong. He has published extensively on modern Chinese literature and culture, and on the relations between Chinese and Western literature.

TERRY SIU-HAN YIP is Professor and Chairperson of the Department of English Language and Literature at Hong Kong Baptist University. Her publications cover topics on gender and Chinese–Western comparative literature.

WIMAL DISSANAYAKE is currently Scholar-in-Residence at Hong Kong Baptist University. He is an adjunct fellow of the East-West Centre, Hawaii and is also a member of the graduate faculty, University of Hawaii. He is one of the leading scholars in film and communications studies.

About the Translators

CHEN CHU-YUN is Associate Professor of English at National Taiwan University. Her English translation of Taiwanese stories have appeared in *The Chinese Pen.*

MARTHA P. Y. CHEUNG is Professor in the Department of English Language and Literature at Hong Kong Baptist University. She received her PhD in English from the University of Kent. She has translated into English stories by Han Shaogong and other modern Chinese writers. She recently published *Hong Kong Collage* (Oxford University Press, 1998).

YUET MAY CHING received her PhD in English from the University of Michigan. She is currently Associate Professor in the Department of English at the Chinese University of Hong Kong. She has published articles on Ezra Pound and modern poetry.

PETER G. CRISP is Senior Lecturer in English at the Chinese University of Hong Kong. He received his PhD in English from the University of Reading. He taught at Jilin University, Changchun, before he came to work in Hong Kong. He has published in English literature, as well as in comparative studies of Chinese and Western culture.

NANCY DU is a freelance translator. She is currently working on an MA in Translation at Catholic Fu Jen University, Taiwan. Her translation of Taiwanese stories have appeared in *The Chinese Pen*.

DONALD A. GIBBS is Professor Emeritus at the University of California, Davis. He has published extensively on modern Chinese literature and translated into English stories by Wang Meng.

JASON GLECKMAN received his PhD in English from the University of Wisconsin, Madison. He is currently Assistant Professor in the Department of English at the Chinese University of Hong Kong. He has published articles on Shakespeare.

HOWARD GOLDBLATT is Professor of Chinese at the University of Colorado, Boulder. He was editor of *Modern Chinese Literature* and has translated into English stories and novels by Hwang Chun-ming, Li Ang, Su Tong, Xiao Hong, and many other modern Chinese writers.

DOUGLAS HUI received his MA in Translation from the Chinese University of Hong Kong and he has translated into English several of Xi Xi's stories.

JOHN KWAN-TERRY received his PhD in English from the University of Cambridge. He was Associate Professor of English at National University of Singapore and Head of the Department of English Language and Literature before he passed away in 1994.

AMY TAK-YEE LAI received her MPhil in English at the Chinese University of Hong Kong and is currently a doctoral student in English at the University of Cambridge.

LING YUAN is Deputy Editor-in-Chief of *Chinese Literature* and has translated Chinese short stories into English for the journal.

NIENLING LIU is a writer and a scholar. She was Research Associate at the Fairbank Centre, Harvard University. She is editor of the book *The Rose-Colored Dinner: New Works by Contemporary Chinese Women Writers* (1988). She has also published works of fiction in the United States and Southeast Asia. Among her works are the novel *The Image in the Bamboo Grove* and the collection of short stories, *The Marginal Man.*

LO MAN-WA is Senior Chinese Language Officer working in the Hong Kong government. She is currently a doctoral student in English at the Chinese University of Hong Kong. She has translated four books from English to Chinese. She also published articles on Chinese–Western comparative literature and Chinese women writers.

LUCIEN MILLER is Professor of Comparative Literature at the University of Massachusetts, Amherst. He has published a collection of Chen Ying-chen's stories, *Exiles at Home*.

JOHN MINFORD is Professor in the Department of Chinese and Bilingual Studies at Hong Kong Polytechnic University. He has translated into English Louis Cha's *The Deer and the Cauldron* and portions of the eighteenth-century classic novel, *The Story of the Stone*.

A. T. L. PARKIN is Professor of English at the Chinese University of Hong Kong. He received his PhD. in drama from the University of Bristol and taught at the University of British Columbia, Canada, before coming to work in Hong Kong. He is a poet and his recent publication is *Hong Kong Poems* (1997).

MADELYN ROSS is on the staff of *Chinese Literature*. Her translations of contemporary Chinese short stories have appeared in *Chinese Literature*.

KWOK-KAN TAM is Professor in the Department of English at the Chinese University of Hong Kong. He received his PhD in comparative literature from the University of Illinois, Urbana-Champaign. He has published books and articles on modern Chinese literature, comparative studies of the theatre, and Western literary theory. He is the author of *New Chinese Cinema* (Oxford University Press, 1998).

TIMOTHY WEISS is Associate Professor in the Department of English at the Chinese University of Hong Kong. He received his PhD in English from the University of New Mexico and taught at the University of Illinois, Urbana-Champaign, and the University of Maine before he came to Hong Kong. He has published books and articles on modern literature.

HARDY C. WILCOXON is Associate Professor in the Department of English at the Chinese University of Hong Kong. He received his PhD in English from Yale University. He has published articles on Hong Kong students' perception of American literature.

EDITH S. Y. WONG received her MPhil in English from the Chinese University of Hong Kong and is Administrative Executive at the Hong Kong Productivity Council. She has published articles on modern Chinese literature.

LINDA P. L. WONG received her PhD in English from the Chinese University of Hong Kong. She is Assistant Professor in the Department of English Language and Literature at Hong Kong Baptist University. She has published articles on Chinese–Western comparative literature.

JANE PARISH YANG is Associate Professor and Head of the Department of East Asian Studies at Lawrence University. Her translations of Chinese stories have appeared in *The Chinese Pen.*

TERRY SIU-HAN YIP is Professor and Chairperson of the Department of English Language and Literature at Hong Kong Baptist University. She received her PhD in comparative literature from the University of Illinois, Urbana-Champaign. She has published extensively on gender and modern literature.

ERIC K. W. YU is Assistant Professor of English at National Dong Hwa University, Taiwan. He received his PhD in English at the Chinese University of Hong Kong. He has published articles on traditional Chinese literature.

ZHA JIANYING is on the staff of *Chinese Literature* and has translated Chinese short stories into English for the journal.

BENZI ZHANG is Associate Professor in the Department of English at the Chinese University in Hong Kong. He received his PhD in English from the University of Alberta, Canada. He has published articles on modern fiction and Asian American literature.